# HOLIDAY HOPEFULS

SERENVALE SPRINGS - BOOK 1

EMMY TODD

# Holiday Hopefuls

## EMMY TODD

Holiday Hopefuls
Copyright © 2025 by Emmy Todd (Madison Mouser)

Cover Design by Rotoscope Design
Author photography by Laura Powers

First edition: November 2025

The publisher is not responsible for websites or their content that are not owned by the publisher.

Library of Congress Cataloging-in-Publication Data
Names: Todd, Emmy, author.
Title: Holiday Hopefuls / Emmy Todd.
Description: First edition. | Fayetteville, Arkansas : Mimosa Bookhouse, 2025
ISBN 979-8-9898236-7-3 (paperback)
Subjects: GSAFD : Fiction.

Printed in the United States of America

Printing 1, 2025

*To anyone who's ever felt like they needed to prove themself to their family.*

*Keep marching to the beat of your own drum.*

# 1

*Callie*

"I simply don't understand how you could possibly be too exhausted to come over for dinner tonight." The sigh my mother manages to physically push through the phone would make any bridezilla proud. "You know we only have these twice a month since all your siblings stay so busy with their work. Though, heaven knows I'd prefer my babies in my home every week. And anyway—Calloway Leora Rutherford, are you listening to me?"

The sound of my name pulls me back to the conversation. "Of course I am," I answer absently. Meanwhile, a student's still-wet finger painting lifts off the stack of papers in my hand thanks to the chilly winter breeze. Right onto my favorite sweater. Why I didn't leave grading our class' craft for tomorrow is beyond me. Especially knowing there's a family dinner tonight.

"Then what did I just say?"

"Uh ... " Reaching my car, I perform a juggling act of monumental proportion in order to unlock the door and hold the offending painting in place whilst managing not to drop any of the other artwork, all while continuing to listen to my mother complain about how I'm just a glorified babysitter. Only when I'm safely inside the vehicle do I find myself able to answer, "You want us all to be together."

A dissatisfied humph comes through the line. "It's not easy to plan dinners with everyone else's busy schedules, Calloway. You could be a little more grateful they're willing to take time out of their busy weeknights to get together."

My engine roars to life, effectively cutting off my mother's spiel. Heat filters through the vents, thawing my fingers that managed to become popsicles in the short walk from the school to my car. Tugging my favorite wool scarf tighter around me, I once again wish I had worn my hair down today for whatever warmth it could have provided.

"Calloway." The chill in my mother's voice rivals the frigid Colorado afternoon.

"Mom, I promised I would be there. And I will," I sigh. Shifting slightly, I'm able to carefully lay the stack of pictures down onto the passenger seat. "Give me an hour. I need to run home and change first."

"I guess that's fine. Your siblings are all coming straight from work. It's very considerate of you, not wanting to show up in pajamas."

*I did that one time. Once. And I came straight from pilates.* But of course, that's what she remembers. Pressing my lips into a firm line, I count to three and take a deep breath. "Yeah. Sure. I'll see you soon." Without giving her a chance to respond, I end the call and haphazardly toss my phone into the cupholder filled with hair ties and bobby pins.

A quick glance around the parking lot shows that nearly

everyone else has headed home to people that actually enjoy their company.

So I decide to do the same.

One of the main reasons I chose my apartment was its proximity to the elementary school. Well, that and its price. As a single woman living alone, those were two factors I simply couldn't pass up on. Not to mention, I knew the vintage exposed brick would compliment my plethora of plants perfectly.

And Gilmore, of course. My perfect Nidularium Bromeliad child I've had since college. My pride and joy. My raison d'etre. The day my life changed, I was walking around the hardware store when boom—there he was. This tiny plant with dark magenta kissing the tips of each inner leaf sitting all alone on the top of a display tower, the grow light acting as a halo. The fluorescence gave his uniquely colored tips a warm glow, calling to me. When I read 'Easy Maintenance and Hard to Kill' on the tag, I knew he was the plant for me.

I'm allergic to cats and I've never been brave enough to get a dog, so that was the beginning of the plant lady madness. Since then, I've rescued bulbs, sprouts and seedlings alike.

No Plant Left Behind—my own personal agenda.

My best friends, Ian and Aaron, only add to the madness, having gifted me a new plant baby every birthday and Christmas since Gilmore came home.

The drive home is short and warm, just the way I like it in the freezing winters. And when I step out of the cozy vehicle, a sheet of snow smacks me square in the face.

*I need hot cocoa, stat.*

"Hi, Mrs. Martinez," I call over, waving enthusiastically. Though my coat hinders my waving ability more than I'd like.

My elderly neighbor turns as she reaches her door, a stack of mail in hand. "Are you just now getting home, Callie?" Dark skin and salty curls highlight every snowflake that uses her as a landing zone, but her pink fleece robe and matching boots dare the snow to outshine this woman's sweet nature.

"Parent/Teacher conference night," I shrug. "But I'm heading out soon. Need anything from the store? I'm almost out of hot chocolate, which is dangerous for everyone."

"Just to the store?"

"Well ... it'll be on the way."

"Family dinner?" *Okay, my schedule has been way too predictable lately, apparently.* The tiny, shrewd woman raises a nearly invisible brow. My lack of response must be more than enough to answer her question. Or my grimace. "They'll see your worth one day, dear. Don't worry."

Heat rushes to my cheeks, matching my hair. "You really need to get out of this cold, Mrs. Martinez." Unlocking my front door and stepping inside, I drop a canvas tote I've used since college right to the side of it.

"I have some fresh chicken tamales for you," she says, half inside her own apartment. "I'll leave them in your mailbox." Raised in a traditional Mexican home, she learned plenty at a young age. Namely, how to cook. I've easily gained ten pounds since moving in next door.

Beaming through the light snowfall, I shake my head. "You're the best."

"Don't I know it." With that, she closes the door and I follow suit.

"Gilmore, light of my life, I'm home!" I call into the warmth of my small entryway. Shedding my coat and scarf, I make quick work of hanging them on the peg by the door before grabbing my bag and heading to the kitchen counter where my first child awaits. "Hello, sweetheart. Did you have a good day?" I coo. Getting no response—typical, but I can always hope—I give Gilmore's leaves a once-over, checking their health before grabbing one of several misters, and set about watering each of my babies in turn.

My apartment is small in a cozy kind of way. One bed and one bath with an open floorplan kitchen and living area makes for overall easy maintenance, which is my kind of living space. With it only being me living here, I don't really have a need for much furniture, just enough space for Ian and Aaron to sit when they come over. And while the exposed brick walls, big windows and light wood floors should make it feel cold, the outrageous number of rugs and blankets I have on every available surface keep the place in coziness overload. From the corner of the living area, my small Christmas tree blinks in greeting with its multi-colored lights as I bounce from one plant to the next.

All too soon, it's time to change my paint-covered shirt and head to the one place I dread returning to.

The Rutherford family home.

Pulling on a fresh purple sweater and jeans, it takes all of thirty seconds to realize my hair needs to stay in whatever birdnest-like bun is happening so that I'm not any later to this ridiculous dinner. I'll be shocked if I don't hear about that one from Mom as it is.

I sigh, the inevitable finally upon me. "Try to get some grading done while I'm gone," I tell Gilmore, "Most were able to keep the paint inside the lines, so I'm thinking A's?" With no response from my first-born, I reluctantly head out the door.

Radio and heat blasting, the drive through the town is something out of one of those cheesy holiday movies that you can never quite get enough of. The square is coated in fresh snowfall and twinkling lights while people walk arm in arm, all bundled up in coats and hats. Storefronts glow, warm and inviting. Couples snuggle together under a blanket of shining stars. Even with Thanksgiving still two weeks away, Christmas is in full swing in Serenvale Springs.

And I love every minute of it.

About fifteen minutes north of town, the coldest neighborhood in all of Colorado greets me with open arms. Estate after estate home passes, silently judging the old sedan I've had since I was nineteen and purchased with my own funds. Since I was young, I've never wanted anything to do with my parents' money. It fueled them and most of my siblings to act as superior as they felt, and I always resented them for it. For how it made our entire family look to the rest of the world. As the youngest, I was supposed to simply fall in line in the Rutherford machine. But I was a surprise for the entire family.

Mostly a bad one—and they've never let me forget it.

So I've worked hard over the years to minimize my footprint on the family finances and lifestyle.

Aaron and Ian's childhood home passes in a blur, begging me to stop at the Fairchild residence, instead. Their mom would welcome me with a warm hug and homemade bread fresh from the oven, even if I only saw her a couple of hours ago as she closed up her own classroom for the night. Mr. Fairchild would tell me the latest news in the business world, kissing my forehead like the daughter he never had. From the day they moved in next door, the Fairchilds have been more of a family to me than my own.

But I'm not stopping at the Fairchild estate.

Up ahead, the Rutherford estate awaits my displeasure. Three luxury vehicles have already claimed their spots in the circle driveway of the largest home on the block.

Clammering out of my car, anxiety rises up into my chest at my tardiness as I make my way to the door. Hand raised to twist the doorknob, I nearly jump out of my skin when the large oak door opens without me so much as breathing in its direction. "Holy crap," I gasp.

"Lovely sentiment," my oldest sister deadpans.

"Sorry, um, do you think you could, you know, move?" Waving my hands, I try to convey that I'm in the process of becoming a popsicle.

Imogene rolls her brown doe-like eyes, stepping out of the way.

"You don't have to look so put out," I say sweetly, stepping inside. "What were you doing, anyway?"

"I heard a noise." Imogene raises mocha brows that match her deep chocolate waves. Tall and willowy with sharp features, my sister looks more and more like our mom with every passing year.

It's freaky. And disturbing.

"And there you were." She shrugs.

"Oh, come on. That door's, like, a hundred feet thick."

Ever the engineer, she squints to look at the closed door. "I'm pretty sure it's a standard 2.25 inches."

Resisting the urge to slap myself in the face, I blink at my sister. "Yes, I know. I mean, I didn't *actually* know that. I just mean"—I sigh—"never mind."

"Everyone's already at the table. Why don't you go sit down before you hurt yourself." Imogene crosses her lithe arms covered in a burgundy sweater by some designer I've probably never heard of, matching new Prada shoes flawlessly. Black darted pants and a perfectly curated ponytail complete the ultimate 'professional woman' look.

Before I can open my mouth for a retort, my heart sinks a little more as another much deeper voice joins us. "Genny, did you figure out—oh, it's you."

Pinning Prescott with my version of a withering glare, my oldest brother hardly bothers acknowledging my presence before turning back in the direction from whence he came. The stuffy smell of expensive cologne lingers even after he's nowhere to be seen. "You all act like Mom didn't invite me, or something."

Imogene only scoffs before following her older brother.

Suddenly alone in the massive entryway, I leave my coat and scarf with the trembling maid who only shows up once

Prescott has retreated. Because, let's be real, he's never been one to appreciate my parents' staff.

Mom's clearly had the decorators here in preparation for the holidays. Sticky notes and the beginning of garland strands hang from random places throughout the front rooms. Christmas trees and ornaments wait in boxes on the floor to become something out of a fairytale at a moment's notice. Paintings featuring snow-covered villages wait to be hung, replacing what is normally stationed on the wall throughout the year. While other kids' moms made homemade gingerbread and left cookies for Santa, ours brought in private chefs for a gourmet meal and told us Santa is for chumps who don't believe in hard work and earning everything they have.

Needless to say, I didn't have many friends that wanted to hang out at my house around the holidays.

Or ever.

Or, really, any friends at all, thanks to the sinister tone that comes with my family name.

Except Ian and Aaron.

As I walk further into the house, every siren goes off in my system and the feeling that I should've brought Gilmore for backup screams in my head.

Noisy chatter comes from the dining room, just at the other end of the front hallway. One deep breath pushes its way out. Then one more, and my feet carry me toward the sound of love and approval that's never quite been extended to me.

Except from one little girl.

"Aunt Callie!" Marigold hops up from the table and sprints across the large dining room in record time. Dark spirals bounce with each movement while her deep skin radiates joy. All conversation ceases as my seven-year-old niece throws her arms around me, her footsteps echoing in the cavernous room.

"Hey, Goldie," I grin, squeezing out all the love I can. "I like the half braids. Did your dad do them?"

Prescott rolls his eyes in my periphery.

She beams up at me. "Thanks, they're new."

In the distance, my father clears his throat from the head of the table. "Calloway, take your seat, please. We've been waiting on you."

"Sorry," I mutter. Quickly guiding Goldie back to her chair next to Prescott, I take my place on the opposite side of the table.

Six pairs of annoyed eyes watch as I scooch around on the uncomfortable chair.

My niece, on the other hand, giggles.

Only when my movements have stopped for a consecutive ten seconds do the salads appear.

"You still look rather casual," Lillian Rutherford says from the opposite end of the table as my father, eyes never leaving the barely-dressed salad.

Not a soul has to waste time wondering to whom she's speaking.

I shrug. "Figured jeans were a step up." Not really. I'd worn a skirt today. Pink tulle—my favorite. But it was way too cold, even with fleece-lined tights. "I know you don't like leggings."

My mother narrows unamused eyes in my direction, mouth pinched as she chews.

To my right, Constance coughs to cover a laugh. Connie, my only semi-ally. In a frumpy gray turtleneck, brown slacks and flats, the investment banker isn't quite the fashion icon of the family. But at least she doesn't throw insults my way at every opportunity. And unlike our oldest two siblings who favor our mother, Connie and her fraternal twin Christopher look like me with their ruby hair and fair skin.

"Imogene," my mother finds her oldest daughter, "any luck with the new aircraft piece you've been working on?"

"We have a few test samples ready for experimentation." Imogene squares her shoulders, pride radiating from her form.

"So that's, what? A few different types of nuts and bolts?" Christopher asks from next to Connie, grinning.

I usually try not to directly piss off my brother since he could probably throw a pretty mean punch with all those muscles, even for a financial analyst.

But Imogene stares at him, undeterred. "Sorry, I can't hear you over my doctorate."

Heat floods Chris' cheeks as he sputters, "Excuse me, but an MBA in Finance is just as good as a PhD in Aeronautical Engineering."

"Chris," Connie whispers to her twin, who angrily chews another bite of salad.

Next to Imogene, Prescott rubs his forehead. "You're all idiots," he sighs.

Imogene cuts angry eyes toward her brother. "Rude."

He shrugs. "I'm just saying, some of us work in fields that directly impact people's lives. And, I'll point out, I have a doctorate, too. But I don't feel the need to bring it up in every conversation. Even if I am thirty-three and already a senior partner at a law firm."

Chris scoffs. "And how sad for you that people don't call attorneys 'Dr.'"

At one end of the table, my father salivates as the rest of his children argue over who's the most successful, while my mother just looks tired.

"Calloway," Connie's soft voice echoes above the rest of our siblings' fervent discussion, "How is the preparation for the holiday program going?"

All other conversation ceases, heads turning my way. As if they all forgot I was there.

They probably did.

"Oh, um, good. Thanks." Smiling at my sister, tension courses through my chest as I wait for what's coming.

"Are your kids excited?" she continues. Since Connie also

holds an MBA in Finance, I guess she can ignore the other conversation with greater ease.

"Yeah, they are," I nod. "They're going to dress up as reindeer. It's going to be so cute. They're still a little young to do too much, but I know the parents are going to love it." Taking a chance, I turn to the rest of our family. "You're all more than welcome to come, of course. It'll be Thursday, December 17th, at the school. 7pm."

"Not getting enough credit as a babysitter there, Calloway?" Chris asks as the salads are replaced with some kind of Beef Wellington. "Need us all to watch you do it now?"

Connie must reach under the table and pinch him because he yelps.

I don't bother hiding my snicker.

Neither does Goldie, but Prescott puts a quick end to that.

"That's enough, Christopher," my father says with false sternness. "Some of us never reach our full potential, and that's okay."

Pressing my lips together, I resist the urge to roll my eyes. Only Imogene and Connie can get away with that one.

"Just because your sister chose a much softer career doesn't mean cruelty is necessary," Dad continues.

Taking bites of food that I don't taste, I mentally tally how much longer this dinner could possibly last. "You know," I say, swallowing, "I don't think that sounded as nice as you think it did."

Ira Rutherford sits back in his chair. Still in his work clothes, he looks the part of an attorney about to win a case. "What would you like me to say, Calloway?"

"Gee, Dad, I dunno." Unceremoniously dropping my fork, the clattering screams in the resounding silence.

"Calloway Leora," my mother warns.

"I'm just saying. I went to school, too." Raising my hands in surrender, I look between my parents. "I have a great job that I love and that pays my bills. And I get to try and make an impact in these kids' lives. What else could I want?"

"To have a job that earns you some respect and where you don't change diapers?" Chris suggests a little too casually.

Rubbing my temples, I count to five. "Look, I need to go. Paintings to grade and such. You people with your big important jobs wouldn't understand." Pushing back my chair, the feet scrape against the hardwood.

"Calloway," Mom calls as I'm halfway out of the dining room. Congenial, as if she's somehow managed to miss the last several minutes of conversation.

Maybe it's just years of practice being a corporate wife.

My feet come to a halt. "Yes, Mom?" I ask as politely as possible.

"Don't forget Thanksgiving is coming up."

Sighing, I turn to my mother. "Believe me, I couldn't if I tried."

"Are you bringing anyone?"

"Like who, the guy who mows the neighborhood lawns?"

My mother purses thin lips. "Anyone of significance," she clarifies.

The laughter that bubbles out isn't familiar to my ears. Incredulity and embarrassment with a hint of annoyance. "I'd have to be seeing someone in order for them to come to Thanksgiving," I snort. Not to mention, I'd have to be insane to bring anyone I care about around my family of vultures.

Except Connie.

"What about Ian Fairchild?" my dad asks from across the room.

"Definitely not."

"Aaron?"

I don't miss the way Connie tenses. So subtle that anyone not watching her would miss it entirely. "One hundred percent no," I answer.

"Okay," Mom sighs, as if my lack of a love life has brought on a bout of extreme melancholia. "Then I guess we'll see you on Thanksgiving."

"Consider yourself warned," I mutter before I hightail it out the door.

# 2

*Oliver*

Glasses clink together at each table I pass, barely heard over tonight's crowd. Friday night in the sleepy town of Serenvale Springs never fails to disappoint in Theo's Place, and tonight is no exception thanks to the constant stream of musical talent they keep lined up.

Blythe would have loved tonight's selection—a female folk duo. But as we left our parents' house tonight, my little sister refused to hear about anything other than taking a hot bubble bath and climbing into bed.

Slipping past one, two and three more people, I make it to my destination with only one almost-stain on my burgundy sweater. Hanging my coat on an empty chair and dumping my work satchel beside it, I drop into the seat across from John.

"You look great," he comments, sarcasm dripping from every syllable. Dressed in gym clothes, the man throws back a big gulp of the ice water resting beside his main drink.

While he had the opportunity to get in a workout after the last client of the day, I had time for a lovely family dinner complete with plenty of love and guilt.

My answer is a pull of the too dark beer he ordered and had waiting for me.

"How were Mom and Pop Rhodes tonight?" John, my best friend since junior high and business partner, is the only one who could get away with calling my parents such juvenile names.

Especially to their faces.

But John and his older sister, Rindy, made themselves at home within my family the day they moved to our neighborhood. Going out with them in tow was always a riot—everyone assumed they were adopted since their appearance is our exact opposite. Where my sister and I are blond with fairly tanned skin, the McNalley siblings flaunt raven hair with skin nearly as deep.

And while their parents still live states away, John and Rindy have both made a home for themselves in Serenvale Springs.

John pops a chip into his waiting mouth. "Did they bring up marriage again?"

"They waited until dessert, at least."

"I'm telling you, man, they're getting antsy for some grand-babies." John pushes the pizza dip toward me, and I impolitely help myself.

"I guess Nacho isn't good enough for them. Poor girl."

"Guess not," he grins.

Speaking of kids, "Where's Cici tonight?" John's five-year-old daughter and all her spunk are nowhere to be seen.

Not that she usually joins us for beers on a Friday night. But thanks to her constant chatter around the office, I usually have an idea where she'll be on any given day.

"Joanna wanted to take her shopping for clothes," he

shrugs. From the relief written on his face, John is more than happy to let his sister-in-law take on that particular experience. It's just as well—Cici's outfits typically look as though they were put together by a colorblind person.

It's safe to say that John isn't the most fashionable man. He'd probably see clients in sweats, if it were left up to him.

In fact, I think Rindy does most of his shopping. That woman and her wife have done enough shopping for Methuselah's lifetime.

"So, Jo and Rindy picked her up from school today. The shopping commences in the morning," he finishes.

"And tonight?"

"An over-the-top slumber party, complete with movies and all the ice cream she can handle."

"I'm sure there will be every other sweet treat imaginable available, too," I grin. Joanna has quite the sweet tooth.

"Don't I know it." Smiling, John shakes his head. "You know, I may never know why Angela left us, but I do know I'm thankful every single day that she didn't take Cici with her."

Swallowing, I nod. For the past four years, this time of year has been nothing short of difficult for my best friend. Tackling the mouthwatering pizza dip between us, I allow John the few moments I know he'll need after mentioning his ex-wife.

Just as the folk duo switches songs, John clears his throat. "Are Marshall and Sandra at least giving Blythe the same kind of grief?"

I snort, rolling my eyes. "Are you kidding? She's perfect in their eyes."

"And yours."

Shrugging, I grin. I may be biased, but Blythe's a pretty awesome sister. And in my line of work, I see plenty of family dynamics.

"You know"—John takes a drink from his frosted glass—"I don't mean to sound like your parents."

"Oh, this is gonna be good."

"But I think you'd be a great dad," he finishes.

"Aw, come on," I plead. "At least let me get through one drink before you start agreeing with my parents."

John laughs, slapping the table. "You know, I think Ci's teacher is single. She's pretty, kind, intelligent."

"Then why don't you go out with her?" I quirk a dark blond brow at my friend.

John peers at me over his nearly empty glass. "Because I'm not interested in her like that."

Having seen my friend's waning glass, a server brings over two more.

"I dunno," I swirl the drink, pretending to be puzzled. "Sounds like she might be a catch. Maybe you should think about it."

John shakes his head. "It's still too soon, man."

"What if the right person came along?"

Crossing his arms, my friend looks over at the band. "Then, maybe. Cici needs someone else she can count on, don't get me wrong. But I'll know them when I meet them."

With this man's reluctance, I'm honestly surprised Rindy hasn't kicked him into next week. But then, even his sister knows when to back off, I guess.

Not that she ever has with anyone else.

But like Blythe and I, those two grew up close and managed to stay that way. It was even Rindy's idea to open a practice together. Only a couple of years older, she had already been practicing. Specializing in marriage counseling, Rindy had no trouble finding a group to take her on once she graduated. It was when they told her there was no room to hire John too that she approached us about opening the practice together.

With my parents fully settled here, and Blythe back from school and opening her studio a couple years ago, there's never been any reason to move anywhere else.

By the time we're on our third glass of water and second plate of wings, John has his phone out and is creating a list of all the reasons I need to get married. Granted we only have four, so far.

"Here." Reaching across the table, I extend a napkin his way.

Buffalo sauce continues to be haphazardly smeared across the screen before John eventually thinks better of it and wipes of his fingers. "Thanks. Okay, onto the fifth one."

"Yup."

"Clearly, Nacho needs someone to listen to her complain about you when you withhold extra treats."

"Sure," I nod. "Clearly. That's a solid fifth reason. Especially behind needing someone who can keep a plant alive."

"Dude, you absolutely suck at that. Instead of a green thumb, I think you just have a death thumb."

Chuckling while attempting to drink water is not recommended. At least, not by my shirt, which is now soaked. "Thanks, man."

Dipping his chin, the level of seriousness exuded by my best friend is hilarious. "Name one plant that's made it longer than two weeks in your care."

"None." I'd pretend to hem and haw, but the fact is, I really am a terrible plant dad.

John scoffs. "Yet, Sandra keeps the dream alive."

Grinning, I shake my head. "Mom has got to quit gifting me plants. Though, sometimes I think their deaths are self-inflicted."

"Only because they probably know their fate," he points out, "which makes you needing help with your plants one of the reasons for you to find someone."

Using the paper straw to push any remaining ice further into the water, my eyes wander to the bar's uninspired ceiling. "I wonder if this is what the next couple of months will be like."

"What do you mean?" John furrows a dark brow, readjusting to clap for the band, who is wrapping up their final set.

"I mean *this*"—I wave my hand between us—"everyone telling me how badly I need to settle down. Surely there's something I can do, some kind of guiding light to help me make it through the holidays." My erratic movements attract the attention of the next table over, earning us confused looks from the large group. While I awkwardly wave to try and deter them from having us kicked out, John keels over the table in laughter. Only when the others finally write us off as harmless, do I turn back to my friend. "Thanks for the help," I say dryly.

"You looked like you had it under control." John wipes a tear from the corner of his eye.

Rolling my eyes, I lean toward him. "What do you think?"

"You mean about people saying that you deserve someone who makes you happy? Yeah, the outrage. You really should do something about that."

If we were in private, I might just flip him off. "I'm just saying, with how much time my family spends together around the holidays—"

"And every other week of the year."

"And every other week," I concede, "it'd be nice to have just a little break."

"I mean, sure. We'd all like a little reprieve once in a while."

"John."

"Okay, okay ... " John nods. "How exactly do you plan to make that happen?" He lifts a skeptical brow.

"Dunno. I guess I just wish there were someone like me. You know, in my position. But maybe that someone could convince my family that my life is fine the way it is."

"It is?"

Narrowing my gaze, I pin John with a playful glare. "Yep."

John chuckles under his breath. "This sounds like something you could monetize, given the right circumstances."

"Convincing someone's family that their life is actually good?" Furrowing my brow, I shake my head.

"Ehh, that's a little broad." John's skepticism can probably be felt two counties over.

Looking up, my gaze catches his. "Even better—my parents see my single lifestyle as a shortcoming, right?"

"Right ... And probably your main one."

"I'm ignoring that. But I'd be willing to argue that their insistence on my settling down may actually push me further from wanting that life."

Across the table, John merely blinks.

"What if that was what I did?" Grinning like an idiot, I hold my best friend's stare.

My friend who looks very confused. "What?"

Leaning as far forward as possible, I whisper, "What if I convinced someone's family that any traits they see as short-comings in a given family member is actually the family's fault? You know, instead of the individual's."

"You can't be serious."

"Think about it." My face begins to hurt from how wide I'm smiling. "As therapists, we're trained to assess, diagnose and treat all kinds of issues within family relationships"—I shrug—"so, I'd go to their holiday celebration with a mental list of every perceived shortcoming by their family. Then, one by one, I would convince whomever necessary how the defect is actually their fault instead of the individual's. Using psychological facts, of course. I'd be the perfect holiday date."

A smile breaks out across John's face. "A holidate."

"A holidate," I nod, crossing my arms. "Charge a small fee—"

"$500?"

Shaking my head, I take another sip of water. "Nah, that's too steep."

"Wow, I didn't know you could put a price on ruining someone's holiday. But here we are."

Ignoring him, I spout a revised offer. "What about $300?"

John laughs. He grabs a napkin, snagging the pen from our bill. "Oh, that's much better." The man scratches down our proposal cliffnotes.

"What are you doing?"

"Making a few notes. You never know, this could make a hilarious story one day," he says, never looking up. John's written short stories on and off for years. He even worked on our college newspaper. But storytelling has always been his passion.

Maybe that's why he loves working with families—he wants to write their happy endings since he never got one himself.

"I thought you wanted to write a mystery."

John shrugs, finally looking up from the napkin. "I could be persuaded to switch things up." He grins.

"You know what"—I reach out and snatch the napkin from him—"I'm not so sure I trust you to hold onto that without doing something insane." Grabbing my bag from the floor, I toss the napkin inside while he protests.

"Come on, man. Not fair."

A quick peek into my water glass lets me know time is just about up. Sighing, I look back at my friend. "Look, it'd be fun. But until then, I guess I need to go home and see if Nacho has any fresh excuses for me to use over the next few weeks."

"Are you and the furchild still coming over tomorrow to watch the game?" he asks as I put on my coat.

"Of course. Will Cici be there? Or will she be too busy shopping?"

"She'll only be there if you bring cookies." John holds up both hands in surrender. "Her orders, not mine."

Chuckling, I toss my bag onto my shoulder. "Then I guess I'd better deliver."

# 3

*Callie*

"You have really got to stop doing gigs on Monday nights." Slurping up more water, I peer across the small table at Aaron in all of his rockstar awesomeness. Despite the week just getting started, Theo's Place is buzzing with energy from the band's last set of the night.

"Sorry, Cal," he shrugs. "Gotta do what I gotta do. Besides, you're here in sweats. It's not like you had to get all dressed up or anything."

"Excuse me, but I came straight from pilates class." Tilting my drink toward Ian beside me, I continue, "The girl running the class tried setting me up with her brother. Again."

Aaron's younger brother scoffs. "How many times does that make now?" His teasing hazel eyes sparkle as his tightly trimmed beard stretches with a grin.

"At least six."

He winces. "Maybe you should just put her out of her misery and meet the poor guy."

Rolling my eyes so hard I nearly give myself a concussion, I reach for another french fry, turning back to Aaron. Like his younger brother, Aaron sports tousled brown hair and a strong jaw. But where Ian looks every part the mortgage lender banking employee, Aaron exudes rockstar rebellion. "Anyway, I'm just saying, some of us have work in the morning." Aaron narrows his eyes as my grin slides into place. "Though you all definitely killed it up there."

Aaron playfully puffs out his chest.

"The new songs seemed to go over really well," Ian offers. Leaning back in his chair, he looks my way for validation.

I nod, grin widening. "Definitely. Can I venture a guess as to your muse?"

"I don't know what you're talking about." Aaron pushes up the sleeves of his Henley, exposing full sleeve dragon tattoos, before digging into the fry basket.

Sharing a quick look with my best friend, we turn back to the locally famous rockstar at the table. The same one who refuses to dress any way but casual on stage. He regularly reminds us that if it's good enough to wear on a construction site, it's good enough to wear while playing music. Of course, Ian and Aaron's side remodeling company has never been known to host paying fans of Aaron's music.

"Any time you're ready to admit it, we're here." I raise my hands in false surrender. "That's all I'm saying."

"Ready for a day full of your family?" Aaron asks, shoving another handful of fries into his waiting mouth.

"Look how smoothly he changes the subject," Ian teases, elbowing me in the ribs.

"Ugh, don't remind me," I groan. "Thanksgiving is a week and a half away, and I'm already dreading it." Propping an elbow on the table, I rest my chin in my waiting palm.

"Everything will be fine." Aaron reaches for his own water. "Connie will be there, so it's not like you'll be totally on your own."

Biting my bottom lip, I refrain from teasing him about my sister. "Sure, but so will Chris."

Aaron snorts, examining his greasy hands. "Yeah, that guy's a prick. Hey, I'm gonna run and wash my hands. Be right back." Since we picked a spot in the back, it's only moments before he disappears down the short hallway to the restroom.

I turn to Ian. "They've started trying to get me to go back to school again. Find a 'real' profession." Crossing my arms, I shake my head. "Maybe I'll just skip it."

Ian laughs. "You can't skip your family's Thanksgiving. No matter how badly Ira and Lillian try to derail your career."

"I could say I'm sick."

He gives me a skeptical look. "Like Lillian wouldn't barge through your door and drag you there herself unless you had the Bubonic plague."

"That woman's definitely a force to be reckoned with," I grumble.

"What if you just say you promised to spend the day with us?"

"Wouldn't work."

"Why not?"

"Because I'm pretty sure they'd notice if I didn't go next door for the rest of the day."

"Check this out." Aaron says as he sits back down at the table, one random piece of paper richer than before.

"What's that?" I ask, scrunching my nose. Taking the proffered flyer, I read aloud, "Has your family been on your case lately? As your date to this year's holiday festivities, I'll use my professional training to convince your family that your shortcomings are their own doing."

Ian chuckles. "What? No way."

"Who's Dr. Oliver Rhodes?" I ask as I skim the rest of the flyer. Looking back at Aaron, a sickening feeling settles in my stomach. "What?"

Caution marrs Aaron's every feature. "So ... "

"Oh no." I wince.

"No, no. Hang on. There's this woman at my gym. Her name is Joanna. Well, her wife and brother-in-law have a therapy practice downtown. I think it's one of those converted historic houses."

Ian leans forward. "Aaron ... "

Casting a glance at Ian, annoyance fans the anxiety flame raging in my chest as he just sits there so damn intrigued. *Why are we even discussing this?*

"She's talked about this other guy who co-owns the place. This Rhodes guy." Aaron points to the name on the paper. "Supposedly, he's super cool."

"Apparently cool enough to help gaslight someone's family," Ian finally says.

Squinting at him, I look back down at the paper. "I think this means the guy has to be insane. I mean, there's no way this would even work." Looking at Ian for any kind of support, my brows join the stratosphere.

The man has the nerve to sit there looking like he's actually *for* this. "It might not hurt to go meet the guy," he shrugs. "You never know."

Incredulous laughter tumbles from my lips. "Excuse me? That's probably how I'll disappear, never to be heard from again."

"Here, Cal," Aaron says, offering me his phone.

Staring back at me from the bright screen is a strange man in his early thirties with piercing blue eyes smiling into the camera. Dark blond hair styled perfectly with some kind of mousse compliments his perfectly shaped stubble, hardly disguising a sharp jawline. Broad shoulders are covered by a suit jacket, finished off with a tie matching those striking eyes. There's no denying the guy is hot.

Then I notice the name of the practice. Rhodes, McNalley & McNalley Therapy Collective.

John McNalley, single father to the sweetest student in my class—Cici. *This just gets better and better.*

"Well, I guess it's settled then." Grinning, Ian claps my shoulder.

"Wait, what's settled?"

"You're going to spice up your Tuesday by meeting this guy!"

∼

MAKING my way toward the door, it's exactly as Aaron described it.

A large, renovated Victorian house nestled among all the corporate offices exuding charm and warmth. Inviting plum paint that covers the exterior walls reminds me of a haunted house toy that once sat on my Scooby-Doo birthday cake when I turned seven. Briefly, I glance down at the walkway to see if it's lined with candy bones. While I would've been shocked if it had been, I can't help but feel a slight pang of disappointment when nothing but designer pavers greet me.

My heeled booties click through the snow on the old, wooden deck. Large windows showcase a former living room that now acts as the waiting room. A large Christmas tree is on display in the frontmost window. Any of my kiddos would drool over it if it was in our classroom. Smiling to myself, I shake my head at the thought of their pure wonder. And their easy distraction.

But approaching the door, my smile rapidly disappears as I'm reminded why I'm here.

The bell above the door dings, announcing my presence in the cozy reception area. "Um, excuse me?"

Across the space, a woman old enough to be my great-grandmother smiles warmly from behind a tall mahogany desk positioned near a hallway. "Hello, dear. You don't have to let the cold in, you know." She makes a point of looking over my shoulder to the door I'm still holding wide open.

Never know when you'll need an exit strategy. "Oh. Uh, right." Letting go of the antique handle, a gust of cool air kisses my cheeks as the door swings closed. My cheeks that are now the color of my flaming hair. When I turn back to face the receptionist, a patient smile waits on her plump, overly made-up face. Expertly coiffed gray hair moves on its own thanks to a space heater placed on the far side of the messy desk. Polished fingers poised over a dingy keyboard, the woman watches while I seem to have some kind of brain malfunction.

Gingerly, I make my way across the restored wooden floors, my boots announcing my every movement.

"What can I help you with, dear?"

Face to face with the reality of what I'm about to do, my saliva chooses this moment to travel down the wrong tube. Esophagus reacting, I quickly pull a hand to my mouth as the coughing ensues.

"Do you have an appointment?" she tries again.

"No." Cough. "I." Scratchy death. "I was hoping to—" Delicate noise of me clearing my throat.

"Would you like some water, sweetheart?"

"Please," I manage to croak out.

The woman swivels to the back side of her desk, opening a mini fridge and retrieves a small bottle with a branded label.

Rhodes, McNalley & McNalley Therapy Collective.

Yep, I am unfortunately in the right place.

Taking a swig from the bottle, my organs finally understand that the assault is over and it's okay to work properly again. All while I pray to the hot chocolate gods that John McNalley isn't hanging out near the waiting area.

"Now then, shall we try that again?" The receptionist gathers up a pleated navy skirt before sitting back down on her perch. "You were saying you don't have an appointment?"

Sheepishly, I shake my head. "No, ma'am."

"I can help get you scheduled, if you'd like."

"Oh, um." Replacing the cap on the bottle of water, I think about the folded-up flyer in my purse. "I was hoping to speak with Mr. Rhodes? Today, if possible."

Heat floods my cheeks as a knowing smile spreads across the woman's face. Lucky for me, she doesn't know what she thinks she knows. "Well, I'm sorry, dear. *Dr.* Rhodes is fully booked today. Nor does he take walk-ins." She peers at me over the obnoxiously tall desk.

"Actually, my next appointment was just cancelled." A deep, silky voice travels from around the corner, and a man whose face matches the photo from Aaron's phone comes into view.

The photo did not do him justice.

Holding up a smartphone, he waves it at the woman. "Texted the automated system. Told you it'd make your life easier, Mrs. Lanahan." The man who can only be Oliver Rhodes smirks at her.

Mrs. Lanahan humphs, plopping into the fanciest swivel chair I've ever seen.

"So"—Dr. Rhodes slides the phone into his pocket, looking between the annoyed receptionist and myself—"what can I help you with?" Bright, sky blue eyes land on my warm cheeks.

"Oh, well, um ... " *A brilliant start, Callie. Really. Top notch.*

Each unintelligible syllable that comes out of my mouth causes Dr. Rhodes' welcoming smile to drop bit by bit.

Thankfully, Mrs. Lanahan comes to the rescue. "I was about

to help this young woman make an appointment to see you."
The receptionist casts a sly grin my way.

I look between her and the handsome therapist casually
leaning onto the desk with wide eyes.

That megawatt smile returns, stretching his closely
trimmed beard to its absolute limit. "Well, I have time now, if
that still works for you?"

Any self-preservation left kicks in right then. "You know, I
can just make an appointment." Nervously, I readjust my scarf.
Which is way more difficult now, thanks to the stupid water still
in my hand.

Dr. Rhodes' thick brows pull together. "I really don't mind.
Why don't you give Mrs. Lanahan your insurance card and she
can work on getting that squared away while we chat?" The
annoyingly handsome doctor rotates to motion in the direction
of what I can only assume is his office.

Somewhere in the background, a gust of freezing air
brushes the back of my neck. Shoes scooting across the floor
signal that I'm no longer alone with the handsome doctor and
the ornery receptionist.

"Mr., um, Dr. Rhodes, I appreciate your willingness to
bend your schedule to accommodate me," I offer. My voice
comes out higher than normal thanks to my elevated blood
pressure.

One of those deep golden brows quirks, giving away the
good doctor's piqued interest.

Breaking eye contact, I unzip my purse to toss in the empty
bottle. Right in time for whoever just walked in to bump into
me on their way to Mrs. Lanahan.

Sputtering apologies from them fill the air as the contents
of my purse spill all over the hardwood floor.

"Here, let me help you." Dr. Rhodes rushes forward,
catching a lipstick tube mid-roll.

"That's really okay," I squawk. As is evidenced by Dr.

Rhodes flinching from the closeness. Dropping to my knees, I begin shoving the runaway belongings back into my bag.

Inches away, Dr. Rhodes grabs a pen and notebook. Pieces of his long, slicked-back honey hair fall forward, which he effortlessly wipes away.

I roll my eyes as loudly as I can, knowing full well I would accidentally smack myself in the face if I tried to look that smooth.

A smirk pulls into the corner of his sculpted lips and that award-winning five o'clock shadow.

Frantically, I search for the most important item—the flyer that brought me here.

Too bad the good doctor finds it first.

Leaning back onto his heels, Dr. Rhodes picks up the once-folded paper, shocked eyes never leaving the advertisement in his hand. "Where did you get this?" he breathes.

Pulling in my lips, I glance back to the front desk, where Mrs. Lanahan is knee-deep in an insurance discussion. That must be her favorite pastime, right after making snap judgments about why people come to visit Dr. Rhodes. Looking back to the doctor, I find those intense eyes already staring back at me.

With his gaze never leaving mine, he stands to his full height. Waiting. When I don't immediately follow suit, a large, calloused hand reaches out. "I think we'd better go have that chat, now. Miss ... ?"

"Rutherford." Quickly, I shove the last errant chapstick into my purse before pushing myself up from the ground. Upright once again, I readjust my green wool skirt, working up the courage to look this man in the eye.

"Ms. Rutherford?" His low, deep voice pulls my attention back to his stupidly handsome face.

Squaring my shoulders, I pretend he's one of my students.

Mainly so I won't run away from embarrassment. "Which way was it to your office again, Dr. Rhodes?"

Those sculpted lips tip down ever so slightly, dark blond brows furrowing. But without another word, he turns on his heel and heads back toward the hallway from whence he came.

After one more look at the occupied receptionist, I take off down the hall after him. Thanks to his ultra-long legs, I have to take about three steps to every one of his.

Despite this being a small practice of only three professionals, the converted house gives the feeling of endless space. Revived hardwood floors follow the length of the hall, as does the deep olive paint with gold filigree covering each closed door. Mauve and cream wallpaper covers every wall, with various pictures layered in a gallery style hung up along them. Moments in time of who can only be a younger Dr. Rhodes and the two Dr. McNalleys.

Our footsteps echo through the hall, barely covering the sounds of a crying woman behind a passing door.

"In here." Dr. Rhodes opens a seemingly random door on the left, motioning for me to go inside.

"Thank you," I mutter, politeness kicking in before I can help myself. Brushing past him, cozy hints of cinnamon and apple lingers in the air.

Given the size, the room was probably a closet at some point. Or a bedroom for the guests you hope don't stay long. A simple, dark chestnut desk sits pushed up against the nearest wall, while a mustard loveseat takes up most of the far wall. Next to it, a bronze floor lamp glows, giving the space an intimate feeling.

"Nice office," I say, taking in the tiny space.

Behind me, the door clicks into place right as the leather rolling desk chair protests its master. "Why don't you have a seat?"

"I'm not here for a session."

"I gathered as much," he says dryly. Turning back toward him, I find an unamused Dr. Rhodes holding up the flyer. "Where did you get this?"

Before he can say anything, I snatch the paper from his grasp as nicely as possible. Opting for the only other open seat, I unceremoniously plop down onto the loveseat and let out an unnecessarily large sigh.

Across the small abyss, Dr. Rhodes waits with a patient mask in place. Ever the professional.

But how badly he wants an answer to his question is palpable.

Taking a moment to gather my thoughts, I carefully refold the paper in question. Meanwhile, the self-preservational instinct gnawing at my insides shouts to make him wait.

Too bad I need his help.

Clearing my throat, I start at the beginning. "My best friend found it in a bar."

"In a bar?"

"Yep."

"On a bar?"

"In it. The bar. On a bulletin board to be exact."

"Your friend found a flyer with my information on it, on a bulletin board in a bar."

"Theo's Place, to be exact." Rolling my eyes, I rub at my temples. "I feel like I'm talking to a kindergartener with the amount of comprehension happening right now."

"Gee, thanks."

Despite the sarcastic comment, I can hear the grin in his voice across the tiny space before I even dare look up. "I just mean, um, never mind. Look, the point is, are you serious? About this?" Narrowing my eyes, I don't back down from the blue storms staring right back.

Dr. Rhodes' calculating eyes flit down to my lap.

My nervous hands twist themselves into a permanent knot above the piece of paper that may as well be on fire.

His gaze finally returns to my face, which has decided to match my hair once again. Wordlessly, he swivels to retrieve a brown leather satchel from the floor. Several moments pass as the man rifles through it, pulling out paper after paper.

All while a frown etches itself deeper into his face.

Deciding to make myself comfortable, I allow myself the smallest moment to lean back into the plush loveseat. The sparse decor doesn't do much to hold my attention. If anything, the glitter embedded in my skirt from my class' craft today may brighten the space up a bit.

Thankfully, Dr. Rhodes decides to give up a clearly fruitless search. Letting out a sigh the size of an upset kindergartner, the obnoxiously tall man wipes a hand slowly down his face. "Okay. Okay," he says, more to himself than to me. "Clearly, this was meant as some kind of joke. Dammit, John."

"The flyer was a joke?" My question seems to remind him of my presence.

Taking a moment to compose himself, Dr. Rhodes folds his abnormally large hands together, placing them carefully in his lap. "I'm sorry. Ms. ... ?"

"Rutherford."

"Right. Ms. Rutherford."—the man's tanned cheeks tint a slight pink—"a friend and I were joking around after a particularly annoying family dinner and we came up with, er, what you have there." He nods to the refolded paper in my lap. "It was nothing more than some bullet points on a spare napkin when I last saw it."

"A napkin?"

"Yes, which has obviously been stolen from my bag. Clearly, he felt the need to tease me."

Unsure what to make of that, I pull my lip inward to assault it with my teeth. I think of the tiniest hope I felt when Ian and

Aaron waved the flyer in my face. How my family might have taken me seriously for once in my life. Calloway Rutherford both in a serious relationship and in a profession which is finally validated to her family?

Absolutely unheard of. And apparently, the trend shall continue.

"Is your family really that bad?" Dr. Rhodes interrupts my mini spiral and I reward him with an honest to God *flinch*.

"Uh," is my brilliant answer.

The man across the way changes positions, crossing his legs and getting comfortable as attention finally shifts away from his strange predicament.

"What makes you think they're so bad?" I try to sound defensive, but it comes out more like a timid chihuahua. The couch protests as I move to cross my arms. Which is no small feat since I still have my favorite white peacoat on.

A smirk threatens at his lips, ultimately winning out. "Come on, Ms. Rutherford. They'd have to be quite the unique family for you to be where you are now."

Sniffing, I gain exactly one millisecond to come up with an answer. "They ... they come with their challenges."

Dr. Rhodes snorts.

"Excuse me, but that's very rude," I protest. "I sure hope you're not like that with all your patients."

"You're not a patient," he points out.

Annoyed, I snap my mouth shut before pursing my lips. His amused eyes track my every movement for exactly five seconds before I've had enough. "You know what, I don't know why I came here."

"You came here looking for help."

"Yes. And apparently from the world's rudest therapist." Standing, I look him straight in the eye and brush excess glitter from today's art project from my skirt, the asbestos of the crafting world. *Serves him right. He'll be finding it for years to come.*

The doctor's chair groans as the man stands, possibly to throw himself down at my mercy for unleashing glitter upon his office. "Could you please—"

"Thank you very much for your time, Dr. Rhodes. I'll see myself out." Scooping up my bag, I try to exude any amount of confidence I can and scurry out the door.

"If you could please just wait—"

I don't stop for anything. Especially not the strong hand that brushes mine, sending shockwaves through my nervous system as I pass its handsome owner on the way out.

**4**

*Oliver*

"Wait, please," I try again, reaching for her. But the woman is past me and out my office door before I can grab hold of her slender arm. Glitter falls from her skirt with every sway of her hips, leaving an iridescent trail in her wake. The smell of chocolate persists in my office, threatening to mingle with the cinnamon apple scent I carefully selected years ago.

Not altogether unpleasant.

Following her hurried path down the hall toward the reception area, I call after her again. "Ms., um ... " Dammit. Why can't I remember her name? Oh, maybe it's because I still feel a little shanghaied from John's prank. A frustrated sigh rips through the air as the front door slams shut behind her.

"Dr. Rhodes, I thought we were starting at 4pm sharp." The nervous mother from a particularly draining case calls from her place on the reception couch.

"I know, Shira," I say, pinching the bridge of my nose. "Why don't you all go ahead and head on back? I'll just be another minute." Doing my best to remain as calm as possible, I give her a reassuring smile as she gathers her family.

Shira Collins and her two surly teenage sons make their way to my office as I turn to stare at the front door.

The one elusive redheads run away through.

"Everything alright, Dr. Rhodes?" Mrs. Lanahan smirks up from her post at the front desk. The bright lipstick and blue eyeshadow only enhances the menacing quality of the nosy woman.

Furrowing my brow, I glance back toward the door, willing the redhead to walk back through. "Did you happen to catch that woman's name? The one who just ran out?"

Suspicious eyes flit to the door, then back to me. "Sorry, she never gave one."

"But—"

"Don't forget about the Collins', Dr. Rhodes." The shrewd woman sends me a knowing look, reminding me of the impending headache waiting in my office.

Pressing my lips together, I nod once. "Right." Sighing, I run a hand across the stubble along my jaw. That's what I get for taking Nacho on an evening hike—the inability to wake up on time and make myself look presentable. "If she comes back, will you send her straight to my office? Please?"

Mrs. Lanahan peers over the desk and nods.

Turning on my heel, I'm nearly halfway back to my office where my most unpleasant appointment of the day awaits, when John opens the door to his own hideout, letting a young couple with a girl who can't be more than four out into the hall.

"Hey, man," he says, almost running into me completely. "Sorry about that. You okay?"

Seeing the reason for all of this nonsense causes my heart to race. "Do you have a moment?" I grit out.

Mouth settling into a deep frown, he casts a glance up ahead to the young family. "Just a sec. Wait in here," he nods to his office.

Rolling my eyes, I retreat into the light space. Not much bigger than mine, John's session space feels much larger thanks to the bright color palette. Pictures of sailboats line the walls, even though the man has never once set foot on any kind of watercraft. A sand play station with multiple levels and toy options rests in the corner right beside a yellow, oversized armchair and matching sofa. Crayons lay strewn about the small dark coffee table, clearly having just been used by the little girl. On the far wall, his whitewashed desk sits pushed into the corner, not a pencil out of place as the scent of clean linen lingers in the air.

I guess he's putting the joke gift basket of air fresheners I got him to good use.

Annoyingly, all the items he's put in place to help calm his patients are also lowering my blood pressure.

"What was with the yelling?" he asks, shutting the door behind him. "I don't think I've ever heard you get louder than an upset librarian. And I've known you a long time." John grins, crossing his arms and stretching the fabric of his sweater featuring a cartoon turkey, the light material making his midnight skin appear even darker.

"Just diving right in, I see."

"Sorry, did you want to talk about the weather?"

Letting a scowl slip into place, I take a seat on the sofa.

John follows suit, sitting in the armchair so that neither of us has the upper ground. "Let me know if you'd like some calming music to play in the background. I think I have Bach on shuffle today."

I unceremoniously flip him off, causing him to chuckle.

"So, are you gonna tell me?"

Considering my words carefully, I finally start with, "You made a flyer."

The grin resting on his face drops into a blank mask. John blinks once, twice. "Maybe."

I snort. "'Maybe.' Dude, I saw it."

Dark eyes widen. "What? As in—"

"As in, someone actually brought it here, looking for me. A woman."

That really does it. John bursts out in laughter, leaning back into the chair for stability. "No way, man," he says between laughing fits. "Are you serious?"

"Do I look like I'm kidding?" I ask, flat expression on point.

Tears gather in the corners of John's eyes at my perfected mask of indifference. "Wow," he says, catching his breath. Somehow, slapping his knee seems to help his respiratory difficulties. "It's only been up a couple of days."

"Days?" I practically shout. "You're telling me any number of people could've seen that?"

He shrugs. "Pretty much."

"What were you thinking?"

"That you were bored and needed a little excitement in your life."

"Then take me bowling or something."

John scoffs. "You hate bowling."

"It would at least be less invasive than posting details of a private conversation on a flyer for anyone to see and track me down from."

"Ok, but you can't take Nacho bowling," he points out.

"An annoyingly good point," I grumble. "But there are plenty of activities we could do where she could be included."

Thinking he may concede, I mentally prepare for a victory lap. Then he hits me with, "You said a woman came to see you?"

I groan. "What does that matter?"

"Did a woman come to see you?" John enunciates each word carefully, like this is my first time hearing the English language.

"Yes. Happy?"

"More than you know." I don't have to look at him to hear his grin.

Slamming into the back of the couch, my hands move to cover my face. "This is unbelievable. I was just kidding when I said all that stuff—you had to know that." With my eyes still cloaked in darkness, I can't tell if John's even paying attention. Then again, I know he has to be eating this up.

"Was she attractive?"

Throwing my hands down, I sit upright. "What?"

"You know, out of all your unique traits, being deaf isn't one of them," he smirks.

"John, be serious."

"I am, man." He leans forward, elbows resting on corduroy pants. "So, I'll ask you again. Ready?"

"No."

John snorts. "At least you're honest."

I don't bother hiding the smile threatening to spread across my face. "Like you'd give me any other choice."

"We just want you to be happy."

Narrowing my eyes, I pin my best friend where he sits. "What do you mean?"

John shrugs. "Me. Rindy, Jo. And if some random woman happens to stumble into your life, that may not be the worst thing."

I give a humorless laugh. "Sure, let's just advertise everything about myself with the hopes of finding Nacho a mom."

"They have that," John nods. "It's called online dating."

"Well, I'm not doing that."

"Why not? You know Rindy and Jo would have your profile up and running if you gave the word."

Leaning back into the couch, I shake my head. "Yeah, I don't really wanna know what they'd put on it."

Rolling his lips inward, John nods. "You may be right about that one."

I look him straight in the eye. "Besides, I'm pretty sure that's how you meet serial killers."

"Okay," John throws both hands up, "you officially need to stop watching those true crimes documentaries. Doctor's orders."

Barking laughter fills the room. "Can't man. Sorry."

"So ... "

Exasperated, I ask, "We're not going to do the 'so' thing again, are we?"

Leaning back into his chair, John crosses an ankle over his knee. "Did you find the woman attractive?"

The redhead barges into the forefront of my mind. Her flustered eyes and rosy cheeks that matched her auburn hair when I clearly surprised her in the reception area. She's on the taller side for a woman, and she has the willowy frame to match, despite her curves. Chocolate doe eyes and soft, pink lips; everything about this woman was inviting. Even her crazy skirt somehow coated in glitter, boots that looked well past their expiration date and multi-colored nails screamed that all are welcome in her circle. Then, in my office when she held her ground, her ferocity was shocking.

And I hadn't meant to be an ass, I was just surprised.

But was she attractive? There's no question.

Just as my mouth opens to answer my friend, a determined knock raps on the door before Mrs. Lanahan pokes her overly coiffed head inside. "I hate to interrupt your Tea for Two club, but Mrs. Collins just came out asking if she needs to reschedule."

Cursing under my breath, I push up from the couch.

"This conversation isn't over," John calls from his chosen seat.

"It is if I can help it," I mutter, closing the door behind me.

# 5

*Callie*

The bar is absolutely packed tonight and buzzing with the usual Friday night energy. It's still early, but the start of the weekend usually means more patrons than normal find their way here thanks to the great live music lineup kept by the owners.

Not that Ian and I are biased, or anything.

Every table and stool is occupied, with a line six people deep at the bar for service. Thanks to the steady stream of tourists and the local university, there's even a small line of people waiting to be fortunate enough to gain entrance. Lucky for us, we're with the band. We even have the stamps on our hands to prove it.

"I think I see a couple of spots near the front." Ian points through the throng of beer and music lovers to a rickety table just big enough for two right by the stage.

Following where he points, I nod while my ponytail tickles the back of my neck.

Dead ahead, Aaron and his band are finishing final adjustments. With his brother and friend basically staring in his direction, the lead singer pops his head up and locates us nearly immediately. He gives us a thumbs up alongside a wide grin before getting back to business tuning his guitar of the night.

"Perfect." I jut a thumb toward the bar. "I'll grab the drinks while you snag the table?"

"Cool. Nothing too dark."

"Coming right up."

"And a water, please."

"Got it. Next time, he needs to put out a Reserved sign."

Ian laughs. "Yeah, I'm sure he'll get right on that."

"A girl can dream."

"Hey, think Connie will come tonight?" Ian smirks.

Rolling my eyes, I groan. "Who knows. But at least she's the most bearable of the brood."

"Not to mention, your phone has been blowing up with texts from her since before we got here asking about the details for tonight."

"That may or may not be a decent indicator."

Ian grins before hightailing it to the unicorn of seats.

Wiping my sweaty palms on my jeans, I'm once again thankful the dark wash hides everything from stray marker, to sweat, to beer getting sloshed from strange mugs. Being around this many people after a full week isn't really my idea of a great time. But Aaron's band has worked hard and I'm proud to be a diehard fan.

Sweat and too much cologne mingle with telltale aromas of bar food throughout the room. Even the air feels sticky on nights like tonight. But the buzz in the air for my friend propels me onward. One careful step, then another. With each one, a tiny sigh of relief escapes me as I avoid running into anyone who's already had too much to drink. By the time I'm ten paces away from the bar, I've managed to only step on two toes, be nudged by one erratic elbow and ward off one unwanted suitor.

Though, my mother would tell me to grab any opportunity that comes my way after Alexander dumped me in the spring.

I can see the whites of the bartender's eyes when I hear, "Ms. Rutherford?"

My feet come to a crashing halt. Cringing internally, I'm suddenly cursing Ian for suggesting I wear this stupid "I Love This Alot" T-shirt. This may be one of my favorite shirts, but not when I get caught by a parent. Intentionally teaching incorrect grammar is no laughing matter. Ratcheting my body one, two and three times puts me face to face with a high top table occupied by little Cici McNalley's dad.

And none other than Dr. Oliver freaking Rhodes.

Shock and panic take hold as my fight-or-flight instinct tries to kick in with little success. Apparently, my frozen feet have chosen to fight. Do I pretend not to know him? That would certainly be easiest. I mean, how well can you really know someone after sitting in their office for all of ten minutes while you try to proposition them for their fake dating services? Not very well, I promise.

My no doubt wide eyes land on each of them in turn before landing back on Dr. McNalley. "Uh, hi. Hello. How are you, Dr. McNalley?" I don't need a mirror to tell me my cheeks are as red as my hair right about now. Cici's dad is often the talk of the teacher's lounge—majorly gorgeous, amazing with his daughter, financially stable with an impressive job. Needless to say, having Cici in my class makes me the envy of all the single female faculty members. The one on one parent-teacher conferences don't hurt, either. Mrs. Johnson, our little old librarian, has suggested numerous times I try to wrangle a date out of Serenvale Springs' most eligible single dad. And while he is without a doubt the most attractive parent in the PTA and checks every box for any sexually active human with a pulse, Dr. John McNalley just doesn't do it for me. Sad, but true.

"I've told you, call me John." He laughs before taking a sip of his drink.

"John," I repeat. Much to my relief, one of the giant elephants sitting on my chest decides to vacate the premises.

To his right, curiosity radiates from the obnoxiously hand-some Dr. Rhodes. Silent questions that I purposefully avoid engaging with. I hate that he's so freaking hot. Every second he continues watching our interaction, heat burns brighter in my cheeks.

Slowly dipping my chin in acknowledgment, I slide my gaze to the other person in the group. Familiarity floods my mind as I try to place her. Sitting next to John, it's impossible to miss the resemblance. "And you're ... Cici's aunt, right? You were at the Halloween party and brought those little cookies with the chocolates smooshed into the middle!"

"That's right," she says, a triumphant grin spreading as she peeks at her brother.

"You were the hit of the party," I laugh, an easy smile stretching across my face. Less easy as I remember the blond man staring at the side of my face.

She nods enthusiastically. "Rindy McNalley." Rindy holds out a delicate hand. "It's nice to re-meet you, Ms. Rutherford."

"Callie, please."

"Well, Callie, Cici absolutely adores you," she gushes. Like her brother, Rindy McNalley exudes easy confidence with her professional pantsuit, heels and sleek bob.

Taking her proffered hand, I ask the first question that comes to mind as I try to keep the focus off the one person to whom I don't want to be introduced. "Do you work with John at the practice?"

"Yep. But where these two choose to focus, for God knows what reason, on families, I only work with couples."

Stifling a laugh, my brows hike up a couple of inches. "Oh, wow. I bet that can get pretty intense."

"Definitely. But, at the end of the day, I feel like I've done something. Helped someone. That kind of thing," Rindy nods, shrugging. "Besides, sometimes a couple just need a mediator while they talk things out among themselves."

"Really?" My nose scrunches. "All I picture is couples yelling at each other while sitting on a stranger's couch."

Rindy and John both let out a full laugh while their physically flawless tablemate continues his blatant staring. "Trust me, there's plenty of that, too," Rindy answers. "But we all need a little help sometimes. There's no shame in admitting it."

From the corner of my eye, a smirk slides into place across Dr. Rhodes' face.

"Sure," I shrug. What else am I gonna say while I try not to choke? You know, especially with all my experience being married to someone who loves and supports me.

"What about you, Callie? Are you married?" Rindy tilts her head, looking for a ring I don't possess. Dark, manicured brows knit together while my own shoot back up and my tongue trips all over itself.

"Me? Oh, no." Strained laughter forces its way out. "Maybe one day." If only the earth would swallow me whole at this very moment. I paste a tight smile that feels more like a grimace onto an already burning face. As an excuse to look anywhere but at the table in front of me, I send a quick look back in Ian's direction.

My dear friend, the astute man that he is, looks up just in time to catch my wide-eyed 'save me' signal. A slight nod passes between us just before I have to return my attention to the most awkward conversation of my day. And that includes one of my students asking if not pooping for nine days would make you explode.

I reluctantly cast my gaze back to the table in question, meeting three pairs of questioning eyes that are begging for answers.

Cici's dad leans back, clapping a hand on Dr. Rhodes' shoulder. "Ms. Rutherford—"

"You really can call me Callie," I insist. If the rest of the staff finds out Cici's dad and I are on a first name basis, I'll rule the school in no time.

John smiles warmly. "Callie, this is our other practice partner, Dr. Oliver Rhodes."

I reluctantly slide my semi-panicked eyes to the most handsome doctor at the table.

He starts, "Actually—"

Full-on panic takes over, and I just barely manage to speak over him. "It's lovely to meet you, Dr. Rhodes." Is my casual voice anywhere in the room? Absolutely not. I sound like I just ran a marathon, and my mind repeatedly chants at me not to succumb to the desire to lean forward and catch whatever breath used to reside in my lungs.

Confusion subtly crosses his chiseled features before a few rapid blinks bring the good doctor back to the present. "Uh, yes." He tests out each word that makes its way into the world. "It's nice to meet you, too."

Fully aware of our intrigued audience, I ask the only rational question that bothers to pop into my mind. "How long have you been practicing?"

"About five years now," he answers smoothly before taking a sip from his frosted glass. Like the McNalley siblings, Rhodes looks like he just came from work in his khakis and navy button-down combo. The man shoots a pointed look in my direction. "How long have you been teaching, Ms. Rutherford?"

Thank God, an easy question. "Oh, um, about six years, I

guess? But, y'know, longer if you count student teaching." Because he would know the intimacies of getting a teaching license. Obviously. Folding my arms across my chest, the silent questions being thrown our way from John and Rindy slowly start getting louder. "Well, it was great to see you two again but I should probably get back to my table."

But Rhodes' inquisition doesn't stop, the warm baritone becoming more demanding. "Did you always want—"

"Hey!" A heavy arm appears out of nowhere, landing over my shoulder. Ian grins at the therapists in front of us. "Everything alright?"

Dr. Rhodes' eyes narrow, bouncing between Ian and myself.

"Yep, all good"—I gesture to John and Rindy—"I was just chatting with Cici's family."

Recognition touches his every feature. "Cici McNalley? Oh, cool. From Callie's stories, she seems like a sweet kid," he directs to John.

"I'm doing my best," John mumbles, a small smile playing on his lips.

Ian's brow furrows, though I'm positive I've mentioned Cici's situation before.

"As Ci's favorite aunt—"

"Only aunt," John interrupts.

Rindy waves him off. "And I am, therefore, her favorite. Anyway—" she squares her narrow shoulders "—I think I get to decide if my niece is being raised properly. And while I think she could do with a few more toys," Rindy deftly ignores a pointed look from her brother, "I can say, in my expert opinion, that Ci is the best kid I know."

"I think she's the only kid you know." Dr. Rhodes peers at his colleague across the tiny table.

Rindy merely shrugs, causing Ian to chuckle.

As both our bodies rock with his movement, Rhodes once

again flits his cool eyes between us. I can practically feel his professional opinion forming, albeit incorrectly.

Not atypical for us.

"This is my best friend Ian," I feel the need to explain to our audience. Slipping out of Ian's hold, I pull a Vanna as I officially introduce the fifth member in this awkward impromptu conversation.

"Hey." Calm and cool as ever. Ian plants both hands on his hips, scanning the intimate crowd of three.

The McNalleys respond in kind, while their business partner simply watches.

"His brother is actually the lead singer and guitarist in the band tonight," I offer.

Rindy's eyes light up. "Oh, Aaron Fairchild? He and my wife go to the same gym. Says he's a great guy. It's actually why we're here." She motions to the group as John and Dr. Rhodes share a conspiratorial look.

"Is she coming, too?" I ask.

Rindy checks an expensive-looking watch. I think I'd have to teach for approximately eighteen thousand years to be able to afford a matching timepiece. "She'll be here, but she's gonna be late. An end of day meeting got put on her calendar last minute."

"Well, I know she'll love it, no matter how much of the show she sees. Aaron's band has worked really hard for years." I glance at Ian. Grinning, he's ever the proud brother. "They put their all into every song."

"Cal," Ian whispers, nudging my elbow, "look."

My eyes follow the direction of his nod, where my sister is heading toward us looking extremely uncomfortable.

Constance Rutherford is many things, but fashionable is not one of them. Fitted black trousers are covered by a lumpy beige sweater while her scarlet hair that matches mine is pulled back into a severe topknot. Being on the shorter side of the height spectrum, Imogene has tried getting her to wear heels time and time again to no avail. And here's good ole reliable Connie in her favorite black flats.

"Lovely," I grumble, pasting on a smile for my least annoying sibling. Just in time for her to reach our group. "Hey, Connie."

My sister casts a suspicious glance around our immediate area, taking in the outsiders. "Calloway," she mutters, eyes landing back on me only when she's sure she's seen all there is to see. "Ian." Connie nods as though she's giving condolences.

"Hey Con," Ian practically shouts across the small distance.

She winces at the volume, even with the overall noise in the bar.

"What brings Serenvale Springs' favorite investment banker here on this lovely Friday evening?" I ask, quirking a brow.

"Easy." Ian's whisper is low in my ear. "Don't spook her."

I can't help my answering grin. He's right—you've gotta treat Connie like a wounded animal.

Her face flushes as she stammers, "Well-well, I've known Aaron for a long time and I know it's important to support our friends."

"Then I think it's a great idea that you came." Ian gives her a wolfish grin. "Callie and I have a table up at the front."

I shoot him a sidelong look, silently asking if he's trying to ruin the fun tonight.

"I'm sure we could squeeze in another chair," he finishes.

With the entire force of Rhodes, McNalley & McNalley Therapy Collective watching our interactions, I force my smile even wider. "Ian's right, Con. Join us." I give a half-hearted gesture in the direction of our table.

Connie looks toward the claimed spot. "Uh, do you think we could make room for one more?" Desperation colors her tone, and I know why before I even look behind her.

"Ah, man." Ian elbows me, but I can't help myself. It slipped out.

"Ian." Chris appears from behind his twin in dark joggers and a gray V-neck covered by a navy zip hoodie. His wet, slicked hair means he definitely just came from the gym, and all because his twin sister is nervous of being around a guy she certainly likes but won't admit it. Crossing his arms, judgmental eyes peer straight at me. "Calloway."

"Connie, do you know the first thing I teach my students at the beginning of the year?"

"How to take themselves to the bathroom?" Chris's voice drips with sarcasm.

"Easy," I warn in my best I'm The Sweetest Teacher Don't You Want To Pet Me voice. Nodding to John, I pin my brother with a look that means business. "This is one of my parents, so this may not be the best time to call me a glorified babysitter, dearest brother of mine."

"And I'm an overprotective aunt who likes to kickbox after a long day." Rindy sits up a bit straighter and squares her shoulders.

Chris scoffs, unfolding bulky arms swollen from lifting.

"Enough," Connie whispers to him. It's soft, but it gets the message across.

A small sense of pride blooms in my chest.

"I'll get the drinks," Chris grumbles, stalking off toward the bar. "Meet you at the table."

Connie nods to her twin. Casting one more look at the group of strangers beside us, she shuffles off toward the table.

"And that guy was?" Rindy pushes back a mostly empty glass.

"My brother," I deadpan.

"One of them." Ian snorts.

Heat rises in my cheeks at the realization of how much insight into my life these people have just witnessed.

Especially the man I was stupid enough to actually go and consider asking for help.

"Yeesh." Rindy's response is automatic, eliciting a dry laugh from myself. "Sorry," she backtracks, "I didn't mean for that to come out."

"Trust me, you're not the first." Ian rubs the nape of his neck before turning back to me. "Think tonight's the night?" He quirks a thick brow.

I snort, rolling my eyes. "Dunno. If it's taken them this long ..."

"I still think it's weird."

"Oh, come on," I insist. "I think they'd be good for each other."

"Who?" Dr. Rhodes tips down his sculpted lips surrounded by a perfect five o'clock shadow.

I wish I could say I'd forgotten about his presence, but that'd be a bald freaking lie.

"Connie and my brother," Ian says. He nods toward the band's setup.

"They've clearly had a thing for one another for years," I chime in.

"But they're both oblivious," Ian finishes.

The good doctor's gaze bounces between us, narrowing a little more with each movement. But the final shift lands on me. "Why do you think it'd work between them?"

Being the focus of his attention makes me itch, just like we're back in his office and I'm making an idiot of myself again.

"Aaron's super laid back." Ian to the rescue. Casual. Calm. Collected.

Too bad my nervous system can't relate so long as the most attractive therapist in the room won't release me from the world's weirdest stare-off. This is probably how Rhodes gets his patients to confess to all kinds of things.

Theft. How they can't stand their family.

Murder.

The good doctor's eyes search mine. "Ms. Rutherford?"

I try my best to hide the gulp I force down. "Like Ian said," I shrug, doing my best to look nonchalant, "and you saw Connie. She looks like she could produce a diamond if given enough time."

The corners of those Adonis-like lips lift upward into a secret of a smile.

"Have you ever just tried getting them to talk?" John's question allows me to finally break away from the intensity between myself and Rhodes.

"Trying to get Connie to talk about anything is like trying to convince Callie's dad there's any way other than his," Ian's grin mirrors mine. We've always managed to crack ourselves up.

"Frustrating, useless, and a complete waste of time," I finish. "Maybe that's how Chris has always kept so close to her," I say. "They don't actually have to *say* anything to communicate."

"Speaking of which," Ian replies, "we should probably head to the table. Looks like we need to grab some new seats."

I smile sweetly as every possibility of how to murder Chris with a chair runs through my mind. "Yep. But it was great to see you both again. And, um, nice to meet you, Dr. Rhodes."

Ian pats my shoulder as his way of warning me he's about to whisk me away.

Smiling one more time at the trio of therapists who now know way too much about me, I manage not to choke while meeting each pair of eyes before Ian guides me back toward the stage.

Relief floods my system with each step we take. And apparently, I'm not quiet about it.

Ian chuckles as the band starts their first song. He guides me to a freshly vacated couch near our original spot. "What was that about?" He has to shout to compensate for the newly added volume of the music.

Shaking my head, I send a warning glance toward my siblings. Raising both brows at my friend, I make sure he understands the message.

Ian nods once. Twice. Then it hits him. "Wait. You're telling me—"

"Keep it down," I remind him.

It's only then he remembers all the noise around us means we have to talk louder. Throwing an arm onto the back of the couch, he leans in to whisper, "You never said you actually went to see the guy." I can hear his mischievous smile without even looking. Ian leans away, pretending to listen to the music.

Immediately in front of us, Chris involuntarily nods along with the beat while Connie looks starstruck.

Pain begins to radiate throughout my face as a grin makes its way from ear to ear. Maybe today will be the day my youngest sister finally does something for her own happiness, rather than the twins' collective duo.

Watching the band, I shrug. "Guess I'm just ready for a little acceptance. Is that really such a bad thing?

I don't have to look to see the mischievous glint that waits in my best friend's eye. "Not at all. But if you team up with this Rhodes guy ... "

"What?"

"There's gonna be all kinds of mayhem in the Rutherford home this holiday season."

# 6

*Oliver*

"I was thinking of taking Cici up to the Aspen Point Lodge in Honeyville again, if you all wanna come." With each song played, John's voice gets a little louder. "Figured we'd head up that way a couple days before Christmas, then come home the day after." John keeps inviting Rindy and Joanna to family things to give Cici a sense of maternal figures, but neither of the women in question ever bother to hide their lack of enthusiasm about the annual trip to the Aspen Point Lodge.

Never mind the fact that it's one of the top resorts for the country's one percent. I can't even begin to imagine what the lives of the lodge's owners are like.

"It's just so expensive," Rindy whines, swirling her third glass of red.

John squints across the rim of his own drink to his older sister. "Did I say you'd be paying?"

Rindy merely pushes out her lower lip in response. Typical.

Joanna gingerly removes the fragile glass from her wife's hand and replaces it on the table. "I think what my well-meaning partner means is that we're not totally sure what our holiday plans will be this year," Joanna rubs her wife's shoulder, "and we wouldn't want you to commit financially if we aren't able to make it."

Biting my cheek, I manage to hide a grin. "You know Rindy, it wouldn't kill you to participate in a conventional family holiday. Many people thrive on yearly expectations and traditions."

"Do you hate me?" she asks, dark eyes narrowed.

I don't bother stifling the laughter. "No. But I do think it would benefit Cici to have something to look forward to each year." Another sip of whatever John brought me last slides down my throat.

John shakes his head, pretending to listen to the music while Joanna presses thin lips together in amusement.

"Just because you specialize in families doesn't make you our therapist. You know that, right?" Rindy snorts.

"I'll send you my bill."

"As long as there's a dozen of those homemade chocolate chip peanut butter cookies included that we all know you make, you can send anything you want right on over." Jo interrupts, grinning. I'm pretty sure I see drool forming.

Holding up my mostly empty glass, I cheers and grin right back across the table. "Deal."

"Whatever," Rindy spits. "If you're so interested in family traditions, what are your plans for the holidays this year?"

Easy. I shrug. "Mom and Dad's for Thanksgiving. Then they're going to visit my grandma in Boston for Christmas, so I'll probably see what Blythe's up to."

"Is she not doing the holiday open house at the studio again this year?"

"I'm not sure," I admit. Annoyingly, Rindy looks awfully

smug at the confession. I let out a sigh before continuing, "Some friends of hers were thinking of taking a tropical vacation. Y'know, to get away from the snow and all that."

"Sorry man." John claps me on the back.

"She's an adult and can do what she wants," I say, leaning forward onto my elbows that are resting on the table. "Besides, I don't think she'll be truly content this time of year until she's married with a hundred kids, all of them surrounding a huge Christmas tree."

John and Rindy burst out laughing, having listened to Blythe talk about wanting a big family since we were young.

"Sure, sure," Joanna nods, "and what about you?"

"Me?"

"You."

My lips pull down in response. "I guess I don't understand."

"Oliver." Joanna levels me with a stern look. Her green eyes sparkle, giving away the underlying teasing.

"Jo."

"Don't you think your baby sister, your parents, and—" she waves around the table "—all of us have it pretty good when it comes to the holidays? Even if we end up sitting at home staring at one another with no fancy resorts or vacations?"

I blink at my friend.

Beside me, John chokes on a laugh. "C'mon, man. Surely you don't want to be alone forever."

Rearing back, I feign outrage. I throw a hand to my chest. "I am hardly alone."

"Nacho doesn't count," he retorts.

"She'll be offended when I tell her that. Besides, she's—"

"Your best girl," Rindy finishes as she rolls slightly glazed eyes before throwing back the last of her wine. "We know. But don't you think you might want, I dunno, a human woman at some point?"

It's my turn to roll my eyes as I take another drink. "It's not like I've never dated."

"No one serious," John mutters.

Sending a few optical daggers his way, I try to come up with a name. Any name. "There was ... no, wait. Okay, well, what about ... no, I don't think we ever actually ended up going out. How many dates count as dating?"

Rindy crosses her lithe arms. "How many women have you taken home to meet your family—" a quick survey of the room "—you know, for the holidays?" She snickers. "AKA the ultimate potential partner test."

Huh. "Well, none as an adult, I guess." I swallow the confession with a mouthful of alcohol. "Unless—"

"High school doesn't count," she interjects. I bite my lip and Rindy slaps a victorious palm on the table. "I knew it!"

Joanna tilts her head toward the dance floor. Long caramel waves kiss the table as my friend zeros in on some target in the distance. "What about the redhead?"

Half of my mouthful of beer is now down my shirt. "What?" The back of my hand becomes a napkin without a second thought. Not that it's really doing much good, but Rindy stole the rest of the napkins earlier when she dumped pizza dip into her lap.

Just like that, three pairs of eyes are on me.

"Yeah, the one you keep watching over. Tall? Pretty? Fills the room with sunshine when she smiles?" Jo nods toward Ms. Rutherford, who's currently dancing with her third partner as the band plays on.

Not that I'm counting.

"Ci's teacher. Callie?" John looks a little too smug for my liking.

Eyes sliding back toward the woman in question, I grumble, "She didn't ask me to call her that." I take another swig.

"That's right," Rindy says, pretending this is fresh information. Turning to her wife, Rindy places a hand on John's shoulder. "John and I can call her Callie—sorry, *Calloway*, if you listen to her siblings."

"Unique name," Jo interjects.

"Right? But Ollie, here, wasn't extended that invitation. So I guess she'll just be 'Ms. Rutherford' to him." An irritatingly smug smile is flashed my way.

Joanna's light brows shoot up, inquisitive eyes finding mine. "And how does that make you feel, Oliver?"

The entire table busts out in laughter, but with the bar this crowded, no one even bothers looking our way. Not that most of them would even know who we are. There are plenty of locals here, but the nearby university and tourists keep a steady stream of new faces around.

Catching his breath, John polishes off the drink in front of him. "And what was with trying to get in a lightning round of personal trivia, anyway?" Like his sister, John's scrutinizing eyes peer in my direction. Our group may have an unspoken rule to not psychoanalyze one another, but that doesn't mean we can just turn it off. "I've never seen you act that way."

"Especially not with someone you just met," Rindy agrees, "unless they're a patient."

My gaze bounces between them a moment too long.

"You've met her before." It's Jo that blows my cover.

"Is she ... a patient at our practice?" Rindy asks, looking to her brother for any indication he knows something she doesn't.

No words form. Not in my head, not from my mouth. Nothing. What am I supposed to say without betraying Ms. Rutherford's confidence when she came to see me? Albeit, about something I said to a friend as a joke. But it was still in my office —a place of privacy and professionalism.

"No," John's confidence is almost overshadowed by his confusion, "she's definitely not seeing any of us."

"And just why not?" Rindy demands, clearly affronted that

Ms. Rutherford seems to be lacking any emotional issues that need sorting.

"Well, she's not married," John starts, "so it's not like she'd come to see you. And I'm pretty sure her family is one of the wealthiest around, so I'm sure they'd just call in a professional privately." That catches everyone's attention.

The women wait for him to continue with rapt attention while I try my best to not create a mental dossier about the woman currently spinning around on the dance floor.

"Yeah, her dad and brother are two of the senior partners at Rutherford, Rutherford, MacCallum & de Luksa. And that's just to start. I know she has a few siblings, and I think they all have pretty intense jobs."

"Have you met any of them?" Joanna asks, leaning around her wife to hear John better. She may as well be listening to a ghost story.

My face remains in a statuesque state, only violating my frozen state to blink.

John shakes his head. "Only the two that stopped by here before the band started."

"And they both seem like a delight," Rindy scoffs. "You think she's anything like them? That certainly wasn't the vibe I got."

"No way, Callie's great. And she's great with the kids."

"How do you know so much about her?" My voice is soft, but the broken silence redirects everyone's attention back my way. Great.

John considers his answer. "We chat during parent/teacher conferences. I help out with the classroom parties and field days. That kind of thing. She's easy to talk to. And with our training, it's not difficult to pick up on certain things." He laughs. "Like the fact that she is obviously the black sheep of her family. Though, she did say something a while back about how being in a relationship may help. Or at least give her some backup at family gatherings. Sounds like she needs it."

"Well, I liked her." Rindy shrugs as she swirls her empty glass. "Maybe a bit young, though. Especially for Grandfather Rhodes, here."

Joanna waves her off, looking back at the dance floor to the woman of the moment. "I'd guess late twenties. Plenty old enough. What do you think, Oliver?"

My wayward eyes slide back to the attractive woman who is apparently old enough for me to date, according to my friends. Callie and the man she introduced as her best friend dance chaotically to a song about a woman coming into some guy's life like a storm he wishes he could've prepared for. Their laughter is easy; years of shared history flowing between them.

A frown takes over my features as I watch their obvious comfort with one another. The ease of their relationship.

That damn flyer.

Why doesn't she just have this guy pretend to be her boyfriend? It's clear they get along and could likely convince everyone they're dating. They look like they're dating. Or have some kind of weirdly close sibling relationship.

Realization hits me. It's because of what else was advertised. The promise to make the family in question believe Callie's flaws are their fault.

That's why Jordan ... Callan ... Ian—whatever his name is— isn't enough. The relationship is only the first part of what could help her be accepted by her frigid family.

The second part is my opinion, which may or may not be totally professional at this point.

Callie stands on her tiptoes and whispers in the man's ear before releasing him and turning to the table where her siblings sit. The brother frowns up at her as she says something he clearly doesn't appreciate.

The brother who apparently calls her a glorified babysitter. He must be a real ass if that's what he thinks of educators. Especially ones like his effervescent sister who works with young, impressionable kids. And who, according to John, is amazing at her job.

My frown deepens.

The sister doesn't pay much attention to Callie, either. All of her attention is taken up by the lead singer. Callie's friend's brother.

And just like in a standard family session, lines start forming. Methods to heal the broken communication in her family begin mapping themselves out.

Callie doesn't have to be an outsider. She chooses to remain true to who she is rather than conforming to the Rutherfords' values.

"Wait a second," John holds up a hand. Twisting around, he looks me square in the eye.

Meaning I have to stop watching what Ms. Rutherford is doing, not totally unlike a newly obsessed stalker.

His gaze flits toward the dance floor as the music continues blaring. "Was it Callie that ran out of your office earlier this week? Callie Rutherford?"

I don't get a chance to answer.

"Why was Callie in your office?" Rindy demands.

"I never said she was," I point out.

"I was pretty sure I recognized her voice, but didn't want to say anything in case it was weird," John says carefully. "Of course, she knows what I do. But I figured, if she was at the office, she'd be there to discuss Cici." A frown works its way onto my friend's strong features.

Joanna cuts in, "You think she was there to see you and got to Oliver first?"

"She wasn't there to see John." The words are out before I can stop them.

One, two, and three of my closest friends look my way. All of them silent, waiting.

But John's eyes widen before I can say another word, raucous laughter pouring from him.

His sister and sister-in-law watch the sudden change, clearly wondering if he's having some kind of fit.

"What's going on?" Joanna asks. Careful, like asking too intently will bring about catastrophe.

Confusion mars Rindy's pinched face.

"Oliver?" Jo tries again.

Rindy pokes her brother's arm. "Any time you'd like to quit your cackling and explain yourself would be fantastic."

I, on the other hand, pray to anyone listening that the music doesn't come to a crashing halt and divert all the attention our way.

Especially one redhead, in particular, who's now dancing with her brother while he looks ready to pass out from boredom at any moment. Sighing, he moves to spin her, nearly causing her to crash into another woman.

With every bout of John's laughter tainting the musical experience, my chest tightens a little more. Tears begin leaking from his eyes with every shake, only increasing in volume as he hunches over the table for stability.

Annoyance flares as my friend finally catches his breath. "No way," he wheezes. The hand not gripping his glass reaches up to wipe away the saline. "I can't believe it." Another choked laugh makes its way into the world.

"Uh, hello," Rindy presses.

I've never been one to embarrass easily, but right now, I'd love nothing more than to crawl under the table and wither away. It doesn't help that my best friend's sister is like a bloodhound—there's no stopping her once she's caught a scent.

Rindy's eyes narrow more, which I honestly didn't believe was possible.

John slaps the table once more before taking a big breath. "When you came to see me ... not that I knew it was her but ... " he blinks. "Wow."

Jo and Rindy are chomping at the bit for answers, and I know we can't hold them off for much longer.

"John," I warn.

"So, what did you say?" My friend quirks a thick brow and I have the sudden urge to shave it right off his smug face.

"To what?" Rindy practically yells, throwing exasperated hands in the air.

It's right then that the band finishes their current song. Only half a second passes before every person in the joint is focused on our table. Even the band hesitates a moment too long before starting up again.

My eyes unwillingly seek out the one person I wish they wouldn't. But Calloway Rutherford is already staring right at me, her chocolate eyes indecipherable as sweat slicks face-framing hairs to flushed cheeks.

"Uh, one, two, three, four," the lead vocalist chants into the mic. And just like that, Mr. Callie Rutherford's Best Friend's Brother leads the entire bar back into a state of normalcy.

Even Callie turns back to her group, taking a drink from a tall pint glass. Cider, judging by the label etched into the side. Sweet with a tart aftertaste, just like I'd imagine she would be after running out of my office, leaving glitter all over my sofa.

The world of crafting's personal virus.

It's been three days and I'm still finding that crap every-where. Even places she didn't touch.

"That must've been one hell of a conversation." John clap-ping my shoulder pulls my attention back to the three nosiest people in the room.

Reluctantly, I turn back to the maniacal grin I already know is waiting for me on John's face.

"Would either of you boys like to, y'know, fill us in?" Calm, curious, and patient. Jo really is the perfect opposite to her wife, who is demanding, nosy and needs information five years before she might use it.

But it's what makes Rindy good at her job.

The roll of my eyes gives John all the permission he needs. "A couple weeks ago, our boy Oliver and I were in this very bar. Mom and Pop Rhodes had been giving him a hard time about needing a wife—again, I might add."

Joanna's brows furrow with each new statement, trying to piece everything together.

Rindy, on the other hand, looks fascinated.

Kill me now.

"After a couple of drinks, we got to talking about familial ideas and projected happiness. That's when Oliver had a bright idea." John's nothing if not a good storyteller. He should've been a damn poet. "With the holidays coming up, there will be plenty of time for families to pressure us single folks into finding love. So what if Oliver were to pretend to be their date to the festivities?"

"Why do I get the feeling that's not all?" Jo's cautious voice eases the tiniest bit of tension in my chest, a small smile breaking out.

"Because this is what sets Oliver apart as the ultimate holiday date—" John McNalley, the ultimate salesman "—as a prominent family therapist in our area, he'll convince their family that everything believed to be wrong with them is actually the family's doing." John crosses his arms, satisfaction written all over his face.

I've never seen Rindy speechless, but even I'll admit it's a pretty nice sight.

"Okay," Joanna nods, "but what does ... holy crap." And two and two are now four. "But wait, Callie?"

My turn. "Remember, I just said this in passing. Then my

good friend"—I look pointedly at the man next to me—"took it upon himself to actually act on the idea."

Both women turn incredulous faces in John's direction.

John simply shrugs. "All I did was open a document, make a flyer and post it in the bar. Anyone could've done it. It's not my fault someone acted on it."

"Well, can we see this flyer?" Rindy presses. She holds out a perfectly manicured hand.

"I only made the one copy and threw the original notes away after I stole it from Oliver's bag."

"And Callie shoved it back in her purse before she ran out of my office," I add. Since we're obviously on a Tell All.

Jo waves her hands in front of her face. "Wait a second, when did Callie come see you?"

"Tuesday afternoon."

Rindy whips around to fully face John. "You've known about this since Tuesday and are just now saying something?"

"I didn't know anything for sure," John reminds her. "I mean, that's when I knew someone came to see him about it. But I didn't know who it was. Besides, it's not like you really would've known who Callie was outside of the Halloween party."

"Of which I was the hit," Rindy gloats.

"Which brings us back to," Joanna redirects at me, "what did you tell her?"

I frown. "What do you mean?"

"Did you tell her you'd do it?"

I may as well be under a microscope with how hard my friends are staring at me. My face flames, but I employ every facility to ignore it. "I mean, she never actually asked me anything." Based on all the blinks I'm receiving, I'm doing a splendid job of explaining myself. Sighing, I try again. "She got there and, from what I gathered, Mrs. Lanahan was trying to get her to make an appointment when I came in. Callie tried to leave when Mr. Klosten arrived and bumped into her, dumping her purse contents all over the floor, including the flyer, which I found. When we got back to my office, I asked if her family was truly bad enough that she'd come looking for what the paper offered."

John snorts. "If the brother we saw tonight is any indication, the answer is yes."

"Yeah, well, she didn't really give an actual answer. Just something about them having their challenges."

"Talk about an understatement." Rindy elbows her wife. "I mean, yeesh."

"So," John sends his sister a playful warning, "how did you leave it?"

"She ran out of my office, man."

"Okay, that's not great." He nods. "But that explains why she pretended not to know you tonight." Yeah, that wasn't my best work.

Running a hand through my hair, I watch with an annoying amount of nerves as the three look between themselves. "What?" I ask wearily. Though I'm not sure I really want to know the answer.

It's like they're holding council among themselves. It's unnerving.

"I think you should do it." If Rindy didn't have that look she gives each and every patient, I'd think she was kidding.

I snort. "Excuse me?"

"Come on, what've you got to lose?" she presses. "And you could always just agree to Thanksgiving. That would give you both an out in case it's too weird."

"You know," John starts, a little too slowly for my liking, "the poster's message was one-sided."

"But?"

"But"—he hesitates again—"what if it was reciprocal?"

Jo and Rindy both look a little too excited at that particular prospect.

"What, like she comes to my family's Thanksgiving, too?" I am now all too aware that the music has stopped and wonder what, if anything, anyone listening in would think our group is discussing.

"Yes, Oliver. That's exactly what that means." He waits for me to process before continuing, "Think about it. It would help you get your folks to cool it for a bit."

"Which is apparently how all this started," Jo laughs. "I think it's perfect."

Rindy nods in the direction of the bar. "Look, she's over at the bar. Just go talk to her." She shrugs. "If anything, it'll be great entertainment for us."

"Lovely," I grumble, since I don't really want to admit that I already knew Callie had gone to the bar, and was being watched by no less than two potential suitors.

John makes a shooing motion.

Rolling my eyes, I push back from the table, a half-full glass in hand. I weave through the throngs of sweaty people waiting to be served and step right up behind her. She hasn't noticed me yet and man, does that make me feel like a creep. Blythe always says she prefers when a guy announces himself so she's not startled. Since I don't have a fancy man in a robe and scepter to proclaim my arrival, I stick with clearing my throat.

Callie doesn't so much as look up from her phone, but a young man about her age standing next to her does. Cutting a judgmental gaze my way, the guy tries to puff his chest to stake his claim. Pulling out my withering glare, it doesn't take long for him to scramble away with his fresh drink.

I don't waste any time taking the open space next to her.

Fully engrossed in looking at pictures of strange plants on her phone, she goes on unaware of my presence.

Here goes nothing. "I noticed you didn't say that I could call you Callie."

She freezes, thumb mid-scroll.

"Of course, I'm happy to call you whatever you'd like," I continue, "but if we do this, I should probably call you something less formal."

Delicate ruby brows knit together as Calloway Rutherford turns my way. How does a human being smell like chocolate and sweat? "If we do what?"

"You know, pretend to date while I convince your family they're crazy."

Throwing a panicked gaze over her shoulder one way, then the other, that long ponytail barely misses slapping me square in the face. "Shh!" She glares back at me.

"What?"

"Could you please not say that so loud?"

"Which part?"

"Any of it."

Now it's my turn to frown. "Sorry, are you not still interested? You did come to see me, after all."

"Everything okay, Callie?" the bartender asks her, eyeing me suspiciously.

"Oh, yeah." She gives him a breathy laugh, waving him off. "He's just a friend. But I'm fine."

The bartender nods to her before setting a giant glass of water down in front of her and heading to the next patron.

I quirk a brow. "Just a friend, huh?"

Callie rolls her warm brown eyes, the same color as the light dusting of freckles coating her nose. "Look, Dr. Rhodes—"

"You should really call me Oliver."

"Dr. Rhodes—"

"Is that how you'd introduce me to your family?" I ask, gaining far too much enjoyment from the lovely blush spreading over her cheeks.

"I mean, not if we ... you know—" she sighs "—but we're not. So it's a non-issue."

"Sorry, when did we decide we're not? May I?" I nod to the water sitting in front of her. "John has a habit of ordering me beers that are a little too dark for my liking." Callie hands over the water without a moment of hesitation. I waste no time taking a large swig before replacing it on the counter.

"I thought the flyer was a joke?" Callie crosses her arms as she leans the side of her frame into the bar.

I shrug. "Originally, yes." Watching her every movement, I choose my words carefully. "But I think we could both benefit from it."

She scrunches her tiny nose. "Both of us?"

"Yep," I nod. "Thanksgiving. You come with me to my parents' house and convince them I can have a steady relationship. In return, I'll go to yours and fulfill the duties listed out on the poster. You introduce me as your serious boyfriend all while I use my professional training to your advantage."

"I'd introduce you as my boyfriend," she repeats, "and you'd basically convince them I'm really a functioning adult."

"That everything they believe to be wrong with you is actually their doing," I correct.

Skepticism coats each angelic feature of the woman's face. "I have a hard time believing your family needs convincing of anything," she finally says.

A laugh bursts from my chest. Her shock, punctuated by widening eyes, isn't lost on me. "My parents think I work too much. And neglect a love life for time spent with my dog."

Callie brightens. "You have a dog?"

I nod. "Nacho."

A musical giggle tumbles from her lips. "What a name."

"She's a golden retriever I rescued when she was just a baby. I can't believe she's three now." A smile I didn't even feel form widens. "My mom wanted me to name her something like

Daisy. When my sister suggested Nacho, my mom begged for it
to be anything else. And it just stuck," I shrug.

Grinning, Callie shakes her head. "So, you're quite the
rebel, then?"

"Oh, absolutely." I flash her my toothiest grin. "Look, I
know things didn't go too well on Tuesday." The way her face
drops at the mention of my poor behavior is like a knife to the
gut. "But I really do think we could help each other."

"I dunno ... " Rolling her lips inward, she glances somewhere behind me.

"I'm not saying it'll be easy, but who knows? If it gets our
families off our backs, even for just a little while, wouldn't that
be worth it?"

Callie takes a drink of the water while I try not to think
about how my lips once touched where hers now deign to
grace. Cautious eyes flit back toward my table. "Do, um, they
know?"

Ah. "Yes," I answer matter-of-factly. "But it can actually be
to our advantage."

This piques her interest. A raised brow gives away her every
worry.

"They can help us build a backstory. Corroborate our story
if needed, that kind of thing."

Callie nods, more to herself than me. Thinking. "And they'd
do that? Go along with it, I mean?"

"They've already agreed." Not really, but I highly doubt they
would object.

Callie raises her brows.

I merely shrug.

She considers this for a moment. But the amount of relief I
feel is annoying when she answers, "We'd need to come up
with a game plan. If we were to do this."

"We can do that."

She bites down on her full bottom lip. "It's Friday."

Slowly, I nod. "Yes ... " Not that I looked too hard at my calendar today, but I believe her.

"Thanksgiving is in less than a week," she finishes.

Got it. "Would you want to grab lunch this weekend to hash out the details?"

Callie shakes her head. "Sorry. I already have plans."

"With your other boyfriend?" I tease. Mainly because I'm trying to ignore how much her rejection stings.

Callie smirks. "Oh, absolutely." But she laughs a glorious, carefree laugh. "No, I'm helping Ian move."

"How about early next week?" I offer.

"I have school through Wednesday," she says, eyes downcast.

Shrugging nonchalantly, the words are out before I can even truly consider them. "I could come and have lunch in your classroom. How about Monday?"

Callie's brows shoot up, clearly unfamiliar with the concept of a lunch date at school. "Fair warning, you may get glitter on you."

I playfully roll my eyes. "I doubt it'd be any more than you left in my office earlier this week."

Somewhere in the background, the band starts up again for their next set.

Callie casts a quick glance back toward her group, raising the water glass to whomever she's sending a message. "Well," she says, turning back to me, "I'll see you Monday? Eleven AM?"

"See you Monday, Ms. Rutherford," I murmur.

Hope blooms in her features for the first time since I've met her. Curious eyes roam my face as a small smile plays on her rosy lips. Without another word, Calloway Rutherford turns and wanders back into the crowd.

# 7

*Callie*

I changed my outfit four times this morning. Four times. The last time I did that was ... well, never. But those four little texts this morning reminded me that Friday night really happened. That this could really be happening. That I, Calloway Leora Rutherford, might have a fighting chance to change the way my family sees me.

Maybe.

UNKNOWN NUMBER:

> Are you allergic to anything at Sandra's Sammies? It's on the way, so I thought I'd stop there and grab us some food.

> This is Oliver.

> Rhodes. I got your number from John's classroom parent phone number sheet. To be fair, I did have to bribe him with donuts.

> I always bring my lunch, but thanks for asking. See you soon.

> See you soon, Ms. Rutherford.

I'D BE LYING if I said I didn't have a mini panic attack standing in my bathroom wearing outfit number three. Because let's be honest, a kindergarten teacher can only look so fancy without drawing attention. And not even from the other staff. If the kids think something's off, they'll have no reservations about telling me to my face. This is coming from a woman who once had a student say my tropical print skirt looked like thrown up candy.

Seriously, zero filters around here.

So, take kids with no brain-to-mouth filters and add one lunch date in my chaotic classroom with a man who is stupidly handsome and going to pretend to be my boyfriend at my family's Thanksgiving, and what do you get?

One frazzled teacher in her only pair of actual work pants and a brand new green sweater that's already covered with a giant hot cocoa stain. Thankfully, my name badge covers most of the chocolatey blob. Oh, and let's not forget how my curling iron decided to quit working halfway through doing my hair, which is now in one very full ballet bun.

Lunch is only ten minutes away and counting, and dot tokens are absolutely everywhere as I attempt the world's most chaotic cleanup. On the tables, on the floor. Stuck to Jack's shirt, thanks to a booger he graciously showed me, and in Maria's pigtails. And that's just the ones I can see.

Checking one of the last two tables and their cleanup progress, a soft knock raps on the classroom door.

Panic wastes no time shooting through my nervous system. *Relax, Callie. It's probably just a literacy coach. Or the janitor.* But a thorned vine winds itself through my ribcage, thoroughly attuned to who waits on the other side of the door. I guess that's just what happens when one gets a fake boyfriend.

Outwardly, I scoff at my own wishful thinking that it could be literally anyone else.

"Ms. Rutherford, there's someone at the door!" And there goes any remaining zen I've managed to gather this morning. Jameson should really be some kind of commentator when he grows up.

Anna giggles into her hand beside me. "He looks like my daddy."

"I sincerely doubt that," I mumble, steeling myself to turn around and face who I know waits on the other side of the door.

Sure enough, through the glass paneling, there stands Dr. Oliver Rhodes suppressing a grin. "Flipper nuggets," I whisper. Marching toward the door with as much confidence as I can muster, I will myself not to take in Dr. Rhodes and all of his obscene handsomeness. It's a lot easier than I anticipated thanks to the dark brown overcoat he's wearing.

Of course, the reflection in his round glasses shows that I'm not lying to myself quite as well as I'd like to believe.

But his soft smile makes me extremely aware that eighteen pairs of eyes from tiny humans are glued to my back. In fact, I think it's the quietest my class has ever been.

Opening the door, a subtle hint of sandalwood wafts into the classroom. Too bad this is the worst time for a drool check. Some kind of delicious food in a tan takeaway bag distracts me enough to remind me that the poor guy is still just standing in the doorway. "Hey, come on in," I say as casually as possible. Though it probably sounds like a train just ran over my foot.

Rhodes looks past me at our audience. Amused eyes slide back to mine, brows raising.

"Don't worry about them," I laugh, "they have lunch in a few minutes. Why don't you go hang out at my desk while we finish up?" I point to my corner sanctuary, which I did try to clean up a bit this morning.

'Try' being the operative word.

"Oliver!" Cici McNalley shrieks. Jumping up from her table, the sweetest girl in the world hurls herself across the room in record time, before throwing tiny arms around his waist.

The man tosses his free arm around her shoulder in a tight embrace. "Hey, Cici." Releasing her, he crouches down so that he's eye-level. "Have you made your dad any new drawings today? With extra glitter?" He sends a knowing look my way.

But my favorite student clearly has her own agenda. "Why are you here?"

Dr. Rhodes chuckles. "I came to have lunch with your teacher."

"Are you friends?"

A secretive smile threatens to overtake the man's face. "You could say that."

Cheeks heating, I turn back to help the other kids finish getting ready for lunch. Though, it's really to ignore whatever Dr. Rhodes is telling Cici.

Not a moment too soon, Mrs. Fairchild and her class knock on the door to pick up my kids and take them to the cafeteria.

I don't miss the double take she does to the good doctor sitting at my desk. Not that I blame her.

"C'mon, Cici," I call to the little girl holding on tight to his neck.

Cici whispers something in his ear before snatching a pink

lunchbox from her cubby and bounding to the line of students leaving without her.

Shutting the door behind them, my classroom is now a vacuum, and I am instantly aware of how very alone Dr. Rhodes and I are. Turning back toward my desk, I find the man of the hour sitting in a student chair about eighty sizes too small, across the desk from mine.

Having shed the overcoat, the man sits there like a modern Greek god in his black slacks and tan sweater. With a paper napkin on one leg, he unpacks a sandwich and chips from the bag marked Sandra's Sammies, while a soda sits already opened beside it.

"I didn't know you wear glasses," I blurt out.

Dr. Rhodes pauses, subconsciously readjusting the thin gold frames. "You've only seen me twice," he shrugs. "There's no way you could have known, unless you're able to divine optometrical records."

"Not currently. But it's next on my list of useless gifts to learn."

Rolling his lips in, the man nods. "What are you currently working on?"

"What?"

"You said it was next, which means there's some other impractical talent you're trying to learn."

"Huh," I say, looking back over my shoulder. Gotta double check I don't have an audience for this meeting of the minds. "Uh, then I guess it'd be how to not have my curling iron die mid-curl."

I turn back just in time to watch his eyes flick up toward my hair. "You'd pick that over mastering how to never spill your coffee?" he grins.

So he definitely noticed the stain. Pressing my lips together, I take a deep breath. "Cocoa. It's an ongoing project," I answer, much to his amusement. My stilted laugh sounds more like I'm being choked as he attempts to readjust in his tiny chair. "Why don't you take my seat? It'll be much more comfortable for you and all your tall ... ness."

The man lifts a thick honey brow before shaking his head. "No, thanks. I'm good here." He beams. "Besides, it's my turn to be in your office."

Crossing my arms, I snort. "Look, if you stay in that chair, you'll have cramps by the end of this. Then you'll be stuck here until maintenance can come and unstick your butt from it. With the holiday approaching, that could be days. And if that's the case, you'll be worthless to me." Shrugging, I do my best to appear nonchalant and not show the extreme panic boiling below the surface about how this stupidly hot man is supposed to be my pretend boyfriend in no less than four days.

In front of my entire family.

Oh, and I'm going to be his pretend girlfriend for his family too. Let's not forget that fun little tidbit.

Dr. Rhodes narrows his annoyingly striking eyes, considering it. Finally, logic wins out.

Or the fear of being left here over Thanksgiving break without snacks.

It takes him longer to get out of the chair than it should, but when he does plop himself down on my adult-size swivel chair, his relief is apparent. "Your classroom is about how I pictured it."

"How's that?" I ask absently while I focus on reaching to the cabinet above him for a stashed lunchbox. Plant-themed, of course. But it's more to ignore how close my boobs have to get to his face mid-reach.

I don't miss how he tenses at maximum boob-closeness.

My face flames as the stupid lunchbox decides to choose today of all days to play Keep Away.

Thankfully, the good doctor recovers quickly. "Colorful,

warm. Chaotic. A little noisy." His point is exacerbated by a flinch as I scoot the tiny chair closer to the desk.

"The chaos would happen with or without my help. That's more thanks to the eighteen children I have running rampant in here five days a week."

"Of course."

"So ... you've been picturing my classroom, huh?" Taking a bite of salad, I do my best to not be envious of the mouthwatering sandwich in his hands. Why, oh why, did I have to be polite when he offered food this morning? A sandwich from Sandra's Sammies would always be better than some dumb salad.

Swallowing, he grins. "Remember, I need to know as much about you as possible. What with you being my girlfriend, and all."

"Fake girlfriend."

Rhodes shrugs. "No one knows that. Except John, Rindy and Joanna."

"And Ian."

His lips tip down. "Your friend from the bar?"

"Yep," I nod, ignoring his slight frown. "He's my best friend. And he's actually the one who found the flyer. Well, his brother is. But Ian encouraged me to come see you in the first place. Aaron doesn't know I actually went to find you."

"Huh."

"So, really, we owe this entire outlandish situation to him." Looking around my classroom as a slight reprieve from the intense stare of the doctor, I swallow and ask the one question screaming in my mind. "Dr. Rhodes, do you really think this will work?" I mumble.

He laughs, bringing my gaze immediately back to him. "Not if you don't start calling me Oliver. Unless they'll think it's some kind of kinky foreplay thing?" Narrowing my eyes must be enough of an answer, because he clears his throat before continuing, "No, seriously, I think it's worth a try. Besides, it doesn't really sound like your family could get much worse. At least, from how John talks about them."

My head snaps up from my grapes. "Wait, what?"

The man has the nerve to hesitate. "John may have mentioned you two have chatted in the past about the social experiment that is your family."

"They're not all bad." Now, it's my turn to frown up at the handsome doctor. "I mean, Prescott's, well, Prescott. Same with Imogene. But they're both always under a lot of pressure at work," I amend quickly.

"Which one is the aeronautical engineer?" he asks around a mouthful of sandwich.

"Imogene. And she's the second oldest after Prescott, who works with my dad at the law firm. Rutherford, Rutherford, MacCallum & de Luksa."

Swallowing, Rhodes peers around the small space of my cramped classroom. "Do they really call you a glorified babysitter?"

Dry laughter escapes. "Among other things. Chris is the worst, though," I grimace. "But our feud's been going on for years."

"And he was the brother at the bar on Friday? With your sister?"

Taking a swig of hot cocoa from my thermos, I nod. "The one and only."

"What does he do?" I don't miss the disdain in his tone, no matter how casual his handsome mask may be.

"He does financial analysis for the Bank of Serenvale Springs. He was really only there Friday night because of Connie. Constance. His twin. She does investment banking and is one hundred percent my favorite sibling. But don't tell the others!"

Oliver's eyes soften. "I won't tell them anything you don't want me to."

"Really?" My eyebrows miss the memo about hiding my shock.

"Of course," he laughs. "You and me? We're a team, Ms. Rutherford."

"Wow. I've never been on a team before." Something swells in my chest. Pride. Satisfaction. Heartburn. Who really knows.

"Never?"

"Never ever."

"You didn't play any team sports when you were younger?" Oliver doesn't bother hiding his surprise. "You're pretty tall. No basketball?"

"Nope. Ira and Lillian were too busy toting around the four other high-achieving Rutherford kids to their many activities. And scholastic events."

Oliver blinks. "Well, that speaks volumes."

"What about your family?" I ask. "Oh, and I guess you should call me Callie. Especially since everyone else does. But, I guess my boyfriend most definitely would."

He smirks. "Not Calloway?"

Rolling my eyes, I groan. "Do *not* call me that."

"Why not? Might be a little, well, formal for you. But it is your name."

"Way too formal," I say, scrunching my nose. "Y'know, stuffy."

He rolls full lips in, considering this. Finally, he nods. "Callie, then." He tests the nickname, causing heat to lick the tips of my ears.

"You've been, uh, still calling me Ms. Rutherford." My strange excuse of an explanation has me working to not face palm myself. I settle for taking another swig of molten chocolate. Gotta balance that salad.

Curious eyes roam my features before a glorious smile

settles on his movie star face. "You never told me I could." He shrugs. "I didn't want to assume."

Wiping my mouth, I give a flourish with my free hand. "So ... your family?"

"Oh," he says, as though he forgot they were even part of this equation. "Right. They're definitely a whole different ball-game than yours."

Feigning shock, I throw a hand to my chest, strategically covering the cocoa stain. "You mean to tell me that they're not extraterrestrial overlords whose society is teeming with cats ready to pee all over your plants at a moment's notice?"

"Shocking, I know," he deadpans. But those eyes sparkle as he suppresses a grin. "But, no, my family is super close."

"Must be nice," I grumble, much to his amusement.

Oliver chuckles, pulling something else from the paper takeout bag. "It—what?" He blinks rapidly. "Did you change your mind?" he winces. Then he notices what I can only assume is the drool forming in the corner of my mouth.

"What is that amazing smell?" I don't even care that my eyes are probably the size of a circus Big Top. Whatever is coming from Oliver's bag can only be a gift from the gods.

The beautiful man blushes furiously, pulling a small Ziplock bag of cookies from their hiding place. With only a moment of hesitation, he holds them out to me. "I made them. Chocolate chip and oatmeal. I'd love to share them with you, if you'd like." Without waiting for an answer, Oliver opens the bag and hands one over.

One bite is all it takes. "Well, I think I'm in love," I sigh.

Laughter bursts from his lips. "Is that so?" he asks around his own bite of cookie.

"Yep," I nod. "In fact, go ahead and warn your family that we're headed down the aisle any day now." Swallowing, I narrow my gaze. "Okay, but really, Rhodes. If you can bake like that, why on earth are you still single?"

"Why are you?" he shoots back. But not until he's handed me another.

"My last name, it takes care of scaring away anyone I'd be interested in. Not to mention, I grew up here. Everyone knows who my family is"—I shake my head—"and anybody would probably have to be crazy to upset them. Which is what would happen if I chose someone they didn't approve of."

"Well, I don't."

My brows knit together. "Don't what?"

"I don't know who your family is. My family only moved here when my sister was a senior in high school." Oliver shrugs. "So, frankly, I don't care if I upset them or not." He grins.

"Will your family be mad?" I whisper, looking down at the half-eaten cookie in my hand.

He considers this. "They won't love the idea of being lied to if they find out. But they just think I work too much and need to settle down. Unlike your family, who just sound cruel and dismissive."

"*Do* you work too much?"

Oliver looks over to the photo collage of Ian, Aaron, and I for inspiration. He must not find any since he frowns before returning his gaze to mine. "When I was in grad school, I witnessed some gross misconduct. And I swore that, when I was finally in a position to do so, I would only be a positive influence on those that came to me for help."

"So, you think helping gaslight my entire family is considered positive?" I ask, quirking a brow.

Rolling amused eyes, Oliver leans back in my chair. "I'll admit, it's not a shining example of my professional goals." His eyes lock onto mine. "But I think this is a pretty worthy cause."

Being on the receiving end of Dr. Oliver Rhodes' open stare is nothing short of flush-inducing, and I stumble all over myself trying to find something, anything, to say. "Well, then," I start, clearing my throat, "I guess your parents are about to meet one awesome girlfriend, since she'll need you to hold up your end of the bargain."

"Marshall and Sandra," he says.

"Sorry?"

"My parents, Marshall and Sandra," he repeats. "My dad owns his own woodworking business, and my mom actually owns a restaurant. Then, of course, let's not forget Nacho, who will also be in attendance on Thursday."

"Got it," I nod enthusiastically. "Nacho'll be there too?"

"Of course." Oliver playfully rolls his eyes. "Sometimes, I think Mom likes her more than me." He pulls out his phone to display the lock screen image of him holding his golden retriever on some overlook.

"She's beautiful," I gush, taking the phone. "How'd you manage to take the picture?"

"John was there with us. Rindy might've been, too," he frowns. "I can't remember."

My brows shoot up. "She doesn't seem much like the hiking type."

He shakes his head. "Not since she met Jo. But back in college, the three of us spent a lot of time on the trails."

"Hm," I hand the phone back over, "the brother and sister hiking duo. Does your sister ever go with you, too?"

"Nah. She prefers indoor workouts," he laughs.

"Oh, how much younger is your sister?"

Oliver crumples up his trash, placing it in the bin by my desk. "She's twenty-seven. And, uh, while we're on the subject ... " That beautiful blush returns. "I'm thirty-two, for reference."

"Okay," I nod, doing my best to suppress a grin. I know he's fishing for how old I am, but how often do I get the chance to make such a gorgeous man this uncomfortable? "Noted." Besides, will he feel weird once he learns I'm the same age as his sister? Would it make him back out of our deal? Feeling his eyes watching my every move, I clean up my mess from lunch and begin gathering worksheets for when my babies return.

T-minus ten minutes.

"How long have you been baking?" I ask, rounding another desk to place some papers. I don't have to look up to know he's watching.

"Forever," he answers. That silky voice is a little too casual. Too relaxed. I wonder if that's his standard my-patient-is-annoying-me voice. "I've been helping my mom in the kitchen since I was little."

"Ah."

"But she learned really early that I had to have ground rules when I did," he continues.

Hating admitting that I'm intrigued, I peek back over my shoulder as I move around the final table. That same intense stare from the bar catalogues my every move. "How's that?"

Lips tipping up, Oliver crosses his arms. "Let's just say I was quite the taste tester. Especially at the most inappropriate times. I usually had powdered sugar all over my lips from sneaking samples."

Easy laughter bubbles out of my mouth and into the world. "I can imagine." Making my way back toward the handsome doctor, a single and sudden thought sends sirens blaring in my mind. "Are we, um, going to … to have to kiss … in front of your family?"

The man who looks way too comfortable in my chair leans back slightly before running a hand through his slicked back hair. "I mean," he clears his throat, "my family is pretty affectionate, sure. They would probably expect to see that from us, as well."

I'm pretty sure my brain short-circuits.

"But we don't have to do anything you're not comfortable with, of course," he adds quickly. "I would never ask that of you."

"Well, I promise you that my family is certainly not the affectionate type. Except for my niece." Pressing my lips together, I consider my next words carefully. "But I guess I wouldn't be opposed if we had to do that for yours to believe—" I wave my hand between us "—this." As if he's somehow missed our predicament up until now.

Oliver snorts.

"What?"

"You wouldn't be opposed," he mimics. Raising deep honey brows, he smirks.

Planting my fists on my hips, I send a playful glare his way. "I just don't think it'd be the worst sacrifice I'd have to make in the name of getting my family to respect me. Really, I'd say it's a notch or two above petting a leper or hugging a cactus or something."

"Or something," he grumbles. Nodding, Oliver stands and tosses his coat over his waiting arm. He hesitates for just a moment before looking back up at me.

Frowning, I narrow suspicious eyes. "What are you thinking over there, Rhodes?"

Oliver sighs before striding across the room, not stopping until he's standing immediately in front of me.

Even being on the taller end of the spectrum, I have to crane my neck to meet his gaze. The mouthwatering scent of a woodsy body wash and cookies sends any kind of coherent thought down the drain, almost making me miss the warmth of his fingertips brushing along my cheek. Heat sings under his touch, so light it may as well be a butterfly tap dancing where our skin meets. "Callie," he whispers, "is this okay?"

I nod rapidly, fully aware that my voice has left the building. Fire races across both of my cheeks, and amused sky blue eyes trace its path as it's forged.

Oliver gives me a soft smile. "I need to hear you say it."

Clearing my throat, I try again. "Yes, it's okay." I've never heard my voice sound so breathy. It's honestly embarrassing.

"Good," he nods, "especially since we'll need to be comfortable casually touching one another, should the situation warrant it."

"If this is your idea of casual, what do you consider intimate?" I blurt, immediately regretting my words as a wolfish grin takes over his face. "Never mind. Forget I asked." Is this what a stroke feels like?

"I'm going to kiss you now," Oliver breathes, watching for any sign I'm out.

"For practice?"

He nods. "For practice." The large hand ghosting over my cheekbone slides behind my ear, making its way down to the back of my neck, where he holds me in place.

Steadying me.

Dipping his chin, Oliver reverently closes the last remaining distance between us. Thoughtful and deliberate. If everyone's first kiss was like this, heartbreak wouldn't exist. Happily ever afters would grow like flowers in the spring.

No one would ever kiss anyone else.

A soft press of pillowy lips molding perfectly against mine. That's all—just one incomparable moment.

And then it's over.

Oliver pulls away, the warmth of his hand going with him.

Holding his gaze, I internally chide my racing heart. "See you soon, Callie." Then he turns and walks out of my classroom, taking every bit of air in the room with him.

"THERE CAN NEVER BE TOO much blue," Ian says, handing me another piece of supreme pizza across the coffee table. Tossing a pile of napkins by the pizza box, he rounds the corner and plops down onto the couch next me.

Aaron snorts from the floor. The first Wednesday pizza night at Ian's new place may not have been the best idea, since most of his furniture still isn't put together. "Dude, the walls. Your couch. The barstools. Your bedding. Any girl you bring here is going to think you're weird."

"Because your place is so curated," I grin down at him. "Your apartment—the one with enough colors everywhere to be a room in Willy Wonka's factory. Ever heard of a color palette?"

Laughing, Ian leans back into the couch. "Blue is calming, man. Aren't you some kind of songwriter? You should know that." I look over just in time to watch as a pepperoni falls onto his white T-shirt.

"So, Ian, sell any houses today?" I ask, picking up the offending slice of meat and dropping it on a nearby plate.

Ian rolls his eyes. "I sell mortgages, not houses. Mortgage lenders assess—"

Snickering, I poke him in the ribs right as he leans forward for a drink of soda. "I know, I know. Just like to annoy you, is all."

"Hey," Aaron says around the chewed up pizza rolling in his mouth.

"Swallow," Ian and I say in tandem.

Thankfully, he does before continuing, "Mom said some guy visited you at work earlier this week. Tall. Blond. Like a hot nerd."

"He is not a nerd, "I frown, "I don't think."

"That's Callie's boyfriend," Ian teases.

"What?" Aaron pops up, pizza crust still in hand. Despite the guy's immense size thanks to muscles on muscles, a full beard and two full sleeves of tattoos, he's pretty agile. Must be all that jumping around on stage. "Why haven't I met this guy?" He feigns outrage, pointing to his brother. "And why have you?"

Ian holds up hands covered in pizza grease. "I only met him last Friday, man."

"Besides," I interrupt while handing Ian a napkin, "it's nothing serious. I don't even know if I really like the guy." I deftly ignore Ian's eyes burning a hole in the side of my face.

Aaron crosses flannel-clad arms. "Well, I need to meet him."

"Absolutely not," I start, but a knock on Ian's door saves me from looking for any kind of excuse as to why Aaron can't meet the man he had a hand in introducing me to.

Rolling his eyes, Aaron crosses the living room to answer the door.

"You didn't tell him?" I whisper to my couchmate.

Ian shakes his head. "Figured the less people that know, the better."

I nod as Aaron opens the door.

"Oh, sorry, I was, um," a familiar feminine voice dances through the air. "Is Ian home?"

Standing, I turn around to see the owner of my home pilates studio holding an electric tea kettle. "Blythe?" Stepping over Ian's legs, I head for the door.

Dressed in a vibrant purple spandex top and pants set, she's clearly come straight from the studio. The petite woman's bright blue eyes widen. "Callie? Hey! What are you doing here?" Her free hand brushes back loose golden hair.

Reaching the door, I unceremoniously swat an imposing Aaron out of the way. "Move." I give him a shove, which does absolutely nothing.

But he's a good sport and heads back to the living area.

Turning back to Blythe, I paste a bright smile on my face. "Come on in," I say, holding the door open for her. "Ian's right over—"

"Blythe." My best friend sounds like he just ran a marathon. Or ate an entire pizza by himself, which he did. "Hey."

I startle at the closeness of his voice, finding him mere inches from us.

"Oh, here," he thrusts my phone in my face, "your phone keeps dinging from messages."

"Thanks," I mutter, taking the phone. Blythe says something to my friend in the background, but I'm too focused on the texts from an unsaved number. One I recognize from this morning.

Oliver.

> Nacho's excited to meet you. Just thought you'd like to know.

> And my parents. The topic came up at dinner tonight, so I thought I'd prepare them.

*Oh, crap. I hadn't even thought about mentioning a guest to my parents.* Shooting a quick text to my mom would be easy, but it may be more fun to see if they panic when their carefully laid plans are disturbed.

With everyone else distracted, I take a moment and officially add Oliver to my phonebook. When my phone alerts the room to another message, my heart lodges in my throat.

> Ready for your family to meet your new boyfriend?

MY RESPONSE IS IMMEDIATE.

> Absolutely not.

. . .

"EVERYTHING OKAY, CALLIE?" Ian's voice draws me back to reality.

Snapping my gaze back to the rest of the room, I'm greeted by three pairs of confused eyes. "Huh? Oh, yeah. Fine. Why do you ask?"

"Because you look like you're about to have a coronary," he says carefully.

"Probably just Cal's boyfriend," Aaron offers from the fridge. The sound of a soda can popping open echoes in the sparsely furnished room.

Blythe's light brow creases as a sly grin slides into place. "I thought you didn't have time for a boyfriend?"

Ian looks toward our mutual friend. "You've tried setting Callie up?"

"With my brother," she nods. "I think they'd be a good match." Her musical laugh fills the entryway. "Balancing."

Groaning, my phone pings again.

> Don't worry, baby. I've got your back.

> "Baby"? Laying it on a little thick, don't ya think? I doubt my family will read our texts.

"WHO WANTS TO WATCH A MOVIE?" I ask, my voice a notch below supersonic. Blushing furiously, I look for any excuse for everyone's focus to be off of me as fast as possible. Especially as my eyes drift back to the new message on the screen.

> Just wait til you hear what I call you in front of them.

# 8

*Callie*

"Are you nervous?"

Leaning back from the bathroom mirror, I pop the mascara wand back into the tube. "Pfft. Why would I be nervous?" Though, I have to admit, the pitch of my voice isn't really one that's been accessed in the natural world as of yet. And I'm pretty sure my heart is beating like a humming bird's right about now. Even if I'm actually totally one hundred percent fine.

Because I really am.

"Because you're about to go to someone's parents' house that you hardly know and claim to be their head-over-heels girlfriend," Ian says. So matter-of-fact. So calm.

"Well, when you put it like that ... " Rolling my eyes, I double check my appearance in the mirror one more time. The deep forest green turtleneck and auburn skirt I'm wearing are a little dressy, with just the right amount of causal thrown in. But my dark leggings and booties say I do have some practicality lurking in my bones, given the snowscape outside. Keeping with the semi-nice feel, I pat my half-up half-down hair, making sure not a single hair is out of place. My favorite small gold hoops finish off the look.

"So, are you totally sure this guy isn't a serial killer?"

"Can anyone ever really be sure?" I tease around reapplying a subtle pink lipstick for the third time.

The sound of something being dropped comes through the phone, followed by Ian cursing under his breath.

"What was that?"

"Trying to get Mom's tree out of the attic." More grunting. "I always forget how big this thing is."

"Make Aaron help you."

"He's still at the bottom of the stairs."

Not bothering to stifle a giggle, the thought of Ian and Aaron struggling with the Fairchild family Christmas tree springs to mind. And neither of them are anything short of fit. "When are you gonna tell your mom to get a smaller tree?"

"Shh!" Ian says into the phone. "You know those kinds of words will have you permanently labeled as a blasphemer in this house."

"Nah, that'll never happen. Your mom totally likes me better than you, so I think I'm safe."

Ian scoffs on the other end of the line. "Whatever. Promise you'll text if you feel uncomfortable, though? I can always come pick you up if you need me to."

Three brief knocks sound on my front door.

Oliver.

He's here. He's really here.

We're really doing this.

Rolling my lips together, I take a deep breath. *Huh.* I really thought this moment would make me want to crawl under my secondhand sofa and pretend to not be home. Instead, an annoyingly suspicious sense of calm washes through my system at the thought of what we're about to do.

Of the thought of having him by my side through this.

"Callie?" Ian's disembodied voice is the slap back to reality I definitely needed. "Did you hear me?"

"Yeah-yeah," I stutter. "Sorry. He's here."

"Go be the coolest girlfriend ever." I can hear his grin through the phone as he hangs up, leaving me all alone with my latest questionable decision.

Flicking off the bathroom light, I make quick work of grabbing my white peacoat and purse from the kitchen counter. I take one last deep breath and then I'm heading to the front door.

Three more soft raps echo on the door right as I turn the knob, each one more insistent than the last.

But when I fling the door open, there stands Oliver Rhodes, mouth parted and cheeks flushed from the cold. In his dark slacks and beige button down shirt, those intensely deep blue eyes stand out, begging to be noticed.

Eyes that flit down my outfit, lingering just a little too long. "You look ... "

"Like the best girlfriend ever?" I smirk, putting on my coat.

He blinks. Shoving his hands into his coat's pockets, the man nods. "Exactly."

A grin breaks out across my face. "You're wearing your glasses again."

Reaching to push them farther up the bridge of his nose, the pinks of Oliver's cheeks deepen. "Oh, I just thought they'd make me look even more convincing. You know, for your family."

Nodding, I pull the door closed behind me. "Right, makes sense." A quick turn of my key and I'm once again stuck facing the stupidly handsome doctor. "Especially since we've only got one shot at this. Better make it count."

Oliver's lips tip down, his thick brow too furrowed to be casual. "Right," he repeats. Seeming to remember himself, he points to the mini SUV parked by my car. "This is—"

"Is that Nacho?" I squeal. Without waiting for a response, I take off toward the sweetest furry face pressed into the windshield.

Oliver laughs behind me, snow crunching as he works to catch up. "I told her all about you," he says as I round the passenger door. "She's been looking forward to the day you two finally meet."

Shooting a skeptical look his way, I wave at the best girl. The stupidly wide grin hurts my entire face, but I honestly don't care. All thoughts have been rewired on how to get this golden girl into my arms as fast as possible.

I feel him before I see him. Oliver's warmth envelopes me, radiating through the crisp November air as he reaches around me to open the door.

Right as my fingers touch the handle.

"Oh, um." Blood rushes to my cheeks as any words currently hanging out in my mind make a speedy exit, with no plans to return. Unsupervised eyes flit to his, which are already watching me.

Oliver gives a low, throaty chuckle. "I think our hands can touch, Callie," a strong brow lifts, "since you're my girlfriend and all."

Clearing my throat, I nod and painfully press my lips together. "That's true." Desperate for any other words to come out of my mouth, I turn back to our furry onlooker. "Will she sit on my lap?"

"Will she? If given the chance, absolutely. But she should probably ride in the back seat. You know, for safety purposes."

"Killjoy."

"Yep, that's exactly what I bring to this relationship." He smirks down at me.

Squaring my shoulders, I hold my ground. "Do I get to meet the best dog ever or not, Rhodes?"

Eyes glued to mine, Oliver opens the door and I'm greeted by a kiss from Nacho's tongue slapping against my cheek like a raw piece of bacon.

My laughter and Nacho's barking intermingle before she goes in for seconds.

"Okay, easy girl," Oliver laughs. "To the back seat. Make room for Callie."

Nacho wastes no time hopping over the console, vacating the front seat. Though, if I had died being suffocated by her fluff, that's just how I was meant to go.

Oliver waits until I'm fully inside before shutting the door behind me and heading to get in on the other side.

Despite having a dog who likely sheds like there's no tomorrow, the man's car is spotless. I could probably even eat off the floorboards. The light interior exudes warmth, just like everything else about Oliver. Even the soft smell of cinnamon apples linger in the air, reminding me of the first time I met him.

Threatening to make me want to stay here forever.

"My parents' house is actually only a short drive from here," he offers, pulling away from the parking spot. "So I thought it might be helpful if we knew a few things about each other. You know, in case they ask anything specific."

I nod. "That makes sense. What do you want to know?"

"You grew up here?"

"Yep. You didn't, right?"

"Right. I grew up in Boston, but I went to college here. My family would come visit, and they fell in love with the natural beauty. So they moved here—"

"When your sister was in high school," I finish proudly. "You mentioned that on Monday."

A small smile tempts its way onto his handsome face.

"Do you miss going home to Boston?"

Dark blond brows raise slightly, as if he's surprised I asked a semi-personal question. "I actually do go back on occasion. My grandma still lives there, so my parents go to see her pretty regularly."

"Does Nacho ever get to go?" I ask, reaching to the back seat to sneak a few pets.

Oliver chuckles. "Of course. Every single time I go."

"I love that," I sigh. "If I had a dog, they'd go everywhere with me, too."

"Why don't you?" He peeks over to the passenger side.

Picking at my nail polish, I shrug. "You'll think it's dumb."

"I would never consider anything dumb that's important to you, Callie," Oliver's voice is soft, kind. "Why would you automatically assume I would think that?"

"I didn't automatically assume that."

"Callie."

Swallowing, I turn to watch our town pass by. Few people are out strolling down the blanketed sidewalks. Instead, they're all warm in their homes with families that love them unconditionally.

Must be nice.

"That's just how it's always been—with little exception," I mutter.

I look back just in time to watch Oliver's knuckles tighten on the steering wheel for the shortest moment. "Well," he says, an easy grin sliding into place, "hopefully that's something I can help."

My own smile is instant. "I hope so."

"Will you answer now?" Oliver whispers. Low and intimate, like he's afraid of learning the answer.

Toying with a button on my coat, I look back at Nacho for courage. "It's something I've always wanted to share with someone else. Someone permanent. Most people in my life become temporary, no matter how hard I work to keep them.

Not to mention, if my family thought I was doing something wrong as a dog owner, I'd never hear the end of it."

"Showing your commitment to another through shared ownership," he nods. "Essentially, having someone else prove their own commitment to you in a way no one else ever has, especially those who should have."

I snort. "I guess I've never thought about it quite like that. But sure." Shifting in my seat, I fully face the man I'm supposedly in love with. "Okay, rapid fire. Ready?"

Though I doubt Oliver's ever looked less sure of anything in his entire life, he nods. "Ready."

"Sweet or sour?"

"Sweet."

"Cool, me too. Coffee or hot chocolate?"

"Coffee."

I don't bother hiding my disgust. "Ew. Maybe we're not compatible, after all."

Laughter bursts through Oliver's lips. "Based on the fact that I like coffee and you don't?"

Tapping my pointer finger to my lips, I pretend to consider the predicament. "Well, I am a hot cocoa connoisseur."

Oliver raises a brow, sliding his gaze my way. "Is that so?"

"Yep. I'm basically world-renowned. My name is probably in an official book somewhere. So I'm sure I can convert you."

He rolls amused eyes. "Next question. Favorite hobbies?"

"Hm. Taking care of my plants, trying new foods and hiking to find new plants. And watching movies snuggled up all cozy at home. You?"

Oliver bites his lower lip, his smile clear as day. "Movies," he nods, "hiking with Nacho, though I can sometimes convince John to go with me. Baking. And, of course, helping women gaslight their judgemental families."

His grin is infectious. "Of course. Okay, last one. Favorite color?"

"Brown." The answer is quick, needing no consideration.

My nose scrunches in confusion just as fast. "Like ... dirt?"

Glorious, howling laughter fills the car. Even Nacho joins in the chorus. "Sure," he nods, "brown, like dirt." Turning onto a residential street, it's mere moments before he guides the car into the driveway of the cutest two-story, white Victorian home I've ever seen, where a familiar red sedan also waits in the driveway.

"Wow," I breathe.

Candles sit lit in every front-facing window while garlands hang in bows along the outside of every windowbox. A large red bow adorns the featured wreath, with mini wreaths hanging along the white picket fenceline.

"Your turn, Callie." Beside me, Oliver waits patiently. As if knowing my favorite color is the most important thing in the world.

"Green. My favorite color is green."

"Like your plants?" Curious eyes roam my face, awaiting my next answer.

Doing my best to stifle the giggle trying to escape, I nod. "Yes, Oliver. Like my plant babies. Now, are you ready?"

He grins. "Let's go." Letting Nacho out, he rounds the car just as I'm stepping onto the fresh snow.

"Does she not need a leash?" I nod to the bounding girl headed up the front porch stairs.

"Nah, she knows the way. I only really use a leash when we're on the trails," he answers.

"There's my girl," a female voice sings from the front door. A woman who can only be Oliver's mom stands with the front door wide open, an enthusiastic Nacho standing to her shoulders and giving her all the doggy kisses. On the shorter side, the years have been kind to her. Soft through the middle, she reminds me of every mom whose natural waistline hasn't been helped by Dr. Whatshisname that the women in my mother's circle all use—which isn't very many of them. Wavy blonde hair floats to her thin shoulders and her feminine features glow with laughter at the onslaught of kisses from the cutest granddog.

"Hey Mom," Oliver calls from beside me, waving to the woman.

Releasing herself from Nacho's iron grip, his mom's eyes widen when they land on me. "You two, get on in here. It's freezing," she calls.

Looking up at Oliver, the love for his mom is evident. Natural. While this man always seems to look perfectly at ease in any situation, something about seeing him come home is truly moving.

A dull ache squeezes in the depths of my chest—a reminder of everything I've never had. But the possibility of one day having that kind of love with my own family propels me forward with this strange mission of ours.

The one where I pretend to be the doting girlfriend.

My hand surprises us both by reaching out and taking hold of his.

This bewilderment continues as his squeezes mine in return.

Then, one step at a time, we head inside.

If it weren't for every nerve currently being lit on fire while I try to remember my sole purpose in being here, I would have thought I was in one of those made-for-TV holiday movies. Traditional furnishings have been given a facelift with all kinds of holiday decor strategically placed throughout the open floorplan. Hints of vanilla, lemon and rosemary hang in the air, with a dining table fully set for Thanksgiving just off to the left. Christmas music plays softly in the background, mingling with football commentary coming from an unseen television.

"Dad?" Oliver calls, letting go of my hand to shut the front door and sliding off his coat. Hanging it on the coat rack waiting beside the door, he holds out a patient hand for mine.

Removing my own, I do my best to ignore the immediate chill once our hands are no longer intertwined.

Oliver guides me further into the entryway when a small door next to the stairs swings open. A tall, older man emerges carrying a dust-covered box that hasn't seen the light of day in years. My fake boyfriend comes by his height honestly. Dressed in jeans and a red plaid flannel, Mr. Rhodes looks ready to take in a football game on the couch instead of eating a fancy, chef-prepared meal like my father undoubtedly will.

I love him immediately.

But Oliver's father also doesn't hide his surprise when he sees me. "You must be Ollie's girlfriend." Mr. Rhodes shifts the box to his left arm, extending a calloused hand. "Marshall Rhodes."

"Nice to meet you, Mr. Rhodes." His handshake feels like a father who has never failed to lift up his kids, no matter how far they fell.

"Any girlfriend of Ollie's can call me Marshall," he insists.

"Marshall," I repeat around a soft chuckle. "It's a pleasure to meet you. Oliver's told me so much about you," I gush.

Raising wiry gray brows, Mr. Rhodes looks at his son. "Is that so?"

Beside me, Oliver shrugs. "Had to warn her." But he grins across the cozy space at his father. "Oh, Dad," his hand moves to the small of my back, "this is Callie Rutherford."

If it's possible, Marshall Rhodes's eyebrows climb to their absolute limit. Recognition gleams behind tired eyes. "Rutherford?" he repeats.

Hackles raised, my smile threatens to wane, but I keep that sucker plastered in place. *Flipper nugget, flipper nugget, flipper nugget. We're screwed.*

"Well, Calloway, technically." Oliver smirks down at me. "But she prefers 'Callie.'"

Marshall Rhodes looks between his son and me. "Oliver, are you telling me you brought home ... a Rutherford?"

Oliver tenses beside me. "You know her family?"

Mr. Rhodes frowns, brow furrowing. "Son, everyone in this town knows her family. Tri-state area, even. And I'd imagine you both will be heading over to their house when you leave here?"

We nod in tandem.

Marshall whistles. "Talk about facing the wolves," he laughs. Questioning eyes appraise me. Only when a toothy grin graces the man's face does my nervous system begin to relax. "Ms. Rutherford, if you think this guy's good enough for you, far be it from me to disagree."

Stilted laughter chokes its way out of me. "Oh, I mean—"I glance up at a rather bemused Oliver whose hand is now firmly pressing into my back, pulling me closer"—I think I'm the lucky one. Personally." And it's true. How many professional therapists would offer to help make your family question everything they've ever known?

"You just keep thinking that, Callie." Mr. Rhodes winks, readjusting the box in his arm. "And please know, you're welcome here anytime."

By no means or standards am I a crier. With my family, it'd just be seen as another weakness. But the immediate loosening in my chest and the breath of relief felt deep in my bones? Those send tears straight to my traitorous eyes. "Thank you," I whisper.

Marshall nods right as a shriek sounds from the kitchen.

"Callie!"

Oliver flinches toward me, fingertips gripping into my back. "Geez, Blythe. I think you just burst my eardrum."

"Did not, you big baby." My pilates instructor barrels

toward us, stopping just short of plowing us down. Fists planted on her tiny hips, incredulous eyes pin me in place. "Callie, what the hell?"

Oliver steps slightly in front of me. "Easy," he warns. Peeking over his shoulder, he catches my gaze. "Do you two ... know each other?"

"I've only been trying to get her to go out with you for *months* now." Blythe rolls eyes that look exactly like Oliver's.

I truly have no idea how I missed the resemblance. I've only seen Blythe about eight times since Oliver and I first met.

My very hot, very fake boyfriend scratches his chin, shrugging. "Well, I guess she took your advice."

Stepping around him, I hold up my hands in surrender. "Also, to be fair, you never said his name." Slowly, a smile replaces the concern on my features. "But I guess you were right—I would like your brother."

Blythe peers at me for the longest minute of my life, and that includes the time Prescott was certain I put a dead fly in his pudding when I was nine, and made me stand there while he strained it.

Fighting the desperate urge to crawl back behind Oliver, I try to practice breathing techniques taught to me by the very woman standing before me.

Crossing her arms, Blythe finally leans back. But that narrowed gaze never lessens. "How did you two meet, then?"

Panic. Choking. Instant death.

We never came up with a backstory. How could I have been so remiss about such an important detail?

"Met her at Cici's Halloween party for school." Oliver slides an arm around my shoulder, giving me an easy grin. The weight of his arm is reassuring, comforting.

My arms snake around his waist as I lean into his side. *And cue the heart eyes to the man pretending to be mine.*

Oliver wastes no time looking at me like we should never be apart ever again.

Skepticism takes over Blythe's every feature. "Why did you go to Ci's school party?"

"She needed to bring desserts." The man shrugs, breaking our faux intimate eye contact. So nonchalant, like he didn't want to just keel over and die when his sister asked such a simple question. "I made some brownies and took them up to the school. Callie asked if I wanted to stay for the party. How could I resist her?"

Blythe's curiosity melts into a satisfied smile of acceptance just in time for their mom to round the corner with Nacho in tow.

"Honey, let your brother and his girlfriend actually come into the house." Sandra wipes her hands on a towel before tossing it over her shoulder.

Rolling her eyes, Blythe makes her way to the couch, where she unceremoniously plops down beside her dad.

Nacho takes the liberty of unabashedly throwing herself across her couch mates. Twisting so she's in the optimal position for belly rubs, Blythe's black jeans and navy blouse instantly gain golden highlights from Nacho's hair.

"I feel like I should be worried," I whisper as Oliver guides me toward the kitchen.

"Why is that?" His breath is warm on my ear, sending shivers down my spine at the unexpected closeness. He must notice my brain malfunctioning, because he applies the smallest pressure from the arm still around my shoulder.

"Because of how good you are at this." *At making me feel like you care.*

"Which part?" he murmurs, pressing a soft kiss to my temple. To the rest of his family, it'll only look like he's whispering some sweet nothing in my ear.

Giggling, I complete the look.

"Coming to help finish the dessert?" Oliver's mom holds out a plate of sugar cookies ready for icing. "Don't tell the others," she winks at me.

Pressing my lips together, I glance up at Oliver, whose hand is already halfway to the plate. Following suit, I bite into the most delicious sugar cookie I've ever eaten. "This is incredible. No wonder Oliver can bake the way he does." Gotta lay it on thick—especially since it's true. Other than the cookies he brought to my classroom the other day, these are the best cookies I've ever eaten.

"Well, there's plenty of powdered sugar ready to be made into icing," Sandra says, setting the plate on the counter. "Callie, do you bake much?"

I laugh. "I can cook decently enough, but it's really a lot of guesswork," I shrug, "and none of my plants have complained." Oliver's mom chuckles, causing my smile to widen. "With baking, you can't quite get away with that same mentality. It's much more specific."

Sandra nods, smiling. "You'll have to come by the shop sometime and cook with me. Anytime you like."

"Mom," Oliver interrupts.

"Wait, the shop?" Peeking up at Oliver, two and two become four. "Sandra's Sammies," I whisper, turning back to his mom, "you own Sandra's Sammies."

Sandra rolls her eyes, whacking Oliver with her handtowel. "I can see you two have had some serious conversations." Shaking her head, she beams at me. "Yep, and you're welcome there anytime. Now, you—"she points at Oliver"—you can make up for your lack of transparency with your girlfriend by icing these cookies." Raising light brows at her son, Sandra shoots me one more wink before heading to check on her husband and daughter.

"Your family is incredible," I say, voice low.

Oliver heads to the bowl of powdered sugar, stopping to

grab milk from the fridge. "They are," he nods, "but they're especially happy that you're here."

Snorting, I lean a hip against the counter. "Considering Blythe repeatedly tried to get me to date you, it sounds like you could've brought home anything with a heartbeat and they'd be happy."

"How long *did* she encourage, um, this?" he asks, voice just a little too casual.

Biting my bottom lip, I try to recall the first time it was mentioned. "Back in April," I nod, "she overheard me talking about going on a hike and said she had a brother who liked to hike, too, and would I want to take him with me. Apparently, he didn't get out much." With almost no space between us, I can feel the laughter rumbling through his very warm body.

"That's some ringing endorsement," he grins. "What did you say?"

"That I only date lepers and pirates. But that was only my excuse the first time."

"Wonderful," he deadpans. "What others did you give?"

"Usually pretty generic ones. I had plans, wasn't interested in dating anyone, may or may not be talking to someone," I count on my fingers, "that kind of thing." Glancing at all the sugar ready to be consumed, my mouth begins to water. "Does your mom get some kind of special holiday sugar or something? Because that stuff smells incredible."

"Wanna help?" He peeks over at me, holding up the bowl.

"I think I better." At the confusion coating his features, I laugh. Sneakily angling my head toward the living area, I whisper, "We're being watched. But I'm not sure what to do."

A wolfish grin takes over his handsome features. "Then let me show you." Out of nowhere, a fingertip glances off the tip of my nose, leaving a powdery trail in its wake down the side of my cheek. "That's better," Oliver declares proudly.

Smirking, I dip my fingers in the bowl as he gloats, making

sure all ten fingers are ready. "You know, I think you have a little something right here." Without warning, I take his face in my hands and pull him close, effectively getting the light powder all over his cheeks.

Oliver tips his head back, exuding light and laughter from every ounce of his being. But just as I try stepping out of his immediate proximity, one hand grabs my waist as the other tips my chin toward him.

Slipping my arm around him, my free hand falls to his shoulder.

Tender eyes trace my sugar-covered face. "Careful, Ms. Rutherford," he murmurs, lips dangerously close to mine.

"Or what?"

"Or they'll think we're headed down the aisle any day now."

Quirking a brow, a coy smile slides into place. "Isn't that the idea?"

"Guess I just didn't think you'd be this convincing."

Feeling the blatant stares of the rest of the Rhodes clan, the next words out of my mouth shock us both. "I think you should kiss me now."

Oliver recovers quickly, pressing perfectly sculpted lips to mine while his fingertips pull me as close to him as physically possible.

My hands take on a life of their own as they secure themselves around his neck. Returning the soft urgency in his kiss, I hold Oliver flush to me.

"When I pictured you dating my brother, I didn't really imagine you two kissing in our parents' kitchen. You know, where all the food is." Blythe's voice sounds from behind, startling me.

Heat rushes to my cheeks while my fake boyfriend looks cool as a cucumber. Clearly, his heart rate has maintained its normal pace.

How annoying.

Clearing my throat, I try to achieve some kind of equilibrium in my overstimulated nervous system. "So, Blythe, is Ian being nice?"

Oliver's sister freezes for the smallest moment, hands full of cutlery headed to the table. "Huh? Oh, yep. He's a great neighbor."

"Good, I'd hate to have to tell his mother on him," I joke.

Oliver raises a quizzical brow. "You know Ian's parents?"

Blythe whirls around to face her brother. "You know Ian?"

My fake boyfriend's brow furrows. "He's Callie's best friend. How do you know him?" Oliver squints at Blythe through powdered sugar-covered glasses that may or may not be fogged up from our kiss.

Awkward laughter bubbles from his sister as she nods. "Uh, right. Right. Well—"

"Let's eat," Marshall calls from the table.

Nacho barks in enthusiastic agreement, settling right by Mr. Rhodes' seat at the table. If there was ever any doubt about who feeds her from the table, there sure isn't anymore.

Blythe hurries to the table without another word while I shoot Oliver a questioning look. Holding out my hand, he wastes no time taking it and leading us to the table of my domestic dreams.

Only when everyone has more than enough to feed no less than six hobbits and I've heard countless stories about Oliver growing up, do I sit back from the table. The deepest ache in my heart constricts my chest, knowing that I certainly got the easy end of this deal with the man sitting beside me. I've spent the afternoon experiencing the warmth and kindness of a family who clearly adores him.

Oliver, on the other hand, gets to enter the middle of a storm that's been brewing for twenty-seven years.

Sandra Rhodes, an astute woman, looks down the table to me. A loving smile waits on her kind face. "Callie, what do you think? Wanna come back again next year? Because I think I speak for everyone here when I say we'd love to have you."

A chorus of agreement sounds from everyone in the room. Even Nacho.

A genuine smile spreads across my face as I take in the family surrounding me. Each one is filled with so much joy and unconditional love for the others that it's almost difficult to believe this kind of a family exists outside of dreams. Looking back at the mother I wish was my own, I answer honestly, "There's nowhere I'd rather be."

"Speaking of," Oliver glances at his watch, "time to face the wolves."

# 9

*Oliver*

Callie walks into my apartment with me to drop off Nacho, and I immediately wish I'd thought to clean up this morning. Not that I'm messy or anything, but you think about things from a different perspective when a beautiful woman is suddenly in your place for the first time.

*Only time*, I remind myself.

Following Nacho and I through the door, Callie takes timid steps inside and closes the door behind her. The overwhelming silence as I fill Nacho's bowl with food in the open kitchen isn't encouraging.

"What do you think?" I finally dare to ask.

Callie looks around as if she hadn't thought to do so until now. Nodding, she says, "It's pretty modern."

A smirk slides into place. "You mean cold?"

"That's not what I said." Those large brown eyes meet mine. "Did it come furnished?"

"But that's what you meant," I say, ignoring her question.

Callie wanders into the living room, carefully examining the white leather seating set and white oak furniture. She takes in the white walls with nothing hanging on display, the dark rug and LED lighting.

"Well?" I try again.

"You could almost use it as a dentist's office," she muses. Based on her shocked expression, I don't think that last thought was actually supposed to come out.

I don't bother holding back my laughter. Shrugging, I move around the white granite counter. "Fair enough. And you're right," I nod, "it did come furnished."

The relief is visible on her lovely face, making me chuckle again.

"You need art or family pictures or something. And a fuzzy throw." Callie nods to the stark couch. "Either would help."

"I'll admit, I've never shopped for a fuzzy blanket before." I smile at her.

"Maybe Blythe can help you. Her place is really cozy."

Lifting a brow, I give her a playful grin. "I thought girlfriends were supposed to help decorate their boyfriend's place?"

"Then maybe you should get a real girlfriend and she will." Callie grins back. "You know, if you're not careful, I may have to join you and your real girlfriend for Thanksgiving when you finally get one. Especially if it means getting out of having a full meal with my family."

"What do you mean?" My brows knit together. "I thought we were having Thanksgiving dinner with your family."

Callie shakes her head. "They eat the traditional meal for lunch. We're joining them for dessert."

Huh. "Will they be upset that you weren't at the main meal?"

"I doubt they even noticed I wasn't there," she answers. Callie glances at her watch, her beautiful smile fading.

"Time to go?"

She nods as though the undertaker is on his way.

On instinct, I hold out my hand, which she willingly takes. "Well, if they ask, at least you can honestly say you've seen your boyfriend's apartment."

When we're back in the car, Callie gives me the address to her parents' home. While I can't say I know the entire area surrounding Serenvale Springs, I know enough to understand that where the Rutherfords live houses only stately homes.

Minute after minute begins to tick by in silence. Finally, I can't stand it any longer. "So, your family isn't really a pack of wolves, right?"

Callie peeks over at me from the passenger seat, confusion marring every gorgeous feature. *Okay, I guess we're fully admitting that we're attracted to her.*

Not that I was really trying to avoid it before.

Grimacing, I clear my throat and try again. "I just mean, even my dad called them that." Forced laughter chokes its way out. "And he basically lives in a cave with his woodworking. Literally, if you consider their garage a cave."

The smallest smile graces her full lips, more polite than anything.

So I try again. "Anything I should be aware of?"

"Like what?" Her voice is small, nerves evident.

"Anything in particular they may try targeting you about? Weird habits or childhood stories they might use to embarrass you?"

Callie twists her fingers into a knot in her lap. Worrying her bottom lip, she answers, "They'll probably ask you if this is real."

*Geez, who are these people?* Doing my best not to show the rising frustration for these people I've never met, I work my fingers around the steering wheel, desperate for a distraction. "Have you brought many fake boyfriends around, then?" I shoot her a goofy grin, but it doesn't land.

Instead, she looks like she could vomit at any moment. "Quite the opposite, actually. I've never brought anyone home for a holiday before."

"Never?"

"Never. So it wouldn't be a huge stretch for Chris to tease you about my hiring you. Don't get me wrong—I've dated plenty. But no one's ever, um ... "

"Made it to the family holiday test?"

She shakes her head. "In fact, they've only ever met one boyfriend."

My brow lifts of its own accord.

"But that's only because our fathers know each other," she continues. "And he's friends with Chris, who was certainly not happy when things ended. You can add that to the list of reasons he provides such a wondrous familial experience."

"Your brother sounds like quite the gem," I grumble. "Is he worse than the older one? Prescott, right?"

Callie straightens in her seat. Eyes wide, she grips her seat belt. "Wait a second. We've never discussed payment."

My hand takes on a life of its own, reaching across the console and enveloping hers. The subtle squeeze is meant to be reassuring, and it occurs a little too late that she may think I'm being creepy.

Blythe always talks about how it freaks her out if a guy randomly touches her. Especially if they're not dating.

And while Callie and I are technically together, that still doesn't give me the right to just assume anything, even if I have touched her before now.

But when I try to pull away, Callie places her free hand onto our intertwined ones, squeezing right back.

"I promise I'm not worried about that, Callie."

She nods. "We'll deal with all of that later."

Discomfort lodges itself in my throat. Trying anything I can to swallow it, I continue, "Anything else?"

Callie shrugs. "Mom likes to be the bride at every wedding and the corpse at every funeral."

I bark out a laugh. "Quite the attention-seeker, got it. What about anything secret I may need to know that would give us away?"

"Don't get me coffee when it's passed around. My family loves their java jolt, so it definitely will be offered at some point."

Lifting a brow, I give her my best look of innocence. "Why would I do that when my girlfriend only likes hot chocolate?"

Callie smiles to herself. "Imogene ... she's pretty standoffish. Don't be surprised if she just ignores you for the most part. She's kind of Prescott's minion, but she's really smart. And I don't know that she would be rude, except to make Prescott like her. She's constantly making sure she has his approval." Her cheeks pinken, and I assume she's leaving things out. For whose benefit, I'm not sure. "But Prescott's little girl is precious," Callie gushes. A brilliant smile brightens her face.

My brows raise. "Prescott has a kid?"

Callie nods. "Marigold. She's seven, and my favorite person in the family."

"Other than Connie?"

She doesn't respond immediately, but the smile leftover from mentioning her niece doesn't fade, either. "I think Connie and I could be close. Maybe."

"If it wasn't for Chris?"

She nods, that burst of sun slipping.

Considering my next words, I phrase my next question delicately. "Why does Chris seem to be so antagonistic toward you? Of all your siblings, you seem to have the most difficult relationship with him." I give her hand another squeeze for courage. Her cheeks pinken at my gesture, which brings me more pleasure than it really should.

So I do it again just to be sure.

This time, Callie tucks her face toward the window as her lovely blush deepens.

Something inside me stirs, making me wish I had a good reason to reach out and touch her cheek. To see if it's as warm on my fingertips as I imagine it is.

"He and Connie were the youngest," she starts, still facing the passenger window, "and they never seemed to need anyone but each other. I always teach my students independence at the beginning of each year, but any attempt to help Connie gain a little distance from Chris has never gone over well. I'm already seen as the interloper in my own family, and Mom and Dad have always made it clear they expected to stop after four, anyway. 'We already had two of each, Calloway. Why would we need more?' That's my dad's favorite answer when asked if he wanted any more kids." Bitterness seeps in, tainting her sweet voice. "Prescott is the oldest—your standard overachiever. Mom and Dad doted on him, but they always pushed him so hard. With Imogene, they often pitted her against her brother. Pushed her to be better, faster, smarter. A couple years later, they had the twins. Connie had some medical issues at birth. There was a collapsed lung and she had to stay in the NICU for weeks. So, while Mom and Dad pushed the oldest two, Connie got all the coddling. Still does, really. And Chris ... "

"Feels unappreciated and like he doesn't receive the same attention," I finish for her.

Callie nods. "From what I've gathered, yeah. Then, I was a surprise. And while I never got the coddling the youngest child tends to receive, I think he feels like I got away with so much more. It's really only because Mom and Dad never actually paid me much attention. He feels like I got off easy. Picked an easy profession. That kind of thing." She shrugs.

I don't bother taming the snort that comes out. "There is nothing easy about being an educator, Callie, and you shouldn't let them make you feel like there is."

"If you truly believe that, then you've got your work cut out for you today." We may only be two feet apart, but her thoughts are years away.

"Callie?"

The amazing woman sitting in my passenger seat turns toward me. "Oliver." Large, chocolate eyes blink at me as we sit at a deserted stop sign.

Everything occupying my mind goes out the window as this woman stares across the tight space, daring to witness my bare soul. So I ask her the first thing that pops into my mind. "What's your middle name?"

Her button nose wrinkles in disgust. "Why?"

Laughing, I resist the urge to reach over and smooth the creases from her kind face. A face that radiates sunshine when she smiles. "In case they ask. You know, as a test."

Callie looks toward the car ceiling. "They won't."

"Humor me?"

She peers at me through narrowed eyes. Sighing, she caves. "Leora."

My chest warms while I grin like an idiot. "Of course it is."

"What do you mean?"

"I took this course on the psychology of names given to children for my degree. One of the things we looked at were the meanings of different names. Your name, it means 'light'," I explain. When Callie continues to blink blankly at me, I elaborate, "I told John—the night we talked about that flyer, actually —that I wished I had some kind of guiding light to get me through the holidays this year."

Callie gives me her best skeptical look.

"I know, I know. It's cheesy. But with my parents pushing me to find someone and settle down, I was starting to dread all the time I'd be spending with my family."

"Which is sad, because they're absolutely incredible."

Her words warm my heart. It doesn't take an expert to see I may just be in trouble when it comes to Calloway Rutherford, knowing that she enjoyed being with them, too."I guess I'm just glad I had you there today, is all. So your name makes sense to me." Releasing my hand from hers, I brush a loose piece of hair from her face. "You deserve a family that appreciates you, Callie," I whisper. "Please don't think otherwise."

Callie blushes furiously. "Then I guess it's a good thing you'll be there."

Brushing my fingers under her chin, I tip it up and bring her eyes to mine. "You better believe it, baby."

She groans. "Not that again."

"Oh, my sweet hot cocoa connoisseur," I grin, "we're just getting started."

"You know what?" Callie straightens as we pull onto the street. "I think I left my stove on this morning. Maybe we should turn around and go check. Just in case. Because I'd hate to be responsible for burning down my entire apartment complex due to such carelessness."

"You're right, that would be bad." A chuckles escapes, one hand on the steering wheel while the other remains firmly in hers. "But the stove wasn't on. Trust me."

"I do," she says instantly, "but you also didn't come in, so there's no real way for you to know that."

"You didn't invite me in," I point out. A fact I'm still telling myself I'm not disappointed about.

Callie frowns. "Fine. But—"

"Calloway."

Her mouth snaps shut while I pull into the driveway of the type of house that used to make peasants revolt.

"Everything will be fine, I promise." Putting the car in park at the end of the driveway, I turn toward the woman I'm supposed to be in love with. *Which is turning out to be a lot easier than I imagined.* Making sure her gaze is locked on mine, I take a deep breath. "No matter what happens in there, you and me? We're a team. Whatever is said, whatever is insinuated, I can hold my own. And while I have no doubt that you can, too, you don't have to. Because I've got your back. Got it, Calloway Leora?"

A small smile cracks that terrified facade. "What's your middle name?"

Shaking my head, I grin while I unbuckle my seat belt. "Grant."

Callie hops out of the car with much more gusto than I'd imagined, humming a Christmas song. "Oliver Grant Rhodes," she muses to herself. Callie looks over at me and smiles that breathtaking smile. "I like that. It just kinda flows, you know?"

Rounding the car, I throw my arm around her before placing a kiss on her temple.

"What're you doing?"

"Playing the doting boyfriend, in case they're watching. Can't be too careful," I murmur into her hair. I breathe in deep, really hamming it up.

"Mm good call," Callie says, wrapping her arms round my torso, "though they don't really bother with me unless they have to. So it's not very likely anyone's looking."

Knowing we already look like the perfect couple in love, I pull her in close. The walk to the door is too short as we pass three luxury vehicles coated in fresh snowfall.

We're definitely late to the party.

"Do any of your siblings have significant others?" If so, it says something about which family home they've been at all day.

Callie shakes her head. "Nope. Prescott used to seriously date this girl back in law school, but they broke up a long time ago. None of the others have anyone, though."

"What about Connie and Ian's brother?"

Playfully rolling her eyes, Callie smiles. "Maybe one day. Oh, there's one other thing I should mention."

"Consider my interest piqued."

"My parents love when my siblings challenge each—"

"There you—and just who is this?" A tall, slender woman in her early sixties stands with the front door wide open. Dressed in a cream blouse and matching slacks, Lillian Rutherford is everything I've pictured as Callie's mother. Thin lips purse as she takes me in, medically enhanced cheekbones prominent with the movement.

"Ready or not," I whisper as I unlatch myself from Callie, immediately missing her warmth. But that woman did an incredible job of holding up her end of the bargain.

Now, it's my turn.

Pasting a smile on my face, I start this bizarre game of chess. "My name is Dr. Oliver Rhodes. It's a pleasure to meet you, Mrs. Rutherford," I hold out my hand, "You have a lovely home."

Lillian Rutherford takes my extended hand automatically, gaze still flitting between her daughter and myself. "Um, it's a pleasure to meet you, doctor."

"Mom, I'm so sorry I forgot to tell you. I just wasn't sure if he'd make it. Oliver is my, um, boyfriend." I can practically hear Callie cringe behind me.

Lillian's eyes widen at the word.

"But I figured, since you asked a couple weeks ago, it would be okay if I brought him today," Callie continues. "If not, I'm sure he can wait in the car or something."

Pressing my lips together, I work hard to keep my scoff internal.

Her mother's manners kick in then, dropping my hand and ushering us toward the house. Well, mainly me. "Please, come on in, doctor. You must be freezing." She keeps a couple paces ahead, overaccommodating with me while all but ignoring her daughter.

Frowning, I hold out a hand toward Callie, ensuring she keeps pace with me.

Reminding her that we're in this together.

She shoots me a grateful smile, one that tells me just how forgotten she feels by her family.

When we meet Lillian at the door, impatience seeps into hawklike eyes as she appraises Callie's appearance.

"Man, I'm glad we wiped off all the powdered sugar before we left," my fake girlfriend mutters to me.

Her shrewd mother cringes in disgust. "You went somewhere covered in food? Calloway Rutherford, you were taught better than that." Lillian shifts a tight smile in my direction as she closes the door behind us. "I promise, doctor, her father and I really did try to teach her some manners."

A timid maid appears out of nowhere, meek and trembling, holding out frail arms waiting for our coats.

Mrs. Rutherford aims to look apologetic for her daughter, landing in the realm of utterly miffed.

Swallowing my thorough annoyance with this woman, I put on a mask typically reserved for difficult patients. "Please, call me Oliver, Mrs. Rutherford."

The woman who's practically taken a bath in Chanel blushes, stammering, "Well-well, then a handsome man such as yourself is more than welcome to call me Lillian."

Callie rolls her eyes as loudly as possible, making quick work of handing off her white peacoat before holding out a hand for mine.

Rolling my lips in, I suppress a smile at the role reversal from my own family's home.

Shooting a knowing grin my way, Callie's cheeks heat while her mother turns on a heel and takes off deeper into the house.

"This way, Oliver," Lillian calls over her shoulder. "The rest of the family will be very interested to meet you."

Taking Callie's hand in mine, I press one more kiss to her cheek. Just on the off chance someone's watching us. Moving my lips to her ear, I whisper, "Showtime."

## 10

*Oliver*

Callie wasn't kidding about Imogene seeming standoffish. Other than the initial shock of seeing me in her childhood home, the woman has practically avoided me. Every time we're in the same vicinity, she looks at Prescott for behavioral guidance.

"Imogene," I say from my spot on the couch, "Callie tells me you work in aerospace engineering. That sounds exciting." I think Callie's right—Imogene has the potential to be a decent human toward my girlfriend, if she can quit worrying about what Prescott and Lilllian think. She and Connie should certainly be the easiest to convince.

Beside me, Callie cuts me a cautious look.

All the Rutherfords sit on the extensive seating that likely costs more than my entire post-graduate education, and are dressed in designer outfits that cost more than my car. While the home is decorated in warm colors, dark woods and bulky furniture that screams aristocracy, it's easy to see why Callie wasn't eager to return. The furniture, though exquisite and finely made, is hard and uncomfortable. Art pieces hanging on the wall evoke anger instead of peace. The air is too still, like the house hasn't been aired out for spring cleaning in nearly thirty years. The large fireplace along the far wall looks like something that could be mistaken for a portal to hell if Ira Rutherford became irate.

It's truly astounding to think this is where my Callie grew up.

Across the living room, Callie's oldest sister nods. "I suppose." I know Blythe and I have strong genetics, but this woman could be Lillian Rutherford's clone. The two share everything from their willowy frame and expressive brown eyes, to their naturally mocha chocolate hair.

Callie's oldest brother also strongly favors their mother's dark features, while his daughter—who is currently perched halfway on Callie's lap and occasionally looks my way with a giggle—is clearly of mixed descent.

The twins and Callie all resemble their father in hair color and complexion. But where Callie and Chris have dark eyes like their mother, Connie has the same vibrant green eyes of Ira.

"Have you worked on anything I might've heard of?" I try again.

Nervous eyes flit toward her brother before finding mine again. "I work on parts for the International Space Station pretty regularly. Nothing major or lifechanging, by any means."

"I dunno," I say, "I'd imagine so much as a single screw failing would be life changing to anyone up there. You shouldn't discount yourself."

A timid smile graces her heart-shaped face.

"I work with a man whose daughter loves space and has

been looking at a program this summer up in Honeyville for her. She'll be jealous I got to meet you."

"Cici?" Callie guesses, grinning from her seat next to mine.

Beaming back at my girlfriend, all I can think of is how in sync we seem to be.

Imogene's eyes light up. "Cosmic Kids," she nods. "I actually help with that camp."

Chris, who sits by Connie on a loveseat, leans forward. "Where did you say you two met?" he interrupts. Ah, yes. Middle child.

I paste a brilliant smile on my face. "In Callie's classroom."

"Why were you in Calloway's class?" he demands.

Connie sets her jaw and whispers something in Chris's ear, a look of contrition coming over him. The two of them have some kind of unspoken conversation over a span of ten seconds before Connie looks back at Callie and I and nods for us to continue.

Interesting.

"He came to help with the Halloween party," Callie offers on my behalf.

My hand automatically reaches for hers, unbidden relief crashing through me when she takes it.

Ira Rutherford straightens in his seat. "Do you have a child, Oliver?"

Callie tenses beside me. As if she's about to find out I have a kid hidden away somewhere.

Biting the inside of my cheek to hold back a smile, I look back at her father. "No, sir. But my business partner's daughter is in that class, and I heard they needed volunteers. Since I work with children regularly, I thought I'd lend a hand."

"So you have only known each other about a month, then?" Lillian asks.

I look down at Callie and answer, "Yes ma'am."

"And you're happy?"

Callie snaps wide eyes to Lillian. "Mother," she warns.

"Well, I only ask because we thought Alexander was happy with you, but then it was suddenly over."

"That's because he's a jerk," Callie grumbles.

Chris smirks. "Maybe he didn't want to marry a glorified babysitter," he says to Callie, "Which is all teachers really are." He yelps when Connie pinches him.

"You can tell a lot about a guy by who he hangs out with," I shrug. "I'm sure his friends aren't the best, either, then."

Across the room, Chris's face matches his hair. "He's *my* friend. I'm the one who suggested they go out in the first place." His tone is restrained, but it's evident his temper is brewing beneath the surface.

"So you're why Callie doesn't date much?" I smirk, turning to my girlfriend. "Thanks for giving me a chance, my hot cocoa connoisseur."

"You're all-around better than Alex," Callie grins back at me, only boosting my ego. "It's no contest."

I turn to Callie's oldest brother, ignoring Chris's fiery glare. "Prescott, you're a partner at the firm? That's impressive for your age."

He nods. "It's been a lot of hard work, certainly."

"And nepotism," Chris smirks.

Prescott narrows his eyes at his younger brother. "But I think it's been worth it," he continues.

"What kind of law do you practice?"

"We have partners that specialize in different areas," Ira interjects, "but Prescott and I tend to focus on intellectual property and corporate law. We handle patents for the boom of technology companies all looking to outdo one another, as well as mergers, acquisitions, that type of thing. You're welcome to come by the firm anytime and I can show you around." Callie's father smiles in a way that feels shockingly genuine.

Even Callie's brows knit together in question.

When a maid pushes a large silver cart with several plates of chocolate cake and three carafes of coffee into the living room, Lillian stands with practiced elegance. "Cake and coffee, anyone?"

Releasing Callie's hand, I hop up to join Imogene and Prescott in passing out the dessert. When everyone else has been served, I grab a couple of plates for Callie and myself. "You don't happen to have any hot cocoa, do you?"

Lillian blinks at me, the sound of forks scraping against fine china singing in the background.

"Callie doesn't like coffee," I explain.

"Of course she does. She's drank it for years." Lillian waves me off.

"Actually," I say, gathering our plates, "I think what you're referring to is when she was younger and would drink it because you expected her to. Did you know studies show that forcing children to eat and drink things they don't like often has the opposite effect, leading to negative associations with the food and, by extension, the parent who made them consume it?" Offering her a tight smile, I make my way back to my girlfriend.

I take my seat next to Callie, handing her one of the plates. Leaning next to her ear, I whisper, "Sorry, no-go on the hot cocoa."

Callie's face breaks out into a beaming grin at my rhyme, causing her to choke on a bite of cake.

"What do you think, Oliver?" Ira's voice pulls me back to the conversation and away from his daughter.

"Sorry," I say, finding him watching us closely, "what was that?"

Ira practically licks his plate clean in between words. "Don't you think it would be worth Calloway's while to consider returning to school to study in a different field? She has so much potential, but it's being wasted in a classroom. She always excelled at sciences—she could've been a chemist or a botanist. But she settled for something so far beneath her abilities."

If this is the way her family talks to her at every family meal, I can't believe she keeps returning.

Taking a deep breath to temper the building frustration, I level Ira with my gaze. "Education is a perfectly respectable field, sir," I say calmly. "If Callie ever decided to return to school, I know she would flourish in whatever discipline she may choose. But if she received this kind of pressure growing up, I'm not surprised she concluded her education at the bachelor level."

Ira narrows his eyes as though I'm a puzzle he can't quite figure out. "And why is that?"

"Parental pressure to perform is a very real issue. I see it often in my practice." I shrug. "Anxiety, burnout and mental exhaustion are pretty common in these types of situations, leading to potentially choosing a path that others may consider the easy way out."

Callie's father leans back in his seat, a secretive smile playing on his lips. Like he knows about our chess game.

But if respect for his daughter is on the line, I'm going to win.

I'll make sure of it.

"Oliver," Connie's soprano voice cuts through the thickening air, "do you have much family in the area?"

"My parents and sister live in town." Sitting forward, I adjust until Callie's knee touches mine. "Apparently, my sister used to bug Callie about dating me." Smirking at my girlfriend, I'm rewarded with her lovely blush.

Connie turns to her sister. "Is that true, Calloway?"

Callie nods. "Yep. His sister owns the pilates studio I go to. For months, all I heard about was what a great guy her brother was." She reaches over, stealing my hand for herself and inter-twining our fingers. "Turns out, she was right."

Looking from Callie back to the rest of her family, I realize something. "Why do you all call her Calloway instead of Callie?" I ask no one in particular.

"It's her name," Lillian answers, polishing off her cup of coffee.

Across the room, Chris smirks. "And because she hates it."

Conversation swiftly turns to Prescott and some cases they're working on at the firm when Callie leans my way. "How much longer do you think we need to stay?" she whispers. "It's been nearly two hours." Wide eyes convey she's hoping for an answer that means we need to leave soon, much to my amusement.

And who am I to deny her?

Pulling out my phone, I pretend to check a text message. "It looks like Nacho had a little mishap," I say a little louder than necessary.

Callie's furrowed brow hangs around for only a moment before understanding dawns on her. "Oh, man. Well, we should probably go so you can check on her," she nods, standing and motioning for me to follow her lead.

Connie turns to us. "Who's Nacho?"

"Oliver's sweet dog," Callie explains. "Sorry Mom, Dad, but we need to go."

Lillian and Ira stand, shaking my hand as I thank them for having me and wish them a happy holiday. Giving a general sentiment to the rest of the Rutherfords, I smile at my girlfriend and offer my hand as we make our way toward the front door.

Just as Callie and I slip on our coats, Chris rounds the corner and heads right for us.

Pushing the remote start, I hand the key to Callie. "Why don't you go wait in the car?" I suggest.

Callie frowns but doesn't argue, and I can tell she's trying not to roll annoyed eyes when she sees her brother. She slips out the front door and I push it shut behind her.

"Hey, what's up?" I ask casually. Though, to be honest, he could be ready to punch me and I wouldn't be surprised.

Shoving his hands in the pockets of his slacks, Chris smiles up at me in a way that makes my skin crawl. "Look man, about earlier."

"Ah." I allow my mask reserved for difficult, narcissistic patients to slip into place.

"I was just trying to impress upon you that Calloway really doesn't contribute as much as the rest of us, yourself included. To society, or our family." The little prick has the audacity to shrug, smirking up at me. "So don't judge my friend too harshly based on my sister's opinion, Mr. Rhodes. She only takes care of kids while the rest of us deal with real issues."

Sighing, I smile back at him, a gesture he wrongfully takes as agreement. "Then consider me unimpressed. Oh, and Chris?" I clap him on the shoulder. "It's 'Dr.'" With a wink to his stunned mug, I slip out the door.

The car ride back to Callie's apartment is completely void of tension and is instead filled with Callie singing along to Christmas songs playing on the radio. I have to admit, it's a great feeling. Both of our families clearly believed our story. My family seems to think my life is going well, and Callie's overwhelmingly egocentric family will hopefully start showing her a bit more respect. By the time we pull up in front of Callie's building, her nosy neighbor is peeking out the curtains, as if anticipating our arrival.

Putting the car in park, I know it's too much to hope that she invites me inside. But the sting still radiates through my system when Callie unbuckles and throws her arms around me. The hug only lasts about three seconds, but her intoxicating scent of liquid chocolate lingers even after she sits back in her own seat.

Bright eyes look back at mine, her smile effervescent. "I, um, I guess this is it."

"I guess so." I don't bother hiding my frown, which she quickly mirrors.

"Uh, I guess so," she repeats. Shifting in her seat, any remaining ounce of happiness seems to dissipate. Delicate fingers fidget in her lap. "Well, thank you for everything, Oliver. You have no idea how much I appreciated you being there with me tonight."

My eyes search her face, trying to discern what she's feeling. "Of course," I nod. "And thank *you*. You know, for everything."

"Oh, my part was easy," she laughs. "Your family really is great. Though, I'm sure Blythe will probably ask for details at my next several pilates classes." Those ruby brows furrow.

I palm the back of my neck, willing myself to think of absolutely anything I can say to make this woman stay with me just another minute longer. "I'll try to see if I can get her to back off a bit. I know she can be tenacious."

"That she can." Callie grins. "Um, I guess I'll let you get back to Nacho."

"She loved you."

If it's even possible, Callie's smile widens. "She's the sweetest girl. Will you give her lots of kisses from me?"

"I will," I promise, trying not to think about the feel of Callie's lips.

And how I'll never feel them again.

"Good. I don't want her to forget me."

I smile at my fake girlfriend, automatically reaching to place a hand on hers before thinking better of it. "Nacho could never forget you."

Swallowing roughly, Callie watches the hand that dared to move toward hers. "Goodbye, Oliver," she whispers. Without waiting for a response, she gets out of my car and heads to her front door.

"Goodbye, Callie." I watch until she slips inside, shutting the door behind her. And when I pull away into the night, her sudden absence in my life makes my stomach roll.

# 11

## Callie

"It's just so frustrating. The astronauts have to be able to kick the box on the spacecraft, which is supposedly a reasonable request. But apparently, just asking them not to kick it is out of the question." Imogene groans into her soup.

"Will it float once they're in space?" Across the table, Chris pretends to look mildly interested in my oldest sister's dilemma. Maybe he's regretting his life in finance and looking for something to take him to new heights.

Imogene eyes him suspiciously. "It's likely, why?"

Chris shrugs. "Maybe they're just trying to plan on it accidentally getting kicked in midair, not necessarily on the ground."

"That is ... mildly helpful ... " Despite the semi-positive sentiment, Imogene looks ready to vomit.

"It may be worth considering," Connie offers. Her soft voice carries in the stupidly big dining room made for company dinners and family parties with relatives you've only met twice in your life.

As the soups are taken away, my father rubs his hands together. "Great news, I've secured the Aspen Point Grand Ballroom for the annual New Year's party again this year."

At the opposite end of the table, Lillian nods approvingly, as if this is something new and noteworthy.

It's definitely not, since we've had the party in the Grand Ballroom every year since I can remember.

Connie looks across me to our father. "Have you decided on a theme, Daddy?"

"Not yet, my darling girl." Dad's tender smile accompanies doting eyes reserved only for his favorite daughter. "But I want something classy, timeless. Prescott, any thoughts?"

My oldest brother looks up from tonight's white alba truffle pasta, mouth completely full with him caught completely off guard. Choking down the bite, heat rushes to his cheeks as he clears his throat. "I'm sure whatever Mom puts together will be perfect," he says, waving his fork in her direction.

Dad pinches the bridge of his nose. "And to think, it's only Tuesday," he grumbles to himself. Rolling his neck, Dad turns back to his oldest. "Of course it will, but that's not the point. The point is for you to care about how our family is presented at our annual gathering, since our most important clients will be there." Disapproving eyes peer down the table at Prescott.

My brother swallows, squaring his large shoulders. If he wasn't a giant booger of a human, I'd almost be intimidated. Pressing a napkin to his lips, Prescott turns to face my dad. "I do care about how we look to the clients, but that's why we have a whole events and marketing team that takes care of worrying about things like that—so we don't have to."

Connie gathers another bite of pasta. "What about gold and

black?" That woman's voice may sound like a bunny, but it carries authority. She's nothing if not sure of herself.

Ira's unamused face stretches into a grin rivaling the crescent moon out tonight. "With mirrorballs everywhere," he finishes. My father claps his hands together, soft from years spent behind a desk. "That's brilliant, darling."

To Connie's credit, she doesn't brag. She doesn't gloat. While all my other siblings would look smug and eternally proud of themselves in this rare moment of validation from our cold father, Connie simply returns to her pasta.

"Oh," I say, speed-chewing my food so I don't lose the thought, "Connie, I meant to tell you. Aaron's band is playing again this Friday."

On the other side of my favorite sister, Chris' jaw seems to clamp down on whatever he's currently chewing.

Connie freezes before remembering she has an audience. Barely turning my way, she shoots me a timid smile. "That's good to know. Thank you, Calloway." Pushing around what remains on her plate, her freckled cheeks show the slightest hint of a blush stain.

"Yeah, several of us are going," I continue. Mainly so the rest of our family doesn't start the Rutherford family inquisition on why Connie suddenly looks extremely interested in her least favorite dish since childhood. "Ian's trying to get Aaron to save us a table. You know, so we don't have to fight our way to a seating arrangement this time." Awkward laughter echoes, filling the stilted silence.

"Don't we already have plans this Friday?" Chris turns to his twin. Ginger brows raised, you don't have to be part of their twin connection to understand his message.

Connie frowns at her partner in crime. "No. Besides, if you want to watch those silly space movies again, you're more than welcome to do so by yourself."

"You said you loved them," he accuses, taken aback.

Across the table, Imogene scoffs. "Oh, please. You're the only one of us who got the super geek gene." She points an empty fork at him with the accusation.

"Excuse me?" Chris's ears match his hair.

Imogene shrugs. "I'm just saying, how many comic books do you have in your collection now?"

"Those are collectibles."

Prescott smirks, taking arms with his sister. "You said the same thing when you were seventeen and couldn't get a date to the prom."

"I had better things to do than go to some stupid dance." Chris puffs up his chest.

"Like sitting at home alone watching your space movies?" Prescott asks, feigning innocence.

Connie's twin sputters, looking for words while Connie glares at the others from across the table.

It's always fun to feel a Rutherford sibling riot brewing. The air gets thick. Blood pressures rise. The animals get really quiet. But as much fun as it can be to watch my siblings hurl every insult in the book at one another, I've got a busy week.

"So, Scotty boy—"I grin at the dark look shot my way at hearing his least favorite nickname"—is Marigold doing okay?"

"Why?" is the curt response I receive.

Shrugging, I look at the empty seat next to him. "Because she's not here tonight and, I mean, with the holiday coming up and being in a single parent household ... "

"She's at dance class."

"But she's doing okay other than that?"

Prescott sighs. "She's fine, Calloway."

"Really? Because it's not unusual for kids in single parent households to feel heightened emotional challenges that may not always be present the rest of the year." I take a big gulp of my water while my brother looks ready to be sick. "Loss, stress and increased emotional strain can be pretty common."

Down the table, Chris snorts. "Where'd you get that? Dr. Hotness?"

Glaring at my self-declared arch nemesis, I count to three. Extra slowly. "No," I say carefully, "believe it or not, I do know some things about children. Since, you know, I work with them every day and all."

While Mom's attention can have the tendency to drift off during conversations that don't interest her—like ones involving the mundane parts of her kids' lives—the mention of Oliver brings her back to life. "Where is Oliver tonight, dear?"

Blinking at my mother, it's all I can do to remain seated. *You're not found out, you're not found out.* "W-why?" If Connie ever tried to ingest some helium, this is about what she'd sound like. Clearing my throat, I try again, ignoring the strange looks I'm receiving from every person at the table. "I mean, why do you ask?"

Mom pushes back her plate, signaling to the staff that we're done. "He may have given me some things to consider—oh, I got hot cocoa delivered from the store today. But you looked so *together* a few weeks ago, and I haven't heard you mention him even once tonight. I'm surprised you're out of each other's sight." She sends a sly grin down the table to Dad.

Gross.

That exact look is probably why I'm even here today.

"Reminds me of when we were young and in love," Mom continues. Man, I guess we did a better job than I realized.

"It's called taking a breather. Some space." But I'm certainly not about to admit how much I've missed having an excuse to talk to him in the nearly three weeks since Thanksgiving.

Not that I've heard from him, either.

"Good," Chris says, tossing his napkin onto the table, "that guy gave me the creeps."

"Rude," Connie chides. Turning to me, her sweetest smile graces those soft features. "I think he was lovely, Calloway."

Heat floods my face. "Oh, um, thanks," I mumble.

Across the table, Prescott leans back in his chair, crossing his arms. "Genny, what did you think about Dr. Streets?"

"Rhodes," I bite out.

Prescott dismisses me with a wave.

Beside him, Imogene shrugs. "I dunno, I thought he was nice enough." A grin slides onto her face as she looks at Chris. "I know you didn't like him because he's in the doctorate club. Isn't that right?"

Chris rolls annoyed eyes as he flips her off.

"Christopher Irving Rutherford, absolutely not." Dad thunders, even as a smirk threatens to break through. "Especially not at the table."

Turning to my brother, I smile as sweetly as possible. "And to think, there may be some poor woman out there who will love you the way Oliver loves me." *The fake way.* "When you do find her, I'll be sure to send her my condolences." I can practically see his middle finger twitching, begging for sweet release. Letting out the biggest fake yawn I can conjure, I push back from the table. "Well, I hate to break up the party, but I have a big week."

"Taking your kids to Munchkinland?" Chris sneers.

"Yep," I reply, not missing a beat, "but before that, we have our holiday program the day after tomorrow. So I'm gonna head home. There are a couple of reindeer costumes that need hemming."

"Calloway," Connie peeks up at me as I stand, "would you mind giving me a ride home?"

Confusion casts a heavy light over both Chris and myself. We even make awkward eye contact to confirm it.

"You do know that I live in the same exact place as you, right? We share a mailbox and everything," Chris asks. If his brow stays furrowed for much longer, it may never look normal again.

I nod. "Yep, and everyone here thinks that's weird," I answer for our entire family.

My brother glares up from where he's seated while his sister stands gracefully. "Please?" she asks again.

Blinking, I realize she's serious. "Um, yeah, of course." Honestly, if we all truly liked each other, the twins and I could carpool every other week—we only live a few blocks from one another. But that would require a stronger relationship than bickering at family dinners every two weeks.

Then again, if Connie continues showing up to Aaron's gigs ... we may just get somewhere, after all.

Or they will.

Connie kisses our parents goodbye while I shift from foot to foot.

"Calloway?" My father stands, dropping a used napkin where his plate once sat. "Is Oliver joining us up at Aspen Point this year?" While the man's face may be open and curious, the underlying sheen of antagonism dares to try and break through the facade.

"I think he'll be with his family for the holidays." A light bulb goes off in my mind. "They usually go and visit his grandma in Boston." I give myself a little pat on the back for remembering that tiny tidbit. "Maybe next time." Shrugging, I smile.

And try to ignore the sting of knowing how false my statement truly is.

Marshall, Sandra, and Blythe invade the forefront of my mind, their faces warm and welcoming. The genuine feeling of home.

*I wonder if they've asked about me.*

No, no. Thanksgiving only. That was the deal.

Dad doesn't bother responding before heading toward the living room, ready to turn on whatever game is on tonight.

"Ready Calloway?" Connie holds out my coat.

Swallowing, I take it from her and we make our way to my snowtopped car. I'm proud of my car. I bought it when I was nineteen with my own money. I'd had a job for three years and, with supplemental money from years of babysitting, I was able to afford it without the help of my parents. While my siblings took the fancy vehicles Ira and Lillian supplied, I wanted to make my own way. And of course, the other Rutherford children were able to eventually exchange their firsts for newer models. But I've had the same trusty Goaty for nearly nine wonderful years.

Goaty, since Mountain Goat is too long for everyday conversations.

But as my extremely successful, prim and proper sister climbs into Goaty's worn interior, I can't help but feel a twinge of resentment. Of their success. Of their financial stability.

Of them clearly all being cut from the same cloth, while I'm just ... not.

The engine roars to life, the trusty heater and radio blasting from having left them on when I was last here. Buckling my seatbelt, I glance over at my sister in her dark slacks and beige cardigan. The excess glitter on my seats may just be what she needs to finally win Aaron over. Though, who am I kidding?

Aaron's been hers for years.

If only they were smart enough to figure it out.

"Maybe Chris needs to get laid," I blurt out. Both my hands grip the wheel with a dangerous amount of tension while I try to not face palm myself.

But Connie surprises me by bursting into laughter.

Wide eyes slide toward her, testing to see if I've upset her.

"Maybe so." Connie grins down at her lap. "I do apologize for his behavior."

"Which time?" I grumble.

"Chris really is a good person. He's supportive, and great at his job. He does his best with any task thrown his way, big or small," she insists. "Not to mention, he has an amazing eye for detail. That's probably why he's so good at his job. But I think he's lonely."

"How can he be lonely?" Brows knitting together, my frown feels less alone. "You two are always together. Well, except for right now. But you sleep next door to one another. You carpool to and from work and Mom and Dad's house. And probably everywhere else. He even came with you to see Aaron's band play last time, and I highly doubt that was his idea of a good time."

"Yes," she nods, "but what you've found with Oliver—I think Chris is a little jealous."

My ribs twist themselves into oblivion at the mention of Oliver and our clearly outstanding job of romantic deception. And here I thought we wouldn't be able to pull it off.

Silly me.

"He knows about my feelings," Connie continues, "for Aaron. Chris has always known." She snorts. "He knew even before I did."

My sister isn't usually this talkative. But I take the shot anyway. "How long have you liked Aaron?" Chancing a peek, I have the privilege of a full-on flush. "I promise I won't say anything."

Connie shifts in her seat to face me. "Do you remember when the Fairchilds moved in next door?"

"I was ten," I nod. "They came to my Scooby-Doo birthday party a few weeks later. Their mom had learned I wanted to be a teacher and they gave me a chalkboard and that student desk?" Remembering Ian sitting in a desk that was much too small for him for all the hours I made him play school with me brings a smile to my face.

Connie's musical laugh reminds me of holiday bells. "That's right. Well—" she sighs "—I remember looking out my bedroom window and seeing their moving van. Their parents were talking to the movers; giving directions I'm guessing. And then he marched out of the van carrying a huge box and wouldn't let anyone else take it from him. While our family was taught to simply hire something out or let workers take care of things for us because we're fortunate enough to be able to afford it, here was this guy. A guy who was clearly from our world, but was also so capable. He wasn't all buttoned up and proper like those hiding behind the ivory walls in the Rutherford mansion. And he understood how music can speak to your soul. It was refreshing."

"But you didn't know right away how you felt?" I ask.

She shakes her head. "No, not immediately. I just knew I found him intriguing." Connie runs a hand through loose hair, freshly cut to shoulder-length. "I started spending more time in the yard, hoping to run into him. Hanging around you when you would see him and Ian so I wouldn't seem out of place." Connie grins.

I can't help grinning right back. "You could've just joined us, you know."

"I know ... "

"But Chris wouldn't have wanted to," I finish for her.

She nods. "And I couldn't just leave him. He's been my partner since birth. I felt like I would be abandoning him—betraying him—if I did that."

"It's okay for you all to have independent hobbies, Connie," I whisper. "Just because you spend time apart doesn't mean you're doing anything wrong."

"Trust me, I have no interest in going to the gym," she laughs. "I'll leave that one to him."

"The space movies?"

"Ugh," she groans, "yeah, he definitely needs another friend for those."

"Or a girlfriend," I snicker.

"Speaking of ... " Connie raises a brow.

Oh no. Please don't bring him up.

"Is Oliver really not going to come to Aspen Point with you? Even I'll admit that I find that surprising."

And there it is. "Why?" It comes out harsher than I mean it, but Connie sits there with her soft-spoken patience.

When I don't give her anything else, she rolls emerald eyes. "Because of how he looked at you the entire night at Thanksgiving."

I don't bother holding back the derisive snort. And silently curse myself for accepting her request for a ride home. Only a few more miles and I'll be home free.

Connie's brow climbs higher. "You disagree? When was the last time you saw him?"

"Look, I don't really know how much more I'll see of him, if I'm being honest," I sigh. There, that's not totally untrue. Especially since I currently have no plans to see him again. And I am one hundred percent refusing to admit how I don't love that to someone I've convinced otherwise.

"Why not?" Connie demands.

Rolling my neck back and forth, I beg the car travel gods to make these last few minutes go by faster. "It-it's just, it's complicated."

"You love him, he clearly loves you—" she shrugs "—what's complicated about that?"

"Because it's fake, okay?" I shout. "There, are you happy? It was all fake. I admit it. We fooled you all." The only sound in the vacuum of Goaty is some folk song playing through the radio. My face burns at the confession, and I keep my eyes locked on the road while I pray that Connie's suddenly become deaf.

Sliding my gaze over to my sister, I watch while she quirks her lips this way and that. Her brows furrow and smoothen, only to reenter the wrinkly zone. Finally, I hear, "Huh."

"What does that mean?" The volume from my previous

shared secret remains. Groaning, I contort my face into what in no way can be considered attractive. I probably look like I'm dying from scurvy. Maybe I will.

But then who would water Gilmore?

I haven't set up a will yet, choosing who to bequeath my botanical babies to when that time comes.

Surely Ian will take some of them on.

"Breathe, Calloway." Connie's tender voice reminds me that we both need to get home safely, so it wouldn't do any good to get in a car crash right now.

"I so should not have told you that. Here, I've been worried about getting caught and I managed to spill my own secret," I ramble. "He told me everything would be fine, that no one would find out. But he didn't count on my own big mouth—"

"Calloway." The sharp tone coming from my timid sister shocks me into silence, which she's probably as thankful for as I am. When it's clear that I don't plan on continuing my verbal tirade anytime soon, she continues, "First, I promise not to tell the others."

Does this woman have a shiny halo above her head, or am I seeing things?

"But why did you feel like you had to bring a fake boyfriend to Thanksgiving?" She frowns. "And, um, where did you find ... him?"

"Come on, you know Mom," I grumble. "She's been asking more lately when I'm going to settle down. Like, if I can't have a graduate degree, I can at least get my M. R. S. or something. I mean, it's not like I don't want to find someone."

"It's the family name," she smirks.

Using one hand to rub my now aching forehead, I pull into the space by Connie's car. "I'm kinda surprised we beat Chris home," I mutter.

Connie scoffs. "You drove like a mad woman. Am I that bad to spend time with?"

Shame floods my cheeks. "No."

"I actually like you, you know?"

Biting my lower lip, I smile at my sister. "Good to know. You're, um ... you're actually my favorite sibling. You don't make fun of me—of what I do."

Connie tilts her head to the side, loose hair draping itself over her shoulder. "Why would I make fun of you?"

"Everyone else does."

Raising light brows, she nods to herself. "The others don't really dislike you, particularly, either."

"Could've fooled me."

"Like I said, I think Chris is jealous—whether or not he'd admit it. Genny and Scott are just so wrapped up in their own worlds, they don't really know any better."

I shoot my sister a skeptical look. "Mom and Dad?"

Connie hesitates. "I don't really know," she admits. "But I do know that they were impressed by Oliver. Even if he did spend the evening dropping subtle hints that were overall pretty well-disguised, if I do say so myself." She laughs.

I can't help but wince. "Was he that obvious?"

"No, don't worry about that."

"Why do I sense a 'but'?" I ask wearily.

"But ... " Cautious eyes find mine, "I do think it would help your case if Oliver came with you to Aspen Point."

"You're kidding," I deadpan.

"There was a reason you brought him home in the first place, right?" she insists. "Well, I don't think it would look great to Mom and Dad if it looks like you couldn't make it work with the only man you've ever brought home other than Alexander."

"No. No way." I shake my head so hard my bun comes loose. "I can't bring him with me. That wasn't the agreement."

Connie shrugs. "What exactly was the agreement, if you don't mind my asking?"

Rolling my lips in and out, I weigh the consequences of

giving Connie the skinny. On the one hand, I could not tell her and keep whatever modicum of dignity may remain. On the other hand, she already knows Oliver's not actually my boyfriend, and that's not really all that great. So I give her the story from the beginning, ending with how awkward I left it when he dropped me off Thanksgiving night.

"Did you ever pay him?"

I knew there had to be another shoe to drop. "That's embarrassing," I mumble. "I wonder if he would take a check."

Ignoring me, she continues, "I'll take that as a no. So you didn't leave it with any other plans to see him or his family?"

"Nope."

"What about Blythe? You're at pilates three to four times a week. And you said she now lives next door to Ian." Crap, I'm gonna have to find a new workout studio. I've carefully avoided the classes she teaches, but I'll need them soon to keep up my stamina.

A look I like to call 'Callie's about to be violently ill' takes over my face.

"Got it," she nods, needing no further explanation. "Does it matter that he texted you about twenty minutes ago?" Connie holds up my phone with a message notification from the one and only Oliver Rhodes. "He said you left your scarf in his car and he just found it today. Then he asked if you wanted to come by the practice tomorrow to retrieve it."

My wide eyes look between her and the phone. Shaking my head, I take the phone from her and toss it in the cupholder. "I can't do that."

"Why not?"

"Because."

"Because why? Because it's against the agreement? The deal is over, Calloway." Connie folds her arms. "Now, you can do whatever you want. But if you want Mom, Dad and the others to continue on this trajectory of 'let's be nicer to Calloway,' then

I think you need to go see him. Tomorrow. Just mention Aspen Point to him—he may surprise you." Before I can halfheartedly disagree, my sister gives me one more knowing look before stepping out into the cold.

FAMILIAR DREAD CREEPS into my chest as I walk up the snow-covered cobble walkway of Rhodes, McNalley & McNalley Therapy Collective.

At least I was invited this time.

The same bell rings above the door as the nosy Mrs. Lanahan looks up, smirking when our eyes meet across the reception area that suddenly feels much too small. "Lovely to see you again, dear."

A timid smile breaks the frozen state of nausea on my face. But just as I open my mouth to defend myself, I hear him.

"Don't forget to practice counting with the breathing. I really think it'll make all the difference. Remember, we don't always want to say what we're feeling in the moment." Dr. Oliver Rhodes emerges from the hallway, looking as stupidly handsome as ever. Apparently, my memory hasn't done him justice since my hormones are halfway to the nearest closet and begging him to follow.

A woman in her forties with two teenage boys walk out with him, one of the boys listening intently to the man who was my fake boyfriend. The sullen teenager nods in confirmation.

"Great," Oliver claps the boy on the shoulder. "I'll see you all after the holiday, okay?"

The family says their goodbyes, walking right past me.

But Oliver finds me immediately. His shoulders relax, like tension has kept him prisoner all day. A grin brightens his face. "Callie, you came."

"I texted you that I would," I remind him.

He strides right up to me, hesitating only when he's within breathing distance.

It's an odd thing, seeing someone you pretended to date. What are you supposed to do for a greeting? Kissing seems a little weird, since we were never actually romantically involved. Even if we did kiss in front of our families. Hugging seems oddly casual. Shaking the guy's hand just feels wrong.

Oliver blinks a couple of times before settling on, "Why don't you come back to my office? Do you remember the way?"

"She doesn't have an appointment, Dr. Rhodes," Mrs. Lanahan calls in protest from her perch.

Oliver grins down at me as I march past him toward his office. "It's okay, she's my girlfriend." He snickers, catching my eyebrow raise.

Only when we're in the safety of his office do I say, "Girlfriend, huh?"

He shrugs, closing the door behind him. "Eh, it's the least likely excuse to be questioned. And it'll make her leave you alone, which I'm sure you'll appreciate."

Snorting, I drop into the familiar loveseat. "You got that right, Dr. Rhodes."

"We're not back to that again, are we?" Oliver leans against his desk, crossing his arms. Between the cozy feel of the office, his rolled-up sleeves and today being a glasses day, my hormones are literally crying right now.

"Nah," I laugh, "it just felt right."

He swallows, cheeks tinting. "So .. how have you been? How is ... everything?"

"Everything is ... getting worked on," I admit. "Things with Connie are better. We actually rode home together last night from the family dinner."

"Wow, that is better." Dark blond brows raise. "Was Chris in the car, too?"

I scoff. "Definitely not."

Oliver chuckles, leaning down to grab his bag. "Didn't think so," he shrugs, "but I figured it wouldn't hurt to ask." He frees my favorite scarf from his bag, offering it to me. "What did you and Connie talk about the whole time?"

"Are you being nosy?" I grin, taking the scarf.

"Maybe."

I sigh. "We talked about her feelings for Aaron—"

"Wow."

"I know, right? Um ... " I knot the scarf around one of my hands as a distraction of what I now have to tell him.

Oliver frowns from his own chair. "Callie? What is it? What's wrong?"

Pressing my lips together, I look anywhere but at the handsome therapist sitting in front of me. "Well, you see ... she was telling me about how she thinks Chris is jealous ... of us."

Across the tiniest office known to man, Oliver squints as he waits for whatever's coming next, nodding slowly.

"And I may have admitted, uh, everything."

He freezes. "So Connie knows."

"Yep."

"Everything?"

"Everything. But it really all came up because Mom asked if you were coming with us to Aspen Point Lodge this year. Otherwise, it's very possible it never would've come up." I flinch, waiting for his outrage, his embarrassment.

But it doesn't come.

"Aspen Point?" he asks, confusion coating his features.

"Uh, yeah." I frown. "It's this fancy lodge up in Honeyville—"

"I know where it is."

"Okay, well, you just looked confused so ... " The scarf may now officially be cutting off circulation, but I don't really need that hand, anyway. "My family goes up there every year for Christmas. Then we always come home for a few days before

Dad's firm has their annual New Year's party there, which we always attend." I don't bother hiding my annoyance at the obligation.

"Your family goes to Aspen Point every year?" he asks slowly.

"Yepper pepper."

Those sculpted lips press together, suppressing a grin. "What did you tell them?"

"About what?"

"About my coming with you."

Picking at a loose thread on the couch, I do my best to hide the hint of disappointment threatening to make itself known in my voice. "I told them you were going with your parents to Boston to see your grandma."

Oliver nods slowly, my heart stupidly sinking a bit more with each pass.

"So anyway," I lock eyes with Oliver, willing myself to think about the new plant babies I know will be coming my way soon from Ian and Aaron, "how do I pay you for your services? Cash? Card? Check? Twenty boxes of designer chocolate?"

His face never changes. Not even when he says, "I think I should go with you."

My heart stops. I'm dead. No longer among the living. Gilmore is on his own. Goaty will never be covered in stray glitter again.

"As long as you're okay with it, of course." Oliver quirks a brow. "Callie?"

"W-why?"

"If it'll help you, why wouldn't I do it?"

"We'd have to share a room."

"I think I'll manage."

I sit up straighter. "What about your family?"

Oliver shakes his head with a dark and quiet chuckle. "Funnily enough, you got that one right. They are going to Boston."

Huh. My brows knit together. "Blythe?"

"She and some friends are going to Mexico."

"Lucky girl. I'd love to go sit on the beach for Christmas instead of being with my family," I mutter.

"Hey—" Oliver leans forward, elbows resting on his knees "—I know for a fact that you won't be alone with your family this Christmas."

"Really?"

"Yep." He smirks. "I heard you've got a pretty great boyfriend that's coming with you."

The smirk I mirror back fades as I lean back into the couch. "But our deal ... "

Oliver rolls his chair across the small space, taking my hands in his. "Callie, I promised you we were in this together, right?"

Nodding, I do my best to ignore how the warmth from his hands runs through the entirety of my body. How desperately I want him to hold me close like he did in front of our families. "Right."

"So, we'll just keep up the pretense through the holidays." Titling his head, Oliver beams. "If something with my family comes up before Christmas, you can attend if your schedule allows. And I'll accompany you to Aspen Point."

Releasing a dramatic sigh, I feign only mild satisfaction. "I guess that would be easier than finding a new fake boyfriend before then."

"Undoubtedly," Oliver grins. "So, my beautiful cocoa connoisseur, what does the rest of your week look like? Anything family-holiday related I can crash?"

"I have my class' holiday program tomorrow," I offer, ignoring how intently he's listening. I've never received such full attention before. It's a little unnerving. "I invited my family, but Connie is the only one who usually shows up."

Oliver twists to grab his phone. Pulling up December seventeenth on his calendar, he opens a new event. "What time?" His voice is patient, sincere.

My brows try their hand at joining my hairline. "You want to come watch my kids act like reindeer?"

Oliver, the handsome man that he is, grins. "What are fake boyfriends for?"

## 12

*Oliver*

The nice thing about tonight is that my best friends will be here, too. And while they should—and will—be here to support Cici the Reindeer, they'll also be getting a front row seat to what Callie and I look like together in action.

"It looks like there are some seats over near the middle." Jo points to where four cafeteria chairs practically have a light shining down upon them. With the number of parents and family members here, it's honestly a miracle that she spotted that many together at all. But the churn of friends and family leaving after each class helps with the seating issue.

John nods, hands glued to his daughter's shoulders. His daughter that truly does look like a little reindeer with her brown fleece suit, antlers headpiece and face paint. "Good catch. You three go save them while I get Cici to her class."

Cici wiggles in place, dancing to the holiday music playing over the speakers before the first class takes the stage.

"I think I better go with you," I offer, clearing my throat. "Since her teacher is my girlfriend, and all."

Beside me, Rindy grins. "Right. Good thinking, lover boy." She holds out her hand, and I grace her with the task of watching my coat. "There's nothing like your face on hers to make a class recital go smoother."

Rolling my eyes, I turn and run to catch up with John and Cici. It's a quick walk from the cafeteria to Callie's classroom and Cici does a pretty good job of giving us show spoilers the whole way.

But my favorite kindergartner's enthusiasm is warranted when her gorgeous teacher squeals as soon as Cici walks through the door. "Cici McNalley, you look absolutely adorable!" Callie kneels so that she's eye-level with Cici, my girlfriend's fitted cocoa blouse and dark jeans accentuating every curve. Her long hair is pulled back into a ponytail, the loose strands telling how much she's been running around keeping order. "How does your costume fit? Are the antlers poking at all?"

Cici shakes her head, causing said antlers to look a little haywire.

With an expert hand, Callie fixes the headpiece in record time and sends Cici over to her desk. "Hey guys," Callie breathes, looking between John and I. Finally landing on me, she blinks. "You came."

The smile already on my face threatens to test the human laws of physics. "Of course I'm here. I wouldn't miss it."

"I'm, um, I guess I'm just not used to that," she laughs. Nerves make her voice higher than normal, but whether it's the stress of managing her class or my presence, I'm not sure.

I know which one I hope it is.

"I mean, Connie's usually here somewhere," she continues,

"but she doesn't come back here or anything. John—" she says, remembering we're not alone "—are you ready for Cici's performance? Got your camera prepped and ready to capture the cutest reindeer?" The questions are rehearsed, as if she's asked them a hundred times.

Grinning, John holds up the silver camera he's had for years. "You bet, Ms. Rutherford. Ci gave us the rundown of when her parts are, so I feel well-prepared."

Callie smiles, shaking her head. "That girl cracks me up."

"You and me both," he nods. I send him my best get lost look, which he astutely picks up on before I have to escort him to the door. He claps my shoulder. "Ollie, you good to get back to the cafeteria by yourself? Or do you need a chaperone?"

Flicking away his hand, I have a hard time looking away from the stunning woman tenderly helping a little boy fix a button on his shirt. "I'm good, man. Now get out of here."

"See you out there." John laughs all the way to the hall.

With the boy's costume back in order, Callie turns to me. A shy smile graces her lovely face. "Hi," she breathes.

I don't bother hiding my own grin. "Hi, Ms. Rutherford."

"Is it weird I still can't believe you're actually here?"

My lips tip down. "We're a team, Callie. If you're up to bat, I'm in the dugout rooting for you."

That soft smile grows into a full-blown grin. "I feel like we should come up with a secret handshake or something."

Laughter bursts through my lips. "If that'd make you feel better, I'll get to work on one. Though—" I peek around her to the kids chattering excitedly among themselves "—you may have better resources for that than I would."

"Maybe," she nods. "Are Rindy and Joanna here, too?"

Nodding, I glance at Cici, who's busy smoothing another girl's hair. "They wouldn't miss it. So," I say, looking back at the amazing woman before me, "where do you wait while they're on stage?"

"Off in the wings. You know, just in case one of them decides to start eating their weight in boogers on stage, or something."

Quirking a brow, I give her my most serious look. "Does that happen often?"

Pressing pink lips together, Callie's face darkens. "More than you'd like to know." She gives me a look of pure terror before it morphs into giggles.

Laughing along with her, I can't help but feel so comfortable. This—being in Callie's class with her, or just laughing together—feels so natural.

Despite our strange predicament, everything has.

While Callie gives directions and her class prepares to walk toward the holding area, a little boy holds up a hand. "Yes, Alex? Do you need to use the bathroom before we go?"

Alex shakes his head, smartly holding onto his antlers during the moment of chaos.

Callie smiles. "Okay, then what is it?"

"Who's that?" The boy points around her. Right to me.

My girlfriend blushes, twisting around to look my way before turning back to her kids. "That's Dr. Rhodes. He's a friend of mine."

"He told Daddy you're his girlfriend," Cici shouts, leading the entire class in giggles.

Callie laughs, peeking at me over her shoulder. "Well, I guess that gives us all something to think about. But for now—" she claps "—we've got some reindeer who need to show their parents how awesome they are."

The kids get lined up in some predetermined order while I watch Callie with nothing short of admiration. I do well to manage the kids in my sessions, but watching her work is something else entirely. It's practically an artform. This woman balances tenderness and holding firm, always taking the time to show each student that they have her entire attention when speaking with them.

She'll be a great mother one day.

A weight gathers deep in my chest at the reminder that we have a timer—an expiration date on our 'relationship'. I won't get to watch her love her own family when that day comes.

And I hate that.

When all the little reindeer are lined up and ready to go, Callie shoots a smile my way, warming my entire being. "Help me wrangle this herd of deer toward the music room?" Tilting her head, those chocolate eyes pin me in place.

Unable to find my voice, I smile and nod while the little girls at the back of the line snicker mercilessly. Somewhere between the classroom and the main hallway, Cici sneaks to the back of the line, taking my hand. And since her teacher has taken up my entire attention since the day she walked into my practice, I need all the help I can get navigating this strange place.

Ushering the kids into the music room, Callie worries her bottom lip, giving me an apologetic look. "I need to stay here with them. Are you good to go find a seat?" Her beautiful eyes widen. "I didn't mean you have to stay. Please don't feel obligated to."

Chuckling, I take her hand. "Of course I'm staying," I whisper. "I'll see you after?"

A breathtaking grin takes over her face, lighting up every feature. "After."

"After," I repeat, kissing her knuckles. Letting Callie get back to work, I take off toward the cafeteria, hoping that Rindy hasn't given up my seat.

But who knew finding a seat would be the least of my worries, because walking into the crowded room, I run into none other than my sister. "Blythe?" Blinking, I squint at the woman in front of me to make sure I haven't lost my mind. But no, my comically short sister really is standing here. In Cici's school. After hours. With a recital going on. "What're you doing here?"

Blythe's nose wrinkles, squinting right back. "Supporting Callie and her class. Duh. Mom and Dad are here too. Just over there." She points somewhere off in the distance.

Alarms go off in my head. "But ... why?"

She shrugs. "Callie's my friend. She's your girlfriend. She, Ian and Aaron are always talking about how her family isn't very supportive. Plus, Cici's in her class this year. When Ian mentioned the recital the other night, I told Mom and Dad about it and we all thought we'd come down to be here for her." Blythe looks up at me like it's the most obvious thing in the world, and I'm an idiot for not anticipating this.

I completely should have.

I should've known Mom and Dad would want to get to know any girl I brought home. I should've known Blythe would know all about this since she regularly hangs out with Callie and her best friends.

I should have known.

But Callie doesn't know they're here.

"Hey Oliver." Ian walks up behind Blythe. "Callie told me she went to see you yesterday." He sends me a look letting me know Callie clearly told him of the new arrangement.

I nod. "Right, good. That's good." My eyes bounce between Ian and a very confused Blythe.

"Look, you should probably know something," Ian leans forward, "the Rutherfords are here."

Brow furrowing, I try to connect all the dots. "Yeah, I guess Connie usually comes."

Ian shakes his head. "No, man. *All* the Rutherfords, from Ira to Marigold."

If my heart didn't stop when Blythe told me our parents were here, it sure does now. The class on stage finishes their set of songs, with the crowd erupting in applause, while I stare at my girlfriend's best friend. "Ian, are you telling me … that my entire family, Callie's entire family, and my practice partners are all … here? Tonight? At the same time?" I have to ask it all pretty slowly for fear my heart may just give out. Running isn't one of my favorite workouts, so I usually skip it at the gym. But I also didn't know my cardiac health would be compromised like it is now. When Ian doesn't respond, I try to come up with any possible way I could get a message to Callie—to prepare her. She won't like walking into this blind.

"What's the big deal?" Blythe asks, grinning. Mischievous eyes sparkle, even in the dim light of the cafeteria. "Just some preparation for the wedding, which I'm sure is right around the corner."

Ian frowns, confusion written all over his face. And his eyes, which are a little too locked onto my sister for my liking.

Blythe turns her bright smile toward him. "You know, since they're obsessed with each other."

"True," he agrees. "Hey, why don't you go tell your parents we found Oliver and I'll be over in a minute." Nodding, Ian slides his gaze toward me.

"Yeah, that'd be great," I throw in.

Blythe shakes her head. "Okay, then." She takes off in whatever direction our parents must be sitting.

When she's out of earshot, Ian steps closer. "Okay, look. Aaron's over there with the Rutherfords."

"You mean Connie?" I smirk.

Ian grins right back. "Basically." Casting a quick glance at the stage, the board showing which class is up next says it's nearly showtime for my girl.

"Why are they here?" Even out loud, it sounds more like I'm asking myself than him.

But Ian humors me and answers, anyway. "I think it was mainly Connie and Imogene. And where Connie goes, Chris usually follows. But I think she guilted their parents into coming, too. Apparently, she and Cal had a little heart to heart the other night."

"Not surprising," I mutter, "Right, Connie knows about us."

Ian nods. "Yeah, I know."

"Of course you do."

He smirks. "No need to be jealous, Rhodes. Callie's like my little sister—always has been."

"I'm not jealous. You couldn't be more wrong." My cheeks flame, which helps absolutely nothing.

"And you couldn't be more in denial."

Narrowing my eyes, I glare across the tiny space between us. "You don't know me, Ian."

He shrugs. "No, but I know Callie. And I know what she's told me about you." *Callie talks about me?*

Pinching the bridge of my nose, I take a deep breath. "Whatever. What about Imogene and Prescott? Should we be worried there?"

Ian motions over his shoulder where, sure enough, the entire Rutherford clan sits, looking uncomfortably out of place in the elementary school cafeteria. "I think she and Connie teamed up, talking up the costumes to Marigold, who then pestered Prescott."

The lights flicker, signaling the next group is about to begin. Callie's group.

"How do we want to do this?" I ask, desperation seeping into my tone.

"Aaron and I can handle the Rutherfords."

"It looks like you might be able to handle Blythe, too?" I ask, raising a questioning brow.

He swallows, hesitating just a moment too long. Maybe I should ask Callie about that, since we're together—for the season anyway.

Doing my best to ignore the excitement about being able to

talk to her without much of a reason, I allow the question to pass. "My friends will be pretty engrossed with John's daughter, though they are very aware of everything going on. I'll let them know about the new developments."

Ian nods. "What about your parents?"

Trying not to think about how much I may regret this, I ask, "Do you think you and I could double team them?"

"Got it. I met them the other day at Blythe's apartment, and they know Callie and I are friends. So nothing about my being here would seem weird." Looking around, Ian's brother catches his attention. Some kind of communication passes between them, the kind only siblings can understand, before Ian looks back my way. "You go warn your friends, so they can help if needed. I'll start with your parents."

Gratitude and relief flood my veins. "Ian, thank you. You know, for helping us."

"Callie's my best friend," he says, "and I just want her to be happy."

"So do I," I say with full sincerity.

"Then you should know," Ian steps in close, "I overheard Chris talking to Connie. Apparently, a few of them are questioning the validity of your relationship." He shrugs. "It probably started with him, but I don't doubt he could persuade the others."

"I really don't like that guy," I mutter.

Eyes lifting to the final flicker of the lights, he says, "Time to go."

Nodding, I ask, "Is this where we say 'go team' or something?"

Ian rolls his eyes, but smiles. "Just do me a favor. Don't break her heart." He doesn't wait around for an answer before hightailing it toward my parents and sister.

Making my way to John and the others as quickly as possible, I barely make it to my seat before Callie steps out on stage, spotlit in moments. Gone is the disheveled kindergarten teacher answering a hundred questions at once that I left in the music room. In her place stands a ravishing and confident woman holding her head up high.

Callie beams at the audience as her kids make their way on stage behind her. "Hello and thank you so much for coming tonight. Parents, I know technology can be a stinker sometimes, and if that happens, please know we are recording the entire performance. So no worries! Just stop by the table at the back or call the office tomorrow and give them your kiddo's name and their teacher—that's me, Ms. Rutherford—and we'll get you squared away. Now, these amazing kids have worked really hard, and I know they're excited to show you everything. Right, class?" Behind her, the kids cheer. Callie laughs, turning back to the parents. "Without further ado, please help me welcome Ms. Rutherford's Little Reindeer!" The cafeteria bursts into applause as Callie steps behind the curtain, the kids taking over the show.

Beside me, John grins from ear to ear with his camera at the ready.

Rindy and Jo fawn over the cuteness overload of Callie's class, taking the occasional photo or video clip.

And I discover that if I lean just far enough to the right, I can see Callie standing off-stage, pride in her kids covering every flawless feature.

Halfway through the set, I get a text from Blythe with about eight hundred heart eye emojis with a few reindeer ones sprinkled in. Peeking around the room, I spot them near the bathrooms by the entrance.

Like my sister, Mom looks like she's on some kind of cuteness overload while Dad bounces along to the beat.

Ian sits on the other side of Blythe, rightly keeping his hands to himself.

But as much as I want to, I don't dare look around for the Rutherfords. That would be tempting fate.

When Callie's kids are done and all the families they belong to begin to vacate for the next group of parents, I update my immediate group of the newest developments. As expected, Rindy rubs perfumed hands together like any good supervillain, while Jo tries not to look ashamed of her wife's behavior.

John, on the other hand, leaves to go grab Cici from Callie's class before the potential clash with the Rutherfords.

Rindy, Jo, and I follow closely behind in the hall, hoping to beat—

"Oliver, how lovely to see you again." Lillian Rutherford's voice sounds from behind me.

Turning, I come face to face with the entire Rutherford family, with the exception of my favorite.

And who I'm assuming is Ian's brother.

Pasting a charming smile on my face, I look at them each in turn. I even manage to not let surprise take over my features when Connie gives me an honest smile. "Mr. and Mrs. Rutherford, what a pleasure. Did you all enjoy the program?"

Ira and Prescott clearly came straight from the firm, still dressed in expensive suits that no mere mortals can afford. Callie's father clears his throat. "Yes, well, it was quite adequate work. But then, you can only expect so much from kindergartners, I suppose."

I stand a little taller. "Callie put in countless hours between the music and the costume creation. I know I certainly couldn't have done better. But I know she'd welcome her father's help for the spring program, if you'd like to help improve their efforts."

"You're Callie's dad?" My own father strides up behind the Rutherfords, who turn to face his deep baritone voice. Dad holds out his hand. "Marshall Rhodes, Ollie's dad. We just love your daughter."

Rindy taps me on the shoulder. "We're gonna leave you to, uh, this," she whispers.

Tossing a grateful look at my friends, they extricate themselves from what may become a terribly awkward situation.

Ira takes the proffered hand, business manners kicking in. "Ah, thank you. This is my wife, Lillian, and our children. Prescott, Imogene, Christopher and Constance. Calloway you know. And then hiding behind our oldest is his daughter, Marigold." He listens graciously as Dad makes the necessary introductions of our family while I silently beg Ian for help.

"Hey Mr. Rutherford," Ian interrupts, "I heard about the new merger with Benedict International. That's quite the whale you landed. Congrats."

Callie's father turns shrewd eyes to the man next to my sister. "Thank you, Ian. It will mean quite the change in staff, especially with some of their own coming to work in our office over the next several months."

Prescott's gaze snaps toward his father, but he says nothing.

Marigold peeks around her dad at me and waves, a shy grin playing on her lips. While the adults continue stilted pleasantries, Callie's niece slips around her father and tugs on Connie's hand. With a wave of her tiny hand, Connie leans down.

"Daddy," Connie's soft voice catches her father's attention. Callie may be the youngest of the family, but Ira definitely considers Constance his baby. "Marigold and I would like to go see Calloway. And—" Connie nods in my direction "—I'm sure her boyfriend would like to congratulate her on a job well done, too."

Clearing my throat, I silently thank Connie. "Absolutely. Uh, this way, everyone." While the others chat behind me, I have to work to not run toward the classroom to ensure I get to her first.

When we reach Callie's classroom, she's helping one of the

final kids scrub reindeer paint from their face as the corresponding parent gathers their things.

"Ms. Rutherford," I call through the doorway, silently cursing myself for the hint of panic in my voice.

Callie looks up, but her smile falls when she sees the look of alarm on my face. "Dr. Rhodes, is everything—"

And both of our families round the corner, pushing me through the door.

"Aunt Callie!" Marigold circumvents the rest of our group, launching herself into Callie's arms.

"Hey Goldie," she laughs, setting down her niece and taking in the sight before her. "Uh, give me just a second."

Ira and Lillian sit somewhere between impatience and annoyance at being put behind a student, but they luckily say nothing. When Ira steps out to take a phone call, I swear the room temperature rises by five degrees.

Our families chatter among themselves while Ian and Aaron—who have obviously been here on several occasions—give them the grand tour of Callie's class.

Imogene and Connie peruse displayed art projects with Marigold while Prescott and Chris whisper among one another, periodically glancing in my direction.

Or Callie's. There's really no way to tell since I've positioned myself in between them.

Whatever they've been whispering about, they finally work up the nerve to blatantly watch me.

Once the final student/parent combo is out the door, I rush over and engulf Callie in a tight hug before anyone else can even get close. Lithe arms close around me as I whisper, "Your brothers are suspicious and they all insisted on coming to see you."

"Come on now," Blythe says from behind me, "you don't get to hog your girlfriend."

Releasing my hold on Callie, our eyes meet, the tiniest nod passing between us.

Blythe elbows me out of the way, throwing tiny arms around my girlfriend and only letting go when my parents get close enough to take turns hugging her.

My mom brushes a piece of hair from Callie's face. "We are so proud of you, sweetheart. And your kids, of course. They were adorable!"

Callie grins, looking around at my family. "I had no idea you were all coming," she breathes, "but thank you so much. You have no idea what this means to me."

"Wouldn't miss it, Callie," my dad chuckles. "And we can't wait to see the next one."

My girlfriend blushes furiously under all the attention— something I get the feeling she's not used to receiving.

Ian and his brother take turns congratulating Callie on another successful program, which is made slightly more difficult by my keeping a tight hold on her hand. But eventually, the rest of the Rhodes family and the Fairchilds finally see themselves out.

Leaving us alone with the lions.

But this is our den, not theirs.

Lillian Rutherford steps up to her daughter. "Well, it seems you made quite the impression on Oliver's family." Anyone walking by would think Callie's mother was admiring her daughter. Good thing Callie and I know better. "Good for you, dear."

Callie squeezes my hand hard, making me apologetic to her future birthing partner.

"My entire family is very proud of her," I say, releasing Callie's hand to throw my arm around her. With every silent, awkward moment that passes, I pull her closer.

Lillian's eyes float between us, that catlike smile never vacating the premises. "How nice."

Footsteps echo in the hallway, announcing Ira's return. "Lillian, we need to go." Mr. Rutherford turns to his daughter. "Congratualtions, Calloway. Oliver," he turns to me, "it's a shame you won't be joining us up at Aspen Point for Christmas. Maybe next time."

"Actually, my parents decided to make Boston a solo trip this holiday," I say, smiling down at Callie who is now firmly tucked into my side, "so it turns out I can make the trip with Callie, after all."

Wiry gray brows raise, and his head corresponds with a nod. "Huh. Well, I guess we'll see you next week, then. Lillian, please?"

His wife gives Callie and I one more once over before making her way toward the door.

Prescott palms the back of his neck. "That was ... strange."

"Thanks," Callie snorts.

He shrugs. "But it was definitely a decent way to spend a Thursday night. So thanks for the entertainment. Besides, it wasn't any stranger than Marigold's program this year where they danced around in pajamas." Prescott moves to let Marigold give her aunt another hug, sprinkling in some kisses, before he guides her out to the hall.

Chris follows his older brother out without a word, hooking his arm and pulling him to the side as he does so.

Pressing a kiss to Callie's temple, I release her and step toward the hallway, allowing some room for her to chat with Connie and Imogene in private.

And to keep an eye on the Rutherford men who are hellbent on making Callie's and my life harder.

Imogene and Connie both radiate pride for their youngest sister as they take turns giving her awkward hugs, relaying their congratulations.

"Hey guys," I say, approaching the two biggest thorns in my

side. And that includes taking Mrs. Collins' family into consideration.

Prescott and Chris turn my way, neither looking too impressed.

"Thanks again for coming tonight," throwing my hands on my hips, I give them my best 'I'm not dangerous' smile, "I know it meant a lot to Callie."

Chris folds his arms over a puffed out chest.

Prescott just looks tired.

"Is everything alright?" I ask, feigning innocence.

Shockingly, Prescott is the first to speak. "So, what's your game?"

Frowning, I look between them, shaking my head. "I don't know what you mean."

"Is it our money? Status? Connections?" Chris interrupts.

My brows only dig deeper. "Excuse me?"

"Because the way I see it," he continues, "you've got a lot going for you. Your own private practice, two entrepreneur parents and a sister following in their footsteps—"

"Did you do a background check on me or something?"

"Now the question is, what does someone like you want with someone like Calloway?" Chris finishes, a stupid smirk leaking across that smug face.

Prescott rubs his temples, sighing. "Oliver. You seem decent enough. But you and Calloway? You don't match. There has to be something in it for you."

Beside him, Chris scoffs, turning to his brother. "More like he's too good for Calloway. The only benefit is the money and status he'd get from being with her."

"Excuse me?" I don't bother keeping the anger from seeping into my tone as heat floods my cheeks.

Immediately behind me, the classroom door squeaks open, Imogene and Connie's voices whispering to one another. And both come to a crashing halt once they gauge the temperature in the hall.

"Look, man, just be straight with us and we'll try to help you out with as little collateral damage as possible," Prescott finishes.

"No, you look—" I straighten to my full height, narrow eyes searing into these two assholes "—I couldn't care less about anything that comes with your family name, no matter what you two seem to think. There is no amount of money or connections that would begin to tempt me. The moment I met Calloway Rutherford, I knew that she was it. That she's the one for me. Callie is the best person I've ever known. She is thoughtful and unyieldingly loyal. Her kindheartedness knows no bounds and she cares for these kids every single day, showing up with nothing but her best, without fail. Callie deserves absolutely everything and, if I'm the one who gives it to her instead of her family, then that's fine by me. I'm lucky she ever looked my way, and I'll be by her side as long as she'll let me." Blood pounding in my ears, I turn on my heel and march past a shocked Imogene and Connie and back into the classroom. Right up to the amazing woman I haven't been able to take my eyes off of all night.

Callie smiles up at me. "Guess what, Connie—"

Wrapping one arm around her waist, the other slides up her back so my hand can shroud itself with her long ponytail. One tug of her hair and my lips crash into hers, violent and demanding. Desperate.

Callie kisses me back just as roughly. She wastes no time running her hands up my biceps before wrapping them around my neck, pulling me closer. Crushing her chest to mine. Those flawless lips mold with every kiss I offer, and when they part, I take whatever access they'll allow.

If I could think of anything rational, I'd be thanking her idiot brothers for finally giving me the excuse to do what I've been thinking about for weeks. But tasting this much of Calloway Rutherford all at once has every sane thought making a run for it.

Callie's tongue tentatively looks for mine as her hands find my hair.

My heart pounds in my ears as my tongue coaxes hers into a dance, causing her to moan and lean fully into me. Hands sliding to her waist, my fingers press into her skin, branding her as mine.

Even if no one will know but us.

Only when we're both out of breath do we finally break apart, chests heaving and begging for air. Grinning down at her, I pepper a few more kisses across her cheeks and nose for good measure.

Her giggles fill the air around us, encouraging me to continue. I only stop when her tender fingertips graze my cheek. Pulling back, I can't quite remember why I haven't kissed her like this yet.

Not until our predicament comes flooding back.

A lovely blush heats Callie's face as she searches mine for an explanation I don't offer.

But in the recesses of my mind, I admit to myself how thankful I am to have a little more time pretending she's mine.

# 13

*Oliver*

"What did you get for Mom again?" Blythe digs through the eight different shopping bags in her hand. "It was that new mixer, right?" The rustling of tissue paper mixes with holiday jingles playing overhead.

With only a couple of shopping bags in my own hands, I guide my sister through the bustling department store. Our annual shopping trip the weekend before Christmas is one of my favorite traditions, even if I always end up cursing us for not making it earlier in the month thanks to the added crowds and stress. "Yeah, the red one."

Flinging her hand free from the bag, my sister manages to barely miss smacking some guy square in the face. "Okay, cool. The knife block I got her will match perfectly, then."

"Do you need any help?" I ask, watching her resituate the bags for the fourteenth time in ten minutes.

Blythe pretends not to be sidetracked by a high-end yoga mat bag on display. "Nope." Performing a quick drool check, she looks back my way. "Excited to go pick out the Rhodes family Christmas tree tomorrow?"

"Always." I grin. "Even if no one will be there to use it for long."

"Mom and Dad aren't leaving until you do. The day before Christmas Eve. What's that, Wednesday?"

I nod. "True, but you're all leaving the day before that. So really, there will only be a few full days for people to enjoy it."

"Hm," Blythe grimaces, "maybe we should convince Mom and Dad it's nicer to the tree if we just enjoy it at the farm, instead. We could go and see the lights, drink hot chocolate. You know, that kind of thing."

A certain beautiful hot cocoa connoisseur graces the forefront of my mind. Not that she's ever very far from it anymore, anyway.

"Is Callie coming?"

Silently cursing the yoga mat bag for not holding my sister's attention longer, I do my best to ignore the rising temperature in the room. "No." Maybe I should take off my coat. *No, wait, it already is. I wonder if management would be opposed to my sweater being removed if I keep on the undershirt.*

Blythe frowns up at me, challenging me about as well as a chihuahua. "And why not?"

"Because I'm sure she's busy," I shrug. We head toward the men's department in search of new work gloves for Dad.

"How do you know? Have you asked her?"

"No, but she's been a little preoccupied. What with the school program last night and the last day of school for the year today, I didn't want to bother her."

My sister rolls unamused eyes, motioning toward my pocket as best she can. "You're an idiot. Text her and invite her."

"Are you inviting Ian?" I lift a brow, tossing a knowing look her way.

Blushing, she presses her lips together. "He and I are just friends. And neighbors. Friendly neighbors. Unlike you and Callie, who like to make out in her classroom."

Recoiling, wide eyes find my sister. "Who told you about that?"

Grinning, she shrugs. "Connie texted me."

"Since when are you friends with Connie?" My face scrunches in confusion as I nearly run into a family with three little kids.

"Callie brought her to pilates earlier this week. Besides, we've all been hanging out at Ian's place."

Smirking, I slide my gaze back to her. "Speaking of ... "

"Who? Ian?" Those baby blues that have gotten her out of so much trouble over the years widen, innocence radiating from them.

"You bought him a gift." I nod toward her purchases.

"You got John a gift," she shoots back.

"Sure," I nod again, "but I'm just friends with John."

My petite sister sighs. "Yep, just like Ian and I." Blythe cranes her neck around the immediate area pretending to look for something. Anything to get her out of this conversation.

"Whenever you want to be honest about that, let me know."

"Text your girlfriend," she finally says.

Deciding picking out a Christmas tree with my family should absolutely include Callie, I mind my sister and pull out my phone. Our text thread isn't difficult to find—I starred it last night when I got home. Once my invite is out in the ether, I only have to wait all of thirty seconds before receiving an enthusiastic acceptance, complete with heart eye emojis and everything.

"Let me guess, she said yes?" Blythe asks dryly, nodding to my phone.

"What makes you think that?"

"Because you're grinning like a fool in love."

Shoving my phone back in my pocket, I try to remember what we're even doing in this store.

"Speaking of Callie, have you gotten her gift yet?"

My feet stop in the middle of the aisle. I'm celebrating a gift-giving holiday with Callie—of course I need to get her a gift. But what if she doesn't get me anything? I don't want to make it awkward and have her feel pressured. Maybe I shouldn't get her anything. Unless we do some kind of gift exchange in front of the entire family. If I'm the only one empty-handed, it would make us both look bad.

Blythe laughs. "I'll take that as a no. Here," she grabs my arm, pulling me into the closest department.

Jewelry.

"Uh, do you know the last time I bought jewelry for a woman that wasn't Mom?"

Her light blonde brow furrows. "When have you ever bought Mom jewelry?"

"Never, but that's kinda the point," I say, panic rising in my throat. "This is so far out of my wheelhouse, it's not even funny. Besides, Callie doesn't even wear much jewelry."

My sister giggles, shaking her head. "Then it's a good thing I'm with you, oh brother of mine." Looping her arm through mine, she drags me from case to case. Watches. Earrings. Engagement rings. Each display only leads to more confusion.

What kind of jewelry do you buy your fake girlfriend that you don't really want to admit you wish was your real girlfriend?

Wave after wave of confusion hits with each new stone that comes across my field of vision.

Then, I see it.

Blythe gives me an approving smile, so I call over the

nearest available sales associate. Pointing at the case, I say with full confidence, "That one."

CALLIE THROWS OPEN the passenger door before I can even send a text that I've arrived. The woman may be covered with fleece, fur, and any other fabric to help keep her warm, but she looks stunning. Minimal makeup and hair thrown up into a wild messy bun completes the look that says she's comfortable in her own skin. Her bright eyes find mine, a full grin on display.

The tension in my body dissipates the moment her sweet smell fills my car. "Hello, beautiful," I say.

She blinks rapidly, blushing as I lean across the console to press a kiss on her cheek. "Oh, um, hi." Flicking her eyes back toward the building, she nods. "Good thinking. Mrs. Martinez was watching. Now, she can corroborate our story, if asked."

My smile drops before I can stop myself, but I manage to replace it almost as quickly while pulling out of the parking spot. "Yep, that was my plan. How was the last day of school?"

The Christmas tree farm isn't far from Callie's apartment, which is nestled on the north side of town. The drive goes by quickly while she tells me all about how a little boy named Alex tried to stuff a red bead up his nose instead of doing the craft project, how Emily tried to make a run for it with a handful of candy canes, and how a boy named Jack incorporated several boogers into his art project, which his parents are bound to love and cherish forever. But when we make the final turn into the farm, the woman in my passenger seat goes silent.

Being careful not to run over anyone trying to find some holiday joy, I risk a glance her way.

Eyes wide and lips parted, Callie leans forward as far as the seatbelt will allow. "Oliver," she breathes, "this is amazing." Her gaze follows every family we pass, toting their chosen tree to the main area where it will be shaken and baled, ready to have plenty of holiday memories made in its presence.

Spanning over ten acres, coming to Benedict Family Farms has been a tradition for our family ever since I've had a Serenvale Springs address. The various sections are home to different types of trees, whether it be Douglas firs, white pines, or blue spruces. At the center of the entire operation are pony rides, face painting, a little cobblestone restaurant and a barn gift shop to round out the holiday experience.

Finding a spot near my parents' car is pure luck, but I'll take what I can get.

"Need me to carry anything?" Callie looks over eagerly from the passenger seat. Her grin is infectious.

"Nope." Reaching into the back seat, I grab an extra scarf and hold it out, my cheeks warming. "I, uh, stashed this for you. Just in case."

Callie takes the offering, turning it over in her hands once, then twice.

Tilting my head, my lips tip down in confusion. "You don't have to wear it if you don't want to," I offer.

"It's not that," she says, securing it around her neck and inhaling deeply. After which she undoes the scarf she's already wearing and holds it out to me. "It's not fair for me to wear something of yours that smells so good. So here, this will make us even." When I hesitate, she leans forward and ties it around my neck. "There," she says, satisfied.

A hint of chocolate invades my senses, mixing with the cold air and smell of pine as we climb out from the car.

Traveling down the walkway and into the section housing the blue spruces, Callie looks this way and that, not wanting to miss a single thing.

In a moment of bravery, my hand swings through the air and catches hers on its pendulum motion.

Her hand immediately squeezes mine in return, sending electric currents straight to my chest.

The dazzling woman beside me beams as the Edison bulbs strung up flicker to life in the late afternoon hour. Falling snowflakes appear iridescent as they trickle to the ground around us. Couples, families, and determined singles pass us by, all too busy creating their own holiday memories to notice us.

"I can't believe how many people are here," she says, looking down another row.

Tilting my head toward her, my lower lip pushes out. "Hm. Have you never been here before?"

Callie shakes her head, bun flopping. "Nope. Mom has the decorators deal with getting our tree. And I'm not sure where the one at the lodge comes from."

"Do you have a tree in your apartment?"

She laughs a carefree laugh. "Just one of those three-footers that hangs out in the corner. But it does the job." Callie watches as a couple passes us with a mini schnauzer in tow. "I'm surprised you didn't bring Nacho."

Pressing my lips together, I make note of her every move, every tiny emotion flitting across her face.

I don't want to forget it when our time truly does come to an end.

"She's great with a few people. But all of this," I wave my free hand, motioning to all the chaos, "would stress her out."

"Poor Nacho." Sympathy echoes in her tone, face dropping ever so slightly.

We'll have to do something about that. "Hey, guess what." Grinning, I stop in the middle of the path, pulling Callie into my arms. "The café here?"

She smirks like she knows right where this is going. "Yes ... "

Holding her this close, our noses graze one another. If she

asks, I'll just say she looked cold. "They have incredible hot chocolate," I whisper.

"I think I may have to be the judge of that," she grins, my breath becoming hers.

Placing a kiss on the tip of her nose, my lips never leave her skin. "I'll buy you all the hot chocolate your heart desires."

Leaning back, she giggles, inflating my ego. "You're way too good at this. It's not fair." Sparkling coffee eyes roam my face.

"Kissing you?"

"Pretending to date me."

Smile faltering, my insides constrict at her words, each one trying to poison what we could have together. Because for her, that's all this is.

Playing pretend.

Peeking around me, recognition lights up her face. "Look, there's your family." Callie points up ahead a few rows, where my dad lays sprawled out on the ground, going to town with the saw.

Mom pops her head up from supervising as we approach, grinning when she spots Callie. "I guess it's clear who they're more excited to see," I whisper to my girlfriend.

Callie playfully swats my arm, releasing herself from my hold. She runs right into my mom's open arms. "Already have Marshall hard at work?" she teases.

Mom chuckles, a mitten-covered hand waving through the air. "Ever the perfectionist, he insisted."

"Not to mention how Mom pretended to—" Blythe snaps her head toward Mom "—have broken kneecaps when she felt how cold the ground is." My sister snickers.

Callie's gloved fingers fly to her face as she tries to hide her laughter. Wide eyes find mine.

Shrugging, I recapture her hand. "Eh, Mom's a little silly sometimes. But there's nothing she hates more than being cold."

Callie raises ruby brows. "Then I'm surprised you all followed Oliver to Serenvale Springs," she says, looking at Mom. "We're not exactly known for the balmy winters."

"She and Blythe missed Ollie too much," Dad calls from under the tree.

"But not you?" Callie lets go of my hand, much to my disappointment. But that woman never fails me. Getting down on her hands and knees, Callie climbs under the tree with my dad. "Here, let me."

Dad gladly hands over the saw, sweat dripping down his face. "If you insist, Ms. Rutherford." Moving to sit upright, he pulls a cloth from a concealed pocket, dabbing his forehead.

My mom and sister take pity, helping him up.

I'm too busy watching my girlfriend.

"Almost got it," Callie calls.

Taking hold of the treetop, I give her a little leverage to help her finish the job. "I thought we were convincing them that we didn't need a tree this year?" I look around for Blythe. "You know, since no one will be there."

The final crack sounds, signaling Callie's treecutting prowess.

And my dad's, I guess.

But if anyone asks, I'm giving Callie all the credit.

Mom puts a hand on my shoulder as Dad takes the tree, freeing me to help Callie up from the ground. "We're not keeping the tree," Mom says, "we're donating it to the nursing home and will decorate it up there."

"That's an amazing idea," Callie beams. Looking the chosen tree up and down, she sighs. "They're going to love it. My neighbor's granddaughter actually works there as a nurse. I can give you her number, if that'd be helpful."

My dad nods, clearly a little out of breath from the strange workout. "That'd be great," he puffs.

Readjusting my scarf she sports so that her chin is protected from the cold, I ask, "The one who was watching us?"

Mom's brows shoot up. "Callie's neighbor was watching you?"

Callie giggles. "Mrs. Martinez is the sweetest. I promise she's not nosy or anything," she assures my mom, "just protective. Besides, she keeps me fed. Her homemade tamales are to die for."

Grinning, I can practically see her drool forming.

"Wait," Blythe frowns, "you're not talking about Zia? She's so sweet!"

Callie nods while my dad wrinkles his nose, leading us back toward the baling station with a new tree in tow. "What kind of name is Zia?"

The woman who has reattached herself to my arm laughs with her whole frame. It's a glorious sight. "Her name is Xiomara—"

"Woah," Dad interrupts.

"But she goes by Zia," Callie finishes. "She goes to Blythe's studio, too," Callie nods toward my sister. "And she's actually working on becoming an instructor."

Blythe leans around Callie, narrowed eyes pretending to scowl at me. "Zia's the other client I tried to get to go out with you."

I don't bother hiding my exaggerated eyeroll. "Thanks a lot. What'd you do, hand out my business card to all your single patrons?"

Callie snorts. "Basically."

"But no one wanted you." Blythe's dramatic sigh will be felt for generations. "Well," a catlike grin spreads across her face, "I guess one of them did want you, after all." She and Callie lock eyes in that way only girls can, thousands of messages passing between them all at once.

My girlfriend finally graces me with a smile. "All it took was one cookie and I was hooked."

Mom looks back at us from where she and Dad are leading the pack. "You're welcome, son." She winks at Callie. "He didn't want to learn to bake, but I bet he's glad I made him learn now."

"You have no idea," I say, grinning down at Callie.

"Oh, oh, look!" Blythe squeals, jumping up and down.

Callie and I flinch into one another—equal parts hilarious and painful.

Up ahead past the pony rides, some of the workers prepare for the horse-drawn carriage rides. Another one of our family traditions.

Complete with a walk underneath a sprig of mistletoe at the entrance.

Mom and Dad always honor the tradition, of course. And I always give Blythe a big hug.

Now, I have Callie.

Callie, who barely even pauses when she realizes what awaits her.

"Not afraid of horses, are you Callie? Or kissing my brother under the mistletoe?" Blythe asks, skipping ahead to claim our place in line.

Tossing my arm around her shoulders, I pull Callie into my side. "You didn't even flinch when she mentioned our famous holiday tradition," I murmur into her hair.

Callie snorts. "Why would kissing you bother me at this point? We've done the deed pretty much everywhere else." Her feet stop short, face flushing at the words before finding any kind of footing again. "I didn't mean—"

My chuckling cuts her off. "I know what you meant, Cal. But it's good to know you're not opposed." Flashes of us kissing in her classroom only two days ago invade my mind, sharp and raw.

Chocolate eyes cut my way. Under the light of the darkening sky, it's nearly impossible to catch the way they darken before flitting back to the carriages.

But it's there.

"Come on, you two," Blythe calls from the front of the line. Motioning like a frantic four-year-old, my sister doesn't bother waiting to see if we answer the call.

Looking down at Callie in the soft glow of the enchanted evening, my voice comes out low, giving away more than I'd like. "After you."

Without a word, Callie leads us hand in hand toward my family waiting in the nearest buggy.

As we reach the entrance to the carriage path, the teenage attendant looks between us and snickers. "Sorry, rules are rules," she says, pointing to the mistletoe directly above Callie's head.

Rolling my lips together, I hold my girlfriend tight. Those plush, kissable lips I've come to know so well quirk up, begging for what they know is coming. Gently pressing my lips to hers, I plead with my senses to remember this isn't real for her.

But they simply won't listen.

The kiss is quick.

Too brief for my liking, but half of Serenvale Springs is in the immediate vicinity and waiting for their turn at the carriages.

When I pull away, Callie grins. "That'll make tonight worth it, even if we don't get around to their famous cocoa."

I beam down at my girl. "Oh, you're getting that cocoa," I promise.

Knocking on the door, I'm met with a frantic Calloway Rutherford. Dressed in jeans, a wool pullover, and a single fur boot, she looks much more casual than I do in my khakis and dress shirt.

*I could've worn sweats.*

With only one shoe on and a hairbrush in her hand, Callie throws the door wide open, completely out of breath. "Hey," she pants, "you're early. Come on in." She doesn't wait for my response before turning on a sock-covered heel and heading back into what I can only assume is the bedroom.

"Is everything okay?" I call from the small entryway. From this vantage point, her apartment is tidy, quite unlike her classroom. But the place radiates warmth, just like its inhabitant.

Callie pokes her head back out, working to tame her wild mane. "Yeah," she smiles, "I just didn't expect you for another twenty minutes, so I'm a little behind. But, uh," she motions to the main room of her apartment, "make yourself comfortable." Then she disappears back into the room of mysteries.

Taking her advice and removing my coat, I move past her small kitchen and into the living area before plopping down onto a small orange couch. Tattered from years of wear, several patchwork quilts lay draped across the few pieces of mismatching furniture. A cream shag rug fills the majority of the floor, while a small oak coffee table sits in the center of the space. And even though she has a TV and several art pieces on the walls, nothing captures my attention quite like the massive overload of plants in the room. They hang from coatracks, from the ceiling and sit on miniature stands. Some kind of vine crawls across the top of the kitchen cabinets, draping itself onto the countertop, where a single pot sits alone and thriving.

Curiosity gets the better of me, the small plant singing its siren song. Reaching out, my fingers are a hairsbreadth away when I hear movement behind me.

"Don't touch him!" Callie cries.

My hand aborts its mission immediately, opting to fly to my chest to check for cardiac activity instead.

"Sorry," she says, reaching around me. Grabbing the pot, Callie takes it over to the sink and waters it. "I'm just a little protective of this one."

"A little?"

Callie rolls her eyes. "Gilmore's special. He, uh," she peeks up, "he was my first baby."

"How old is he?'

"About eight years old," she declares proudly. Setting him back on the counter, she moves to grab a bag sitting on the floor by the bedroom door.

Palming the back of my neck, I blow out a breath. "Wow. Mine usually last about two weeks. Then they run for the hills." Taking the bag from her, I place it by the front door.

Callie frowns, watching me.

Panic seizes my chest. "What? Were you not done with this one?"

"I didn't see any plants in your apartment on Thanksgiving," she says, words laced with suspicion. "Not gonna lie, your place could use all the plants you can handle. "

"Which is none, if I'm the one caring for them."

"But then your place wouldn't be so cold," she grins, "with the exception of Nacho being there, of course."

"Of course. Maybe I just need you to come and redo my house." I shrug, looking around her chaotic and warm home. Other than Nacho's presence, the only reason mine is a home is because I'm there every day.

But Callie's home is full of life, of love.

Something mine could desperately use.

Callie laughs, producing another smaller bag from right inside her bedroom door. "Just say the word. I'll happily redo my fake boyfriend's house. It would definitely help us sell things even more." She pauses, considering something. "Not that we'll need to for much longer, though, I guess."

Swallowing the lump in my throat, I actively fight the urge

to ask her to reconsider as she turns out every light except for a small lamp in the living room.

"Remind me," Callie shakes her head, "Nacho really will be okay while we're gone?"

My heart warms at her concern, resulting in a smile trying to take over my face. "She'll be fine. My neighbor, Cory, will take good care of her while we're away."

Callie nods. "Okay, only if you're sure. Are you ready?" she asks, reaching where I stand by the door with her large bag in hand. "You know, you really don't have to do this. It's ... a lot."

Pasting a smile on my face, I scoop the second luggage piece from her grip. "I've always heard Aspen Point is some kind of swanky place. When am I gonna get another chance to see it?" Winking, I'm rewarded with one of her sweet giggles.

While Callie locks up and waves to a spying Mrs. Martinez, I tote both of her bags to the car. By the time she makes it down the walkway, I have the door open and waiting for her.

Callie beams up at me as she slides into my passenger seat.

Making my way to the drivers side, I give Mrs. Martinez one more wave before joining my girlfriend.

"What's in the tumbler?" Callie points to the two travel mugs waiting in the cup holders.

I shrug. "In case we get thirsty along the way." Pulling out onto the road, I add, "Don't drink from the one in the back spot. It's coffee, so you won't like it."

"And the other one? The one in the prime cup holder, the princess parking of all cup holders? The one covered in pictures of plants?" A perfect ruby brow lifts, taking the corners of her lips with it.

Pressing my mouth into a line, I shrug, never taking my eyes off the road. "Not coffee."

"Oliver, did you buy me a plant tumbler?"

"Do you like it?" My words are cautious as I glance at the captivating woman in my front seat.

Callie holds up the travel mug, turning it this way and that way. "I'm surprised you picked plants instead of glitter or puppies or something."

A smile tugs at my lips. "Your favorite color is green. Two of your favorite hobbies involve plants." Heat rises in my cheeks. Clearing my throat, I regrip the steering wheel. "And Blythe likes online shopping, so I put it to good use." Chancing a peek at my girlfriend, I ask, "How does one accumulate so many green things, anyway? Your apartment's like a jungle."

Callie, who is currently taking a swig of the Williams Sonoma hot chocolate Blythe helped me pick out, smiles. Looking down at the mug, unshed tears glisten.

Alarms go off in every corner of my body, horror clinching my heart. Gripping the steering wheel as hard as I can, I silently curse such a stupid idea. "Callie, sweetheart, I'm so sorry. I really didn't mean to—"

She laughs.

My entire system freezes, with the exception of my driving capabilities. Thank all that is holy.

But even those become endangered when Callie reaches across the console and rests a dainty hand on my leg for the briefest moment. "Thank you," she says, her warm voice melting away any residual anxiety. "It's perfect."

If my face was heated before, it's undoubtedly on fire now. *I hope she likes what's in my bag as much as she likes the mug.*

"And, uh, Ian and Aaron always get me a new baby for birthdays and Christmases." Callie takes another sip from her new mug. "Since they usually go in together, I've got some expensive plants," she laughs.

Indulging in the twinge of one hundred percent irrational jealousy, I ask the question I've wondered since that first night in the bar. "How did you and Ian become so close? And, I guess, his brother too, for that matter?"

My girl puts the tumbler back in the cupholder, and resituates herself to get comfortable in her seat. "Nothing too crazy. They moved in next door—"

"To the next mansion?"

"Pretty much. Their dad is one of the big wigs in Benedict International's software division. And they have family money, too." Callie shrugs, as if it's all so normal. But to her, it is. "Ian was right between the twins' and my age, while Aaron was Connie and Chris's age. Since the twins had each other, they really weren't interested in anyone else. At least, that's what I thought until Connie told me otherwise. I'd decided at a young age I wanted to teach. I would play School with my stuffed animals since no one else would play with me."

"Not even Connie?"

Callie hesitates, considering her next words. "She did, sometimes. But I think she always felt guilty leaving Chris, so it was usually pretty brief. It was fine—I was typically left to my own devices. So when I found out that their mom was an elementary teacher, I suddenly found their home much more interesting than the Rutherford ivory tower." She scoffs. "That's what all the kids in our classes called our house, anyway. No one was allowed over."

"I'm surprised you all weren't homeschooled," I admit.

"You and me, both," she laughs. "Their mom is amazing. Their dad, too. Mrs. Fairchild actually teaches right across the hall from me. I eventually conned Ian into playing School with me and, I think, he's the one who got Aaron involved. Even with the age difference, the three of us became inseparable. If I wasn't at my house, I was at theirs."

"I'm guessing your parents didn't mind," I say dryly. It's not a big leap for Ira and Lillian.

Callie quirks her lips to the side. "I honestly don't think they noticed. If you were to ask, they probably wouldn't even remember."

*Man, my girlfriend's parents are frustrating.* That's what I'm here to fix.

Hopefully.

Something Callie said sticks out. "Did you say their dad works for Benedict International?"

That lovely face scrunches. "Yeah. Why?"

"Last week, at your program—" shaking my head, I try to remember the exact details "—Ian congratulated your dad about something to do with that company."

Callie nods. "Oh, that's right. They signed a merger. My father's firm now oversees BI's legal division while still maintaining their outside firm, as well." Snickering, she bites down on her lower lip. "Should be fun for Prescott." With a quirk of my brow, Callie answers the unspoken question. "The owner of BI, Charles Benedict? Prescott used to date his daughter back in law school. But she was a little younger, I think. Still an undergrad at the time, even. Rumor is she's an attorney now, too. And working at her father's company."

Snorting, I roll my eyes. "Is this what first-class gossip is like?"

Laughter fills the car. "Pretty much."

"Then I guess I'd better catch up," I grin, "since we're headed to a premier winter resort, and all."

Grinning right back, Callie is stunning. "Don't worry, Rhodes. I've got your back."

## 14

*Callie*

"Wow," Oliver mutters under his breath. "This place. This scenery. It's no wonder only a handful of people can afford to come here regularly."

Stepping out of his car, I'm met with all the reasons I've come to love returning to this place over the years. Birds singing off in the distance, the smell of pine lingering in the crisp air. The complete and utter lack of noise pollution made even by a town as small as ours. Aspen Point Lodge has found perfection in its seclusion.

Oliver turns himself in circles trying to take everything in, awe written all over his handsome face.

Brow furrowing, I glance around the parking lot for any sign of the Rutherfords.

"Callie, this place is incredible." He's not wrong.

Situated in the mountains a couple hours west of Serenvale

Springs, the main hotel is stunning. With its colonial revival influences, the impressive Aspen Point Lodge truly does command respect from all who visit. Crisp white paint coats the outside, and columns line the front porch spanning the entire front of the building. The dark interior contrasts the bright exterior, creating a welcoming feel with its roaring fireplaces and intricate carpets.

But we're not stopping at the main building.

Opening the trunk, Oliver pulls out a medium suitcase and sets it on the ground before doing the same with my bags. It's clearly new because a tag fastener is still attached near the handle.

"Really leaning into your love of brown there, Rhodes." Brows raised, I nod to the case.

Pink tints his cheeks, eyes locking on mine. "I needed a new bag and it's a great color. Warm," he says, voice quiet.

"It's your favorite, like dirt, if I recall." Of course I recall. My mind is a dang steel trap. I remember everything, and man, is it annoying.

Must be all that broccoli I've eaten over the years. You know, once I decided it wasn't toxic or anything.

Though it would be nice to not remember Alfred Robert Jensen's great-grandkids in alphabetical order because I happened to look at his obituary one time fourteen years ago. But I do hope Brandon, Jake, and Kirsten are all doing well and have come to terms with the passing of their great-grandfather.

Oliver says nothing, opting instead to take in the view rather than answering his fake girlfriend's awkward comment.

"Reception's this way." We may not be stopping here, but it'd be nice to not have to walk the rest of the way. Motioning toward the front door, I reach down to grab my bags, but he beats me to them. "I don't think so, Rutherford." Tossing my glitter-encrusted backpack over his annoyingly broad shoulder, he adjusts the handle of the green roller bag to suit his height.

Planting fists on my hips, I take in the sight before me. Even all bundled up, Oliver Grant Rhodes is still the most handsome man I've ever seen. "I'm perfectly capable of carrying my own bags."

"I know," he nods.

Holding out my hand, I await the massive boulder that is my backpack to hit my palm.

Oliver juts his chin toward the main entrance. "Reception, right? Lead the way, my cocoa connoisseur."

"No bag?"

Lowering his chin, a tiny smile teases his lips. "No bag. Not if I'm around."

"This way, then. But I get to carry my new mug," I say with false sternness.

"Wouldn't have it any other way."

Biting my lip to keep a stupid grin in check, I take off toward the front door. Christmas is in full swing at the lodge. Warm white lights line every door and wrap around every column, fluffy wreaths dot every window in sight, and picturesque trees stand erect on either side of the double door entrance. The snow-covered mountains in the background are just the star on top of the tree.

As we approach the front doors, the doormen open them like a well-oiled machine, while Oliver whistles under his breath. Though I'm not sure if it's the doormen, the iron chandelier, or the full-size fireplace surrounded by wooden carvings that elicits the reaction.

"Good afternoon, Ms. Rutherford." The familiar voice of Thomas Carson comes from behind the massive front desk at the opposite end of the lobby.

"Who's that?" Oliver whispers.

"One of my favorite people here," I answer in the same hushed tone, "Mr. Carson. He's been the General Manager since I can remember."

A man of sharp style, Mr. Carson is always dressed to impress. In his late fifties, Thomas has lost some of his native French accent since coming to the States. But he still makes mean madeleines from scratch and never fails to have some ready in our accommodations when we arrive. He meets us in the middle of the foyer, arms open in welcome. "It's lovely to see you again, Ms. Rutherford. I can't believe it's been eight weeks since you and your family were last here."

"It's only been eight weeks?" Oliver asks.

Mr. Carson chuckles. "And who do we have here? Your significant other, I presume?"

Looping my arm through Oliver's, I give him an encouraging smile. "Yep. This is my boyfriend, Dr. Oliver Rhodes." Pride drips from my words while I wish in the deepest recesses of my soul that they were true.

Oliver holds out a hand, which Mr. Carson takes without hesitation. "It's great to meet you, sir."

Mr. Carson smiles, his tender-hearted nature reaching his dark eyes. "The pleasure is all mine, Dr. Rhodes. You must be quite the special man. Ms. Rutherford never brings her male friends on family getaways." His eyes twinkle mischievously as they take in my shock at his admission.

Using my free hand, I rub my forehead and try desperately to avoid looking at Oliver. "I don't think that's information that he necessarily needed, Mr. Carson. But thank you for breaking the ice."

Mr. Carson folds his hands together, ever the proper manager. Supposedly. "My apologies, Ms. Rutherford. I hope the madeleines will make up for it. Fresh from the oven this morning and ready for your arrival."

Oliver's brows shoot up. "The chefs make madeleines?"

Laughing, I shake my head. "Not the pastry chefs here, though I'm sure we could request them. But Mr. Carson makes them himself."

"From scratch," he amends, holding up a finger. "My grand-mother's recipe."

"I should have known Oliver would find someone to discuss baking with." John McNalley says from behind us.

Oliver breaks out into a grin. "Hey man." They proceed to do that weird clap hugging thing that men do.

"Fancy running into you here. Hey Callie, how are you?" John pulls me into a hug.

"Good, thanks. What're you doing here?"

John casts a glance toward Oliver. "I'm surprised it never came up. Cici and I have been coming to Aspen Point the past couple of Christmases. Rindy and Jo are coming up on Christmas morning."

My brows dip in confusion as I look at the empty space beside him. "Um, does she have her invisibility suit on?"

John chuckles in response. "She loves the big tree over by the fireplace, so she's busy counting ornaments while I get us checked in." He points to the far end of the lobby where Cici dances from foot to foot, mostly concealed by the giant tree while singing and counting perfectly in order.

Talk about a proud teacher moment.

John looks between Oliver and I. "Ollie mentioned your family comes up here every year, but we didn't see you here last Christmas."

"Apparently, they stay here pretty regularly," Oliver amends. He sends a sly look my way. One I'm used to from anyone and everyone growing up.

People who know the truth about my family's affiliation with Aspen Point Lodge.

Mr. Carson clears his throat. "Ms. Rutherford's family doesn't stay in the main building, sir. The Rutherfords stay in the residences when they're on campus."

Oliver rears his head back. "Really?" Definitely forgot to mention that one.

John whistles, brows raised. "Schmancy."

Stilted laughter chokes its way out. "Well, you know. With nine people, it's just easier, staying somewhere off the beaten path."

"Dr. McNalley," Mr. Carson frowns, and I know he's about to deliver the blow I've been trying to avoid. "The Rutherford family owns Aspen Point Lodge."

John's jaw drops just like a cartoon, gaze bouncing between Oliver and myself.

Oliver freezes, ratcheting so that he's facing me entirely.

And my face feels like it's fresh out of the oven.

"So it's a good thing we don't have to bother everyone else here while we stay in a different area," I offer, turning to Oliver. "Speaking of, why don't you give Mr. Carson your car key and he can have it pulled around so it's right where we'll be?"

My boyfriend blinks at me like he no longer understands the words coming out of my mouth.

"Oliver," I say a little louder.

That seems to do the trick, snapping him out of whatever state of confusion he was hanging out in. Reaching into his coat pocket, Oliver produces his key, dropping it into Mr. Carson's waiting palm.

"Very good, Dr. Rhodes," Carson nods before turning to me. "Ms. Rutherford, I feel I should prepare you."

"You're never making madeleines again?"

The man chuckles, getting those narrow shoulders involved and everything. "No, dear. I think my grandmother would roll over in her grave, if that were the case."

John takes the opportunity to grab Cici and check in, leaving us alone with Mr. Carson, the good news sharer.

I can't decide if I want the man to spit out whatever it is, or keep us here long enough that Oliver forgets the lovely information Mr. Carson decided to impart on my fake boyfriend and his friend only moments ago. But the longer I keep my gaze away from Oliver, the warmer my face gets under his blatant stare.

"Then I'm sure I'll survive whatever it may be." Let's get this over with.

"Well," Carson adjusts his already perfect tie, "your mother mentioned you were bringing a guest with romantic intent."

Only in my dreams. "Okay."

"But then we received your phone call earlier this week with the specific accommodation requests." The phone call. The one I made on Monday afternoon, when I was last-minute Christmas shopping with Ian and Aaron.

They were teasing me mercilessly about this trip. Talking about how romantic it would be in the mountains. How the magic of Christmas would be all around us.

And Ian mentioned how we'd have to share a bed to keep up the pretense.

During the panicked phone call, I was assured my room in our residence would have two twin beds in place of the absurdly large king that normally stands in its place.

Because I don't want Oliver to feel any more awkward. Or pressured.

Or tempt myself into believing any of this is real.

"Yes … " Gritting my teeth, I brace myself for what I already know is coming. And work twice as hard to ignore Oliver burning a hole into the side of my head.

"The mattresses that would have served the purpose for separate beds in your room were destroyed because they had biohazardous material that simply could not be extracted appropriately."

Throat closing off, I barely choke out, "So kids peed on them?"

Mr. Carson nods. "Among other things, yes."

"When?"

"Yesterday, Ms. Rutherford."

"Yesterday," I repeat with a defeated laugh. Sighing, I press my lips together. "So, it's the regular accommodations, then?"

"Yes, miss." Mr. Carson leans in conspiratorially. "If it makes you feel any better, you're my favorite of the Rutherford children."

Brows raised, I nod. *At least there's that.*

"That has its … privileges. For instance," Carson reaches into his breast pocket, producing two pristine madeleines in a clear baggie, "more sweet treats than your siblings receive."

Despite the desire to never set eyes on Oliver again, purely out of total and utter embarrassment, a small smile breaks through my dread-filled mask. "Carson, you honey-fingered devil. You're too good to me." Opening the bag, the lemony aroma that fills my dreams consumes my senses.

Carson chuckles. "Why don't you save those for when you need a little pick-me-up? I know spending time with your family isn't always the easiest."

Too bad it's not spending time with my family that has me wound so tight I could produce a diamond at this exact moment. In fact, that sounds like a freaking cake walk right about now.

Nerves have me swallowing anything intelligent I have to say, so I stick with nodding.

Mr. Carson snaps his fingers, summoning two bellhops. "Now, let's get you to the residence, yes?"

A tight smile forces its way onto my face as Oliver hands over our bags. "Sounds great." Walking out to the enclosed golf cart complete with snow tires, I take a chance. Not much space is between us to begin with, but I tentatively cross the remainder of the void and take his hand.

The side of his cheek lifts from a hidden smile, his fingers intertwining with mine.

Our ride to the residences only takes a few minutes—the

path is one I could drive with my eyes closed. To my shock, disbelief and gratitude, Oliver doesn't let go of my hand once.

The driver pulls up to the permanent Rutherford residence at Aspen Point Lodge, a humble and meager six thousand square foot luxury cabin with seven bedrooms, eight bathrooms, twenty-foot ceilings, a private pool and hot tub, gym, and home movie theater, all overlooking the mountains that surround us.

A starter home, really.

Oliver's jaw drops as we climb out back into the cold. "Holy sh—"

"Calloway, Oliver." My father walks down the brick driveway in his annual holiday loungewear. Somehow, the sweaters keep getting worse. But the pajama pants have pictures of dachshunds all over them this year, so it's one for one, really. "We were wondering when you'd get here."

I groan internally. "Who's already here?"

"Everyone but the twins. They should be here in a little while. Some meetings came up."

From the corner of my eye, Oliver sweetly tries to help with our bags.

My father, on the other hand, stares at him in confusion.

"Meetings?" I ask to pull his attention away from Oliver. "But Christmas is the day after tomorrow."

"The world of high finance doesn't stop for a holiday, Calloway," he chides.

I can sense a lecture coming on when Oliver drapes a protective arm around my shoulder. "I think Callie's just ready to have everyone together, is all."

Nodding, I look from Oliver to my dad. "What he said."

Oliver's fingers trace invisible circles on my shoulder, causing my body to shiver in response. Peeking down at me, a smile tugs on his lips. "Well, Mr. Rutherford, we appreciate the personal greeting, but I better get this one inside before she freezes."

Deciding to really ham it up, I let another shiver rattle my teeth.

Unamused, Dad simply blinks before motioning for us to follow, as if I haven't been here multiple times a year since I was a kid.

Inside the door, the temperature difference is like walking into a brick wall.

Mom does love the fireplace here.

"The bags should be in your room by now," Dad tells Oliver before turning to me. "Calloway, I trust you remember the way?"

"I have a Bachelor's degree, Dad, not amnesia." I honestly have no idea how I refrain from rolling my eyes. "I know you see both as afflictions, but I promise, one is so much worse than the other."

Dad's eyes narrow, but he only sends a curt nod my way before heading off to the master bedroom.

"So, would you like the grand tour, or the condensed version for now?" I ask, giving my fake boyfriend the toothiest smile I can manage. "Because I'm nothing if not an excellent tour guide."

Oliver snickers. "Oh, I'm sure. But after that last comment to your dad, we may want to lay low for a bit."

"Good point," I mutter. "And there's no telling who else we would run into. Okay, the condensed version it is. On the middle floor, we have the main living areas. Kitchen, living room, the Christmas tree of all Christmas trees, that kind of thing. Oh, and the master bedroom is that way." I gesture around the general space, earning myself a breathtaking smile from the man who will likely need to have himself committed when we get home. Taking Oliver's hand, I lead him toward the stairs. "Down on the first floor is the gym and movie theater. That's also how you get to the pool and hot tub."

"Good to know," he nods along.

"And upstairs are the other bedrooms, each with their own bathroom."

"It's really modern," Oliver observes, looking around as we pass through the living room.

My free hand ghosts the brown leather sectional. "Mom has it redone every couple of years to keep up with trends." And boy, has she outdone herself this time. Floor-to-ceiling windows along the wall looking out over the mountainside, stonework climbing to the tallest point on the opposite wall where the fireplace emits heat straight from Hades, all while cedar panels, shined to perfection, line themselves in perfect order on most other surfaces within eyesight. Adding all the holiday decorations is just the cherry on top.

Climbing the stairs, he says, "I thought your dad said it's only Chris and Connie that aren't here yet."

"He did."

"Then, where are the others?"

"Ah, you mean that immaculate silence surrounding us? The one where you could hear a pin drop?" It's true, the builders did an amazing job soundproofing the place.

He chuckles. "That's the one."

"They're probably in their rooms or downstairs some-where," I shrug. "Who cares." Then it dawns on me. "Oh, of course. If we're being watched, then we need to pretend like we're in love. Otherwise, we can act normal."

A slight frown mars those award-winning features. "Right," he says.

Taking that confirmation as my disheartening cue, I drop his hand as we reach the landing. "We should be safe, for now." Even if I instantly miss his warmth. *Maybe he'll hold me if I act cold.*

Oliver nods, running a hand through his hair.

"Come on, we're at the end of the hall." Muscle memory takes over as I make my way toward my room.

Our room.

Each step is one step closer to staring our strange predicament in the face. Up until now, it's been relatively easy. Hypothetical.

Looking at Oliver like my life depends on it, complete with hugging and handholding? Easy peasy lemon squeezy.

Kissing him in places that our families couldn't miss if they were legally blind? No problem.

Making out in front of those who might give us trouble? Pass me that sign up sheet, babe.

But this—sharing a bed with Oliver—is something else entirely. We'll both be at our most vulnerable. We'll both be so *aware* of the other person. And it may just make me confront those tiny thoughts deep inside about how this all feels too easy with him.

Dangerously easy.

Like it will never be this easy with anyone else.

The flyer Aaron found in Theo's Place rears its ugly head in the forefront of my mind, causing me to swallow down the bile that accompanies it. Because none of this is real for him.

Only me.

Reaching our door, I rip off the bandaid and turn the knob. "Home sweet home," I say, my voice sounding like my foot's been clawed up by a rabid hyena. The bedrooms aren't typically privy to Mom's remodels, so the features are a little older up here. A large, deep red chest of drawers with a flat screen mounted above it sit against the wall to the corridor while two plush chairs and a small bistro table wait to be used by the large glass sliding door leading onto the private balcony. Cedar paneling follows the downstairs trend, with matching nightstands on either side of the intricate wrought iron bed. "Mom only updates the bedrooms every five years or so," I admit, "but the bathrooms were updated during this last round of overall updates."

Oliver discards his coat in the closet and peeks into the sleek bathroom with all-white marble, the clawfoot tub and designer shower.

But the light at the end of this tunnel waits for us on the dresser, with our bags resting on the floor beside it.

Mr. Carson's madeleines.

While Oliver checks out the rest of the room, I drop my coat on the bed and unwrap a madeleine, heading to the sliding glass door. At this time of day, the remaining sunlight hits the snow perfectly, as if it's glittering. The familiar sight helps the rolling nausea.

Mostly.

"Callie," Oliver says from the other side of the room. "Will you look at me? Please?"

Swallowing the last bit of my cake, I turn to face him.

Oliver leans against the dresser just like the last time I was in his office, and I'm tempted to ask him to roll up his sleeves and put on his glasses.

"Are you okay?" he asks, folding his arms over his chest.

"Of course. Why wouldn't I be?"

"Because you tried to ensure we had separate beds only a couple of days ago."

"Oh, that."

Oliver dips his chin, eyes never leaving mine. "That."

*All the flipperiest nuggets.*

Jutting out my lower lip, I shake my head. "Just wanted to make sure you were comfortable with, um, everything while you were here, is all." I clear my throat with a little too much vigor. "I know this is all a lot to take in."

"Do you?" He lifts a brow.

"I mean, I'm guessing. But I've always been a good guesser."

"I'll admit, it was quite the surprise to hear that your family *owns* this place," he nods.

Running a hand down my face, I groan. "I was gonna tell you, honestly. I just ... other than when I'm actually with my family, I live so far outside of that world. I know what everyone thinks about us."

"That's not entirely true."

"Your dad called them wolves," I point out, "and he's not wrong."

Oliver snorts, pushing off from the dresser that's been holding him upright. A few long-legged strides later and the man is only a breath away. Tender eyes roam my face, asking for permission. My brief nod is all he needs before wrapping those strong arms around me.

Resting his chin on top of my head, I breathe in the scent that is purely Oliver.

"Callie," he murmurs, lips pressing into my hair, "I don't want you to worry about my comfort here. If you're around, then I'm perfectly at home. I'm here to make sure you feel safe, to make sure there's someone here you can count on, no matter what." Leaning away, curious blue eyes pin me in place. "You know that, right?"

Swallowing, I nod. "Oliver?"

"Yeah, baby?"

His instance on the pet names even when we're alone brings a smile to my face. "Will it be a problem that I prefer to sleep in the nude?"

Oliver's entire body freezes. I don't even think I can feel his heart beating. The man finally blinks, a rush of blood flooding every visible inch of skin. I've never seen someone look like a tomato so quickly. "Uh-uh, that may, um, complicate—"

Bursting into laughter, I move out of his hold. "Just kidding!" Through squinted eyes, I can just make out the relief written all over his face. "Don't worry, I definitely look like I'm hanging out on the frozen tundra when I sleep."

Oliver swallows. "I mean, I want you to be comfortable ... " If he was wearing a turtleneck, he'd be pulling at the collar right about now.

Placing a hand on his arm, I grin up at the most wonderful man. "Thanks, but I'm good in my eight hundred layers of fleece." I use a time check as an excuse to look away from Oliver's residual shock.

Otherwise, I'd be tempted to kiss it away.

"Surely the others are here by now. I'm starving." Stepping around him, I head toward the door. A quick look back shows that only his gaze has moved, watching my every step. "Ready to go act like we're halfway down the aisle?"

Piercing blue eyes snap to mine. "You have no idea."

# 15

*Callie*

When we make it downstairs, Connie and Chris are walking through the front door. Mom and Dad greet them with open arms and kisses to the temple. They're asked about the drive, how the meetings went and are informed of dinner plans.

According to my world-renowned eavesdropping skills, we're having steak. My niece and her father already sitting at the table with a fork and knife in their hands only confirms this, since my oldest brother would eat steak at every meal, if he could—a trait he lovingly passed on to his daughter.

A trait he received from our father, who is making a beeline for his own chair at the table.

"Hi, Aunt Callie," Goldie calls from the table. "Come sit with us. Mr. Oliver can come, too."

Beside me, Oliver chuckles under his breath. "She really is adorable," he whispers in my ear.

Ignoring how his warm breath feels brushing against my ear, I try focusing on how kind he's been to my niece.

Turns out that doesn't help anything.

Lodge attendants rush past us on the stairs. Arms full of the twins' luggage, I'm sure they're both well-informed of Chris's fiery temper.

"Hello, Calloway. Oliver," Connie calls as she moves farther into the house, "it's lovely to have you with us." A broad smile reaches across the room, practically hugging me already.

Behind her, Chris peers at Oliver and I in turn. At least he's not scowling. Entirely.

"Hey Connie," I grin. Once my eyes leave my favorite sibling, I allow my smile to become so wide I'm practically the Cheshire Cat. "Christopher."

Chris grunts in response as he passes by to head upstairs.

Oliver watches my brother walk by with an amused expression, the corners of his lips twitching.

"Ignore him," Connie says, "he just got out of a pretty abysmal meeting. The stakeholders decided to give him a call on the drive up here and go for a second round."

Smirking at my sister, I roll my eyes. "Aren't all meetings about finances a drag?"

To her credit, she laughs. "Something like that, I guess," she says, stepping around us and heading up the stairs after Chris.

Oliver frowns. "Do they share a room?"

"Not since they were ten. Why?"

"Huh. Based on their interdependency, I'm honestly kinda surprised."

I shrug. Taking his hand, I lead him toward the dining table that's already set for dinner. I make the executive decision on our seating choice and motion for him to follow. "They live together, if that makes you feel any better."

Oliver looks at me, clearly trying to tell if I'm kidding or not.

Steak, mashed potatoes, corn, carrots, green beans, bread,

and butter await us, giving off a mouthwatering aroma as we take our seats.

"We always eat dinner together when we're here," I explain, sitting down. "Breakfast and lunch are usually on our own, but dinner is supposed to make us feel like a family."

Prescott scoffs from across the table. He looks up from helping Goldie stuff a napkin into the front of her Scooby-Doo shirt. "That's because we are a family, Calloway."

"Hello, Oliver." Mom's velvet voice typically reserved for important business associates is on full display for my fake boyfriend that I am currently trying to deny some very real feelings for. Making her way from the kitchen with a second full bread basket in hand, she stops just short of falling completely over Oliver in adoration. "I'm so glad you were able to join us after all. I'll admit I was disappointed when Calloway told us you would be out of town for the holiday."

An easy smile slides onto his face. "Thank you so much for having me, Lillian. This place is amazing."

"Have you never been up to Aspen Point?" she asks, the thought incomprehensible to her. Placing the bread on the table, she moves out of Imogene's way as my sister transports more food in our direction.

Oliver fluffs his napkin, placing it in his lap. "I've never had the chance. My family has always been fairly modest and, when we have traveled, it was usually to see my grandmother back home."

Mom takes a seat on the opposite end of the table from Dad, settling in for the meal. She waves a hand toward us. "I don't know what you're all waiting for. Dig in. The twins will be down whenever they're ready."

I don't wait for any further invitation, spooning some corn onto my plate. I'd be lying if I said my mouth wasn't watering like I haven't eaten in days.

The chair beside me scoots back from the table, Imogene gracefully slipping into it before preparing her own food.

Oliver and I settle into a steady rhythm of passing around food and accidentally bumping into one another on purpose.

Gotta look like that couple that's sickeningly in love and whatnot. Which is annoyingly easy. Especially since every time Oliver touches me in any capacity, blood rushes to my cheeks, making my little niece giggle.

One time, Oliver even winks at her, clearly considering my blushing some kind of new toy he's discovered.

If those two get in cahoots, I don't know what I'll do.

By the time Chris and Connie come back downstairs, the sun has set and nearly half the food has gone to a happy place. "Gee, thanks for bothering to save us some," Chris grumbles.

"Uncle Chris, I saved you this carrot," Goldie declares. She stabs her fork into the only vegetable still on her plate—a baby carrot Prescott has tried three different times to get her to eat.

My surly brother smiles, rounding the table to sit in the empty seat next to her. "Thanks, Goldie. I knew I could count on you."

I can't help my grin as Chris eats the carrot from Goldie's fork. Feeling eyes on me, I look around to find Oliver watching me.

Cue another blush.

*Flipper nuggets, he didn't even touch me that time. Get a grip, Callie.*

Oliver is clearly trying to one-up himself since he leans into the miniscule space between us.

A single peck on the lips is all it takes, and my entire face is absolutely on fire. With my luck, the Honeyville fire department will show up any moment, only to discover it's just me and my stupid feelings.

How humiliating.

Across the table, Marigold Rutherford snickers into her hand like the little gremlin she is.

Just when I think my oldest brother is a lost cause, he shoots his daughter a look that silences her immediately. Prescott is a lot of things. Most of them aren't all that amazing.

But he is a great dad.

An unbidden image flashes in the front of my mind— Oliver, years from now, happily married to some awesome woman and holding a daughter of his own. Holding her, protecting her. Supporting his wife, whoever the lucky woman ends up being.

Tears prick at my eyes. The thought of him spending his life with someone else and my never seeing him again invites a bitter taste to my mouth. Keeping my head low, I blink back the tears and shove in another forkful of mashed potatoes.

"What do you think, my dear?" Oliver asks, voice low in my ear.

In the most unflattering way humanly possible, I turn to him, wide-eyed and cheeks stuffed to the brim with buttered carbs.

He coughs to cover his laughter. "Your mom asked what you thought about her putting a reserve on the Grand Ballroom here."

"For what?" I ask, managing to swallow the remaining potato. Reaching for my hot cocoa, I take a big sip.

Oliver rolls his lips together. *This can't be good.* "For our engagement party."

My brain short-circuits and I choke on my drink, causing Oliver to gently pat me on the back. When I finally regain brain function, I spin around to look at my mother. "Why would you ask such a thing?" I demand.

Mom primly dabs her napkin against her lips. "We have to think about these things, Calloway. Venues don't just book themselves. Nor do they just wait around, chock full of availability on a moment's notice. And wedding venues are even trickier. At least, ones worth having are."

Rubbing circles into my forehead, I sigh. "Look, let's just take one thing at a time. Okay? And not put any pressure on this?"

Mom purses her lips. "Fine. But don't blame me when your dream wedding venue isn't available because you waited too long to book it."

"Believe me, I won't."

"Oh, Callie," Oliver leans back in his seat, tossing an arm over the back of my chair, "tell them about the grad program you were looking at the other day." He shoots a megawatt smile my way, knowing exactly what he's doing as he draws circles on my shoulder.

The only problem is that I've never actually looked into any graduate programs. I know my university offered them for my department, but I was never interested. Apparently, I am now.

Oliver raises expectant brows.

Heat rises in my face. I stumble over my words, struggling to maintain concentration. "Oh, yeah, um, right. The program. The one I was looking at."

"Yeah, we got that, Calloway," Chris interjects.

I narrow my eyes at the nuisance.

My dad leans forward, intrigued. "This is a graduate program? At what university?"

"My alma mater," I answer. "There are two options I'm considering, a master's or a doctorate in education."

Frowning, my dad considers this. "What can you do with that?"

"I'd like to go into administration." That part is actually true.

Oliver shifts closer, tucking me into his side. Pressing a kiss to my temple, adoration I'd give anything to be real gazes down at me. "You'd be amazing," he nods.

Smiling up at him, I let myself pretend, for just a moment, that he'd be there through the entire journey.

By THE TIME the credits roll on Goldie's favorite holiday movie, more than half of my family is asleep on the seating in the home theater.

Including Goldie.

Oliver and I sit tucked into the bend of one of the two sectionals, cozy and snuggled up under a blanket with his arm around me. For the sake of appearances, of course.

Not that any other part of me except my brain got that memo. No, and the only organ that is actually functioning properly is a little busy trying to convince the rest of me that this isn't real.

Oliver shifts to see if I'm still awake, as if I would fall asleep during such a classic. A soft smile graces his face. "Hey," he whispers, "ready to call it a night?"

I nod, pretending alarm bells aren't blaring in my head about sharing a room. About sharing a bed. *It'll be fine, Callie. It's not like you* actually *sleep naked or anything weird like that.* But the shock on his face was pretty great when I said that earlier.

We get up as quietly as possible. Replacing the blanket on the couch, we say goodnight to Imogene and Mom, the only Rutherfords left awake on this Christmas Eve eve.

By the time we reach our room, panic is slowly leaking back into my system. I try reciting the list of presidents but I only make it to Millard Fillmore before Oliver locking the door behind us sends my nerves into overdrive.

"Do you think Chris would've eaten that carrot if he knew Goldie licked it before offering it to him?" Oliver asks.

Twisting around to answer, every word I've ever known flies out of my head.

I need an escape. Fast.

"I need to shower," I blurt much louder than necessary.

The man visibly *flinches*. "Yeah," he clears his throat, "no problem. I can clean up after you're done." He kicks his shoes off while I grab my things, including the world's ugliest but comfiest pajamas, and scurry into the bathroom.

Inside the safety of the tiled sanctuary, I let out a deep breath. "This is going to be a long Christmas," I mutter. Turning on the shower to maximum heat, I take care of all other necessities and step into the scalding water. But even the fiery water licking my skin does nothing to abolish these undeniable feelings growing for the man waiting on the other side of the door.

When I've spent as long as humanly possible in the shower without turning into a pile of goo, I resign myself to my fate. It's only minutes later that I'm toweled off and standing in the middle of the bathroom in my old, ratty, fleece pajamas featuring potted plants, trowels and shovels all over them. With nothing left to do in my safe haven, I brace myself and open the door. Steam rolls out of the bathroom like the beginning of an improv rock concert.

Oliver peeks up from where he lays stretched out on the bed. Setting his phone down on the nightstand, he takes in the hideousness of my favorite pajamas that have been patched up more times than should be legal before throwing them out. "Have a good shower?" he asks. Rolling in his lips, he suppresses a smile.

"Don't make fun." Sniffing, I march proudly to drop off the wad of dirty clothes in my suitcase.

"Wouldn't dream of it," he smirks. "But the length of time you were in there was truly impressive." The click of a lamp sounds behind me, following the bedsprings protesting Oliver's movements.

"A lot happens in there on hairwashing days."

I don't even have to look to know he's eyeing my completely dry ballet bun. "*Did* you wash your hair?"

"Nope. Did that this morning." Spinning around to face him, I plant my fists on my hips. "Any other inquiries you'd like to make about my bathing routine?"

Oliver looks at me much longer than necessary, before shaking his head.

"Good," I breathe a false sigh of relief, "because I've always heard the key to healthy relationships is excellent communication. And, frankly, I'd hate to have to give you the hairy details about how difficult it is to get a decent shave. Pun intended."

Oliver bites down on his lower lip, a grin daring to creep into place. As soon as Oliver's in the bathroom with the door shut behind him, I flick off the main light, snagging my phone and charger from where I dropped them on the dresser earlier. Turning on the other bedside lamp, I climb into what will obviously be my side of the bed. Oliver may have been laying on top of the comforter, but his signature cinnamon apple scent lingers in the air. Groaning, I throw my head back onto my pillow, pulling my phone to my face for any kind of distraction.

Eight texts from Ian and six from Aaron await my viewing pleasure in our group chat. Each one ranges from concern about why I haven't responded in hours, to suggestive things I may be doing with my boyfriend, in which case, it's okay that I'm not answering and to update them in the morning.

Rolling my eyes, I decide they can wait. Switching to Pinterest, I scroll through endless pictures of my ideal greenhouses, plants I can't afford, and all the best tips for making my new Monstera love me. Ads for indoor greenery subscription boxes tempt me, continuing to perform their seductive dance as they appear on my screen. Hot chocolate recipes find their way into my algorithm, and I discover no less than four new concoctions I now need to try when we get home.

When Oliver and I are officially done pretending to be in love.

Here, all alone in my room, the thought guts me. My vision from earlier dares to wiggle its way back into my consciousness, making my eyes burn. Fury brings heat to my cheeks. Anger at my family for driving me to do something as insane as this. Irritation at Aaron for finding that stupid flyer and at Ian for pushing me to go meet the advertiser.

Rage at myself for letting my ridiculous heart become involved, no matter how hard I've tried to keep that from happening.

Sniffing, I roughly wipe away the saline that dares to show itself to the world.

"Callie? Are you alright?" Panic laces Oliver's tone as he rounds the bed to sit on the edge beside me.

Not having heard him even open the bathroom door, my fight-or-flight instinct tries to kick in, and I have to repeatedly tell myself that this man is not an intruder that's come to steal Gilmore away in the dead of this wintery night. Nope, it's just this amazing guy who looks criminally good in a white T-shirt and red pajama pants.

"Callie?" he tries again, voice soft as he reaches up to brush away a hair gone wild. A tender thumb gently wipes my stray tear.

Sighing, I shut my phone off and give him a weak smile. "Don't worry about it," I say, waving him off. Placing my phone on the stand, I resituate so I'm sitting up.

Oliver drops his hand. "If something concerns you, it concerns me."

"A parent ... They just posted something stupid on social media. That's all," I lie.

Those stunning blue eyes search my face behind his glasses.

"Really, it's nothing," I insist. When it's obvious he doesn't believe me, I switch topics. "I like your glasses. I don't think I told you that before. On Thanksgiving."

A light pink tints his cheeks, doing funny things to my insides. "Thank you," he murmurs. Apprehensive eyes dart over me to the empty side of the bed. "Um, let me just grab my pillow and—"

"Why?"

"Well," he says slowly, "I know you were concerned about being uncomfortable with sleeping arrangements earlier." Oliver gets up and moves to the other side of the bed, grabbing the unsuspecting pillow. "So I'm happy to sleep on the floor or in the chair."

Rearing my head back, I'm surprised by the amount of annoyance flooding my system. "Don't be an idiot."

He frowns. "I usually try not to be."

"I just mean—" I dig the heels of my palms into my eyes, sighing "—you don't have to be so chivalrous all the time."

"I'm telling my mom you said that."

I look up to find him grinning at me. "Oliver."

"Callie."

"Get in the damn bed."

He watches me for a long moment, trying to discern whether or not I'm serious.

And while the space from him is good for my heart, his intense stare does nothing for my already shredded nerves. In one last attempt to end this interaction, I yank back the covers, displaying the inviting sheets prime for the taking.

Oliver gingerly climbs in beside me and I realize I've never been this aware of another human being in my entire life.

Which probably isn't great since my profession has me around tiny humans all day long.

But regardless, Oliver Grant Rhodes sitting in bed beside me makes me hyperaware of his every movement.

Oliver removes his glasses, shifting to face me. "I think this is going well. Really well."

Jutting out my lip, I nod and try to tell myself I'm imagining the earnestness in his voice. "Definitely. Even Goldie really likes you."

"So, Goldie ..."

Lifting a brow, I check the time on my phone. Mainly to get a reprieve from seeing Oliver comfortable and undone from the day. Here, in bed with me. "What about her?"

"Her mom is ... ?"

Shrugging, I shake my head. "We don't know. Actually, we don't even know who she is."

"Are you serious?" His brows knit together.

"I mean, Prescott does, but he won't tell us. Only he and our parents know. A woman knocked on Prescott's door one day with a six-month-old baby in a carrier and handed him a note."

Oliver's head rears back. "Was it the mom?"

"Nope," I sigh. "It was a friend of hers, apparently. She told him she never wanted to be a mother and that this little accident from their one night stand didn't change that."

Oliver's jaw drops.

"The birth certificate was included in a bag she sent with her friend that had shot records, some diapers and formula," I continue. "But Prescott was listed as the father."

"Oh my gosh," he whispers. I can't help the easy smile that spreads across my face, thoroughly confusing him. "What?"

"I like that you don't hold back with me," I admit. "Your reactions are honest. At least, they are when we're alone."

Oliver breaks into a shy smile. "You make me comfortable."

In the process of internally denying every warm and fuzzy feeling buzzing around in my stomach, I beam back at him.

"What did he do? After that?" he asks.

"Prescott? He, um, went to our parents' house and showed them everything. They went to the doctor to confirm paternity.

Obviously, it was positive." Sighing, I search Oliver's expressive eyes. "It's honestly crazy how one tiny moment can change your life forever," I muse. "And then the rest is history."

Oliver watches me intently, cataloguing every emotion I try to hide as they flicker across my face. Something intense lies behind his outward expression, something trying its hardest to break through to the surface. He finally nods. "And then the rest is history."

# 16

*Oliver*

The sun eventually breaks through the curtains, dancing to its own perfect rhythm on our ceiling. Based on the relentless teasing from the clock on my bedside table, I've been awake for nearly four hours. Four tortuous hours. Thinking. Recalculating.

Hoping.

The bed creaks as Callie stirs, and the leap in my chest is honestly ridiculous. Sighing, the woman sleeping beside me settles back into her peaceful dreamstate.

Rubbing my hands back and forth over my face, there's no use lying to myself anymore. There's not a single part of me that's left unconvinced, that hasn't already succumbed to the reality in front of me. Or beside me, I suppose. What was supposed to be nothing more than a simple transaction has turned into this. And if I'm really being honest with myself, I think I knew I was done back on Thanksgiving. It would've seemed premature, sure. But looking back, there was never any other path.

When Calloway Rutherford walked into my office that first day, I was a goner.

I just didn't know it yet.

One more glance at the clock and I know John's awake. Even on vacation, the man never sleeps. It drove me crazy back in college. He would be up before dawn with his workout done, breakfast eaten, and ready for whatever the day held.

But I'm taking advantage of his insanity this morning.

Careful not to wake the woman who has my heart, I climb out of bed and slip on my houseshoes and coat. Grabbing my phone off the charger, I pad over to the sliding glass door and step onto the balcony, shutting the door softly behind me. With one more peek back through the window to make sure I didn't disturb Callie, I dial John's number.

Like the early riser he is, he answers on the first ring. "What's wrong?" The man sounds as if he's already had a couple cups of coffee.

Much too alert for this early in the morning.

"Why do you assume something's wrong?"

John scoffs through the phone. "Gee, I dunno. Maybe because you're calling me at six in the morning on Christmas Eve while you're on a trip pretending to be a boyfriend in love?"

The morning landscape is breathtaking, but it doesn't fully distract from the bitter cold of the winter dawn. Shuddering, I mentally curse myself for not bothering to throw on a hoodie, too.

Or socks.

"Spit it out, man." John's voice has officially transitioned into Dad Mode.

"You've always been too in tune with me, you know that? It's annoying."

Silence rings through on the other end of the call. When

my best friend speaks again, the weight of his words nearly knocks me off my feet. "You're in love with Callie." John chuckles under his breath, trying to cover it with a cough. "Well ... can't really say I'm all that surprised, man."

"Thanks for the marvelous insight. Can we try again, please?" I snap.

"Easy, Oliver," he says, voice calm. "Tell me about how you're feeling."

Pinching the bridge of my nose, I exhale slowly. "I don't know."

"You do."

I really hate it when he's right. "I ... I don't want to scare her."

"Did you bring your *Friday the 13th* mask?"

A reluctant laugh forces its way out. "That was one Halloween, dude." I sigh. "I haven't seen that thing since I was seventeen."

"Sure, but you still showed it to Candace Mason and she dumped her punch down your shirt at the school dance."

"Yeah, that wasn't my best work."

Laughing, he says, "So, are you afraid she doesn't feel the same way?"

Scrunching my face, I consider his question. "Not exactly."

John hmms through the phone. "Do you think she does feel the same, then?"

"I don't know," I admit. "Everything feels so natural between us. So real. If she doesn't share my feelings, she's a good actress."

"The only way you'll know is if you ask."

"What if she feels pressured?"

John scoffs. "Have you met Callie? That woman has grown up under tremendous pressure and has become an incredible person in spite of it all. I highly doubt you telling her about your feelings will make Callie want to shove a cactus in your face."

"I don't want to make things awkward between us, though."

"Had you planned to see one another anytime after the holidays?"

Scratching my second-day beard growth, I exhale loudly. "Not exactly."

"Then what do you have to lose? If you tell her and she feels the same, then great. Welcome to your forever. If not, you don't have to see her after these next couple days and then you can move on."

"You make it sound so easy," I snort. "Too bad I don't think it's quite that simple. And if you really believe that, then you've never felt like this."

"Look," John's voice lowers to barely a whisper, "I didn't think I would ever be able to feel anything again after Angela left."

My heart drops in my chest. "John, I'm sorry man. I didn't mean—"

"Oliver, it's fine." He sighs. "Because you're right. What Angie and I had ... that wasn't love. At least, not like it should be. Everything was conditional, and you and I both know better than that. We tell other families every single day what loving relationships should look like, and I can admit that what we had wasn't it. But I know that if I ever got the chance to have something real, I would do everything in my power to keep it. For my sake, and for Cecilia's." The weight of John using his daughter's full name isn't lost on me. He only opts for it when he means business. "What's really scaring you, Ollie? Surely it's not the commitment?"

Shaking my head, I answer with a strong, "No, not at all. I'd buy a ring today if I knew she felt the same way. I think it's more that I didn't, um—"

"You weren't expecting this deal to lead to her," he finishes, "and so quickly."

"It was always supposed to be a transaction," I whisper, "nothing more. Don't get me wrong, I'm not even trying to deny what I'm feeling. I ... I've wanted this. With her. For a while now ... I've only ever felt like this with her."

"But what if Callie doesn't think any of this is real." John sighs, already aware of my answer.

"Right."

"I think you know what you have to do next."

A soft knock against the glass behind me sounds through the crisp air. Turning around, I'm welcomed with the sight of Callie's warm smile grinning at me from the other side of the thick door. The smile that takes over my face is instant, a reflex.

And she beams right back.

Raising a finger to signal that I'll be right in, Callie nods and points to the bathroom before leaving me alone again.

"Oliver?"

"Sorry, Callie's awake," I breathe. "Listen man, thanks for this. For talking through everything."

John chuckles on the other end of the line. "Of course. Let me know how it goes."

Saying our goodbyes, I head back into the warmth of our room that welcomes me with open arms. "Callie?" I call. Kicking off my houseshoes, I hang my coat back in the closet.

The woman of the hour emerges from the bathroom, dressed in a garnet sweater and jeans with wool socks, carrying a small cosmetic bag. "Hey," she smiles. "Merry Christmas Eve." Her long hair falls in effortless waves down her back as she places the miniscule bag on the dresser.

"Merry Christmas Eve."

"You're up early." Callie lifts a brow in my direction as she makes her way back to her side of the bed.

Shrugging, I watch as she unplugs her phone and stuffs it in her back pocket. "Couldn't sleep. Thought I'd check on John and Cici."

Her perfect brow furrows. "You woke him up?"

"He's an early riser," I explain. "By the time I called, it's very likely he had already been to the gym, fed the hog, solved world hunger and won a Nobel Peace Prize."

"Wow."

"And that's just since we saw him yesterday afternoon."

Callie blinks, crossing her arms. "That sounds like quite the itinerary for what's supposed to be a relaxing vacation."

"Speaking of which, what's on the agenda today?" I ask, clearing my throat. "Anything particularly romantic?"

"Oh, plenty of activities that will require lots of lovey dovey PDA since we're madly in love and all," Callie snickers.

Forcing myself to swallow, I think about John's words. "Callie, I think we should—"

Three brisk raps on our door ring out through the room. "Calloway, open up," Chris calls through the thick door, "unless you and Dr. Hotness are naked. In that case, just talk through the door."

My interest piques at this new nickname that has clearly been used before.

Heat floods Callie's cheeks. Groaning, she rolls her eyes and goes to open the door. "What?" she demands.

Chris, fully dressed and ready for the day, stands in our doorway, scowling and looking completely unamused to be in our presence this early in the morning. Like Callie, he wears jeans and a sweater. But where her top perfectly compliments her ruby hair, Chris's looks like the machine exploded in the middle of the pattern. "I thought I told you to just talk through the door if you were naked."

Callie frowns, glancing down at her attire. "You're an idiot."

"I meant him." Her brother nods in my direction.

Plastering on the fakest smile, I salute the biggest prick in the Rutherford family. And that's saying something. "Good morning to you too, man."

Casting a quick look my way, Callie swings her gaze back to him. "Chris, have you ever seen a naked person? Because that is clearly not what's happening here," she says, motioning to me.

Chris rolls his eyes. "Whatever. Mom wants to know if you'll help with the cinnamon rolls this year since Imogene nearly burned the kitchen down last time."

My love rears back. "Really?"

"For breakfast?" I ask, brow furrowing. "Those take hours to make from scratch."

Callie sends a warm smile my way. "Whoever's the designated baker of the holiday works on them throughout the day while everyone else is out, then we have them while we sit around the tree and thaw out from spending all morning in the snow."

Unable to help myself, I grin at my girlfriend. "Now that sounds like a tradition I can get behind."

Callie lifts a brow. "You won't miss skiing or making snow angels?"

In a few short strides, I'm across the room and wrapping my arms around her. Placing a kiss on her temple, I say into her hair, "I'm not a big fan of the snow. Besides, if I do feel the need to be senselessly cold, you and I can just warm up together, later."

Chris looks ready to vomit as Callie giggles. "Right, well. Everyone else is already up and out the door, which means you're already late. So I'd move it, if I were you." With that, Chris turns and stalks back down the hall as Callie closes the door behind him.

As soon as the door clicks into place, I ask, "Dr. Hotness?"

Callie groans. "Trust me, you do not want to know."

"Oh, I really think I do."

She sends me a side-eye that would make Nacho proud.

Lifting my brow in response, I fight to keep my amusement from showing.

Tapping a finger to her chin, Callie weighs something in her mind. The moment she decides is clear as day. Her lips curl up into a mischievous smile. "You know, I think I'll keep that one to myself. But thanks for the offer." With that, she turns to the suitcase lying open on the floor.

Shaking my head, I make quick work of grabbing some khakis and a sweater that happens to be Callie's favorite color. As I head toward the bathroom, a moment of bravery shows itself. "Cal?"

Sitting on the bed, she glances up from the middle of slipping on her shoes. "Yeah?"

I know what's supposed to come out, but instead I ask, "Do you know how to bake cinnamon rolls?"

Callie bites her bottom lip, shaking her head. "Nope. That's what the recipe book is for," she laughs. "Cooking, I can do. Baking, not so much." Narrowing her eyes, she looks across the small space to me. "Luckily, I have a boyfriend who's pretty awesome in the baking department."

"I'd be happy to help." Not that I could deny this woman anything at this point. "In fact, I'd prefer it."

"Believe me," she laughs, "my entire family would enjoy whatever you'll make more than anything I could produce." Callie turns back to find her other shoe.

Pressing my lips into a flat line, I try again. "Callie? One more thing."

"What's up?" Curiosity coats every flawless feature as she takes me in, still clad in my pajamas.

"Um, I'd like to talk later." The anxiety weaving through my chest loosens as I search those warm, inviting brown eyes. "If that's okay."

A small smile lifts her lips. "We can talk now."

"We need to get downstairs," I shake my head, "and I don't really want to rush this conversation."

"Are you being drafted?"

Laughter bursts from my lips. "Not this time."

Callie stands, shrugging. "Good. I'd miss you too much, Rhodes."

Hope blooms in my chest, that dangerous little bastard. A grin threatens to split my face in two. "Right back at ya, Rutherford." *You have no idea.*

"BATCH NUMBER THREE, DONE," Callie sings with pride as she pulls another set of rolls from the oven. Taking a deep breath, she inhales the heavenly aroma. "I don't think I've ever smelled such perfection. You know, other than you."

My brain glitches. "Oh, uh great," I say, making space on the counter. "I'll grab the icing."

Setting down the piping hot dish, Callie moves to where the finished batches wait on a large red platter featuring the big man himself. The holiday-themed dish overflows with newly iced cinnamon rolls, their mouthwatering aroma filling the kitchen.

"You think I smell good?" I dare to ask. Chancing a peek in her direction, I nearly expire on the spot.

Plucking a roll from its obscurity, Callie runs a finger along the icing. The woman nearly gives me a heart attack as she sucks the liquified sugar from her finger, groaning in appreciation. "Is there anything you don't bake?" Either she didn't hear my question, or is choosing to ignore it.

Forcing my eyes back to the task at hand, I do my best to process the question. "Macarons," I choke out, the image of Callie's lips wrapped around her finger still seared into my mind's eye.

Wide, innocent eyes pull my gaze back to hers like gravity. "Why?"

"They're delicate and I tend to burn them," I confess, cheeks flaming.

"Hm. I imagine they don't like that very much."

Her comment makes me chuckle. "You know, they don't. They tend to become rather angry, actually."

"Yeah," she sighs, "there's nothing angrier than burnt macarons." Cinnamon roll in hand, Callie makes her way back to my side.

Forming my lips into a flat line, I slide my eyes toward her, where a dollop of icing rests on the tip of her perfect nose. Without giving it a second thought, I lean in and press a kiss on the stray sugar. Returning to my full height, Callie blinks up at me, bewildered.

"What was that for?" Widened eyes dart around the room. "Is someone else here?" she whispers.

"Only the icing on your nose. Thought I'd use a surefire method of helping you out. If someone else sees, that's just a bonus," I laugh, shrugging.

Callie considers this, setting down the remainder of the treat. "So, if no one sees, then it's just for practice?"

Turning toward her, I ask, "Do you think we need more practice?" It takes my entire focus to keep my hands on the icing tube and not on her.

"Oh, I think we've gotten pretty good at that particular part of being a convincing couple," she says thoughtfully, eyes roaming my face. Her plush lips curve into a smile. "But I don't think we're anywhere close to perfect, yet."

Setting down the icing tube, I wipe my hands on my apron. "And practice does make perfect," I whisper, closing what little distance remains between us.

Chocolate eyes settle on my lips. "Did you know you have some powdered sugar on your lips, Dr. Rhodes?"

"We can't have that," I murmur. "Think you can help me out?"

Callie lifts onto her tiptoes, winding her arms around my neck as mine wrap around her waist. Smirking, she presses soft, pillowy lips to mine. "Much better," she breathes, leaning back.

I shake my head, following her. "I think there's still some left." My lips find hers with ease, their siren song calling me home. Her arms tighten around me as I deepen the kiss.

Callie's fingers dance up my neck, entangling themselves in my hair.

"I hope you remember to wash your hands when you're done."

Callie flies off me like shrapnel, throwing a hand to her chest. The one that was just in my hair. "Geez, Connie. You scared the crap out of me," she pants.

My favorite sibling of Callie's removes her wool scarf and gloves as her smirk only grows wider. Moving further inside from the garage, curious eyes flit between Callie and myself. "Sorry," she says, "just thought I'd warn you that everyone else is headed in. You know, in case you two needed to get cozy." Connie's hawk-like vision doesn't miss the heat rising in my cheeks.

At least she can't hear how hard my heart is pounding.

"But it doesn't look like you need any reminders," Connie finishes.

Clearing my throat, I plead with my nervous system to relax. "We'll take all the help we can get. So, thank you."

"Um, right," Callie nods with a little too much vigor, "thanks, Connie."

Connie shrugs out of her coat, hanging it on a peg. "I may have had to bodyblock Christopher, but he thinks I'm just excited about the sweets."

"Why does he think that?" I frown.

She snorts. "Because I talked them up all morning.

Calloway mentioned your baking mastery, so I figure they can't suck."

Beside me, Callie nods. "They're awesome," she confirms. Hands on her hips, Callie grins at me. "Man, I really lucked out in the fake boyfriend department."

"Shh!" Connie glances over her shoulder at the closed interior garage door.

As if on cue, the rest of the Rutherford women come barging in, shedding a layer per footstep.

"Merry Christmas Eve, Calloway. Oliver." Lillian removes a snowcovered beanie, dropping it in a nearby laundry basket. "It smells wonderful in here."

Imogene and Marigold scoot around Lillian, making a beeline for the overflowing platter of goodies. In a very Marigold fashion, she makes a pit stop to give Callie a tight hug and me a giggling smile before taking a roll in each hand.

"Calloway," Imogene grabs a treat for herself, "I had no idea you could bake so well." Callie's oldest sister sends her a mischievous smile.

"I mainly made the icing." Callie places a hand gingerly on my arm as I work on icing the final batch. "Oliver's really the one you should be complimenting."

Grabbing a napkin, Imogene looks from her sister to me. Her features soften. "Calloway's lucky to have found you."

The sincerity ringing through every word nearly knocks me off my feet. Blinking, I look at the oldest Rutherford sister. "Thanks, Imogene."

Since both of Marigold's hands are occupied, Imogene takes her by the shoulder. "Come on, Goldie. Let's go grab a spot by the tree."

Callie's niece looks back our way. "Are Aunt Callie and Uncle Oliver coming, too?"

I'm pretty sure my heart stops completely.

Callie, in the middle of downing some hot chocolate, chokes.

Tossing the icing tube aside and wiping off my hands, I pat Callie on the back as she coughs. Never taking my eyes off her, I say, "We'll be over there soon, Marigold. Be sure to save us a spot."

Marigold giggles as she and Imogene head to where Lillian and Connie wait on the fluffiest rug known to man.

"Are you okay?" I ask, smiling. "Need some cinnamon rolls to help soak up all that errant hot cocoa?"

My girlfriend clears her throat. "Yeah, yeah. Make fun of the person choking to death." But she grins up at me. "I'm good. Thanks."

"You and Imogene seem to be getting along much better." I nod to her oldest sister, sitting on the couch with Marigold on her lap.

Callie nods. "That's definitely improving." She takes the icing from where I'd dropped it, picking up where I left off. "Imogene's always been so awkward when it comes to me. I think she's finally understanding we can have a relationship without her feeling like she's betraying our parents, or Prescott, too."

"Who's betraying me?" Prescott asks with only a mild edge in his voice. Cool eyes slide between his sister and I.

"Goldie," Callie answers with ease, "when she eats eight cinnamon rolls instead of five, like you told her she could."

The oldest Rutherford sibling merely sighs before narrowing his eyes at me. "They must be good, then. Good thing, too. Connie went on and on about them this morning."

I shrug. "I know my way around a kitchen."

"Daddy!" Marigold screeches. "Aunt Genny and I saved you a seat."

Prescott's generally icy demeanor melts for his daughter. "On my way, sweets." Turning back to us, his smile falters slightly. "Thanks for all your hard work on these, Oliver. If they're as good as Constance and Calloway say, you may have just secured the gig for as long as you're around."

"Prescott," Callie warns.

He grins, making his way toward the platter. "Relax, Calloway." Prescott scoops up a couple of rolls. "I'm sure the good doctor will be around for a long time."

Throwing my arm around Callie, I pull her in close. "Only if I can help it." I force a grin onto my face.

As Prescott stalks off toward his daughter, I lean down so that only Callie can hear me. "How's that one going?"

Callie pipes on the last of the icing. "Fine," she shrugs, "not super awesome, but better than it was."

"His comment may be my fault," I admit.

Her brows knit together. "What do you mean?"

"I may have snapped at him the night of your kids' program."

Crackling from the fireplace mingles with the chatter from everyone in the living area. Ira and Chris make their way inside with only a nod in our direction as they wander over to the sectional.

"Should we take the rest of the cinnamon rolls over there?" I ask, removing my apron and hanging it on a peg by the state-of-the-art refrigerator.

"What did you argue with him about?" Her voice is so soft, I'd have missed her question completely if I wasn't so attuned to her every breath.

Turning toward the pull from my heart, I find Callie regarding me curiously. No judgement or anger, just quizzical.

A tentative step brings her closer to me, and I immediately regret every molecule of air floating between us. "Oliver," she presses, casting a quick glance toward the rest of her family. Callie takes one more step and I can feel the heat radiating from her pinked cheeks. "Tell me."

"Just making sure he knew my intentions were honorable is all, sweetheart." Brushing a strand of hair behind Callie's ear, I beam down at her. "Trust me, he won't make that mistake again."

Callie's eyes flit down to my lips and I work to suppress a groan.

"You can't look at me like that, Callie," I murmur.

Her eyes widen. "Why not?"

"Callie, I—"

"Calloway, Oliver, come on over here," Connie calls from the couch.

My girlfriend's eyelids flutter, remembering we have an audience. Pulling away, she turns to her family. "Just-just a second. We're getting some more hot cocoa." At this rate, I'm honestly shocked it's not flowing through her veins.

Then again, it very well could be.

"Yep," I confirm, "does anyone else want any?" When I'm met with a bunch of headshakes, I turn my greedy eyes back on Callie, who is most certainly avoiding my gaze.

Gathering the platter in my hands, Callie prepares two hot chocolates in record time thanks to the electric kettle resting on the counter. Face still flushed, she leads me to the living area where the rest of the Rutherfords are talking about Marigold taking on the bunny slopes today.

"My goodness," Lillian breathes, looking over at the platter of treats, "how many did you make?"

"My favorite recipe makes about forty per batch," I offer, placing the platter on the oversized coffee table.

"And we made three full batches," Callie finishes proudly.

Connie laughs from her place beside Imogene. "Then there'll be plenty for tomorrow, too, which is good," she holds up a mostly eaten roll, "because I'll be thinking about these for years to come. Whoever has next year's shift has some big shoes to fill." She nods to the rest of her siblings.

With the couch being at capacity, I guide Callie to a spot on the rug nestled right by the tree. Holding her cocoa as she gets settled, I look around at the family surrounding me. There's the making for a close knit family here, but they have to want it as much as Callie does. And I'm going to help her get the family she deserves if it's the last thing I do.

Connie and Imogene watch their youngest sister with warmth in their eyes as she finds her own place in their tiny Rutherford world.

Even Lillian seems a little more attentive today.

It's the men I have to keep an eye on, especially after the conversation I had with them at Callie's school. Prescott will probably be the easiest to persuade that Callie really is worthy of her family name. Chris and Ira, on the other hand, will take some convincing.

"Oliver?" Callie looks up at me from the floor, hands open for her turn holding the mugs while I sit down beside her.

In one fluid motion, my knee is touching hers as I cuddle up as close as possible. Taking my cocoa, I press a soft kiss to her hair.

She hums in appreciation, though I honestly don't know if it's for my kiss or the hot chocolate topped with extra mini marshmallows.

Despite our objective of gaining her family's acceptance, Callie snuggles into me, completely at ease in her surroundings.

Desperation to talk through everything with her rears its ugly head, and I take a quick inventory of my features to make sure I don't look like I'm anything but a fool in love. And with Callie, that's like breathing.

*Later. That will come later.*

Ira leans forward, taking one of the rolls. "I still can't believe Calloway helped make such perfection." He turns the treat this way and that way. *You think he'd be less obvious about looking for imperfections.*

"Callie and I bake together regularly," I shrug, "we've definitely taught each other a thing or two. Didn't you say you've been baking since college?" I ask, turning to my girlfriend.

"About then," she answers around the half of a roll currently in her mouth.

Ira frowns. "Really? I had no idea you were so talented, Calloway."

"She's very talented," I interject. "For instance, she managed to both flummox my annoyingly astute receptionist and trail glitter all through the practice the first time I met her."

Callie shoots me a grin. "Are you all still finding glitter?"

"In the most obscure places," I smirk.

Prescott frowns. "I thought you met in Calloway's classroom?"

Dammit.

Red crawls up Callie's neck, blending with her hair. Tension radiates through her frame and into mine.

"That was when we officially met," I clarify. "But she had come by the practice first to talk to one of my partners about his daughter. I saw her that day and knew I had to meet her."

Callie tilts her head back, eyes searching mine. "What can I say? I know how to make an impression. Especially when someone is a bit of an ass." She grins. "That's when glitter really comes in handy."

"Just wanted to make sure you stayed on my mind?" At this point, I don't even care if the rest of her family is watching us.

"You caught me," she says, voice low. The sparkle in her eyes just about does me in. "It's how I get all my guys."

Leaning my lips down to her ear, I murmur, "You sure got me, Ms. Rutherford." Even though the others have forgotten us once again, I don't want them to hear what's only for Callie to know. "And I hope you'll never let me go."

Callie shivers, and I tuck her in as close as possible.

It's the sound of my name that pulls me back into the larger conversation happening around us. "Sorry?" I reluctantly tear my eyes away from the woman consuming every part of my being.

Lillian reaches for a napkin, wiping off professionally polished fingers. "I asked if you were planning to join us at the firm's annual New Year's party? I'm sure Calloway would love your company." Here, Lillian almost looks like a normal mother and not the privileged woman less concerned with her daughter and more concerned with the fact that the man she is dating has a doctorate. "And I know Ira and Prescott's colleagues would enjoy getting to meet the impressive man Calloway has miraculously managed to snag." There it is.

The immediate acceptance of the invitation sits on the tip of my tongue. Anything to guarantee more time with Calloway Rutherford. But as I glance down at Callie, something unreadable crosses those mesmerizing features. Something that gives me pause.

Something that causes my heart to clench.

## 17

*Callie*

Oliver Rhodes is ... everything.

Everything I've hoped for, dreamed of, imagined. All in one perfect package. I mean, the man can't keep a plant alive. No, that's what I bring to the table. No one is *actually* perfect, I guess. But it's really all about balance.

And right now, my heart is perfectly off-kilter from the balance this man brings to my life.

"Calloway?" Connie slips up beside me at the electric kettle, causing me to jump.

Stilted laughter tumbles from my lips. "You scared me."

A soft smile graces her lovely face. "Sorry. Oliver's doing really well," she whispers, nodding to my fake boyfriend lounging on the couch with Prescott, Imogene, and our parents.

I frown. "Where's Chris?"

Connie lifts a brow. "He went to bed a while ago."

"No wonder there seems to be so much more air in here," I grumble.

Connie chuckles. "He said he walked in on you two this morning ... right in the middle of things?" Dainty ruby brows reach her hairline.

I don't bother hiding my blanche. "We ... he ... clothed ... " I sputter.

Her musical laughter surrounds us. "Relax, Calloway. He only said it privately to me."

My relief is euphoric. "Thank all the hot chocolate gods."

Clearly not done torturing me, Connie leans in closer. "How is all that going?"

Any of my remaining relief flies out the very large windows across the room. "What do you mean?"

"I mean, when I walked in on you earlier, it didn't look ... fake."

"Psh," I wave her off, "you are *loco*, girlfriend." I force out some laughter for good measure. Returning to my cocoa, the weight of her stare practically rips my head in two.

"Calloway." Apparently, she's had enough. "Talk to me. Please?"

A quick glance around the kitchen tells me what I already know—that no one else is paying us any attention. Sighing, I look my sister square in the eye. "We only promised to do this through the holidays." Sorrow weighs down every syllable.

"Do you love him?" she asks. So simply, as if that's the only question that matters in the entire universe. Connie has always been my favorite. Though her loyalty has always remained with her twin, she has made sure I've been seen my entire life by someone in our family. She's made sure I have never been forgotten in the midst of life with my overachieving siblings.

And I love her dearly for it.

But she thinks in black and white. Absolutes. Right and wrong.

Why and why not.

If I tell her the truth, she'll think it's as simple as telling Oliver how I feel.

If I lie, she'll say it should be easy to move on.

Setting down my favorite blue mug with snowflakes all over it, the one which Oliver currently holds the mate to, I look at my closest sister. Nothing but care waits in her eyes when they meet mine. "Connie, I've only known him for about a month."

"So?"

"So, how can you fall in love with someone in such a short amount of time?" Pursing my lips, I furrow my brow.

My sister sighs. "Sometimes, you just know. And there's no other way to explain it."

"What about you?" I ask pointedly.

Connie's eyes search the depths of mine, her own pain begging for a front row seat. "I know there will never be anyone else for me, either."

Nodding, I add Cool Whip to my cocoa. "Do you think you'll ever do anything about that?"

"I think—" Connie runs a hand through her loose hair "—that I don't want to lose my best friend."

"He loves you too, you know." My comment is only met with silence. When I finally peek in her direction, my heart breaks a little more.

Wiping a single tear from her cheek, Connie sniffs. "I want him to be happy," she says, "and he's chosen a career that's not really suitable for our kind of family life. He's amazing at what he does and I'm not going to stand in the way of that. But you, on the other hand, have a chance at a real relationship. That man over there has feelings for you—anyone can see that. And I don't mean the fake kind to put on a show for our family."

Following her line of sight, I'm met with an image I've never even let myself dream about. Someone here that's on my side, no matter what. Someone I can trust. Someone who might truly love me back, despite my last name.

Oliver holds Goldie by the tree, their faces glowing in warm white lights as she regales him with stories about each ornament and how they came to our family.

Goldie catches me watching and waves, whilst Oliver beams at her.

"Uh-oh," Connie snorts. "Mom and Dad have officially had enough eggnog that they're busting out the records."

Sure enough. Dad dances his way from where the record player rests, an old holiday album crackling to life as the familiar lyrics echo throughout the room.

Mom tipsily climbs up from the couch, taking Dad's hand and swaying in time to the song.

Connie takes the mug from my hand, replacing it on the counter.

"I was looking forward to that, thank you very much."

"I know, little sister, I know. But I think there's something better waiting for you." Connie steers me away from the kitchen and toward the others.

When we're only a few paces away, Goldie beams. "Aunt Callie, guess what."

"What's up, sugar lump?"

She giggles into her hand, leaning onto Oliver.

I'm pretty sure my ovaries explode. His magnetic pull is undeniable, and my feet don't stop until we're practically connected at the hip.

"Uncle Oliver knows the legend of the Christmas pickle."

"Really?" My brows shoot up, looking between them. "Did you find it?"

Goldie juts out a tiny lower lip. "No."

"Don't worry, honey," Imogene says from the couch behind me, "we'll find it in the morning." Imogene laughs out a hiccup. "Ope, warning sign." Another hiccup bubbles out.

Prescott grins at his little sister. "Marigold, go kiss Aunt Genny goodnight."

"Do I have to go to bed?" Goldie pouts.

"Yes, sweets. But Aunt Genny needs to, as well," he says, pulling Imogene up for a tight hug. "Otherwise Santa won't come see her."

Marigold slaps both palms to her little cheeks. "Not Santa!"

"Tell everyone goodnight," Prescott nods.

Still in Oliver's strong arms, Goldie leans out and gives me a tight hug. "Night Aunt Callie, I love you."

"I love you too, sweet girl."

My niece releases her boa-like hold, looking back at my fake boyfriend. "Night Uncle Oliver, I love you. Now you say it back."

"Marigold," Prescott chides, mortified. "Oliver doesn't have to say it if he doesn't want to."

To his credit, Oliver only laughs. "It's all good, man," he says to my brother. Then, he turns that beautiful smile toward Goldie. "Goodnight, Marigold. I love you, too," he whispers.

"And you love Aunt Callie, too?" my niece asks boldly.

Off to my right, Prescott looks ready to wither away from embarrassment.

Oliver's eyes never leave mine as he nods. "Yeah, I do."

Eyes wide, my heart stops as my niece looks proudly from Oliver to myself.

Imogene moves toward the stairs. "Marigold, wanna help me sprinkle the reindeer food on your balcony?" The urgency in her voice would make me laugh if I wasn't ready to vomit.

Goldie wiggles out of Oliver's hold. "Aunt Genny, we have to put out the cookies before we go to bed, too. Come on!" Goldie grabs onto Imogene's closest hand, attempting to lead her to the stairs.

"Night," Imogene calls from halfway up the staircase.

Connie snickers as our older sister is led away by the force of a seven-year-old. "I think I'd better go make sure Imogene doesn't get hurt. Especially if she wakes Chris." My sister tucks me in for a quick hug before turning back to the others. "Prescott, let's go." Giving a pointed look to our brother, she motions to the stairs.

Frowning, he looks between us. "When did you become so bossy?"

"Since your daughter led our tipsy sister upstairs," she states as he walks past her. "Goodnight Calloway, Oliver." She grins at each of us in turn before following him.

"And then there were two." I can hear the grin in Oliver's voice without even looking at him.

My brow furrows as I finally allow myself to take him in, ethereal in the Christmas tree glow. Did seeing him play with my sweet niece make him even more attractive than he already was?

Without a doubt.

Am I now extremely aware that Connie may just be right? That I should probably tell him how I feel, regardless of the timeline we gave ourselves?

Annoyingly so.

Besides, even if he doesn't feel the same, we could always just be friends. I don't think I can picture my life without him there in some capacity at this point, anyway.

So will I survive if he doesn't feel the way I do?

Doubtful.

"Two?" But as I twist to take in the rest of the room, the sound of the master bedroom door shutting echoes throughout the living area. I huff. "Two." The familiar record continues filling the cozy room when a hand appears between us.

"Dance with me?" Oliver gives me an encouraging smile.

Swallowing, I shake my head. "I, um, I don't really dance much."

Dark blond brows lift. "You sure did that night at Theo's when Aaron's band played."

"That was different."

"How?"

Shrugging, I fold my arms. "It was comfortable. I didn't care if I looked like an idiot."

"I promise not to let you look foolish, Cal," he says, voice tender. Light blue eyes search mine. Nodding to his still-outstretched hand, he whispers, "Please?"

My arms disentangle themselves without my permission, reaching out for the warmth I know waits in his embrace.

Stepping forward, Oliver takes my hand in his while the other snakes around my waist, moving us to the winter rhythm. The intoxicating blend of cinnamon apples and sheer masculinity envelopes me.

Heart fluttering, I lay my head against Oliver's strong chest as he pulls me closer, obliterating any remaining space between us. Outside, snowflakes dance to the ground, tempting me to fall right along with them.

My fake boyfriend, who told my niece that he loves me, rests his cheek against the top of my head. Surrounding me, his every motion is sturdy and sure.

Too bad it has red-hot awareness raging through my insides like a vine tightening through my entire nervous system.

Oliver spins me in a circle in one smooth, swift motion, pressing me back into his chest one more time. The corners of his mouth lift.

Mine follow involuntarily, mirroring his smile back at him. "What?"

"Do your parents always hang mistletoe from the side of the tree?" He nods directly above us, where a sprig of mistletoe hangs from one of the highest branches.

Snorting, I roll my eyes. "Yep. They take any excuse to gross out their kids, especially around the holidays. But then again

—" I peek up at him from underneath my lashes"—who are we to buck tradition?"

"Calloway Rutherford, are you asking me to kiss you?" Leaning back, he smirks.

Heat races through my veins, threatening to give me away. Grinning, I lift a shoulder. "More like picking up where we left off in the kitchen. It was just starting to get good." Before I can even process the audacity of my own statement, Oliver's lips are on mine.

Pressing. Demanding.

His large hands roam slowly down my sides as our mouths open, each inviting the other in. Stopping just below the dip of my waist, Oliver's fingers wrap around my hips. His grip tightens, pulling me flush to him.

Fire courses through my body, enveloping me in an all-consuming heat. I can't tell if it's from the overzealous fireplace or the stupidly attractive man holding onto me like his life depends on it. As my hands fist themselves in the front of his sweater, one of Oliver's releases its iron grip.

Entangling his free hand in my hair, the best man I've ever known holds me in place just as my knees threaten to give out. A wild rumble of appreciation shudders through his chest as our teeth clash together, each begging the other for more.

Brazen fingers slide down his firm chest and stomach, finding the bottom of his shirt and dipping themselves inside. Underneath the hem, the warmth of his skin scorches my fingertips as he shivers at the contact. In a moment of bravery, my hands slide down to his waistband, where his button and fly open with ease.

Oliver follows suit, his lower hand sliding around to unfasten the button of my jeans.

Somewhere behind my parents' closed bedroom door, another door slams shut.

My heart drums against the walls of my chest as we break apart, both taking in as much air as we can manage.

Oliver's typically light eyes have been taken over, possessed by a darkness felt deep within me, as well. Chest heaving, those eyes pin me in place. "Callie—"

The weight of our situation comes crashing down. Humiliation floods my every nerve. "We need to go," I pant, nodding toward their room, "just in case they decide to come back out." Without waiting on an answer, I move faster than I have in my entire life, taking the stairs two at a time.

The sound of Oliver's footsteps follow me up the staircase and down the hallway, pausing just long enough for me to reach our bedroom before I die from embarrassment.

Throwing open the door, my panicked eyes bounce between my two options for safety. On the one hand, I could lock myself in the bathroom. But if Oliver needs it at any point in the night, that would only make things more awkward. On the other hand, I could potentially freeze to death out on the balcony. It would be difficult for Oliver to explain my frozen carcass, but at least I wouldn't have to worry about embarrassing myself further. Besides, this infernal fire in my core needs to chill the hell out.

I make a beeline for the balcony.

The sound of the door clicking shut behind Oliver only makes me move faster. "Callie, where are you going?"

Yanking the balcony sliding glass to the side, I step out into the Christmas Eve air. My eyes burn, begging for an emotional release from whatever just happened downstairs.

Whatever was about to happen.

Sliding the door back into place, I close my eyes and take a deep breath of the frigid winter midnight. Light snowfall bites at the tip of my nose as I reach the railing, but it does nothing for the heat lingering in my cheeks. Wiping away the single tear forging a trail down my cheek, I sniff right as the balcony door slides open once again.

He's silent as he steps out onto the snowcovered balcony, shutting the door behind him. Soft crunches from the piled snow hints at his movements. Finally, his warmth seeps into my back as he reaches me. "Callie," he tries again, "look at me. Please."

Blinking to ensure there are no other stray tears, I take a deep breath, steeling myself as I turn around.

Oliver's tender eyes take in my face, no doubt catching every single thing I wish I could hide from him.

But he's always seen right through me.

A hand gingerly lifts, cradling my cheek and rubbing a thumb across my skin. "Talk to me, sweetheart," he breathes.

Forcing a smile onto my face, I shake my head.

Oliver's lips tilt up. "It's just you and me, baby. Tell me." He shifts closer, using his free hand to pull me close. "You'll freeze if we stay out here much longer."

"Not likely."

Using a finger to lift my chin, Oliver brings my gaze to his. "Come inside with me. I promise to let you hide in the bathroom if you start to feel the least bit awkward."

Biting my lip to hide my smile, I cast a quick glance over my shoulder. "The view was getting a little old, anyway." I'm not about to admit that I'm already turning into an icicle.

Oliver gives a low chuckle as he ushers me back inside. "That's my girl."

Letting him take care of shutting the door, I plop down onto the bed, kicking off my shoes and socks one at a time.

Oliver leans back onto the dresser, pulling off his sweater to reveal a white T-shirt underneath. The traitorous mirror reflects every flex of his back muscles on display through his shirt.

I'm tempted to check for drool, even if that's about the least appropriate thing to do right now.

Setting the sweater down, Oliver folds toned arms over his broad chest. Mimicking my own movements, the man steps out of his shoes and socks one by one. He makes no secret of watching me carefully, as if afraid I'll bolt at any moment.

Not sure where he came up with that idea.

"Callie, we need to talk about that kiss." His words are slow, deliberate. Each one heavy with the weight of what remains unspoken.

"Why?" I ask innocently, with one sock on the floor and the other halfway off my foot. I'd imagine this is what marriage must be like—having awkward conversations forced on you when you least want to have them.

All while half-dressed.

My wandering eyes drift down to where his khakis hang perfectly from his hips, unbuttoned and right where we left off.

Oliver follows my gaze and smirks. "That's why."

"Do you think it's some big secret that you're super hot or something?" I ask, rolling my eyes.

"You think I'm super hot?" His grin widens.

"Objectively, you'd make just about any woman toss her underwear at you. Don't act so surprised. I've seen your apartment—you own mirrors." Leaning back against the headboard, I weave my fingers together and rest them on my stomach. "And that's not even including all your other obvious attributes," I groan.

"Other attributes?"

I can look at him so long as I take myself out of the judging process. No feelings, no problem. *Think objectively, not like you're in love with the guy.* "Between your career where you get to make a difference daily, your amazing family and the fact that you own the dog of the century, you've just gotta face facts, Rhodes."

"And what exactly are these facts, Rutherford?" His brow furrows, trying to keep up with my logic that is closely aligned with that of the clinically insane.

Shrugging, I resituate to a sitting position while my legs remain kicked out on the bed. "You're a catch."

That beautiful smile drops. Something else takes over his expression, softening it. "You think I'm a catch?"

"The ninety-year-old gas station clerk on the way up here thought you were a catch, Oliver."

He hangs his head, shaking it. "That's not what I asked, Callie." When Oliver brings his eyes back up to mine, every single nerve lights itself on fire. "I want to know what *you* think."

"About the fact that you should definitely be married with eight hundred kids by now?" I ask, quirking a brow. "And that in no way should you have to dupe your family by having a fake girlfriend?"

A wolfish smile pulls at Oliver's lips. Pushing off from the dresser, he takes slow, measured steps toward the bed. "Maybe it'd be easier if I started."

"Started?" I repeat.

"With my assessment of your ... " his heated gaze travels the length of me. "Attributes. Since you were so kind as to share some of mine."

My heart kicks into high gear, thrashing more rapidly with each step he takes. And when he reaches where I lay and holds out his hand, my entire nervous system hums in anticipation.

"Callie."

Needing no further urging, I place my hand in his. The effect this man has on me is criminal. The moment his skin touches mine, my entire body sings.

Outwardly, only my breathing gives away any discomfort from the need growing in my core.

He doesn't miss it, biting back a smile as he pulls me to my feet. Oliver adjusts so that I'm standing toe to toe with him, those long fingers intertwining with mine by our sides.

Blush rapidly staining my cheeks, I chance a peek up at him. "You wanted to discuss, um, something?" I whisper. Air catches in my throat as his intensely blue eyes hold mine.

"Yes, Ms. Rutherford. I've spent a good deal of time with you, you see."

"I'm aware," I nod.

He grins. "And I believe I've gathered some notes worth sharing."

"Oh?"

Oliver brushes his nose along the length of mine. "Oh." Swallowing, I shiver at the featherlight touch as his cheek lifts into a smile against my face. "First, there's your dedication to a career you love." He presses a kiss on the tip of my nose. "You take care of all those plants." Another kiss lands on my right cheek.

"You would consider that a feat," I tease. This close, his scent is intoxicating and I have to work twice as hard to keep my mind from wandering. Worrying about if he still thinks this is fake for me.

If this is still fake for him.

Or what would happen if I just started peeling off my clothes.

*Focus Callie.*

His smile widens as he continues. "There's your courage in standing up to your family at every turn." A third kiss warms the other cheek as Oliver wraps my arms around his middle. Only when my hands are linked does he release me from his hold, palms moving to press into my back. "But then there's my favorite one."

Leaning back, I raise my brows in question. "You have a favorite thing about me?"

"Callie, everything about you is my favorite." Despite my teasing, Oliver's voice only holds gentle sincerity.

*I love you.* The words catch in my throat, clawing for freedom. But that lingering doubt screams in the back of my mind.

One of his hands reaches up, tracing my cheekbone with delicate fingertips while his blazing blue eyes remain my entire universe. "You don't understand, do you? You work so hard to accommodate everyone else that you don't even realize there are people who would turn their lives upside down to make sure you stayed there forever." Oliver leans in, closing the distance remaining between our lips as his other hand presses me deeper into him. His heartbeat thrums through the thin shirt, every hard plane melding perfectly with my curves.

My hands move from his waist. Curling around, they grab at the loosened front of his pants, gripping as tightly to them as I'm trying to hold on to my sanity.

A battle I'm quickly losing.

Breaking the kiss, my apprehensive gaze finds him. "Oliver, I feel like I need to tell you something."

Two large palms cup my face.

"This ... this is—"

"Real," he finishes.

I nod. "So, I don't really know if this is a good idea. You know, if it's still fake for you. And I completely understand if it is." Silently pleading with the hot chocolate gods to make the word vomit stop, Oliver proves he knows how to answer my every prayer.

Those kind eyes holding my gaze come to life. Pressing his unyielding groin against my stomach, the fire staring back at me only burns brighter. "Is this *real* enough for you?"

My breath hitches, eliciting a wicked grin from the man before me. Swallowing, I nod to myself before peeking up at him. "I'm sorry, Dr. Rhodes, but I think I'll need to take a better look before I can adequately answer your question."

Every ounce of blue vanishes, his beautiful eyes eclipsed by midnight. "I'm all yours, Callie. Only yours. Take every part of me."

Holding his gaze, I push his pants to the ground, thanking my downstairs self for getting me this far. I don't think I could even locate his zipper otherwise, with how fast my head is spinning. A bold moment makes me ghost my hands up Oliver's toned thighs, sinking into the waistband of his briefs. One sharp intake of breath from him and I'm sliding them down.

He bobs free as they join his pants pooled around his ankles. Oliver's hand presses down on my shoulder as he steps out of each leg.

Biting my lip, I smirk up at him. "You, uh, should lose your shirt, too. Makes for better research."

"Help me, then," he croaks.

My fingertips grab at the hem of his undershirt as I rise. In one swift movement, Oliver stands before me completely bare. Dragging a finger down his chiseled chest, I murmur, "You're beautiful."

Oliver hooks a finger under my chin, bringing my eyes to his. "*You're* beautiful, Calloway."

Unable to help myself, I grin. "I'm not even naked yet."

"Then I say we fix that."

The only answer I can conjure is to shimmy down my jeans in about the most unattractive manner possible. But if the heat raging in my lower belly is any indication, they were about to spontaneously combust, anyway.

Oliver gives a low chuckle as he leans in to kiss me. Without breaking the connection, his strong fingers dance down my ribcage, his tongue swiping along the seam of our lips. Grabbing my sweater and pulling it over my head, Oliver traces the goosebumps rising across my exposed skin. "Looks like I'll need to help you warm up," he whispers into my neck. As he peppers kisses down the column of my throat, my fingers knot themselves into his hair while he reaches around and unclasps my bra.

I disentangle myself from him long enough to drop it on the floor unceremoniously, before snaking my arms back around his neck.

Oliver guides us back toward the bed. "You can always say no, Callie," he pants. His large hands rub up and down my sides, holding me together.

"Do I look like I'm saying no?" Lifting a brow, I reach between us, taking him in my hand and beginning to pump.

Oliver sucks in a breath, pushing himself deeper into my grip. "I need to get something, if we're really doing this," he chokes out.

"I'll warm up the bed," I grin, releasing him. He nods, making quick work of locating his toiletry bag while I slip between the covers. The cotton rubs against my sensitive skin, which nearly weeps when Oliver makes his way back to the bed, foil packet in hand.

Tossing it on the nightstand, the man takes his sweet time joining me.

"Dammit, Oliver," I groan, "are you trying to kill me?"

He has the audacity to smirk. "Death by sex? Probably not the worst way to go." Oliver climbs in beside me, pulling me up so that I'm sitting between his legs, my back to his chest. Gathering my hair, Oliver pulls it all over to one side and presses kisses along my bare shoulder.

"I don't know who you think you're sleeping with, but I am definitely not employed by the Cirque de Soleil cast." I press my hands onto his thighs to emphasize my point. "I can't reach you from here."

Oliver nips at my ear. "That's the point," he says, his warm breath sending heat radiating throughout my entire body. His hands rise to my peaked nipples, taking one in each hand and working them with expert precision. "I want to take care of you."

A moan slips out as I push my breasts further into his firm grip. The ache between my thighs grows more uncomfortable with each passing moment, causing me to squirm. My nails bite perfect crescents into his flesh.

"What do you need, Callie?" Oliver's low voice rumbles through his chest, the vibrations only making my desire more potent. "Tell me."

"You," I mewl while he continues his exquisite assault.

He grins into the nape of my neck. "Where, Callie? You have to show me." While one hand continues teasing me, the other finds my own.

Taking his hand in mine, I guide it to my center.

Scraping his thumb along the lace of my panties, he hums in appreciation. "I hope you're not too fond of these," he says, releasing my other nipple. Hooking his thumbs into the front of my underwear, Oliver rips them open so that they lay flat beneath me.

Looking back at him with a playful glare, I jut out my lower lip. "Those were my favorite ones."

Dipping his chin, Oliver pins me in place. "I'll buy you more. In every color, if that's what you want. So long as I can do this," he smirks. Spreading my legs with his own, Oliver presses a finger right where I need him most.

My hand flies behind my head, holding onto his neck as he touches me. Circles me. Claims me like a man obsessed.

As if he's trying to memorize every part of me.

Oliver nips along the shell of my ear while pressing his other hand flat onto my stomach to keep me still. Dipping one finger inside and then another, he stretches me as I climb higher with each pump of his fingers. "That's it, baby. I know you're ready. Let go."

A ragged breath drags itself from my lungs when he hooks

his fingers inside me, finding the perfect spot and triggering my release.

Oliver continues lavishing me with pleasure through my orgasm, shifting so that I'm laying beneath him when he finally pulls his fingers out of my body. He shifts to sit on his knees, greedy eyes taking me in.

A sated grin consuming my face, I loll my head toward the nightstand. Reaching out, I grab the packet, ripping it open. Turning hungry eyes to the man I love, I roll my lower lip between my teeth. "That was amazing. You're amazing," I sit up, taking Oliver in my hands and rolling the condom onto him, "but now I want all of you."

He wastes no time as I lay back, positioning himself between my legs. Oliver shifts his weight to impressive forearms. Pressing a single kiss above my heart, his lust-filled gaze meets mine. "You're the most amazing woman I've ever met, Calloway Rutherford."

Taking his face in my hands, I pull him up into a sloppy kiss as he pushes inside me.

Oliver's tongue demands entrance, which I happily give him. All too soon, he breaks the kiss, panting. He nods above my head. "Grab the headboard," he growls.

I immediately do as he says. Wrapping my fingers around the iron, I fold my legs around Oliver's sculpted waist, securing him to me.

He begins to move, driving me wild. His hands drift over my body, learning every part of me.

Tenderly at first, then demanding.

And when he flips me over, holding my hips and driving deeper, I scream his name into the pillow while he bites at the curve of my neck. Only when I've come again does a string of profanities accompany my name, falling from his lips like an everlasting oath.

## 18

*Oliver*

It's official—I never want to wake up without Calloway Rutherford draped across me ever again. Whether we stay in this moment forever, we're married with kids or we're old and gray, I want Callie by my side. I spend my working life listening to families spill their unhappiness about their situation so I can give them the tools to make a change for the better. People tell me about finding an ideal life and goals that they'll spend a lifetime chasing.

My new life snores softly on my chest as the Christmas morning light shines through the curtains.

Checking the time on my phone, I can't believe we haven't heard Marigold running down the hall declaring it's time to open gifts.

Maybe the soundproofing really is that good.

Judging from how loud we got last night, and the fact that no one came running, I guess it is.

Smirking to myself at the memories, I draw circles on Callie's bare back while I check messages from my family. Mom's eighteen pictures of Boston at Christmas and my grandma's house decorated for the holiday remind me that I still need to wrap their gifts for when we have our holiday celebration after they return. Dad's messages talk about some less than stellar meatloaf they ate for dinner the night before and how he's out of antacids. Blythe sent a picture of a small Christmas tree next to a palm tree along with one of her and another girl in dresses on the beach, both flanked by guys in pants and Hawaiian shirts. Annoyingly, I don't recognize the guy with his arm around my sister.

My neighbor, Cory, has sent me no less than twenty pictures of Nacho by his Christmas tree, having breakfast, being walked around the town square and enjoying countless treats.

Messages from John and Rindy also demand attention, letting me know they're having lunch today in the restaurant of the main building of the hotel, and asking if we'd want to join them.

Callie's hair tickles my chest as she stirs. Her eyes open, heavy with sleep as she looks around. Gaze landing on me, a lazy smile spreads across her face. "Good morning, Dr. Rhodes."

Replacing my phone on the nightstand, I turn my full attention to the enchanting woman before me. "Merry Christmas, Ms. Rutherford."

Those delicate ruby brows raise as she looks toward the balcony. "It's Christmas morning."

"Yep."

"Hm," Callie says, tapping her chin. Propping herself up on her elbows, her breasts graze my torso.

I shift so that my erection doesn't make her uncomfortable. Clearly, I have nothing to worry about since Callie drags a foot up my leg before tossing her entire limb over my waist—all the while rubbing whatever part of her is closest along my hardened length.

"I don't know about you," she continues, "but I kinda feel like I got my gift last night." Callie grins at me. "A few times."

Heat floods my cheeks. "Actually, I have something else for you, too," I admit sheepishly.

Callie's grin widens. "I know. I can feel it."

"Not that," I laugh, "but hold on to that thought." Bracing her with one arm, I shift to grab the gift box from my nightstand. Holding the little box wrapped in green paper featuring cartoon plants, I offer it to her. "Merry Christmas, my love."

Callie leans onto her side, taking the gift. Big doe eyes meet mine. Her silent question emanates from every feature.

Tucking her in close with my palm already on her back, I grasp her hip with the other. One deep breath, and here goes nothing. "I love you, Callie."

"You love me?"

The disbelief still lingering in her voice takes hold of my heart. Channeling all my love for her into my grip, I pull Callie flush to me. I make sure I have this woman's full attention before continuing. "I do, Calloway," I nod, "I really do. I love you." My chest feels a little lighter each time I utter the words.

So I don't stop.

"I. Love. You, Callie," I whisper, a smile taking over my face.

Tender eyes trace my eyes, nose, and lips.

"And I don't want you to feel like you have to say anything—"

"I love you, too," Callie beams, "so much." A breath of sweet relief rushes from her lips, as if she's been holding in a secret that's desperately wanted out.

My answering grin nearly splits my face in two. Unable to help myself, I crush her to my chest, Callie's arms winding around my neck in the process. Pressing a kiss into her hair, I exhale my own sigh of relief. "So this is real?" I ask, just to be sure.

Callie giggles. "This is real, Oliver." Pillowy lips stamp a tender kiss over my heart.

Her leg still draped over my waist, I help her resituate to a sitting position so that she's straddling me. My fingertips graze her flushed cheek, and Callie's empty hand steadies herself on my abs. "Open it," I say, nodding to the box.

Callie leans back, excitedly untying the green velvet ribbon. She slips a thumbnail under the paper, carefully removing it, and by the time only the unwrapped box remains, we could reuse the silly gift wrap if we wanted. She opens the green velvet box and gasps. "Oliver, it's beautiful." Callie gingerly lifts the necklace from its holder, placing the box on the nightstand. Her bright smile shines my way. "Help me put it on?"

Taking the delicate chain from her, I secure it around her neck as she holds her hair out of the way. The yellow gold of the four-point star shimmers off her skin, perfectly high-lighting the superimposed half carat marquis ruby. The short chain allows it to lay just below her collarbone, glimmering with every movement. "The stone reminded me of your hair," I admit.

Tipping her chin to get a better look, her fingers gently brush the pendant. "It's absolutely stunning, Oliver, really," she gushes, "thank you." Callie leans down so that our lips meet in the small amount of space I've allowed to remain between us. When she pulls back, a beautiful blush stains her cheeks. "I actually have something for you, too."

Curiosity gets the best of me as I lift my brows.

"But there's something I'd like to take care of first," she says, a wicked grin taking over my sweet girl's face.

Heat races through my system, my entire body flushing with anticipation. "Callie … " I warn. But my grin doesn't falter.

Walking her hands up my chest, one wraps around the

nape of my neck as she pulls me into a kiss. The other grabs the last unopened foil packet from my nightstand. Breaking the kiss, Callie rips the pack open with her teeth. I help lift her so she can roll on the condom before she sits back down, sheathing me within her warmth.

"That's the last one," I tell her.

Callie smiles, the backs of her fingers brushing along my face. "Then we'd better make it count."

When we're both spent once more and Callie has collapsed on top of me, my love runs her hand through my hair. "You're in pretty good shape, you know."

Snorting, I rub my palms along her back. "Gee, thanks."

"You just seem to be busy," she says, adjusting so that I can get up to take care of the aftermath. Callie wraps the blanket around herself as I head into the bathroom. "I guess I'm just surprised you have time to go to the gym."

Twisting the shower knob, warm water sprays to life. "I get the feeling I'm about to have a lot less time," I call.

The sound of mattress springs whining rings through the air as Callie gets up, joining me in the bathroom. Her necklace glistens even in the fluorescent bathroom lighting. "Only if I can help it." She grins up at me as she slips past and gets into the steamy shower, gathering her long hair into a bun. The shower door remains open, and my love bats criminally long eyelashes at me.

Shaking my head, I groan. "If I get in that shower with you, we'll never make it downstairs."

"Maybe that's the point."

A gruff chuckle slips between my lips. "As tempting as that is, we're out of protection."

Callie scrunches her nose in acknowledgment. "Should've brought more, Rhodes. Did you ... plan on getting lucky?" she asks hesitantly, eyes dropping.

Marching forward, I grasp her chin between my fingers and

bring her gaze to mine. "Believe me, I never dreamed I'd get this lucky." Pressing a kiss to the tip of her nose, I smile down at the woman I love. "But we do need to hurry—we've got a lunch date with John, Rindy and Jo at the lodge after the family stuff."

Callie salutes me before shutting the shower door. "On it, Rhodes."

We're both showered and dressed in record time, with jeans and ugly Christmas sweaters on full display. Between the two of us, Callie's hot pink top with a raccoon holding a present definitely beats out my sweater with a llama in a Santa hat.

Flicking off the light in the bathroom, I'm met with the most amazing woman waiting for me with a small gift box in those precious hands.

My love beams. "Merry Christmas, Oliver."

Even after everything we've already shared, pink still tints my freshly-shaven face at the thought of her taking the time for something so thoughtful.

And just for me.

Callie holds out the box, that glorious grin widening with every passing moment. "Open it."

Turning the box over in my hands, I examine the paper she's chosen. "Brown?" I laugh, my brow lifting.

She shrugs. "It's your favorite color."

I laugh, nodding.

"Um, why exactly do you have such an exciting color choice as your favorite?" she asks, pressing her lips together. She's clearly trying not to judge and failing miserably.

A soft smile takes residence on my face as I look into my favorite eyes in the entire world. "Reminds me of someone I love."

Understanding dawns on her as I proceed to tear open the paper, uncovering the box hiding beneath it. Lifting the lid, a few items wait inside the box. My lips part in awe as I pull out a stunning cocoa brown leather collar and leash set with Nacho's name debossed into the material.

"I thought the color would look nice on her fur," Callie whispers shyly. "And it's sturdy for when you take her on hikes."

"When *we* take her," I amend.

Callie's face, open and honest, displays a love she's never been shown before. A love that I will spend the rest of my life giving to her. "We?"

Nodding, I grin. "She'll want her new mom to come with us, of course."

Those delicate brows reach her hairline. "I think I missed the part where we're getting married, Rhodes."

"I don't really see any other way forward," I shrug, "but don't worry, I'll get an official proposal lined up when we get home."

Callie smiles, rolling amused eyes. "There's more." She points to the box.

Setting Nacho's new gift on the bed, I reach back into the box. My fingers grip something soft and I pull out a sage green ballcap. Callie giggles as I flip it around to the front where the words 'Team Nacho' are embroidered. My full belly laugh fills the room. "I love it." Tossing the empty box on the bed, I situate the cap on my head, grinning proudly. "What do you think?"

"A perfect fit." Callie grins right back. Lifting it off my head, she carefully places it by the leash and collar. "You can wear it to bed tonight." She winks, eliciting another laugh from me.

"We're out, remember?"

Callie spins slowly on the ball of her foot, turning back toward the door. "I'd bet the gift shop in the lodge can take care of that."

Smirking, I shake my head. "Insatiable woman."

"Only when it comes to you. Now, come on. They probably think we fell off the balcony or something."

"Would that be the worst thing?"

She scoffs. "Maybe not." Callie's hand pauses halfway to the doorknob. "You never told me," she says, looking back over her shoulder.

My brows knit together as I look at the love of my life. Someone I, in no way, deserve. Someone I ended up in the strangest situation with, only to have the rest of my life unfold before me. "Told you what?"

"What's your favorite thing about me?" The corner of her mouth lifts, her eyebrow following suit.

A soft chuckle fills the air. Tucking a stray hair behind her ear, I smile. "How you can make anyone fall in love with you."

Callie blinks. Uncertainty is written into her every feature. "Even you, right?" Her voice is small, quiet. Like she's afraid I'll recant my feelings.

Moving so that I'm standing behind her, I wrap my arms around Callie's shoulders and pull her into my chest. Callie reaches up, taking hold of my forearms as I press a kiss to her temple. "Especially me, Calloway. My love."

Tension releases from her shoulders as she slumps against me with relief.

"I love you, Callie," I whisper in her ear. My new favorite words, just for her.

My favorite person glances up, eyes meeting mine. Love blazes in the warm amber peeking up at me. "I love you too, Oliver."

PRESCOTT LEANS BACK into the sectional, exhausted from trying to keep up with his daughter's impressive gift-opening speed.

All while wearing a Barbie sweater, just to make Goldie happy.

Apparently, Ira and Lillian are the only two who are allowed to abstain from that particular tradition.

Christmas music plays softly in the background, mingling with the quintessential crackling fireplace. Sugar and cinnamon swirl in the air, surrounding the Rutherfords, who look the happiest I've seen them to date. If they were my patients, I would certainly feel good about their progress.

The love of my life leans into my arm that's tucked around her shoulders, taking a sip from her hot chocolate.

"Look, Daddy!" Marigold holds up a doll with historical clothes and a corresponding book.

A tired smile graces his features. "That's so neat, sweets. Who got you that one?" Prescott takes the book, flipping through it.

Marigold gives the doll a tight hug. "Aunt Connie." The little girl hops up from her spot on the floor, bounding over to her aunt and giving her a big hug and kiss.

Ira snaps numerous pictures of Marigold with each new gift while his wife steadily supplies her granddaughter with Christmas morning treats.

Callie and I watch from the opposite end of the couch, curled up into one another.

My girlfriend glows as she watches her sweet niece.

Pulling Callie closer with the arm around her shoulders, I lean down to her ear. "That'll be us one day."

"Having Goldie thank us for a doll?"

Biting back a grin, I roll my eyes. "Watching our kids open gifts on Christmas morning."

Callie's chocolate eyes snap to mine. Love coats her kind face as she nods. "I want two. Enough that they could have a buddy, but not enough for them to get lost in a crowd." My love smirks. "Or for them to outnumber us."

My heart soars at the 'us.'

Leaning down to kiss the tip of her nose, my heart nearly bursts. "Anything you want, my love."

I'm in the middle of wondering if my parents will think I've lost my mind when I tell them I want to propose, when Imogene turns to face us from the other side of Callie. "Do you think Mom's trying to fill Marigold with snacks so she'll sleep the rest of the day?"

Callie laughs as my brow furrows. Looking between the two women, I ask, "Does that actually work?"

Imogene frowns. "I thought you spent a lot of time with kids."

"Only short timeframes," I answer. "My business partner, John, has a daughter about Marigold's age, though."

"Right, the one in Calloway's class."

"Yep," I nod. Frowning, I think about all the times Cici has hung out at the practice. "Now that I think about it, he is always feeding her."

Callie's sister lets out a light laugh. "I just know that trick always worked on Calloway and the twins when they were little. So I think Mom's just sticking with what she knows. If they were all asleep, we could watch holiday movies with a little more of a bite to them."

"So *Christmas Vacation*?"

"Exactly," she grins. Pulling a knit blanket further up her legs, Imogene offers the afghan to Callie, as well. A reserved smile warms Imogene's face as my love accepts the offering.

I can't help but wonder if it was really just a way to hide her red, bell-embellished monstrosity of a sweater.

Leaning down to Callie's ear, I whisper, "Imogene isn't seeing anyone, correct?"

Callie quirks a brow, moving so that her lips touch the shell of my ear. "Tired of me already?"

Smirking, I roll my eyes. "I was thinking about John."

Callie peeks over at her oldest sister, who has gone back to watching Marigold frenzy at the stockings. "Huh." Her brows knit together, and Callie bites her lower lip in concentration. "Maybe. She's never really dated much. I don't even know what kind of partner she would like."

Turning my attention back to the tiny center of Lillian and Ira's world, I can't help but wonder what John would make of Callie's oldest sister.

"Here, Goldie," Chris says, handing his niece another gift box featuring a large red bow. "Aunt Connie helped me pick this one out to go with your doll." It's the only time I've ever seen the man crack a smile that wasn't at his youngest sister's expense.

Though how the man could remain serious wearing a sweater with an oversized rabbit holding a cake is beyond me.

Marigold plops to the floor in front Chris and Connie, tearing into the gift and producing a white plush dog and accessory kit. The little girl squeals in delight, inspiring laughter from everyone in the room. "It's Coco!" Goldie jumps up and shows off the dog. Clutching Coco to her chest, Goldie pounces into Chris's lap and plants a big kiss on his cheek.

To his credit, the man who's been nothing but a giant pain in my ass blushes at Marigold's affection. Holding his niece, he helps her open the dog's accessories from the packaging while Connie opens the doll.

Checking my watch, I nudge Callie. "We're supposed to meet the others in about twenty minutes." I murmur in her ear. "We don't have to go if you want to stay here."

Nodding, she smiles. "I want to. I'll get my coat."

"Where are you two going?" Imogene asks as Callie stands and heads toward the kitchen.

Still not used to Imogene speaking much, it takes a moment to understand she's talking to me. "To meet my friend John. He and his daughter have been here the past couple of days." I stand, following Callie's example. "And now his sister, the other doctor at our practice, and her wife are here for lunch. So we're going to go meet up with them for a bit."

Movement from the kitchen catches my eye. A glimmer in the sunlight thanks to all the massive windows.

Callie is showing off her necklace to Connie.

Pressing my lips together, I try to suppress the irrational pride of having Callie be excited to show off something I bought her. And then attempt to keep my thoughts away from ring shopping on a day when all the stores are closed. Instead, I make a mental note to ask Ian about what kind of ring Callie would like best.

Connie's eyes meet mine, a satisfied grin greeting me. She gives my love a hug before leaning to whisper something in her ear.

A clap on my shoulder brings my attention back to the Christmas chaos taking place in the living room. Ira Rutherford stands beside me, watching his daughters interact.

I've never been jealous of what another man was wearing before, but Ira's Oxford button-down has never looked better than right now.

"You know, I think you've had an interesting effect on our family, Rhodes." He shakes my shoulder, grip tightening.

"I promise, it's all Callie, sir," I say, nodding to the woman of my dreams.

He laughs in the skeptical way men like him do. "Whatever it is, keep it up."

"I'll do my best." Silence fills the space between us until Ira realizes he's missing Marigold searching for the Christmas pickle ornament.

Callie makes her way back to me, coat in hand. "What was that about?" She casts a glance toward her father's retreating figure.

I follow her gaze. "Proof that this whole endeavor was a

good idea, after all," I say and offer her my hand as we head to the garage in search of my car.

The drive up to the main lodge is short. Thanks to the several snowplows Aspen Point keeps on hand, we have no problem maneuvering to the main parking area and making it to the restaurant with time to spare.

Aspen Point Lodge's restaurant is packed full of people ready to spend some quality time away from their beloved families. With bright walls, ample windows, and expensive furnishings, it's easy to see the appeal—especially if you like spending an insane amount of money on a salad.

"Oliver! Callie!" John waves us to a table tucked back in a corner. My best friend, in his very normal attire. "Woah, nice sweaters," he says as we drape our coats on the chairs.

Rolling my eyes, I take a seat by Joanna while Callie sits by Cici, who waves at me before wrapping her tiny arms around her teacher.

Rindy's unwavering eyes bounce between us. "Something's different," she mutters. Dark eyes narrow while her slender fingers mess with the noisy golden bangles on her wrist.

Fighting the instinct to shield Callie from my friend's shrewd gaze, I pin my colleague with a stare. "Yes, but nothing you should say in front of the present company." Brows raised, I nod toward Cici.

Jo turns to her wife. "I knew I liked her."

Pretending to ignore us, Callie blushes beside me while Cici shows her a drawing.

John leans back in his chair, a smug look accompanying crossed arms. "Glad you finally decided to tell her."

"You knew?" Rindy accuses her brother.

He snorts. "Of course I knew. He called me yesterday morning."

That piques my love's interest, her brows raising as she grins at me. "That's right, you mentioned all of John's early morning activities." Her enchanting laugh rings through the air as she turns to my friend. "I'm so sorry he interrupted your feeding a hog and winning a Nobel Peace Prize all before seven AM."

John waves her off. "If it got him to pull his head from where the sun doesn't shine, then it was worth it."

Cici pokes her head up; her eyes nearly as bright as her red Christmas dress find me immediately. "Oliver, are you and Ms. Rutherford like Aunt Rindy and Aunt Jo now?"

Callie suppresses a smile.

"I'm working on that, missy ma'am." I grin at the little girl who is practically my niece. "But we're on our way."

Cici beams up at my girlfriend. "Good, because I love Ms. Rutherford."

"Me too, Ci," I say, leaning my elbows onto the table, "me too." My gaze sweeps to the woman beside me, a smile tugging at my lips.

Rindy snorts. "I never thought we'd see the day Ollie fell in love." Her joking narrowed eyes peer across the table. "Well, with anyone other than Nacho."

Cici perks up. "I drew a picture of Nacho for you," she tells me. That girl's grin is infectious as she turns to Callie. "Guess what, Ms. Rutherford—"

"Calloway Rutherford?"

Our entire table turns toward the male voice behind Callie and I.

A brunette man about Callie's age in a white dress shirt, slacks, and navy sportcoat gives my girlfriend a look that's a little too friendly for my liking. His small but fit frame tells me he's never experienced hard labor a day in his life, while his tanned leathery skin reeks of too much baby oil at the beach. The man's thin lips pull back into a sleazy smile, dull gray eyes raking over Callie's sweater and stopping exactly where they shouldn't.

"The Rutherfords still adhere to the worst tradition, huh?" He nods to her top.

"Hello Alexander." Callie's cool but polite tone tells me exactly who this is.

Reaching between us, I hold out my hand. "Dr. Oliver Rhodes. And you are?" My tight smile feels like I just sucked a lemon, but I'm not about to let this guy think he has the upper hand.

His lifeless eyes slide to me as he takes my hand. "Alexander Lawrence. How do you do?" Reclaiming his hand, Mr. Lawrence's hungry eyes slide back to a disinterested Callie.

"Lawrence," Jo mutters. She looks up at the newcomer. "As in one of the industry leaders of mining fossil fuels and actively conducting research on artificial duplication of renewables? Lawrence Efficiency Corporation? *That* Lawrence?"

The smug prick puffs out his chest, clutching the slim lapels of his jacket. "It's my family's company, but I am first in the line of succession when my father retires."

Callie's lips form a flat line as she sighs. Taking her hand under the table is the least I can do—a gesture that earns me a sly smile. "Is there something you needed, Alex?"

"Alexander," he corrects.

It takes every ounce of my willpower to not haul him outside to learn a little respect.

"Just thought I'd see what other Rutherfords I could find before I sat down with my family," he shrugs.

Doing my best to swallow the simmering irritation of Alexander's presence, I sling an arm around Callie. Never taking my eyes off my girlfriend, I dismiss him. "Thanks for stopping by, man, but I need to feed this one. See you around."

Callie grins, mirroring my growing smile.

Alexander grumbles some excuse about cold salad as he heads off into the crowded restaurant.

Rindy, that dear woman, doesn't bother with formalities. "Ex-boyfriend?"

"Our fathers are friends," Callie groans. "They thought we'd be good together. My brother encouraged it."

My grip around her shoulders tightens at the thought of her with another guy.

Especially that one.

"Geez, if that's the kind of guy your family set you up with, then I'm glad Oliver agreed to a fake relationship—"

Beside his sister, John's eyes widen. "Rindy, be quiet."

Following his stare, my entire system short-circuits. Jaw dropping, I can't tell Rindy to shut up fast enough.

Eye twitching and nostrils flared, Chris Rutherford is rage incarnate.

"Because if that's how the rest of your family treats you, they deserve to be gaslighted."

Chris grinds his jaw. "I knew it."

# 19

*Callie*

Opening the interior garage door to the residence is like walking into a funeral parlor. A thick, heavy silence hangs over the main room with every single occupant feeling bereft and confused. There are no records crooning softly in the background. No fire popping in the hearth. Despite the warmth, a chill sends shivers down my spine.

My parents and siblings, with the exception of Prescott, all sit on the sectional, and I send a quick thanks to the hot chocolate gods that Goldie must be upstairs taking a nap.

It feels like the night I told everyone I wanted to be a teacher.

Disappointment.

Condescension at the audacity to choose something so mundane.

Only Connie showed me any kind of encouragement for something so outside our family's standards.

No matter how fast Oliver and I ran from the table and back to the car, Chris was faster. The volume of the crowded restaurant only made our pursuit that much harder. Anyone who knew me tried to stop us, looking questioningly at Oliver and primed for Rutherford family gossip. Unfortunately, I'll have to tell my parents there will be some social relationships they may need to repair after I all but shoved one of Dad's sleazy business associates out of the way.

Even if I would never admit that I've wanted to do just that for several years now.

Connie peeks up at us from her spot on the couch. Eyes wide, her face conveys every horror I've dreaded since that night in Theo's. The night my world shifted.

The night Oliver and I agreed to deceive our families.

My heart and stomach fight to be the most dramatic organ, twisting themselves into knots and becoming lodged in my throat.

Oliver stops half a step behind me, yielding to my judgement of how best to proceed in the Rutherford minefield. His warm knuckles brush against mine.

Despite the cold seeping into my bones at the situation before us, Oliver being right here with me does strange things to me.

Like giving me confidence knowing I don't have to face this alone.

Imogene rings her slender hands together, a brow furrowed in concentration. She furtively glances at our stoic and cautious mother, clearly hoping for some kind of direction on how to proceed about something so unprecedented.

Mom lifts her face from the veil her hands have been providing. Sighing, her glazed look makes its way to me. "Calloway ... "

My feet take me further into the space, reaching the back of the sectional where I have a front row seat to the back of Chris's head. "Please, let me explain."

My father's voice cuts through the air, causing me to startle. "No." The word is sharp, threatening harm to any who dare contradict it. An unnatural shade of red paints his face as he turns to look at us. Dad stands slowly from the couch with an expression I've only seen on him during litigation that's going poorly.

Or when he would berate any of the older Rutherford children for showing anything short of extreme excellence.

One that reads as calm and collected while he rages below the surface.

"Ira," Mom cautions.

"Not now, Lillian." Dad holds out a hand to silence whatever was going to come next.

The gesture has Imogene recoiling, as well. Worried brown eyes flick from us, to Dad, and back while my oldest sister is clearly churning through some kind of internal turmoil.

"Why don't I go first?" Dad says politely, each word more clipped than the last. His hawk-like eyes are trained on my rapidly heating face. "My son just told us how you and—" angry eyes cut to the man standing beside me "—that man have been using a bogus romantic relationship to manipulate our family. Now, I can't really say I know why you would want to do that, exactly, but I would sure be interested to learn. Calloway, start talking. Now."

Oliver tries to step in front of me, but I manage to keep the front position. If anyone should be in the direct line of fire here, it shouldn't be him.

"I'm waiting." My father's voice is low, ominous.

I look my father in the eye when the next words leave my mouth. "No one has called me a glorified babysitter since

Thanksgiving," I whisper. It wasn't something I'd been aware of until this very moment.

But it's a truth that Oliver has helped bring about.

Dad's face contorts in disgusted confusion. "What?"

"The family joke that nearly everyone else has been in on since I graduated college?" My voice comes out stronger this time. Despite the slight tremor in my words, I can feel the flush rising in my cheeks. "Or rather, since the day I announced my major. That was the first time. And one time was all it took." My fists clench, pressing into my sides.

Oliver places a steadying palm on my lower back.

The calming effect on my nerves is instantaneous.

Dad's eyes don't miss the movement. Pointing an intimidating finger at my boyfriend, his eyes bulge. "You," he roars, "get your hand off my daughter. This is all your fault."

"Dad—"

"My family is hurt because of *you*," he spits.

When Oliver tries to step in front of me this time, he succeeds. "Because of me?" Incredulity colors every syllable. Anger rolls off of him in sheets. "What about Callie? Your entire family has done little except hurt her for years."

Dad scoffs, waving him off. "If Calloway can't take a joke or live up to her full potential, then that's on her."

"Calloway is the strongest person I've ever met. You should all be ashamed of how you've treated her over the years, some of which I've had the misfortune of witnessing firsthand." Oliver fumes. "And that is my professional opinion."

Imogene leans forward in her seat while Dad tries to gather his jaw from the floor. "So Calloway brought you in to ... what, exactly? I mean, you really are a therapist—and a good one. We looked you up after you came to Thanksgiving. What was the end goal here?"

Oliver reaches backward until his strong hand finds mine, unfurling my fist and intertwining our personal universes. "I was supposed to help balance the family dynamics, however that needed to happen."

Chris, who has been annoyingly silent throughout this entire discourse, snorts. "And you needed to act like you're in love with her to do that?" He looks over his shoulder with narrowed eyes, finding our point of connection immediately. "No offense but, like we told you at the school that night, you could do way better than Calloway."

Oliver's hand inadvertently strangles mine while he clearly focuses on not punching Chris in the face.

Something I've only had the satisfaction of doing once when we were teenagers. It didn't end well.

For me.

Our parents took Chris's side, naturally.

Connie, on the other hand, smacks Chris on the arm. My sweet, timid sister who dominates the financial world and acts like little woodland creatures help dress her each morning absolutely radiates fury.

Chris yelps. "Connie, what the hell?"

"I've told you for years to quit being such an ass to Calloway."

"Only because you have feelings for one of her best friends," her twin sneers.

Connie rears back like she's been slapped. "Excuse me, but I've never needed a reason to be kind to my sister, thank you. You, however, have only ever taken pleasure in ridiculing her for something she's passionate about. What if you have kids one day?"

Chris snorts, and Connie slaps him again.

I'd find it hilarious if I wasn't so stunned.

"Have you ever considered that your younger sister may actually have a more difficult job than you and I do?"

"No," he retorts.

"That's because you're an idiot," she bellows. "Our jobs are stressful because they involve other people's finances, sure. But Calloway? She spends her working hours molding the next generation. I know I couldn't do that job. I know for a fact that you wouldn't be able to, either." Connie pokes her twin in the ribs. "Yet, year after year, you and Prescott have made fun of her profession, never letting her forget that you two think she's beneath the rest of us."

Chris gapes at her while the rest of us hold our breath.

That's the most Constance Irene Rutherford has ever said in front of everyone at once.

And she's defending me.

Dad stares bewildered at his favorite daughter. "Darling," he starts in a tone I've heard five thousand times. As if Connie's some wounded animal, like her voice makes her out to be.

But she turns on him, too. Whirling around to face our father, Connie stands. Setting her jaw, Connie folds her arms across her chest. "And you, Daddy, you've done nothing but encourage them this entire time." Her voice loses some of its previous edge, replaced instead by heartache that her favorite parent would dare to be so cruel, as her frame begins to tremble.

Releasing Oliver's hand, I move to stand by my favorite sibling. Gently, I grasp her shoulders. "Connie, it's okay," I whisper.

Sorrowful eyes cut to mine. She shakes her head. "No, it's not, Calloway." Those large emerald eyes swell with unshed tears.

Swallowing, I push down the guilt building in my core. All I wanted was to be seen as worth something in my family. Instead, the only one who has ever seemed to care about me within the walls of our childhood home is hurting. All because of me.

"You were right to enlist Oliver's help," Connie insists.

Dad rubs his face in disbelief. "Darling girl, are you saying you knew about this?" His soft eyes reserved only for Connie turn hard as they slide to me.

"I found out after Thanksgiving."

Wide eyes take in his newly defiant daughter. "And you didn't say anything?"

Connie lets out a humorless laugh. "What would you have wanted to hear, Daddy? That Calloway is finally happy? Because that was the main thing that changed. The man she brought to dinner did nothing but help her."

Movement directly behind us lets me know that Chris is a lot closer than I'd like at this very moment. "By lying to us, Connie," Chris interjects, "and through complete manipulation." His hand clamps down on my shoulder, turning me toward his glare.

Connie snaps her heated gaze back to her twin. "You mean by not humoring your jokes at his girlfriend's expense?"

"They're not actually dating!" Chris shouts. "Or have you miraculously somehow missed that part in your crusade to rescue Calloway?"

"Actually, we are." Oliver's calm voice slices through the tension in the air. Silence falls over the room at his assured tone while strong, confident steps echo with each stride as he reclaims a spot by my side. I twist around to face him, those eyes that always seem to anchor me never leaving mine. "Christopher, your continued lack of observation and concern for your family members outside of Connie are quite the disappointment. Especially considering Callie and I have done nothing but flaunt our relationship the entire time I've known you. But I suppose I shouldn't be too surprised." Oliver shrugs. "It's not totally uncommon inside of twin relationships, particularly when one is often found to be more co-dependent than the other."

"But-but that woman," he sputters, "in the restaurant—"

"My colleague was operating on old information, which you

would know if you had bothered to speak with us directly instead of running off with nothing but hearsay." Oliver turns to my brother, crossing his arms.

I don't think I will ever get over hearing this man refer to this as an 'us' situation. In spite of this insane predicament, my insides become increasingly in danger of liquifying.

"Now," Oliver nods to where Chris's hand is still pressing down on my shoulder with more force than necessary, "take your hand off my girlfriend. And take note, Christopher, this is the only time I will ask nicely."

Chris peels his fingers off me one by one. It only takes Oliver dipping his chin to stare at my brother before Chris takes a couple of measured steps back.

Dropping my other hand from Connie, I shift closer to Oliver until his unmistakable warmth seeps through my sweater.

Imogene and Mom watch us from the couch like a film they hadn't planned on seeing and are about to demand their money back.

But it's Dad's look of resolve that bothers me most. "It's Christmas," he says matter-of-fact, "with my family, that I've worked to provide for for nearly forty years." His eyes flit over our heads. "And that means that I get to determine how our holiday goes."

Rustling comes from behind me and sets my every nerve on edge. "I think I got everything." Prescott stops at the foot of the stairs, Oliver's packed bag in hand.

That little weasel.

He nods to our father.

I don't bother stopping my bitter laughter. "What?" Standing straight to my full height, I narrow unamused eyes at my dad. "Are you kicking Oliver out or something?"

"You know, Calloway, I am," he replies calmly. "And if he refuses to leave, I'm happy to press charges. It's his choice."

Nothing. No sadness. No fear.

No anger.

No regret.

I feel absolutely nothing as my father looks at me like an attorney holding court. Like he's reached checkmate. As if he holds all the cards.

Because in his mind, he does.

Oliver shifts behind me, placing a hand on my shoulder. "It's okay, Callie. I'll go."

Dad's smug grin deepens at Oliver's concession.

Nodding, I turn to look at the man I love. Resting my palms on his chest, the beat of his heart gives away every ounce of fury he's holding back. Even knowing what's coming next, I can't stop the swell of emotion the man brings out of me. "I understand. And ... I just want to thank you for everything you've done for me."

Oliver's brow furrows. Blinking rapidly, he swallows. "Um, of course, Callie. I love you, and I'd do anything for you."

Someone in the background, probably Chris, makes a disgusted noise.

A soft smile forms on my lips as I look into the loving eyes I've come to know as my home. It quickly turns into a full-blown grin as Oliver's eyes narrow, attempting to determine the sudden shift in my demeanor.

Then Oliver Grant Rhodes, the amazing man that he is, understands. "You're sure about this?" His voice is low, cautious.

"Sure about what?" my father demands.

Beside me, Connie smiles approvingly.

"Yep," I nod. Sighing, I take his hand. "I guess that means you're good with driving me home, then?"

"Of course, my love," he beams, fingers intertwining with mine. "That was always the plan."

"Calloway Leora Rutherford," my father plants tense fists on his hips, "you're not going anywhere."

Spinning around to face him, a sense of calm I never thought I'd feel when faced with this very moment washes through me. "Actually, I am."

My dad's face takes on a fifth shade of red. "Have you lost your mind?"

"Nope," I say, shaking my head around in a stilted motion, "it's still rattling around in there."

He scoffs. "All of your things are still upstairs."

"Yeah, Calloway," Prescott interjects, "I only packed Oliver's things."

Connie perks up, turning to me. "I'll bring all your things over tomorrow," she says, further wounding our father. She pulls me in for a tight embrace, which is made slightly awkward since neither Oliver nor I let go of the other.

"Thank you," I whisper in her ear.

Connie leans away, giving me a short nod in acknowledgment.

Looking back at my father, I deliver the checkmate. "I'm twenty-seven years old and can make my own choices. And if I'm faced with a choice between spending today with people who don't see me as an equal, or with someone who has been supportive of me since we met, I believe I'd choose the latter every time. Merry Christmas, everyone." I take a moment to look everyone in the eyes, only letting the tiniest bit of guilt leak in when I reach Imogene and Connie.

To my intense surprise, Imogene doesn't look the least bit upset, instead opting to let slivers of pride break through her stoic exterior.

Connie just acts like she's ready to shoo us out the door herself so that we can get back to enjoying our day.

Oliver and I share a look as we head back toward the garage door. One that says neither of us are backing out now.

That we're a team and we're in this together.

When we reach Prescott, he hands over Oliver's bag, unable

to look my boyfriend in the eye. "Calloway," he says as we start to walk away.

My feet stop, tuning in to my annoying penchant for curiosity.

Oliver's protective eyes never leave my face, watching for any sign Prescott's upset me.

My brother palms the back of his neck. "I'm sorry," he mutters. His guilty brown eyes meet mine before finding something interesting on the floor.

"Tell Goldie I'm sorry we had to go, okay?"

Swallowing, he nods without another word.

Oliver and I walk hand in hand to the car we parked haphazardly in our haste to get to my family before Chris could. If everything wasn't so messed up, I'd probably find the poor parking job entertaining.

He makes quick work of tossing his bag in the back and opens my door for me, when a noise from the house catches our attention. Tucking me in close, his stance relaxes when Connie comes into view.

Stepping out of Oliver's hold, I watch as my sister's nose pinkens with every passing second. "What's wrong?" The worry I've tried to bury colors the words more than I'd like.

Oliver presses a kiss to my temple. "I'll warm up the car," he murmurs into my hair before walking around to the driver's side. Moments later the car roars to life.

Connie's arms wrap around herself in an attempt to keep warm as she reaches the car. "I just, I'm so sorry," she says, shaking her head.

"This is so not your fault."

"I never thought ... he's such an idiot."

"Dad? Or Chris?"

Wet laughter bubbles from her lips. Unshed tears glisten in her eyes and I pull her into a hug. "Well, both I guess," she laughs, wiping her running nose.

I don't bother stopping my dark chuckle.

"I'll talk to them."

"Connie, no."

"Yes," she insists. "They'll want to discuss it, anyway. Let me make that conversation useful."

Nodding, I look at my older sister.

"If it makes you feel any better, Imogene was already prepared to claw Prescott's eyes out for helping Daddy," she laughs.

I grin across the small space between us. "You know, it does."

"Text me so I know you got home safe?"

"Yes, Mom," I tease, rolling my eyes.

Connie runs back into the warmth for dear life as I climb into the car, all my bravado suddenly slipping.

Oliver reaches over, taking my hand. His thumb rubs circles on my skin, calming the nerves threatening to take over.

We drive in silence for nearly twenty minutes. Only the sound of the car's heater keeps us company and the farther away we get from Aspen Point Lodge, the higher my anxiety creeps.

Oliver must sense the change as he peeks over at me from the driver's seat. "Are you okay?" he whispers, squeezing my hand.

"Can I ask a favor?"

"Yeah baby?"

"I need you to pull over, or I might just throw up in your car."

## 20

*Oliver*

After dropping Callie off at her apartment, I make it back to my own in record time. Callie had asked if I would want to stay at her place tonight and, while there's no way I'm going to pass up an opportunity to be in her presence, I do need fresh clothes. Especially considering what's left in my suitcase is a little fancier than is necessary to hang out at her place.

And I need to get Nacho.

I think Callie's as excited to have Nacho there as she is to have me around, which is fine. It just further confirms she's the right woman for me.

Callie said she'd be more than fine on her own for a bit. In all honesty, I think she needed a little time alone to start processing everything.

I'd be lying if I said I didn't.

Unlocking and opening my front door, I'm greeted by the

familiar bark of my favorite furry companion. "Hey girl." I grin down at Nacho and her ever-wagging tail. I make a quick mental note to send Cory another thank you text for taking her out one more time just a bit ago before bringing her home.

Nacho barks once more, just in case I somehow missed the first one.

Dropping my bag on the kitchen table, I turn my full attention to the best girl. Kneeling to the floor, I receive plenty of welcome kisses while rubbing and scratching any part of her I can reach. "I missed you too, little one," I coo.

Nacho's enthusiastic tongue slaps at my face like a raw slice of bacon, her tail thumping the wall in a rhythmic pattern.

Looking into her joyous eyes, it's almost impossible to believe that today really happened. But it did, and now there's an incredible woman waiting for us to return to her. Standing, I ask, "Wanna go see Callie?"

The best girl jumps to stand on my shoulders with one more bark of confirmation.

Chuckling, I set Nacho back on all fours before preparing her supper and grabbing food for tomorrow at Callie's. I use the time she's eating to take a quick shower and pack a bag of fresh essentials.

By the time I zip up the overnight case and grab my bag for work tomorrow, Nacho is waiting impatiently on my bed. She lets out a sigh of great despair when I head back into the closet.

"Hang on, little missy," I laugh, "I know you want to see Callie as bad as I do."

Sweet, amber eyes that remind me of someone else I love practically roll when I finally emerge. She eyes the belt in my hand.

"Figured it wouldn't hurt to have an extra. My other is on its last leg," I explain. "You wouldn't want my pants to fall down, would you?"

Nacho ignores me, clearly unimpressed by my potential fashion dilemma.

"Alright, alright," I say, securing the belt in my bag, "one more thing." Picking up the new collar, I make the swap from Nacho's bright purple nylon one to the thoughtful gift from Callie. "What do you think? Do you like it?"

Nacho hops up and struts around on the bed.

Giving her a solid pat on the side, I chuckle. "I think that's a yes. You ready?"

One bark later, and we're in the car heading back to the newest member of our family.

Callie texted me saying her front door would be unlocked, so Nacho and I let ourselves in when we arrive.

"Hey," Callie calls. Her sigh of relief doesn't go unnoticed, making me smile.

"Hey baby," I say, shutting the door behind me. That trademark Callie scent of hot chocolate floats in the cozy apartment air. This woman really does know how to make a house into a home.

*And now she's become* my *home.*

Nacho walks right in like she owns the place. That girl has always known when she's wanted.

I, on the other hand, come to a halt inside the small foyer at the sound of additional voices.

"Hi, sweet girl," Callie squeals, hopping up to greet Nacho. "Oh my goodness, your collar looks so beautiful!"

The sight of them together gives me pause, thinking back to that night at Theo's. The night John and I first came up with this crazy idea.

The one that ultimately led me to Calloway Rutherford.

Forgetting all about us not being alone, a bright smile takes over my face while Nacho and Callie share their moment.

"Hey man." Ian Fairchild pops up from the chair on the far side of the living area.

Another man twists around to look at me from the floor. A man I've only seen a couple other times—Aaron Fairchild.

Nodding to Aaron, my eyes shift back to Ian as he approaches.

Ian reaches where I stand in the entryway, extending a hand. Clasping it for the shake, he nods toward the bedroom. "Here, let's put your stuff in there." Ian leads me into Callie's bedroom and I can't help but wonder how many times he's been in here.

The same warm colors and feel from the living area brings the room to life, her modern boho style exemplified through a sleek walnut bed and dresser suite, sage and cream bedding, and various art prints hanging in strategically-spaced mini galleries.

Ian takes my bags and sets them in the corner. When he turns back around, concern colors his anxious eyes. Leaning in, he whispers, "Connie texted Aaron, letting him know what happened. So he knows, too."

"He didn't before?" My brow furrows.

Ian shakes his head. "Callie and I thought it'd be best if he didn't. You know, the less people who knew, the better? That kind of thing."

I work to push down the irrational jealousy of his referring to Callie and him as a unit, instead focusing on what the man is actually telling me. "Was he upset?"

"Nah, just confused. I think he was a little hurt since he loves Callie like a sister, too. But when I explained everything on the way over, he was good."

"How was she when you got here?"

Ian hesitates, choosing his words carefully. "Quiet at first. But hot chocolate is like liquor to that one," he grins.

My own smile mirrors his. "Right."

"She told us what happened at Aspen Point—most of which we already knew, but I think it helped her to talk through it—and we were talking about where she thinks they'll go from here when you got back."

I nod, taking everything in. "She definitely seems more at ease now. Thank you for that."

Ian shrugs. "Of course, man. Anytime."

Narrowing my eyes, I take in Ian Fairchild. Tall, fit, a neatly trimmed beard. Nice, casual clothes that says he cares about how he presents himself, but doesn't take himself too seriously outside of working hours. And on top of it all, he seems like a genuinely decent guy. No wonder Callie and my sister hang around him. Speaking of which ... "I'm, um, kinda surprised you didn't go with Blythe."

Frowning, his brows knit together. "To Mexico?"

"Unless she went somewhere else I don't know about, yes."

"Why would I go with her on her trip?"

Palming the back of my neck, I do my best to word this delicately. "Because I thought you two were, well, together. Especially at Callie's school that night."

His frown deepens. "We're friends who hang out a lot because we live in the same building and have Callie as a mutual friend." He shrugs. "I mean, she's amazing. But Blythe and I are just friends. Come on," he claps me on the shoulder, "Callie's got a nose for secret conversations."

As we head back out into the living room, my love sits squarely in the middle of the couch wrapped in no less than two blankets, a fresh cup of hot cocoa in one hand while the other pets a resting Nacho. Upon our entrance, she beams up at me.

"Are you trying to steal my dog?" I ask, grinning like an idiot as I round the furniture to sit beside her.

Ian follows suit, reclaiming his spot in the single chair.

Callie glances down at Nacho, whose head is nestled up against her leg. "What can I say? The heart wants what the heart wants."

Placing my hand on her leg not currently occupied by our dog, my eyes search hers. "How are you?"

She swallows, nodding. "Better."

"Good. Have you eaten?"

"Nope," she says, shaking her head, "I was waiting for you."

Aaron perks up from his spot on the floor. "We did offer to order pizza and have it waiting for you, but she wanted to wait until you got back." He absently rubs Nacho's butt, earning him her eternal love and devotion.

Looking between the brothers and back to my love, I can't help but smile when our eyes meet. "Sounds great to me."

Ian pulls out his phone. "I'll put in the order."

As he does, I can't help but take in the comical image of Aaron on the floor, rubbing Nacho with one hand while the other grabs the TV remote. He's a big guy. Despite having seen him all of two times, I'd forgotten his immense size.

Picturing him with Connie is actually a bit comical.

But no matter how much this guy adores my girlfriend, there's no way he can be comfortable down there, regardless of how fluffy that rug may be. I get the feeling this isn't the first time the poor guy has had to sit on the floor here. And given his importance to Callie, I highly doubt it'll be the last.

Leaning in toward Callie, I whisper, "My love, remind me to buy you another chair."

$\sim$

"That was the last one for the day, Dr. Rhodes." Mrs. Lanahan peeks up at me from behind her new glasses. Apparently, her prescription read 'whatever glass used to be a Coke bottle.'

Shoving a paper into the Collins' file, I tap it on the desk twice to ensure no fallout before handing it over. "Great." It's only eleven, since the practice only opens for half days between

Christmas and New Year. But being away from my girls makes this half day feel like forever.

Especially when I know they're both cuddled up in bed watching movies without me.

"I trust you had a good holiday?" The woman is fishing. Worse, she's not even being sneaky about it.

"Why do I get the feeling that's not really what you're asking?"

The nosy receptionist gives me a cheeky grin. "I don't know what you mean, Oliver."

"Mrs. Lanahan," Rindy rounds the corner, shooting a chastising look at our receptionist, "I should tell Jo you're up here causing trouble." A teasing smile slides into place. "Besides, John is still up at Aspen Point, so he's not here to take your side."

Jo would be mortified—Nettie Lanahan is only our receptionist because she was Jo's neighbor as a kid. But she became a surrogate grandmother and remained close throughout Joanna's life. When her husband passed, she needed something to do to pass the time. The practice was just about to open. The rest is history.

"Joanna loves me and would never believe it," Mrs. Lanahan says, batting her eyelashes.

Handing over her own files, Rindy playfully rolls her eyes. "Either way, leave poor Oliver alone."

"Uh-oh. Trouble with the redhead … " Mrs. Lanahan sings as I turn to walk away.

Rindy grimaces in my direction, walking with me back toward our offices. "Have I apologized enough yet? If not, I will." Every single conversation between us today has included at least three apologies. "Because I truly am so sorry, Ollie."

Holding up my hands to silence her, I stop in the middle of the hallway. "Rindy, it's really okay."

"Really?" This woman's sarcasm knows no bounds.

Sighing, I lower my hands. "Yes, really. It was something that was likely to come out anyway. It's really okay. Neither of us are upset. I promise."

Rindy nods. "So ... when are you seeing her again?"

Pressing my lips together, I can barely suppress my smile. "I actually stayed with her last night."

"With Nacho?"

"Of course."

"Of course," she waves, "go on."

"I don't want to ever be without her," I continue, "so I was thinking about asking if she wanted to move in together."

Rindy's professionally tweezed eyebrows raise. "Are you sure about that? I mean, are you sure that's not a little fast? How will Callie feel?"

I frown. "I don't think it's too fast."

"And Callie?"

Hesitating, my frown deepens. I know it feels like the right decision. But could Rindy be right? Could Callie feel like this is moving too fast?

"You are obviously welcome to do what you like," she says, "but I encourage you to think about all the factors here."

"Like what, exactly?" I lean against the nearest wall for support as my friend lays out all the ways I might be an idiot.

"Like," Rindy sighs, "do you know if she even wants to live with anyone before she gets married? Have you two even discussed marriage as a possibility? Or, she lives alone, right? What if she's not ready to give up her personal space yet? You've really only known one another for a little over a month. Are you going to be okay if she doesn't immediately jump at the chance to consolidate assets?" My friend's eyes roam my face with each dooming question. "Look Ollie, I want you to be happy. I just don't want you two to set yourselves up to fail."

"What do you suggest I do?" Folding my arms across my

chest, I do my best not to act like she just ate the last piece of pie.

Rindy shrugs. "Maybe you should talk to someone else who's been through a, um, whirlwind romance. And who's successfully remained married for several decades." She gives me a pointed look.

After thanking her, I finish up in my office and head to my car. Pulling out my phone, I dial the number and let them know I'm on my way.

As per tradition, my parents are home the day after Christmas and waiting for me in the living room when I arrive. Since neither are working today, they're sitting in their respective chairs in lounge clothes when I walk through the door.

"What's wrong?" Mom's panicked voice would make me laugh on any other occasion.

"Geez, Sandra. Let the boy get in the house before you bombard him." My dad takes a sip of his coffee. The twinkle in his eye is unmistakable.

My mom turns a withering glare in his direction. "My son called me to say he has something important he needs to discuss, Marshall. What do you suggest I do? Bake him a cake?" She raises thin eyebrows at my dad who, smartly, remains silent. She turns her worry back to me. "Do you want some coffee? Tea? Brownies?"

Unwinding my scarf and removing my coat, I shake my head. "No, thank you," I say and take a seat on the couch.

Mom smacks Dad on the arm. "See? I told you. Something's wrong. He's refusing my brownies."

Leaning forward, I place my elbows on my knees, wrapping my hands together. "Mom. Dad."

Dad, whose eyes have been glued to the television, snaps his gaze my way. Slowly, he lifts the remote, pressing the power button.

"How did you know?" I ask. It feels like a frog has taken up residence in my throat. Maybe one of Callie's plants invites all the neighborhood frogs to her apartment.

I'll have to check when I get home.

Home.

"Know?" my dad repeats.

I nod. "You two barely knew each other. Only a couple of months, right?"

My parents exchange a look when Dad breaks out into a grin. "Can't say I'm too surprised, my boy. You looked head over heels for that girl the moment the two of you walked into this house on Thanksgiving," he chuckles. "And the way she doted on you, well," he takes my mom's hand, "all I can say is, it reminded me of someone else I know."

Mom looks at him as if he's the only other person on the planet before seeming to remember my presence. "Oliver, you just have to decide what's right for you. And for Callie, of course."

Wringing my hands together, a knot forms in my stomach about what has to come next. Especially since the Rutherfords know. "Well, there are, um, some things ... that you aren't ... aware of." Biting my lower lip, I feel like I'm in high school again.

Mom releases Dad's hand, leaning forward. "Is Callie pregnant?"

Waving my hands around like a lunatic, I shake my head so fast my glasses nearly fly off. "What? No, nothing like that." I don't think.

"Then, Oliver Grant Rhodes, I would start talking." That stare only a mother can accomplish threatens to burn a hole right through my head.

Sighing, I launch into the story from the beginning. With each new revelation, my face grows hotter. But to my parents' credit, they sit there in silence as I spill my guts. By the time they're up to speed, I feel ready to pass out.

Mom rubs her temples. "Oliver ... "

I flinch, waiting for the yelling to start, like with the Rutherfords. But it never comes.

Sighing, Mom lifts her head. "Honey, I am so sorry you felt like that's what you had to resort to in order to make us happy." After a couple moments of silence, she pokes Dad on the arm. "Marshall, say something."

Shocked eyes look at his wife. "Like what? It's honestly kinda hilarious. But it's clearly turned into something that's actually ... something."

"So," my gaze flits between them, "how mad are you?"

Mom and Dad look at each other before looking back at me, but it's Mom who speaks for them both. "We're not mad."

"Really?" Hope dares to bloom in my chest at not being sent to my room without supper.

"Really," Dad answers. He sits up straighter in his chair. "Now, you wanted to know how we knew."

I nod.

He beams at my mom, my favorite example of what love should look like.

Like what I've found with Callie.

"Son, everyone will have their own opinion on what you should do when you're in love," he continues. "Where you should live, how long you should date, what steps you should take. Where you should try and meet your partner." He gives me a pointed look. "But, ultimately, it comes down to what you feel like is right for you and the person you decide to choose every single day for the rest of your life. Oliver, do you really love this girl?"

I've never been an emotional person. But my father's question nearly brings tears to my eyes with how much love exists in my heart for this woman. "Yes."

My father leans forward in his chair, eyes trained on me. "Then, son, what are you going to do about it?"

# 21

*Callie*

Sunday afternoon, the oven timer and a knock on my door sound at the same time. Looking at the microwave clock, I frown knowing Oliver should still be with John right now. Besides, he already let me know he was planning to stay with Blythe tonight since she's back from her trip. That way he can fill her in on everything.

But I get to keep Nacho with me. So, really, I win.

An insistent knock hammers on the door again.

"Just a sec," I call. There may be someone freezing outside, but burning down my apartment by leaving my food in the oven too long won't do anyone any good. So they can wait.

Nacho barks, clearly siding with me.

Glancing down at my favorite green sweats and Oliver's old university shirt, I shrug to myself. If people don't want to see me dressed down with no makeup and a messy bun, they should really call first.

Depositing the chicken casserole on the stovetop to cool, I make quick work of wiping my hands on a dishtowel and rush to the door. "No way," I mutter, checking the peephole. Confusion settles deep in my stomach, curious about what ball is about to drop here in my own home. Especially considering the last time we were all in the same room, when things did not go supremely well.

I open the door and sure enough, there waits all four of my siblings.

"Geez, Calloway, let us in." Connie's teeth chatter in spite of her being wrapped up in a down winter coat and boots. Moving me aside, she leads the pack into my apartment.

Each of them look around the space in wonder. Never having been here before, they all take in the insane amount of plants, no doubt wondering if I've lost my mind. Or if all the plants have kept too much oxygen in the place and have thus made me the defective Rutherford they've come to know.

"Make yourselves comfortable," I grumble, heading back into the kitchen to cover the chicken in case Nacho gets any bright ideas while I'm distracted by having the entire Rutherford legion in my living room.

"You didn't attend that school," Connie teases, smirking down at my shirt, "but I bet I can guess who did."

Rolling my eyes, I grin and turn to grab the tin foil.

They all remove their coats, hanging them off the two barstools as they wander farther into the space that's much too small for the five of us.

Prescott hightails it to the single chair on the far end of the living room, as if he's been on his feet all day and can't wait to sit down. Given that it's the weekend, I know he wasn't in court today. Maybe Mom had him walking from place setting to place setting at their house to help with the New Year's party planning.

Frankly, that would exhaust me, too.

Prescott clears his throat. "Man, something smells good, Calloway. I guess you really can cook?"

"How else do you think I eat?"

"Take out?"

I snort. "All the time? On a teacher's salary?"

His lips form a flat line. "Fair point. Are you ever sorry that you didn't choose something more lucrative?"

"Money's not everything, Scotty boy."

The nickname he usually despises earns me a small smile. "No, but then you wouldn't have to cook all the time."

Shrugging, I put some fresh water in the electric kettle. If I'm going to make it through having my siblings spend time in my apartment, I'm going to need some gourmet hot cocoa, stat. "I really like cooking, actually. I even grow some of my own herbs." I nod to the row of basil, thyme, rosemary and oregano on a shelf above the sink.

Imogene sits down on the couch ... right in my spot.

I try not to dwell on that fact.

"I didn't know you have a dog," Imogene says absently. Nacho leans into the timid pets my oldest sister offers.

"Or so many plants," Chris gripes.

"This is Nacho, right?" Connie asks. She takes a place on the couch next to Imogene, leaving the last spot for Chris.

The sweet baby's tail wags in confirmation, making Connie giggle.

Chris huffs. "Is she Dr. Hotness's dog?" But the gruffness of his voice is diminished by the smile threatening to take over his face as Nacho delivers a wet kiss right to his waiting cheek.

What can I say? That girl's quite the charmer.

Ignoring the edge in my brother's voice, I nod. "Yep."

"Where is he?" Prescott glances at the only other interior door, leading to the bedroom. "You're wearing his clothes, and I'm surprised he's not attached to your hip."

"Believe it or not, we can still function as individuals," I laugh. "But he's out with friends right now, and will be seeing his sister later tonight. Since she doesn't know about, well, everything, he's taking this opportunity to tell her." My cheeks flush at the taboo mention of our strange predicament. "So Nacho and I are having a girl's night in." With the casserole securely covered and the hot water almost boiling, I lean onto the counter facing my unexpected visitors.

While none of them look particularly comfortable in my home, no one looks oddly out of place, either. It's a little unnerving to have this situation feel so commonplace. I'll be the first to admit that I have no idea what the Rutherford siblings get up to in their evenings, but it sure isn't sitting around in their youngest sister's apartment watching the latest episode of their new favorite hyperfixation.

I briefly wonder if I should snap a quick picture for Ian and Aaron—they sure aren't going to believe this without some proof.

Sensing everyone in the room is now in love with her, Nacho makes her way back to the kitchen and collapses in a furry pile at my feet.

"So," I clap my hands together out of the pure need to do absolutely anything other than just stand here like a moron in my own home, "what brings you all here on this lovely Sunday afternoon?" I think my smile comes across a bit more manic than I intend, but my nerves are only leaving me so much to work with here.

Connie shifts to face our brothers. Her delicate eyebrows raise, and her shoulder-length waves swish through the air with each sharp turn of her head as she looks at each of them.

"What?" Chris grimaces.

"I think one of you should start."

"Why?"

"Christopher Irving Rutherford."

"Constance Irene Rutherford."

"Fine," Prescott interrupts, "I'll start. You two, shut up." My oldest brother sits up straight in his chair. Squaring his shoulders and taking a deep breath, he looks at me and begins speaking. "Calloway, we had no idea about how you've felt all these years. I mean, we knew what we were saying, but we never realized how much it affected you. And we're sorry. Right, Chris?" Prescott kicks our brother's foot.

Chris grunts in disapproval. Still glaring and making his displeasure known, he nods at me.

"Say it," Connie commands.

Her twin cuts his annoyed eyes her way and sighs. "We're sorry, Calloway."

"Thank you," I mutter, brows furrowing further in confusion.

Chris sighs in exasperation. "Relax, there's no ulterior motive. We're not recording this to blackmail you or anything weird. Like to, I dunno, gaslight you later on." He doesn't stop the grin from spreading on his face.

"If you don't mind my asking," Imogene says, sitting up, "when exactly did you and Oliver actually start dating, since you weren't at Thanksgiving? Even though you could've fooled us."

"They did fool us," Prescott interjects.

Imogene nods while I fight the urge to crawl under the counter. "Right. Were you dating when we were all up at the school for your program?"

Biting my lip, heat flushes my cheeks. "Actually, not until Christmas Eve."

Connie grins from the couch like a proud mother.

Prescott rears his head back. "Wow. Well, I feel like an idiot."

I wave him off. "Eh, I hear that's good for you once and a while."

Imogene, my stoic oldest sister, bursts out into laughter

while Chris groans. "Ugh, that means you were probably being gross just down the hall, right? You know what"—he waves his hands in front of his face, shaking his head—"you're my baby sister and I don't wanna know."

"Smart man," Connie snickers while I try to not die from embarrassment.

Prescott rubs his forehead and sighs. "Look, we're having a family dinner tonight," he explains and glances at his watch, "in a couple hours, actually."

"I know," I answer, "Mom left me a voicemail." I still feel kind of bad for not answering her call. It was Dad who was so loud and upset, after all. And while I don't blame Mom for siding with her partner, I still didn't feel prepared to talk to her just yet. Then I outwardly cringe as I make the connection. "Did she send you all here to drag me to dinner gagged and bound?" I gasp. "Am *I* what's for dinner?"

My oldest brother rolls his eyes. "Mom didn't send us." He looks around my tiny living room at each of our siblings before landing his gaze on me. "We wanted to come talk to you and apologize. And then ask you to come to dinner."

"Why?" My voice is quiet, unsure. I admittedly don't know how to handle my siblings being decent to me all at the same time.

Connie stands and makes her way to where I am floundering in the kitchen. Stepping around Nacho, my sister places her palms on my shoulders. "I know how hard this whole thing has been for you," she says, "but I don't think you realize it's been difficult for us, too. We were raised in the same house as you, but you had vastly different rules than the rest of us. You always felt like Mom and Daddy overlooked you. But the entire time, the rest of us were struggling to survive."

"Not to mention," Imogene pipes up, "that they were always pitting us against one another. It made it hard to know who to trust a lot of the time."

Nodding, I look at my oldest sister. "I knew that. Or, well, I figured." Worrying my bottom lip, I fold my arms across my chest. "I just always felt leftover, for lack of a better word. You had Prescott to team up with, while Chris and Connie had each other. Mom and Dad have always been a team, so who did that leave for me?"

"Calloway," Connie brings my attention back to her, "I'm not saying anything we did was right or wrong in the past. But we are sorry we hurt you for so long. And we'd like you to come to dinner tonight. It'd mean a lot to us."

Imogene shifts in her seat. "Like the start of a new chapter. For all of us."

"But maybe don't bring Oliver around just yet," Prescott grins. "Dad might just have him shot. I mean, are you two planning on actually staying together?"

I nod. "I love him. I ... I didn't even know it was possible, feeling this way about someone. Especially so quickly." Swallowing, I do my best to keep the tears gathering in my eyes from spilling over.

"Oliver really is a great guy," Imogene says. "And it's obvious he loves you, too." Her soft laughter fills the room. "If you get married and have kids, are you going to tell them the truth about how you got together?"

"We actually haven't talked about that yet."

Imogene frowns. "About getting married?"

"No, we've talked about that. And kids." I blush furiously. "I meant about the whole deception part."

My brothers sitting in my living room look ready to vomit at all this talk about love.

Connie shakes my shoulders, forcing my attention her way. "Calloway, dinner's in less than two hours. What do you say?"

"Well," I say, looking back at Connie, "I guess I need to go take a shower."

"The Beef Wellington is really good tonight, Mom." I offer her the best smile I can around my mouthful. Though I'd be lying if I said I wasn't a little jealous of Goldie's spaghetti and meatballs substitution since she doesn't enjoy this meal.

My mother's tight smile greets me. "Thank you, Calloway." Her voice is soft, polite.

It makes me want to throw my chair across the room.

In spite of the tension radiating from my parents, this is truly the most comfortable meal I've ever had in my parents' house. It's amazing what a difference not feeling like your siblings hate you can do. I guess nothing brings a family together like the youngest child enacting a massive gaslight campaign.

The Rutherford family home is warm in that post-Christmas way, with all the professional decorations still in place. But unlike at our residence at Aspen Point, Mom's returned us to classical music existing softly in the background instead of those old holiday favorites.

Turning to the opposite end of the table, I try again with my other opponent. "Dad, how are the plans coming along for the New Year's party?"

My father, in his Sunday slacks and sweater vest, sends me a chilly frost from the north. "I'm sure they're fine. If you're truly interested, I would ask your mother," he says, swirling his glass of red. "She has more to do with it than I do."

"Right, sure," I nod. "I just remember how excited you were about the potential color scheme."

Dad humphs without looking up from his plate.

I take the opportunity to stab another broccoli and toss it in my mouth, earning me a grossed out look from my niece.

Across the table, Prescott clears his throat. "I was going over the final guest list today. Looks like it'll be quite the turnout."

"Will you be bringing anyone, dear?" Mom asks him. It's an innocent enough question, but everyone at the table can hear its undertone.

Except Goldie.

Prescott's brows knit together. "Does my daughter count?" He gestures to my favorite kid sitting between Imogene and himself.

To Goldie's credit, she peeks up at her dad with half a spaghetti noodle hanging from her mouth.

Biting the inside of my cheek does little to hide my amusement.

Mom ignores his retort, turning to Imogene expectantly. "What about you?"

"Trust me, Mom, you don't want to meet any of the guys I work with." Imogene makes a face depicting the horror of working with a bunch of guys who are all smart and who know it.

"Well, what about men you don't work with?" Mom tries again.

Imogene simply blinks back at her.

Maybe Oliver was right about Imogene and John. From what he's told me, John doesn't sound all that interested in *looking* for someone. And based on her reaction to our mother's inquiry, neither is Imogene.

Mom sighs and looks at her two oldest children. "You two do realize your father and I aren't getting any younger, don't you?"

"Especially not with the crap some of you like to pull," my father grumbles under his breath.

Rolling my lips together, I take a deep breath as quietly as I can.

Connie squeezes my hand under the table. Shooting me a quick smile, my sister looks at our mother. "I actually went out on a date last night."

I narrow my eyes and slide them toward my sister. Clearly, Aaron and I have some chatting to do.

Mom's entire face brightens while surprise takes over Chris's every feature. He looks at his twin as if blindsided. "I didn't know you were actually going out with him," he says. "I thought you were just considering it."

Connie shrugs. "I did consider it. And then I followed through. It went pretty well, actually."

"What's his name, Constance?" Mom drops her fork and clasps her hands together. This particular brand of excitement is usually only reserved for new clothing line releases. I wonder if Mom's personal shoppers have been notified about their competition.

"Careful," I mutter to my sister, "or she might just start planning your wedding."

"I heard that, Calloway." Mom's shrewd gaze pierces me before looking back at Connie.

Connie, on the other hand, ignores both of us. "His name is Andrew Weston. He's a hedge fund manager in our building," she explains.

My eyes widen and it takes every ounce of willpower to ask why on earth she isn't dating Aaron. And whether or not he knows about this development.

I'm gonna guess not, because I sincerely doubt he would've been texting me about *SpongeBob SquarePants* reruns earlier if he did.

"Is he from the area?" Mom asks.

Connie shakes her head. "He moved here after school on the east coast."

"And you're planning to see him again?"

"We have another date tomorrow."

"Well," our mom breathes, "you must bring him to the party." I think Mom just mentally picked out Connie's wedding dress.

Connie nods in agreement, deftly ignoring my pointed stare.

Across the table, Imogene and Prescott glance at one another and each look across the suddenly much smaller table at me. Surprise and concern intermingle as we all think the same thing. While Connie has been more reserved about her feelings for Aaron over the years, the older Fairchild brother has been less than subtle about his feelings for her.

As long as you're paying attention.

If Connie's at all serious about this guy, Aaron needs to know.

Soon.

"I can't wait to hear more about him, my darling girl." Dad beams across me to Connie. "I'm so glad you don't feel like you need to bring someone you're pretending to date to the party. Or have them convince us you're living up to your potential."

Staring hard at my plate, I count to ten in my head. Silence rolls over our family while I ensure my wits aren't scattered all over the floor. Wiping my napkin across my lips, I turn to fully face my father. My heart takes up a new residence in my throat as I begin. "Mom, Dad, I really am sorry about everything that's happened. Truly. I'm sorry I lied to you. That I had Oliver lie to you. All of it. Not that it should really make you feel any better, but it was only supposed to be one time. Thanksgiving. That's it. I had no other plans to bring him around. But you know what?" I don't bother stopping my smile. "I ended up falling in love with him, as silly as that may sound. He made me feel like I was worth something, which is more than you've ever done. He's never overlooked me or discounted me. He believes in me. He supports me. Oliver and I, we're a team. That's something I've never felt before I met him."

Dad opens his mouth to speak, but I hold up a hand to silence him. Miraculously, it works.

"I know I've broken your trust, if I ever had it at all. But please know that Oliver's not going anywhere and, if you reject him, you might as well reject me, too. Which would be a shame, because I'd like you all to be there for my next graduation." I chuckle to myself. "Whenever that may be."

Mom frowns from the other end of the table. "What are you talking about?"

A broad smile takes over my face. "I've decided to go back to school." Peeking around Connie, my grin lands on Chris. "For my doctorate in education. I've seen how hard our admin works to make a difference in our kids' lives. For years, I've admired their constant dedication to making our schools a better and safer place and now, I want to help them. There's a great program through my alma mater that can be mostly completed online and part time while I continue teaching in the meantime."

Every single one of my siblings beams with pride. Even Chris cracks a smile.

Nodding, Mom asks, "How long will it take to complete your program?"

"Part time, about five years. But I don't want to give up my time in the classroom to speed up the process. It's the connection with my kids that drove me to this decision—I don't want to lose that."

"Congratulations, Calloway." That soft, cool voice begins to thaw.

Offering my mom a genuine smile, a small breath of relief pushes through my lips. "Thanks, Mom."

Dad keeps silent, but I'm really okay with that. Nothing about moving forward with him will be easy anytime soon. I recognize that.

"I should probably go," I say, pressing my napkin to my mouth one more time. "I have some hot cocoa to drink."

"And some plants to water," Chris interjects.

I smile at my brother. "And plants to water." Scooting back my chair, I stand from the table.

"Calloway." My father's voice is rough, unsure. In my twenty-seven years, I've never heard him sound like this. "Are you still coming to the New Year's party?"

"Of course," I say, "I will always show up for my family."

# 22

*Oliver*

There's nothing like walking into the office of your girlfriend's dad ... who probably hates you. And it's Monday morning, so there hasn't even been time for his first coffee of the week to kick in just yet.

Awesome.

But surely four days is long enough to have stayed away. Besides, I'm going to be in Callie's life as long as she'll let me. That means there's no better time than the present to have this conversation. No matter how much it makes me want to vomit. With any luck, my favorite blue button-down and tan slacks will give me some of the confidence I'll need.

Rutherford, Rutherford, MacCallum & de Luksa is housed in a stunning multi-story building on the outskirts of Serenvale Springs. White marble floors run the length of the front lobby, appearing even brighter with sunlight streaming in through the floor-to-ceiling windows all along the front wall. A sleek modern desk accommodates two put-together receptionists typing furiously on their keyboards. Even though Christmas was just last week, no tree adorns the lobby, adding to the cold, business feel of the intimidating space. No background music plays overhead. No abstract art hangs on the walls. From being here all of ten seconds, it's clear that Lillian has taken care of decorating the Rutherford home if this is Ira's idea of homey decor.

The nearest receptionist, a sharply dressed kid who can only be about twenty, and is probably hoping to enter law school in the next year, holds up a finger indicating he'll be with me in a moment. He never even bothers to actually look up.

This kid gives me whole new respect for Mrs. Lanahan.

A large group enters the lobby through the front door, chattering amongst themselves. They head toward the elevators without so much as an acknowledgment of the cold administrators that will, apparently, be with me in a moment. When half the group enters one large elevator and half enters another, I seize the rapidly closing window of opportunity.

Hopping into the closest elevator car, I stare straight ahead as if I've been with them all along, doing my best to ignore the only two people who bother to notice my sudden appearance. While the building only has four floors, that's four more than I know how to navigate. I make the executive decision to exit when everyone else does. But I also manage to move to the side just enough so that everyone else will have to get out before me. This way they don't know that I have no idea where I'm going.

That's the right choice, as it turns out.

"Did you push the button?" one woman, probably forty and all business, asks another.

Her colleague, a woman older by a few years with a sharp

bob cut and sharper suit, nods. "Yes, we're on the expressway to the morgue." The older woman gives a dark chuckle.

A worried-looking man next to me in his mid-thirties in desperate need of antiperspirant visibly shivers. "The morgue?" He looks up at me and I have the sudden urge to cover my shoes in case he gets sick right here and now.

I only shake my head and pray to Callie's hot chocolate gods that he doesn't ask me a direct question.

The older woman gives him a skeptical look. "You've never met the partners, have you?"

He wipes a sweaty hand on his cheap blue suit. A tic he probably developed from an overly aggressive father who liked to regularly berate him. "Only de Luksa. Just once during some litigation. He wasn't bad, just really serious."

The woman scoffs. "He's the nicest of the partners. Everyone calls the floor with all the partner offices the morgue, because they'll work themselves to death if it means they'll win their cases."

Mr. Sweaty Hands gulps right as the elevator dings to announce our arrival.

The group shuffles out of the car, and I follow them out into a much warmer version of the downstairs lobby. Instead of bright whites and frigid blacks, sunny golds and calming greens cover every surface. Where tile lines the floors downstairs, expensive carpets cover the walkways here, deadening the clacks of each skyscraper heel being worn by every woman in the building. The smell of disinfectant lingers in the air and fresh flowers wait to be admired on a round glass table just outside the elevator doors. No receptionists wait to assist anyone here, but it doesn't take long to discern in which direction Ira Rutherford's office waits.

Just follow the constant trembling and ever-present look of nausea.

Several associates and paralegals work tirelessly at desks covered in meticulously placed stacks of folders, typing as if their life depends on it. Some rush past me with arms full of loose papers, while trying to not spill overly full mugs of stale coffee. Others look like they slept in their clothes and haven't showered in two days.

The farther I walk, the higher my stomach lurches into my throat and the weight of what I'm doing begins to sink in.

But I know I've reached the point of no return when a striking Latina woman in her mid-thirties looks my way. "Can I help you?" she asks. Her soft features don't match the sharp tone she offers, keeping in line with the all-business blouse and skirt combo she wears. Dark brows raise when I don't immediately answer. Equally dark eyes follow my gaze over her head, right to the giant office waiting behind her.

The office of Ira Rutherford.

The man himself sits behind an obnoxiously large mahogany desk in an oversized black leather chair, talking animatedly on the phone as he stares at something on his desk.

She turns back to me. "Are you here to see Mr. Rutherford?"

"Sorry, yes."

"Do you have an appointment?"

"Um, no. Sorry," I say again.

The woman doesn't waste her time with any kind of empathetic expression. "I'm sorry, but Mr. Rutherford only sees people by appointment. In any case, he has a full schedule today." With that, she turns back to her computer, ultimately dismissing me.

"Look," I say, leaning onto the desk, "I really need just a few minutes with him. Then I'll go away. Promise."

She slides annoyed eyes back my way, not bothering to hide any ill feelings about me. "Like I said before, Mr. Rutherford is completely booked."

"I understand that," I say, doing my best to not let frustration seep into my tone, "but I need to talk to him."

"Make some time in my calendar, Lucy." The sound of Callie's father drags my attention from the unhelpful woman. Ira stands in his office doorway dressed in pristine black slacks and a white dress shirt, arms crossed and looking like someone just spit in his coffee.

Lucy's eyes widen, glancing back at her boss. "But sir, you have a meeting at nine with Carlton."

"Move it." Ira's voice is unyielding as he continues staring at me during his conversation with someone else. "I'd like to hear what Dr. Rhodes has to say. Oliver." The man nods toward his office, signaling me to enter the dragon's lair.

I stand back to my full height, sending an automatic "thank you" to the rude assistant.

Ira turns and heads back into his office, not waiting to see if I follow. Taking a seat behind the gargantuan desk, he leans back in the expensive and ergonomic chair.

His office is more like one would expect from a movie set of an attorney's office, instead of from a man with an entire family and who goes home to his corporate wife every day. Bookshelves line the closest wall while the farthest two walls are made completely of glass. A modern buffet sits against the fourth wall, decorative knick-knacks strategically placed for a sense of a warmth I'm not sure Ira Rutherford possesses. Art pieces not found in the downstairs lobby have found homes here, even though not a single family photo graces the walls.

"Have a seat, Oliver." Ira gestures to the chair opposite his.

If I thought I was nervous before, then this is a whole new level. I'm really glad I skipped breakfast right about now. Sitting down in one of the most uncomfortable chairs I've ever had the displeasure of occupying, I force a tight smile onto my face. "Thank you."

"Why are you here?" No preamble. Got it.

Sitting up as straight as humanly possible, I look Callie's father right in the eye. "First, I want to personally apologize for everything that's happened."

Ira gives nothing away. Nor does he throw me out.

So I keep going. "I stand by my position that Callie deserves better than how she's been made to feel over the course of her life, intentionally or not. I'm a firm believer that among family is where someone should feel the safest. Supported. Ira, Calloway is the most amazing person I've ever met. No matter what has happened in the past, know that you raised a truly incredible and strong human being. And she fully deserves to feel those things. Please don't misunderstand—I'm not saying our methods were right, but I'm not sorry her feelings were brought to your family's attention."

Ira's hands rest on one another, elbows pushing into the chair's armrests. So many of his features resemble my love's that it's a little unnerving.

It's like looking at what Callie could have become if she'd chosen a different path. If she'd given in to the cold, ruthless life of her family name.

"And I am sorry for how you all found out," I nod.

"Were you two ever going to tell us?"

Swallowing, I work to hide my shock that he actually spoke. And in such a steady tone. "Honestly? I'm not sure. Because here's the thing—" I shift just enough to reach into my pocket and pull out its occupant, setting it on the desk "—I fell in love with your daughter during this crazy charade. And if I can help make sure she's treated right by the people she calls family, then I will do anything in my power to make that happen. Including letting you believe it was always real." Despite the absolute trainwreck happening with my heart at the moment, I manage to keep my voice steady.

Callie's father looks at the engagement ring peeking out of

the open box staring up at him. When his eyes finally reach mine again, that stoic face gives nothing away.

"I've spent my life avoiding love. I had a great example set by my parents and I never thought I would find anyone who would measure up so entirely. But then, one day, I went to work, just like every other day. I remember it was a Tuesday, because a family I see every Tuesday at four had canceled due to their little girl being ill that day. I walked out into the front of the office and there stood this beautiful woman trying to make an appointment to see me. Me, of all people. When I offered to see her then, some kind of panic came over her. It was like she couldn't leave fast enough. But I knew I wasn't ready for her to go. And when a particularly clumsy client walked in and bumped into her, subsequently spilling the contents of her purse all over the floor, I rushed to help her." I sigh, rubbing a hand down my face. "I love my parents. Dearly. But they're ready for grandchildren and they want to see my sister and I happy. My friend and I had joked about this idea that I could spend the holidays helping someone in a similar situation— someone whose family thinks there's some shortcoming to be fixed in their life. Because that's how my parents viewed my lifestyle. As a shortcoming. The offer was to ultimately convince that person's family that any of their perceived short-comings were the fault of the family itself, rather than that of the person in question." A humorless chuckle leaves my lips. "It was only ever a joke to me. But my friend actually made a flyer. And when I found it among the contents of Callie's purse, I couldn't believe what I was seeing."

Ira shifts in his chair, leaning forward onto the desk. "When did things change?" he asks, eyes never leaving my face.

I nod, thankful he hasn't kicked me out of the building yet. Yet. "When we said goodbye after Thanksgiving, that was always supposed to be it. That was all we had agreed to. But the moment I drove away, I missed her. I missed the way she made me laugh, her hot cocoa obsession. Watching her face light up when she talked about work. Every single thing she did was magic." I can't help but grin thinking about Calloway Rutherford and how she's changed my life forever. "When she came to see me after Lillian asked about my plans for the holidays, I jumped at the chance to spend more time with her. I *needed* more time with her. But everything changed on Christmas Eve. That was when we both fully realized that things had changed. And now that I have Callie in my life, I don't plan on ever letting her go."

Ira stares hard at the ring that Ian and Blythe helped me pick out yesterday afternoon.

After my sister was done yelling at me for feeling like Callie and I had to lie to her.

"You've only known each other a month," he says. Voice neutral, the man gives nothing away. "Why on earth would you think this relationship can make it in the long run?"

Leaning back in my chair, I smile at Callie's father. "Because it runs in my family."

"Excuse me?"

I chuckle. "My parents. They were set up on a blind date by mutual friends and had their own whirlwind romance."

Ira appears extremely unimpressed. "So? That happens all the time." He taps a particularly thick folder laying on his desk. "Here's an example of that. I don't normally take on divorce cases, but this one is exceptionally messy." The man smirks at the silent question from my raised brows. "What can I say? I like a challenge. But both were born into wealthy families and were introduced by friends. They let passion overtake them and eloped after three weeks. Never even took the time to sign pre-nups. But they just knew everything would work out. One's a workaholic and the other started to feel neglected. One issue led to another and so on until finally, the marriage fell apart." He shrugs. "Now, they're both hurting. Their families are suffering. And all because they threw caution to the wind."

Nodding, I pull my ankle over my knee. "Mr. Rutherford, Callie and I aren't throwing caution to the wind. And we're not eloping. At least, not unless that's what she wants. I'd give her the biggest wedding she can plan or take her to the most secluded beach, if that's her choice. But Callie and I aren't like those poor people that folder represents. We didn't meet one crazy night and fall in love. We bonded over events that put us at our most vulnerable. We saw the best and the worst of one another very quickly." Picking up the ring box, I look at the piece waiting to be placed on my love's finger. "I spend my days listening to those seeking help in their situations. In a way, that folder on your desk represents those I end up failing. But Callie ... " Determined eyes lift back to Ira Rutherford. "I will never fail her. I'll work until my hands bleed and I breathe my final breath. I'll stand by her side until she sends me away, and even then, I'll beg to keep a place at her feet by the grace of her mercy. There will never be another for me. Failing Calloway will never be an option. I love her and I wholeheartedly plan to marry her."

I make a mental note to never play poker with Ira as he continues sizing me up from the power side of that massive desk. Just for the sake of not falling out of my chair from nerves, I count the seconds of the world's strangest stare-off. I make it to seventy-four before Ira blinks.

Sitting back in his chair, Ira juts out his lower lip, nodding slowly. "I don't love this."

"I understand." And I truly do.

"Your candor, though. That's something I don't often see. Not in my position and not with the prestige that comes with our family name," he says. "Everyone always wants something from us. Wants to take advantage of the empire I've worked so hard to build for my family."

"I can't imagine how hard that must be," I admit. "You never know who you can trust."

He nods. "You're right." Callie's father regards me carefully. "What do you think?" The words are louder than he's spoken thus far, eliciting a frown from me.

"Sounds sincere to me." The words come from behind me.

Turning toward the voice, I watch as Prescott strides into his father's office.

His navy slacks lift, exposing socks with unicorns, as Prescott crosses his legs sitting in the chair next to mine. "Hello, Dr. Rhodes." Prescott looks across the small space between us, an alarmingly pleasant smile resting on his clean-shaven face.

My frown deepens. "Prescott."

"You're serious?" He nods to the open ring box in my hand. "About this?"

"Yes."

"Good." Prescott leans back casually in his chair. "When do you plan on proposing? I'd imagine the sooner the better?" His voice is calm. Too calm.

I don't bother hiding my shock, brows shooting up at his question. "Are you saying you're good with this?"

"Of course. Why wouldn't I be?"

"Because I figured you probably hate me."

Prescott shrugs. "I don't hate you. I even think there's potential for us to be friends. I'll admit that I don't love the trouble you helped create for my family. But Calloway was right—there were issues that needed to be addressed. And you made her stronger." He casts a quick glance at his father. "That's something the rest of our family clearly failed at. So I'm on Calloway's side. And if her side includes you, then great."

Man, that dinner last night must've gone better than Callie let on. Of course, I did rush her a bit since Blythe and Mom were busy gushing over Callie's ring in the background.

Heaven forbid they waited until I was off the phone.

"Now," Prescott says, "the proposal?"

Looking over at Ira, I shake my head and turn back to Prescott. "I haven't really decided yet. Preferably as soon as possible. I just need to figure out the logistics."

Callie's brother grins. A quick nod between father and son before Prescott's mischievous eyes return to me. "Oliver, how would you feel about having an audience?"

## 23

*Callie*

The firm's New Year's Eve party is in full swing. Mom knocked Dad's vision out of the park with glittering golds, midnight blacks, and mirrored surfaces covering every inch of the Aspen Point Grand Ballroom. Sparkling golden tablecloths shimmer under the low lights, diamond centerpieces dripping in crystals that flow gracefully onto the nearly one hundred tables. Candles glow on every tabletop, highlighting the glasses of champagne abandoned for the onyx pool of a very full dance floor. The flower choice is a little odd for the occasion, but if Mom decided red roses were the flower of the party, then no one was going to tell her otherwise.

A full buffet lines the back wall, filled with all kinds of amazing hors d'oeuvres, finger sandwiches, and sweets. Every beverage from soft drinks, to champagne, to hot chocolate wait to be served, with an entire wall of greenery bringing a serene levity to the glitz and glamour of the rest of the room.

But I have to admit, the hot chocolate fountain may be the coolest thing I've ever seen. I've already taken three pictures on my phone and sent them to Oliver.

He returned the favor by sending back pictures of the cutest dog named after concession stand food.

Since he thought it'd be best if he stayed away for a bit longer, I am officially dateless for New Year's Eve. I think the only time Oliver was actually sorry for missing tonight's shindig was when he saw the outfit Connie and Imogene put me in. One look at the simple long-sleeve black blouse and shimmering gold miniskirt featuring a diamond pattern, and I could tell he was thinking about all the ways we could celebrate the new year when I returned. Imogene added her own level of glamour by zipping me into thigh-high black suede boots, and finishing me off with minimal makeup and small gold hoops. Connie did manage to hold me down long enough to pull my hair into some kind of fancy bun, which was only accomplished by Imogene handing me a third cup of hot cocoa.

I added the final touch of Oliver's necklace.

Having left Aaron by the buffet, I wander back toward the crowded dance floor. As I watch everyone mingle and laugh and dance the night away, I can't help but revel in the lightness in my chest. I've been in this ballroom a thousand times for a thousand different occasions. Every time, I spent the entire event worried about what my brothers or dad would say about me in front of others, and how well I would be able to temper my reaction. I spent so many years tirelessly monitoring my every expression, my every word.

It was truly exhausting.

Our family still has a long way to go. But I know we're headed in the right direction. If anything, having all four of my siblings in my tiny apartment without ripping each other's heads off is a great starting point.

And with Oliver's support, I have no doubt the journey will be worth it.

Maybe one day, we'll even have a family of our own.

Taking a seat at the closest empty table, I nibble on a chocolate chip cookie I picked up on my last trip to the dessert bar.

"What do you think?" Connie asks, taking a sip of champagne. My sister shimmies her way into the chair beside me. She looks absolutely stunning in a fitted black dress that accentuates full curves with raven pumps to match. The long sleeves and plunging neckline have definitely kept her date's attention all evening.

And Aaron's.

My sister swishes her fiery hair that kisses her collarbones in soft waves, drawing the eye to a simple gold choker and matching earrings.

I frown. "About what?"

The woman lifts a brow, her answer obvious. She makes an exasperated gesture to the rest of the largest ballroom known to man. The same room we've spent every New Year's in our entire lives.

"It's beautiful," I answer, "but Mom always kills it with the decor. Why should this year be any different?"

Connie rolls her eyes. "Because it's absolutely gorgeous. Besides, I figured you'd like all the plants and flowers and everything."

Snorting, it's my turn to roll my eyes. "I do. If I'd been asked to help plan this shindig, it's basically what I would've picked. But what does that matter?"

"What does what matter?" Imogene makes her way to our group, placing delicate hands on the backs of our chairs.

"Calloway's being difficult."

Rolling in my lips, I puff out my cheeks in response to that insane accusation.

"Surely not." Imogene grins down at me. Long hair forming perfect retro waves, her sleek copper silk gown glistens under the lights.

I can't help but smile up at my oldest sister. "You look beautiful," I tell her.

Under the atmospheric lighting, Imogene is positively radiant. "Thank you, Calloway. So do you."

My smile breaks out into a full-blown grin. "Well, I had help."

Chris ambles up to our table, plopping into the seat next to his sister, threatening to wrinkle his black designer suit. "Are we having our own separate party over here?"

"How'd you know?" Connie smirks at him.

Her twin shrugs, clearly bored. Slouching back into the chair, he looks around the immediate area.

Connie spins back to me. "Wanna go dance?"

Shaking my head, I try to ignore how much I'd rather be at home with Oliver and Nacho than stuck here without him.

Connie sets down her champagne glass. "You do know it's okay to have fun without Oliver here, right?"

"Of course," I chuckle. "It's important for couples to still cultivate individual interests. But that doesn't mean I can't miss him when we're apart."

Heavy hands fall on my shoulders and I know who it is before I even turn around.

Connie sighs in relief. "Ian, thank goodness. Get this girl up and make her go dance." My sister waves at me in false annoyance.

Potentially false.

"Why?" I challenge her.

Chris sits up in his chair. "You know what, Connie's right. It might be a fun story for the future if we were all out on the dance floor at midnight on the year our family started a new chapter."

"You hate dancing." Narrowing my eyes, I peer across the table at my brother. "Are you actually Chris Rutherford? Or are you an alien who just looks like him?"

He smiles, which just further confirms my alien theory. Connie must pinch him under the table, because he jumps a couple inches off his chair. "Ouch! What was that for?"

Connie gives him a hard stare in lieu of a response.

They must be doing that twin communication thing because understanding immediately floods Chris's features. "Right," he nods. Chris turns back to me. "I danced with you that last time Aaron's band played at Theo's," he points out.

Laughter tumbles from my lips. "And you hated every moment of it."

Chris wiggles his nose around like he's suddenly dealing with some serious sinus pressure. "Hey, I'm all for some family bonding."

"Sounds great." Ian squeezes my shoulders before pulling out my chair and dragging me to my feet.

I spin around to face him. "You're not even in this family."

"Come on, Cal. Connie's orders." My best friend grins, guiding me toward the dance floor.

"And you're not even the Fairchild who's in love with her," I grumble, too low for anyone other than Ian to hear.

He doesn't disappoint, bursting into laughter as we move away from the table.

My siblings follow, watching us with a little too much interest for my liking.

"What's wrong?" Ian asks above the pulsing music.

Frowning, I nod back in the direction of my family. While certainly still trailing along behind us, they whisper among themselves like scientists on the verge of some kind of break-through. "They're being really weird."

He laughs. "Aren't they always?"

"Yeah, but not like this." Grimacing, I nearly run right into my dad and the other partners, with Prescott nowhere in sight. "Oh, sorry Dad."

My father chuckles, champagne nearly sloshing onto his tie. Clearly, he's a few glasses deep. "I guess the others enlisted your help?" he asks Ian.

Raising my brows, I glance between them.

Ian lifts a shoulder. "Just doing my part to make sure Callie enjoys tonight, is all." Mr. MacCallum and Mr. de Luksa look plenty amused as my friend steers us away and into the heart of the crowd.

"I'm a little surprised Prescott wasn't with them," I muse. "Being a partner is so important to him that, anytime Dad and the others are together, Prescott's somewhere close by."

Ian hmms. "Maybe Goldie needed to go to the bathroom or something."

"Maybe. But she normally asks Mom or one of us."

"Well, I doubt Prescott's career is in any danger. So I wouldn't worry about it."

Just as we're nearly to the center of the dance floor, a brilliant flash of blonde catches my eye and I bring us to a crashing halt.

Literally.

Ian definitely crushes my toes in the process, cursing under his breath.

"Sorry, I just ... did you see that?" Craning my neck, I try to see through the dense crowd. "I thought I just saw Blythe. Did she come with you?"

Ian's dark brows knit together, lower lip jutting out. "Nope. It was just the parents, me and Aaron McGee in the car."

I snort, grinning up at my friend. "He really hates it when you call him that."

"I know," he grins right back. "That's what makes it fun."

"Where is he, anyway?"

Ian juts his chin off to our right. "Over there dancing with some paralegal who's been flirting with him all night."

I wince. "How's he doing with the whole, um ... "

"Connie dating someone else thing?" he finishes.

Nodding, I roll my lips together. "Yeah. That."

Ian sighs, finally dropping his hands from my shoulders. "I think he's in denial. He says he's fine and that they've always been just friends, so that's how it'll stay."

"Wow," I snort, "how convincing."

My oldest friend grins down at me. "Right? Anyway," Ian bows, extending his hand, "may I have this dance?" He wiggles his thick eyebrows, making me giggle. "I know I'm not Oliver, but hopefully I'll do for the present."

Taking Ian's hand, a wave of gratitude washes through me. With a sigh, I look up at him and rest my palm on his shoulder. "Thank you."

Confusion takes over Ian's features as he tilts his head in question. "For dancing with you?" We move together to the rhythm in that easy manner we've always had.

I shake my head. "For everything. For always being there, from that very first day when you moved in next door. For not letting my family scare you away from hanging out with me. For supporting me when no one else did. For pushing me to go meet Oliver. I wouldn't have him if it wasn't for you." Tears threaten to fall from my eyes, and I blink them away.

"Callie ... " he whispers. My dearest friend looks back at me with nothing but love. Releasing his hold on my waist, Ian spins me around. "I'll always be there for you, don't worry. You're the little sister I never wanted. But I am so proud of you," he says, catching me. "And you deserve to be happy. Never forget that." I watch my friend's eyes flicker to somewhere above my head toward the front of the room.

The song comes to a close, no new tune replacing the

previous melody. But no one questions the DJ. No one moves. No one breathes.

A quick look to my left and right reveals that Ian and I are surrounded by my family, each one of them watching us.

No, not us.

Me.

I turn back to my friend, a confused frown in place. "What's going on?" I whisper.

Ian says nothing. Instead, he pulls me in for a tight hug before spinning me around to face the stage.

A gasp catches in my throat. Goosebumps break out across my skin. My heart ceases all movements, unsure if it even remembers the most simple of operations.

There, on the raised platform, stands Oliver.

My feet beg my mind to remember how to move, if only to run to Oliver's waiting arms.

But Ian keeps me anchored in place, holding me steady while my knees threaten to give out.

With a wireless microphone in one hand, Oliver waves to the crowd with the other. No longer in his university lounge pants from earlier, my favorite person somehow manages to look effortlessly stylish in dark navy chino pants and a fitted gray sweater. "Hello everyone," he says, "I apologize for the interruption. I promise this will only take a moment." It takes less than a single breath for the lights to come up and my love's eyes to meet mine. A breathtaking smile breaks out across his handsome face. "You see, I met this woman. This incredible woman. For all intents and purposes, we began seeing one another. Now, we may not have gotten together under typical circumstances, but I knew I continued to crave her company each time we would part ways. Over time, I began giving in to little indulgences here and there where she was concerned, before I was finally able to admit the truth to myself." Oliver's eyes lock onto mine. "I had fallen in love with her."

My heart kickstarts, waking from its ill-timed slumber and taking off in a gallop. Eyes wide, I watch as Oliver descends the small staircase from the platform. The crowd parts for him in a manner so reverent, it's almost biblical—my personal salvation coming to claim my heart and soul here for all to see.

And I'll let him.

Step by measured step, Oliver makes his way to me.

Each stride is a test of my patience. A trial that I am actively failing.

When Oliver is only a few paces away, he continues, "Then, one day, and for only a single moment in time, I found out how I would feel if I were to lose her. And I knew then that this was it. That she was it for me. If there had ever been any doubt in my mind, logic and love cast it out." Oliver closes the remaining distance between us, stopping only breaths away. His familiar scent of cinnamon and apples holds me captive as Ian steps away. Oliver beams down at me, his gentle hand brushing a piece of hair from my face.

In my periphery, a figure steps out from the crowd and heads toward us.

When Prescott is close enough, Oliver moves to hand him the microphone, exchanging it for something smaller and more easily concealed under those large fingers. "Thank you," Oliver murmurs to my brother.

Prescott takes the microphone and steps away, giving us a false sense of privacy.

I never believed the fairy tales—the princesses who spoke of time slowing or stopping altogether when their true love asked for their hand. But as the man I love drops down to one knee, tears stream down my cheeks while the rest of the world falls away.

Here, it's only Oliver and I.

Here, in this perfect moment, we are infinite.

Taking my hand in his, ocean blue eyes filled with adoration and longing search mine. "Calloway Leora Rutherford, from the moment we met, we were a team. We looked out for one another, protected one another. Defended one another. Callie, you are strong, fiercely loyal, and wholly good. I don't believe I'll ever be able to thank John and Ian quite enough for bringing you into my life."

Wet laughter bubbles from my lips, Oliver grinning right along with me. My hand not in his wipes away my tears, doing its best to clear my vision so I won't miss a single moment.

"I promise to always trust you and support you. You will never have to wonder where my loyalty lies, because it will always be with you. My love. Callie." Using one hand, Oliver opens the tiny blue box with gold filigree around the edges. Nestled among the cushions sits the most beautiful ring I've ever seen. A large oval center diamond surrounded by tiny teardrop diamonds on either side rests on a thin yellow-gold band, sparkling under the lights. "Will you marry me?"

A permanent smile takes over, erasing years of confusion and doubt. The tears flow freely now, and I no longer bother trying to stop them. Sniffing, my head nods of its own accord. "Yes," I laugh blissfully.

Relief evident on his face, Oliver removes the ring and slips it onto my waiting finger. My favorite laugh is quickly drowned out by the clapping and excitement of everyone in the room. Standing, he slides the box back into his pocket and I simply can't hold back any longer.

As soon as he's at his full height, I launch myself into Oliver's arms.

And he catches me, just like I knew he would.

Lifting me from the ground, Oliver's arm wraps around my waist to tuck me as close to him as possible. Desperation and joy and love pour from his lips as they find home with mine, while the other arm snakes under my seat, giving me additional leverage.

My hand slides around Oliver's neck and into his hair, pulling him closer still. The other moves to his chest, where the wild beat of his heart causes the rhinos stampeding through my ribcage to frenzy, heat and excitement surrounding us.

When he brings me back to Earth and sets me on the ground, that beautiful smile greets me as he leans away. Fingers linked at the small of my back, those blue eyes sparkle. "Hi," he whispers.

My cheeks ache from my grin threatening to break the laws of physics. "Hi."

"Are you ready?"

I laugh. "To marry you?"

"For our engagement party," he grins. Oliver's gaze breaks away from mine, willing mine to follow. "You didn't think your Mom originally wanted a hot cocoa fountain and dessert bar, did you? Or all the plant babies?"

Looking around, both of our families, John's family, and the Fairchilds all rush toward us, arms open in congratulations. As we get pulled in every direction for hugs and kisses and overwhelming love, the countdown to midnight begins.

"10! 9!"

Sandra kisses her son on the cheek and looks at me with shining eyes before wrapping her arms around me. John, Rindy, and Jo take turns hugging us tight, saying their congratulations.

"8! 7!"

Connie, Imogene, and Blythe manage to squeeze me within an inch of my life, giving a whole new meaning to loving someone to death.

"6! 5!"

Prescott and Chris clap Oliver on the shoulder and take turns shaking his hand while welcoming him to the family. Marshall congratulates his son, pulling us both in tight.

"4! 3!"

Ian and Aaron encircle me in one giant hug. They give my sisters and soon-to-be sister a run for their money when it comes to lovingly depriving me of air.

"2!"

Mom and Dad each press a kiss to my cheek. Their excitement may be more understated than everyone else's, but I still wouldn't change them being here for the world.

"1!"

Finding the man I love among our sea of loved ones, I drift back into his arms. "I love you, Oliver," I whisper.

"I love you, too, Calloway," he murmurs against my lips.

My grin widens, and his follows my lead. "You know, this holiday was better than I ever could have hoped for."

Oliver chuckles as he closes the final breath between us.

"Happy New Year!"

Our lips meet across every challenge we've faced, joining where our future begins.

# EPILOGUE

*Six And A Half Years Later*

*Oliver*

Champagne pops across the room as laughter fills the air. My wife's graduation party is in full swing, the Aspen Point Lodge Grand Ballroom decked out to the nines and full of our closest friends and family, all of whom are ready to congratulate Callie on her latest amazing accomplishment.

My wife glows with every hug from her siblings and their respective spouses. She laughs with every embrace from each of our nieces and nephews.

We've spent plenty of time talking about it over the years— how our little stunt almost ruined everything Callie had worked so hard to build over the span of her life. But in the end, she was able to voice her own feelings and stand her ground.

Even if I wasn't there to witness that part, it will always be one of my proudest moments for Calloway Rutherford-Rhodes.

"Daddy, can I have another cupcake?" A tiny hand tugs on mine.

Though, the birth of our daughter certainly outranks Callie standing up to her family. I don't know that Ira and Lillian will ever be able to fully give my wife what she needs emotionally, but I'm thankful they're finally on the right path.

I know their granddaughter has been a significant part of that. They want to be part of her life as much as we'd like them to be, as well.

Ivy beams up at me, the spitting image of her mother.

I'd be lying if I said that grin missing its two front teeth doesn't have me wrapped around her little finger. "Only one more, honey," I say, giving my daughter's hand a squeeze. "We're having dinner with the whole family once Mommy's party is over."

Ivy throws both arms around my middle before running off to sneak more treats with her many cousins.

At five years old, Ivy Jane Rhodes is bright, confident and compassionate. Nacho is her best friend in the entire world, always staying right by her side during our family hikes and every other moment of her life. Ivy's been pretty bummed that her mom won't be her kindergarten teacher this coming fall, but the newest doctorate holder in the Rhodes family has graciously accepted a new position.

When the Serenvale Springs school district heard Callie was graduating, they were quick to ask about her plans and aspirations. Callie was ready to say goodbye for the time being to leading a classroom, but she wasn't ready to leave her home-town in search of a new title.

Especially as our family has grown closer over the past several years.

As luck would have it, the tenured assistant principal of

Serenvale Springs Elementary School had just notified the school board of her impending retirement last December. Two rounds of interviews later, and Callie graciously accepted the position pending her graduation this May—on our sixth wedding anniversary.

"Hey man," Chris claps my shoulder, "congrats."

Lifting a brow, I look at my brother-in-law. "It was all her. No question."

Chris chuckles. "Oh, that I know. But you, uh—" he swallows "—you've supported her every step of the way. Well, you have since you met her, I guess."

"I'm just glad you finally came around. You were definitely the hardest one to crack."

Chris looks out across the ballroom, his gaze landing on his very pregnant wife. He smiles. "Sometimes, it just takes the right push."

I snort. "Don't I know it. I probably would've stayed alone forever if Callie hadn't come along."

Barking laughter comes from behind. "You mean if I hadn't made that flyer?" John nudges me with his elbow, hands full of his toddling two-year-old son.

As if she knows exactly what we're discussing, my wife's eyes find mine on the opposite end of the room, a lovely blush tinting Callie's cheeks. The sage crushed velvet floor-length dress she's wearing highlights the added radiance.

Beside Callie, Blythe chatters away as my sister rocks her newborn, while their older son sits beside Ivy at the table.

Folding my arms, I watch as our kids sip their juice pouches with Grandma and Grandpa Rhodes, sneaking grapes off my mom's plate.

"Sure," I tell John, "I guess at this point, I can thank you for making that ridiculous flyer."

John scoffs, looking around me at Chris. "Yeah, only after he's married with a five-year-old and a son on the way."

Chris's eyes widen just as Connie walks by. "What's wrong?" she asks. Her panicked expression flits between us.

"Calloway's having a boy," her twin grins. "Pay up." Chris holds out an open palm.

Shaking my head, I look at them, incredulous. "You two were betting on that?"

Connie digs into her pocket, producing a bank note. She shrugs. "Gotta keep life interesting somehow. Especially since we don't have people trying to infiltrate our family and gaslight us anymore." My favorite sister-in-law smirks, shifting one of her tiny daughters from one hip to the other.

I can't help but laugh. "You try to fool a woman's family one holiday season and they'll never let you live it down, huh?"

Connie shrugs. "Nope, sorry Oliver." Her smile softens. "But for what it's worth, I'm really glad she picked you to help dupe our family."

John rests his free hand on my shoulder. "That makes two of us."

Rolling my eyes, I can't help but smile at my oldest friend. "If you all are finished, I'm going to go see my wife now." Not waiting to see if there are any protests, I take off toward my own personal beacon of light. Deftly ignoring anyone trying to get in my way, I manage to scoot right up next to Callie as Blythe explains her stance on some new health trend. Sliding my arms around my wife, I pull her into my side. "How's my newest nephew?" I ask, nodding to Harrison snoozing in Blythe's arms.

"I forgot how exhausting newborns can be." My sister rolls her eyes, but the megawatt smile never leaves her face.

Hudson turns in his seat at the table and holds up his empty juice pouch. "I made it full of air, Mama!"

Sitting down next to her older son, Blythe finally turns her attention away so that I have Callie all to myself.

My wife peeks up from underneath dark lashes. "Hi, stranger."

"Hello, Dr. Rhodes," I murmur into her hair, pressing a kiss to her temple, "and little Alder, of course."

Callie turns, resting her forehead on mine as my hand finds the gradually growing bump.

"I was thinking ... "

"That's dangerous," my wife laughs, leaning back. "The last time you were *thinking*, we ended up announcing I'm pregnant again."

Grinning like an idiot, I shrug. "Yeah, but we had fun, at least."

Callie rolls those warm chocolate eyes. "So, is this idea something the rest of our family can overhear, or should we go somewhere more private?" I don't miss the mischievous sparkle in her eyes as she lifts a brow.

"Why don't we start a new holiday tradition?" My hands interlock behind Callie's back, securing her to me.

Settling her hands on my chest, Callie nods. "We could go to Boston and see your grandma. I think she'd like that. Then we can see my family when we return." My heart warms at the relationship that has been built between Callie and my grandma.

Gran insisted on meeting Callie once she heard about everything. One trip to visit was all it took before she and the love of my life were in cahoots. But then, that's pretty normal for Calloway Rhodes.

"She's moving here this summer."

Shock coats Callie's features. "Really? I hadn't heard that."

"You've been a little busy," I chuckle. "Finishing grad school and growing a human are no small feat. Not to mention our other little gremlin. And Nacho. And Gilmore."

"I hope Ivy doesn't feel like I've abandoned her." Callie's expression softens from the guilt I know she often feels.

"Never," I say, taking her chin between my fingers. Making

sure I have her full attention, I smile. "You are an amazing mother. She's just as proud of you as I am."

Callie looks at our daughter, who is busy teaching Hudson how to stuff five crackers in his mouth all at once. Sighing, my wife shakes her head, returning her gaze to mine. "Then what's the new plan, Dr. Rhodes?"

"I was thinking something more tropical might be fun this year."

She smirks, raising both brows. "You'll never get it past our parents."

"I've got plenty of time to come up with a game plan. All I need now is a willing partner." Trying to be as subtle as possible, I shoot my wife my best suggestive look, waggling eyebrows and all.

Callie presses those flawless lips together, nodding. "It'll be quite the scandal."

"Without a doubt," I concede. "Know any volunteers?"

"Maybe ... So, what does this new tropical tradition entail? A beach? Cruise? Traipsing through the rainforest?" Callie thoughtfully tilts her head, amused eyes tracing my confident expression.

Taking the opportunity, I press a quick kiss to my wife's lips. "I'm not sure yet. But I'm hopeful it'll be a holiday to remember."

# ACKNOWLEDGMENTS

Coming from an entirely different genre (and author name), this one really allowed me to test new muscles. I was knee-deep in finalizing another holiday book when Callie and Oliver's story started forming in the back of my mind and before I knew it, an entirely new universe of stories was begging to be written. So here we are, with a new name and a whole host of new characters. Welcome to Serenvale Springs.

To **Matt**, my absolute best friend in the entire world (and you know, my husband)! I simply cannot thank you enough for your constant encouragement with my every hope and dream. Having your support truly means everything. I love you today, tomorrow, and every day after.

To **Gee**, my incredible editor who helped me bring Callie and Oliver to life. Thank you so much for your expert eye and for calling me out when I had no idea what I was even *trying* to say. Every suggestion and comment truly helped bring together the best version of this story, and I could not have done it without you.

To **Luz of Rotoscope Design**, your talents never fail to impress me. Once again, you've taken my abstract and completely vague ideas for a cover and turned them into something beautiful. Thank you so much for everything. Six covers down, so many more to go!

To **LB**, I can't thank you enough for helping keep me sane throughout this entire process. Seriously. I probably would have forgotten half of the standard things with this release if it weren't for you. I'm so grateful to have found you!

To my dear friend **Tay,** AKA the person to whom I sent a picture of myself crying when I finished the first draft. Thank you so much for your constant support. I love you dearly and I hate that we live so far apart.

To **Solo and Ripley,** thanks for once again sitting with me all those hours it takes to carve a book from my soul. You two are the best babies. Ready for the next one?

And to all the wonderful authors, bookstagrammers, and everyone else who has been so encouraging throughout this process. Thank you so much. For everything.

# ABOUT THE AUTHOR

EMMY TODD writes, watches movies with her husband and pups, and drinks coffee in Northwest Arkansas. When she's not writing, she can be found reading, crafting, cuddling her creatures, or trying out a new recipe.

Author Image by BelArt

Follow her for updates and cute pictures of creatures:
    @emmytoddauthor